WONDER VALLEY

WONDER VALLEY

IVY POCHODA

ecco

An Imprint of HarperCollinsPublishers

This is a work of fiction. Names, characters, places, and incidents are products of the author's imagination or are used fictitiously and are not to be construed as real. Any resemblance to actual events, locales, organizations, or persons, living or dead, is entirely coincidental.

WONDER VALLEY. Copyright © 2017 by Ivy Pochoda. All rights reserved. Printed in the United States of America. No part of this book may be used or reproduced in any manner whatsoever without written permission except in the case of brief quotations embodied in critical articles and reviews. For information address HarperCollins Publishers, 195 Broadway, New York, NY 10007.

HarperCollins books may be purchased for educational, business, or sales promotional use. For information please e-mail the Special Markets Department at SPsales@harpercollins.com.

FIRST EDITION

Designed by Renata De Oliveira

Library of Congress Cataloging-in-Publication Data has been applied for.

ISBN 978-0-06-265635-3

17 18 19 20 21 LSC 10 9 8 7 6 5 4 3 2 1

TO THE WRITERS AND ARTISTS IN
THE LAMP ARTS PROGRAM

**WHEN THEY SAID REPENT REPENT
I WONDER WHAT THEY MEANT.**

LEONARD COHEN, "THE FUTURE"

PROLOGUE

He is almost beautiful—running with the San Gabriels over one shoulder, the rise of the Hollywood Freeway as it arcs above the Pasadena Freeway over the other. He is shirtless, the hint of swimmer's muscle rippling below his tanned skin, his arms pumping in a one-two rhythm in sync with the beat of his feet. There is a chance you envy him.

Seven A.M. and traffic is already jammed through downtown, ground to a standstill as cars attempt to cross five lanes, moving in increments so small their progress is nearly invisible. They merge in jerks and starts from the Pasadena Freeway onto the Hollywood or the Santa Ana. But he is flowing freely, reverse commuting through the stalled vehicles.

The drivers watch from behind their steering wheels, distracted from toggling between radio stations, fixing their makeup in the rearview, talking to friends back east for whom the day is fully formed. They left home early, hoping to avoid the bumper to bumper, the inevitable slowdown of their mornings. They've mastered their mathematical calculations—the distance × rate × time of the trip to work. Yet they are stuck. In this city of drivers, he is a rebuke.

He runs unburdened by the hundreds of sacrifices these commuters have made to arrive at this traffic jam on time—the breakfast missed, the children unseen, the husband abandoned in bed, the night cut short on account of the early morning, the weak gas station coffee, the unpleasant carpool, the sleep lost, the hasty shower, last night's clothes, last night's makeup.

He ignores the commuters sealed off in their climate-controlled cars, trapped in the first news cycle and the wheel of Top 40. He holds a straight line through the morning's small desperations, the problems waiting to unfold, the desire to be elsewhere, to be anywhere but here today and tomorrow and all the mornings that run together into one citywide tangle of freeways and on-ramp closures and Sig Alerts, a whole day narrowed to the stop and go.

His expression is midmarathon serene, focused on the goal and not yet overwhelmed by the distance. He shows no strain. But the woman in the battered soft-top convertible will say he looked drugged. The man in a souped-up hatchback claims he was *crazy-high, totally loco, you know what I mean*. A couple of teenage girls driving an SUV way beyond their pay grade insist that, although they barely noticed him, he looked *like a superhero, but not one of the cool ones*.

THE DAY IS AN INDETERMINATE, WEATHERLESS GRAY. THE SUN IS JUST another thing delayed this morning. Beneath the 10, the air over the bungalows of West Adams and Pico-Union is a dull, apocalyptic color. The color of bad things or their aftermath.

The other city—the remembered and imagined one—stretches west, past the sprawling ethnic neighborhoods where Koreans overlap with Salvadorans and Armenians back into Thais. It begins on the big-name crosstown boulevards lined with deco theaters, faded tropical motels, and restaurants with sentinel valets, and ends where the streets run into the ocean. But in this trench where the 110 sinks through downtown, that place is barely a memory. Here there is only the jam of the cars and the blank faces of the glass towers.

The runner is on pace for an eight-minute mile or so it seems to the man behind the wheel of his SUV who woke up late and didn't have time for his own jog. He missed his predawn tour of Beverlywood, the empty silence of the residential neighborhood when he visits other people's cul-de-sacs, peering into the living rooms of dark houses as his pedometer records his footsteps, marking calories and distance until the morning's ritual is complete. He wonders what went unseen—coyotes slinking home before sunup, a car haphazardly left in a driveway after one too many, a man sleeping in the blue glare of his TV, a teenager sneaking through her back gate, liquor bottles shoved into bags and left at someone else's curb. During these stolen hours before his wife and kids need him, he believes he glimpses his neighborhood's secret soul, seeing beyond the façades of the bungalows and the manicured squares of unremarkable lawns into hidden discontents.

There is never anyone to encourage him on his early morning runs, no one to witness his labored breathing in the sixth mile, his heroic triumph over his ebbing willpower. Watching the runner navigate the stationary cars, this driver is aware of the jellied muscles of his own legs after a weekend's drinking.

He wants to reach back for the hour he cheated from himself, when he lay in bed and instead of lacing up his shoes, rolled over, checking the clock to see how long before others needed him. Without his run, today will belong to the commuters in their cars, to the team waiting for him at work, and now to this shirtless jogger cutting through traffic on the 110.

He rolls down his window and wedges his torso out to watch the runner pass. The man's mechanics aren't bad—his chest upright, shoulders relaxed, hands not balled into fists. He cups a hand over his mouth, shouting at the man to keep going. Then he sees that the runner is naked. He pulls back inside, raises the window, and busies himself with his cell phone, moving on to the next thing in his day.

THE FREEWAYS WELCOME SPECTACLE. JUST THIS YEAR AN UNDISCOVERED rock band closed down the 101 between Sunset and Hollywood to play a concert on the back of a flatbed, three poodles escaped from a stalled station wagon and chased each other down the 5 between Burbank and Los Feliz Boulevard, and a truckload of onions was released onto the 405 blocking all four northbound lanes. There were two car chases that ended in gunfire and flames and the prop plane that landed on the 10 just shy of the Santa Monica airport. The unlikely, the bizarre, and the tragic grinding people to a halt and capturing the attention of the city.

And even though you are stuck, you want to write yourself into the story, listen for your experience on the radio. You want to be near the action instead of miles back in the jam. These commuters are already translating their experience of the naked jogger into a story they will tell when they get where they are going, figuring how to play it for their audience, exaggerating their part in it, making it a thing of annoyance, insanity, or beauty, depending.

A helicopter climbs over the towers of downtown and hovers over the 101/110 split. It lingers above the runner, before dipping to the right to circle the interchange. The percussive beat of its blades fades in and out with its approach. The chopper is just another addition to the anxiety of the morning, its aggressive sound suggesting a danger more exotic than a man jogging through traffic.

The runner passes through two cars logjammed between their lanes, one trying to move into the fast lane, the other trying to exit. He jumps the narrow space between their front bumpers with only a "fucking perv" to urge him on.

A woman shields her daughter's eyes. Another stops applying lipstick and turns to admire his butt as the runner heads south. People lean out of their windows, holding up cell phones, making videos, hoping this thing goes viral.

The man who missed his run phones his wife. It's a reflexive gesture, mindlessly executed. He keeps his cell on speaker, tucked into his shirt pocket. When she picks up, he says nothing, listening instead to the sounds of his family's morning. "Tony? Tony?" she says. "Tony!" There is the ding of the microwave, the clatter of a dish set down on their granite countertop. "Tony, you're pocket dialing me." He listens to the opening of the microwave door. "Anthony, you're pocket dialing me. Again," she says, even though they both know his phone won't register an earlier call. He fumbles in his pocket and disconnects. He puts the car in park and flexes his calves.

All around him people are tuning their radios, searching for the story of their delay. They crane their necks toward the chopper, following its tight circle, trying to see whether it's news or police.

The first radio reports are low information, tucked into a growing list of citywide slowdowns. *A vehicle stalled in the right lane on the 710 near Artesia Boulevard. An accident reported on the northbound 5 at Colorado Boulevard. The 110 through downtown stopped between Fourth and Hill Street due to a pedestrian running against traffic. The southbound 101 slow over the Cahuenga Pass. On the 405, drive time between Getty Center Drive and the 10, fifteen minutes.* No elaboration. No explanation. A fact tucked into facts.

REN'S NOT BIG ON DRIVING. HE CAME TO IT LATE AND NEVER GOT THE FEEL. He doesn't have a proper license, let alone a vehicle. Which is why this car is hot, reappropriated, boosted from an alley off Mateo. Ren trusts the universe to correct the balance.

Not that he's out for himself, planning a joyride or intending to drop the Honda at a chop shop and make bank on the parts. It's only for a couple of hours max, enough time to take Laila to the beach like he promised. Then he'll leave the car somewhere for the cops to find without a scratch, like the Honda wandered away on its own.

But this jam wasn't part of the plan. The first wail of sirens is making his palms sweat and his heart beat time with the copter. *No good deed*—and doesn't he know it?

Ren's instinct is to jump, abandon the car, thread his way through traffic, clear the guardrail, and lose himself in the grid of downtown. But family is family and he can just imagine Laila's tone should he bail. *Can't keep a single goddamn promise, no matter how simple. Say you're gonna take me to the beach and then cut and run when things get hot.*

He checks the clock on the dash. It's been less than thirty minutes since he boosted the Accord.

"Be cool," he says to the rearview.

Ren doesn't live in the car city, but in a place where people walk, crawl, and straggle. Where they roll into the streets and stagger off sidewalks. Where they don't have houses, let alone cars. A place where too many possessions are nothing but a problem.

Just look at these people in cars that are overflowing with living. Backseats piled with extra clothes, emergency snacks, a lifetime of objects lost under the seats. Cords to charge the electronics that they're not supposed to be using. TV monitors on the seatbacks. Everything to distract them from where they are. Ren wipes his hands on his jeans. He fiddles with the controls, letting the air cycle from hot to cold, an entire weather system in the shift of a dial.

In the cars ahead of him drivers are rolling down their windows, straining to watch something coming down the freeway. Ren keeps his seat belt on, his window up, his eyes on the digital radio display—another commuter marking time until he's set free. He's just like you or me, fussing with buttons and switches, searching for some combination of temperature and music that will make this moment pass. He's so focused on acclimatizing that he nearly misses the show, a naked man jogging between the cars going in the opposite direction. Ren glances up in time to get a good look. He knows the runner, a white face in the Skid Row panorama. Not exactly of the place but in its orbit. Before Ren can get his window down, call out to the jogger, pull him to safety, he has disappeared between two box trucks.

THE RUNNER CROSSES INTO THE FAST LANE AS HE PASSES THE SIXTH Street exit. Then he jumps the barrier so he's running with traffic now, continuing south on the 110. He keeps pace with a steady flow of cars that are heading toward the exit for the 10. But behind him, traffic is stalling, slowing, unwilling to pass him.

Asshole.

Put some clothes on!

Fuck you think you're doing?

Looking fine.

The first images appear on the local news, the runner, a beige blur, streaking through the gray downtown streets.

Northbound traffic is now backed up the ramp where the 110 slides off the 10 and is working its way west, past Hoover, Western, and Arlington, cars slowing as they approach Crenshaw, unable to work their way into the exit lane. Soon it will be stopped as far back as La Brea.

A man with full sleeve tattoos, driving a yellow diesel Mercedes east on the 10, coming home from the after show of an after show, watches a second helicopter heading for downtown. He can't hear its blades, but sees it circle like a hawk hunting over the freeway. Instantly his thoughts are back in the desert ranch where he grew up, where hawks silently hunted rabbits and mice above his parents' land, the spread of their wings creating shadows across the sand and scrub. He was terrified of the moment the birds struck, rocketing downward with their talons outstretched, their wings making a sound like ripping fabric as their shadows grew larger.

He lets his foot off the brake and collides with the car in front of him creating another slowdown within the slowdown as he and the other driver struggle over to the shoulder to exchange information.

TONY IS STARTLED BY HIS PHONE RINGING IN HIS SHIRT POCKET. "DO YOU know about this?" his wife says. "There's some psycho running down the 110. Naked. Who does that? At rush hour?" He can hear sirens approaching from the opposite direction, threading their way through traffic that's slowed to a crawl in appreciation of the facing jam.

"Tony? Did you see him?"

"I saw him."

"And?"

"He was running."

"That's it?"

Every day the same route. The city streets to the 10 West. The 10 West to the 110 North through downtown. The 110 North to 5 North into Burbank—his car passing above or through or along neighborhoods whose names he's unsure of, whose streets are unfamiliar. A city thoughtlessly traversed.

"Tony? You should lock your doors. It's on the news."

From television to television, computer screen to computer screen, the jogger will cover the city. He'll enter living rooms and appear on kitchen countertops. He'll be watched by people burning off last night's calories on treadmills. He'll pop up on smartphones, his journey in the palm of your hand.

"Did you lock your doors? You don't know what's going to happen."

"I'm not locking my doors."

It's too much to be sitting in this traffic jam while the runner moves freely, part of the city, in it, not just passing through it.

"What time do you think you'll be home?"

THE RUNNER EXITS THE FREEWAY, CUTTING UP THE EMBANKMENT JUST after Seventh Street. Only a few drivers see him as he scrambles up the hill dotted with exhaust-choked trees, skirts the dismal shrubs sheltering a gaudy Italianate apartment complex. He emerges on Bixel, then pauses for a second before doubling back to Seventh and continuing west.

He begins to leave downtown, emerging into the no-man's-land of medical buildings, drab apartments, and off-brand restaurants. He passes businessmen in flashy cars headed for the glass towers of the financial district, delivery trucks returning to the warehouse district, cyclists darting between the stop-starting buses.

It's an odd crowd that watches him: arrivals for the first shift in the sweatshops, homeless who've wandered up from Skid Row a mile or so to the east, hospital workers—medic techs and tired nurses—leaving their overnights, residents of the few tumble-down apartments, undocumented workers hustling gigs in the Home Depot lot. To those who see him over here, the runner is an apparition.

THEY ARE TRACKING HIM FROM THE HELICOPTER, SWOOPING DOWN Wilshire over to the park, the police chopper just ahead of the news crew. *The 110 still stalled through downtown. A two-car collision on the 10 has moved to the shoulder. Drive time over the pass twenty minutes. The southbound 5 slow between the 710 and the 605. A mattress on the 105 blocking the right lane near LAX.*

TONY WATCHES THE TWO CHOPPERS CUT TO THE WEST. HE UNDOES HIS seat belt and opens his door. He peels himself from his seat and leaves the keys in the ignition. He doesn't bother to stretch. He begins to run, following the path of the jogger through the stalled cars and onto the city streets.

He's a gearhead: trail shoes, barefoot shoes, energy boost footwear, heat-tech in the winter, moisture-wick in the summer, iPod, sports headphones, GPS watch, calorie counter, heart-rate monitor, dozens of gadgets and outfits to make his run go faster, seem more professional, more meaningful. Still, on his morning runs Tony experiences a tightness in his quads that drops to his calves until he's fully warm. There's an ache in his right knee and a click in his hip. No matter how much he spends on gadgets and gear he never feels as good as he should.

But running down the 110 in his button-down, twill pants, and loafers he is lithe. His limbs are loose. He's not lost inside the music from his headphones but buoyed by the sounds of the city. Even the hard slap of the asphalt underneath his flat-soled shoes is an inspiration.

You too, motherfucker?

You can't leave your damn car like that. You can't leave your damn car.

You running after your boyfriend?

The hecklers urge him on. He cuts up the embankment at Seventh and heads west. At the intersection of Lucas Avenue he catches sight of the naked jogger a block ahead and continues his pursuit.

The jogger enters the outskirts of Pico-Union, a tangle of Salvadoran and Honduran shops, indoor swap meets, and calling centers. He jogs north for one block before cutting into MacArthur Park where homeless and those who didn't make it home are stretched out on the grass like body bags.

Back on the shoulder of the 10 the tattooed dude in the old Mercedes is sweating. He tries to count the hours between now and his last drink, desperate to estimate his BAC, trying to guess the cost of this accident. His phone's been going mad in his pocket, buzzing and buzzing, making his leg itch. It's his mother. He holds it to his ear.

"It's your brother."

"What?"

"The man on the news? Are you even listening to the news? It's all over the radio and the television. He's running. On the 110. Or he was. Now he's downtown somewhere." His mother exhales into the phone. "There's something else," she says.

The man clenches the steering wheel and sits up a little in his seat, craning his neck toward downtown as if he might be able to see his brother running through those streets.

"He's naked."

REN'S SWEATING HARD AS THE POLICE CHOPPER CIRCLES ABOVE AND TWO cruisers honk and bleat their way through the stalled cars. He recites the directions in his head—110 to the 10 all the way to the end. He checks on his mom in the backseat, making sure she's covered, comfortable. He hopes the cruisers pass by quick. But he's getting antsy, anxious to get out of this jam. He tells himself to chill. He can't afford to drive aggressive, draw attention to himself, even in this nondescript car.

"It's cool, Mama," he says. "It's cool."

TONY'S HEART LUNGES IN HIS CHEST. HE SEES THE NAKED RUNNER CUT into the park. He watches him make a circle of the pond. Tony crosses to the west side of the street. He's about to run onto the sidewalk when a cop car squeals at his back and another jumps the curb, blocking him from the front.

Tony stutter-steps. Then the police bring him down.

"I almost got him," he says, as his cheek hits the asphalt.

The cops are cuffing him, but he manages to lift his torso and look into MacArthur Park.

"Where is he?" he says.

Because the runner is gone. He'd been there, at the eastern edge of the pond, making a counterclockwise circle. Tony could swear it. "Where—" he says again as the cuffs pinch his wrists.

He watches a few of the cops fan out into the park, split into two groups, circling the pond in opposite directions. He hears the news come over the crackle of walkie-talkies—the jogger has vanished.

The city was watching and then it wasn't. A seam of wildfire began to threaten Malibu State Park. A singer was found dead in the Peninsula Hotel. And everyone's attention turned west away from the naked man running down the 110. But he was there—Tony and Ren know. And he's still somewhere, running, naked. He will be found. He has to be. Because no one can vanish for good. Not in Los Angeles. Not with so many people watching.

1

BRITT, TWENTYNINE PALMS, 2006

She should have considered herself lucky that so far the trucker had limited himself to glancing at the shadowed triangle just below the hem of her miniskirt, the dark V where her thighs parted and sweat pooled. Now his hand was fiddling with the radio, more often than was necessary. Soon it would be on the glove box. Soon on her knee.

Britt knew. She knew the way men's hands moved incrementally, making staggered inroads their owners thought would go unremarked. Always the same routine—tennis camp, frat party, team bus, lecture hall. Their hands crept over her like she might be too dumb to notice.

They passed a Circle K market. Then a sign that warned NEXT SERVICES: 100 MILES. The sun had set behind them and they drove into nightfall on the two-lane highway. Britt craned her neck trying to distinguish anything from anything in the darkening desert.

The radio was on AM talk, a rattle of static and barrel-voiced anger. The road curved and the truck banked right. The trucker reached out his hand to keep Britt from hitting the window. And there it rested on her hip. Like nothing. She glanced over at the driver—a watermelon stomach resting on his thighs, red and gray stubble, and eyes shrunken from too many nights behind the wheel. His gaze didn't leave the road, like his hand had a mind of its own. Like maybe he didn't even know what it was up to over there on her hip.

Britt pressed against the window, staring down from the cab as the sturdy adobes and flat ranch houses of Joshua Tree and Twentynine Palms gave way to makeshift homes cobbled together from tumbledown cabins, corrugated iron, shipping containers, and trailers. They passed yards littered with the refuse of desert living—heaps of scrap metal, shells of cars, rusted-out water tanks—signs of all the things that could go wrong out here.

"You're out here now, ain'tcha," the driver said.

"That's the plan," Britt said.

"A girl with a plan." He tightened his grip on her hip.

They passed a tiny airport with winking purple lights. And then nothing.

The road curved again and again one more time, a dramatic right-hand turn.

"Stop," Britt said. "This is it."

The truck hurtled on.

"Stop."

The driver hit the brakes. The truck squealed, shuddered, then skidded off the road, rumbling to a rest on the soft sand shoulder. Britt screamed.

"Jesus, girl," the driver said. "You sound like we got hit head-on."

Britt grabbed her duffel and swung the cab's door open. She tumbled out, landing on her knees.

The driver leaned out of his seat. "You're not gonna thank me for the ride?" He slammed her door. His wheels spat sand and gravel and the truck lumbered off.

There was only a thin seam of light back west, pinking the distant mountain ridge. Britt backtracked to where the road had curved. If she hadn't guessed right about the turnoff she didn't want to think about the next driver who'd come along.

BRITT HAD MET CASSIDY AND GIDEON THAT MORNING AT THE JOSHUA Tree farmers' market where they were selling chickens inexpertly sealed in plastic. While they rambled on about the beauty of the soul and the health of the spirit to their customers, the birds' blood leaked over their forearms, running down their lariats and beads.

They were both the sort of dirty tan that comes from too much time in the desert, like the sand had worked its way into their skin. Their hair was long, dreaded in places with beads that often vanished in the tangled mess. Cassidy wore two necklaces— one with a large feather, the other with a tooth. Gideon had a bird claw on a leather braid. *Life is beautiful even in death,* he'd said when he caught Britt looking at it.

Gideon and Cassidy moved like they were dragging their limbs through soft butter, slow, heavy, and deliberate as they reached into their blue cooler, bagged the birds, and made change. Their math wasn't very good.

Britt had been waiting for a ride—a guy she'd known from a tennis club in Palm Springs who'd promised he'd be passing through Joshua Tree on his way to Arizona. But the sun had crept east to west and he hadn't shown.

She was checking the highway one more time when she'd felt Cassidy's fingers in her hair. "Are you on a trip or are you just going from point A to point B?"

"I'm waiting for someone," Britt had said.

"The world turns while we wait," Cassidy had replied. Then she invited Britt to come smoke a joint with her and Gideon. They'd driven into the Joshua Tree National Park to a site called Jumbo Rocks, which Cassidy explained was her and Gideon's power place. The weed had made the landscape of red rocks and rows of spindly Joshua trees seem like a hallucination.

Cassidy had picked up a small stone and placed it in Britt's palm. "Do you feel that? The universe is a heartbeat in the palm of your hand."

"If you join us up on the farm, you will learn how the warrior spirit can be found in a grain of sand," Gideon had said.

That's when Cassidy had told Britt about Howling Tree Ranch, the chicken farm where she and Gideon lived with a bunch of other people she'd called interns. But it hadn't sounded like a farm, not really. And the owner, Patrick, didn't sound like a farmer. More like a swami or a cult freak, one of those guys they make documentaries about when someone escapes and tells everyone about the magic mushroom omelets, the daily naked baptisms, and the tantric chanting.

"It's not like that," Gideon had said. "He can reach deep inside of you and pull out things that you hadn't even known you'd buried."

"He can heal you without touching you," Cassidy had promised. "He can see inside you, figure out what's broken, and then fix it."

Britt thought this sounded more painful than helpful. She didn't say that there was no way that "the earth laughed in flowers," as Cassidy had proclaimed, because that didn't make any fucking sense. Nor did she point out that the garden of her soul was probably beyond tending. Instead, when the joint was done, she'd asked for a lift back to town so she could wait for her ride. "Maybe we are your ride," Gideon had said as he pulled her into a long hug in order to exchange energy.

Cassidy had tugged on his arm. But he'd waved her off. "Chill, Cassidy. I'm just vibing off my high."

Britt watched them climb into a Volvo station wagon.

Her ride never showed. And now here she was, twenty miles east of Joshua Tree looking for the fallen sign to Howling Tree Ranch Cassidy told her was just after the sharp curve in the road.

She almost missed it—a pile of trampled boards and a spray of paint on which the last strike of the sun showed the word *Ranch*.

The farm was a mile up from the road—too far to see from the highway. The sun had slipped away leaving the desert purple-dark. Without her duffel and in her running shoes, Britt could have made the walk in fifteen minutes give or take. But at night, in her sandals and miniskirt and lugging her bag, it was going to be rough.

The sand kicked up over her toes, wedging between the straps of her sandals. She carried her phone in front of her, its weak blue glow showing her the road or what she hoped was the road, a sunken depression of vague tire tracks lost beneath the gravelly sand.

She had played a few tournaments on the opposite side of the national park, where the harsh landscape was tamed by golf courses, midcentury architecture, cocktail hour, and spa hotels. She thought she knew desert. But a few steps off the Twentynine Palms Highway was all it took to prove her wrong.

Something was scuttling through the brush, a scraping, scratching sound that tracked Britt's progress. She tightened her grip on her bag and tried to pick up her pace. Then the dogs began to howl, volleying their lonesome call-and-response across the thick night.

It was pitch dark, darker than she imagined possible. The silhouettes of the distant mountains and the nearby bushes were absorbed into one impenetrable black that the light from her phone could barely puncture. She could feel her heart beat in her hand as her bag's strap cut into her palm.

The sun hadn't taken the heat with it. Sweat slipped down her back. It beaded down her legs, running over her ankles. She could tell she was going uphill, a slight incline that stretched the back of her calves and made her feet lose traction. She could hear the rustle of palm trees somewhere off the road.

Since she'd wandered away from college she prided herself on winding up places where she couldn't be found or, rather, where no one, especially not her parents, would think to look. Until now she'd never felt lost.

When you hitch in a truck with a stranger, when you let a group of guys drunk-drive you up the coast, when you knock on the door of a house deep in South Central because some kids on campus told you that's where the real party's at, you don't show fear. But Britt didn't think she could hide the way this nighttime desert was making her heart race and her breath come quick.

The road leveled. And she saw the farm—a modest ranch house to the right and a smattering of cabins straight ahead. The whole way out from Joshua Tree, she had been fooling herself into imagining some sort of midwestern dairy operation, all red barns and green fields. Hoping, really. But the light coming from the various windows of Howling Tree Ranch brought up a place not much different from the forbidding compounds she'd passed on the highway—mismatched buildings, jury-rigged electricity, and moats of junk.

From somewhere on the property came the rhythmic creak of metal, a constant one-two beat and the chug-chug of an air conditioner or swamp cooler. Behind her were the chickens, their frantic scratching making their desperation even deeper. She smelled their hay and ammonia tang. She couldn't imagine that scent in the full force of the midday sun. The birds noticed the intruder in the yard and they flapped their wings, crying out, and crashing into their wire enclosure.

Across the driveway the porch light came on, then a flashlight beam cast in the direction of the coop, catching Britt.

"You new?"

Britt shaded her eyes and squinted into the light.

There were two boys sitting on the porch, each in a metal glider. Britt crossed a hard-packed driveway. The one holding the flashlight never took it off her face.

"Are you new?" he repeated when she was closer.

"At what?"

They were twins, fourteen or fifteen years old, their skin the same dirty desert tan as Gideon's and Cassidy's. They were both barefoot. The one holding the flashlight was bare chested. His brother wore a tank top a size too small.

"Are you the new intern?" the boy with the flashlight said. He drew tight, fast circles with the light over Britt's face. "One of the others said we were getting a new intern."

"When were you talking to the interns?" his brother said.

"Shut up." The kid switched off the flashlight. "Mom," he called, "there's someone in the driveway." He turned on the light again. "It sucks here, by the way. We don't know why you guys come."

"I'm not planning on staying," Britt said.

"So why are you here?" He switched off the light again, then he punched his brother on the shoulder. "James, let's go."

James rocked a beat in the glider until his brother hit him again. Then they went in the house, letting the screen door bang shut. The porch light went off.

Britt waited in the driveway, listening to the chickens resettle in their coop. Only one dog still howled in the distance—its call more desperate each time it went unanswered.

Finally, the screen door opened and the porch light came on. A woman in denim cutoffs and a large T-shirt with a picture of a jackrabbit stepped out and stared down at Britt. Britt guessed her hair had once been blond and wavy, but the sun had dried it to a pale frizz. There was a chance she had been beautiful before she let the harsh climate have its way, creasing her skin, drawing lines around her full lips and light eyes. Now she looked like the other creatures Britt had noticed out here—devoid of softness, whittled down to the brute essentials necessary for survival.

The woman held out her hand. Her grip was strong, her palm dry and calloused. Ropy veins popped on her forearm. "Grace," she said. "You're a new intern?" Wine had soured on her breath.

"Maybe," Britt said.

"Or are you just here for Patrick?"

"I'm Britt."

Grace let go and Britt caught sight of a doorknocker ring swinging loose on her finger. "You're the one Cassidy met in town. She'll be surprised."

"She thought I wouldn't come?"

"She thought she wanted you to come. She'll learn her mistake. As Patrick says—reap the intention you sow in the world."

"But she didn't want me to come?"

Grace laughed. "Isn't that why you're all here? So that my husband can tell you what you really want?"

"I don't even know why I'm here."

"You'll figure it out. They all do. Or they hang around and keep trying."

"We'll see." But Britt was pretty sure she wouldn't.

"My husband will tell you that the soul is a flower you have to water daily or else it will wither and dry."

"For real?"

Grace put a hand on Britt's arm. "You think you're different from the rest. But you're not." In the distance a dog howled. Britt flinched. "You're lucky it's not a wolf," Grace said. "Come on, I'll show you around." She switched on the flashlight the twins had left on the porch and cast the beam around the yard. "This is Howling Tree Ranch. The main house is off-limits to anyone but Patrick, the boys, and me. Our property runs from here for two miles toward the park." The light danced south over the outbuildings toward a vast, black expanse. "There's nothing I'm going to say that will prevent you from running around out there. But we get coyotes, bobcats, and even wolves. My husband might be a healer, but there are some things he can't fix."

Most of the lights in the cabins had gone out. "You got here on a special night," Grace said. "Tomorrow is our biggest chicken slaughter of the year. You saw the birds?"

Britt followed as Grace showed her the enormous wooden coop with its chicken wire fortress. Grace pointed out the separate enclosure for the meat birds and the stump where they would slaughter the broilers tomorrow. "After the first twenty, you get used to the blood. After fifty, the smell," Grace said.

They left the coop and processing area and headed for the cabins. They passed a large fire pit and a dead Joshua tree where a plastic bag filled with water and a makeshift nozzle stood in for a shower. "Most of you just rinse off in the oasis."

Now they turned away from the cabins and main house and headed for a large stand of palms Britt hadn't noticed before. Between the palms a slick pond was handing back the moonlight. "Normally I'd expect to find a few of you in the pond, but Patrick insists on a quiet night before the slaughter," Grace said.

Grace led Britt to her cabin, a small adobe between two prefab sheds. "It's one of the nice ones," she said. And without another word she left.

Britt dropped her bag and flopped on the narrow bed. The springs complained and bowed toward the floor. Next to the bed was a large window that gaped out at wilderness that stretched to the national park.

The air in the cabin clung to her skin, crawled down her throat. There was a bedside fan that did little beyond spin the heat in different directions. She didn't want to crack the window, and certainly didn't want to open the door even though that might have created a cross-breeze. She didn't want to know what might come calling in the night, what she might hear passing her cabin.

In fifteen minutes she could be back on the highway. In three and a half hours Vegas, four and a half hours Phoenix—places where the desert was defeated by light and climate controlling. But she had to admit, at least to herself, that she couldn't brave the walk down from the farm and she didn't want to know who might be willing to stop for her once she made it to the blacktop.

She closed her eyes, pressed the skimpy pillow over her face to black out the blackness beyond, and tried to focus on the uneven whip-whir of the fan. She wasn't stupid—she knew Grace was trying to scare her with her talk of the chicken blood and all the things that could kill her. Anywhere else, she would have stuck around to prove Grace wrong. But tomorrow Britt would be gone.

2

Nine days he'd been on the Greyhound breathing the cold canned air, banging his chin on the metal window ledge. Passengers came and went. Some talked for hours. Some slept deeply, spilling their drinks and food and making the floor stickier than when they'd rolled out of Port Authority.

Ren had booked an indirect route from coast to coast, a meandering path that cut south for a while before it turned west. He had some bank in his pocket, about seven hundred or so from his various hustles. He figured he could afford the detour.

Eight years in juvie and he'd lost perspective on the outside world. All the kids ever talked about was space, of getting out into the wide-ass world, seeing the things they were missing on the inside. Problem was, when you're incarcerated at twelve, outside becomes abstract. Proportion gets screwed. Big becomes the common room instead of your cell. Wide open is the rec pen.

The outside world was shrunk to fit on the communal television where the sky was perfect, the weather weather-free. Being inside made it hard enough to remember the hush of snow and the skin-splatter of rain. Anyway, all the other boys ever wanted to watch were shows set in police stations or the ones that made criminals into kings. Up to Ren, that communal TV would have been tuned to the nature channel or something else that would revive an actual sense memory of what freedom felt like. Because inside everything smelled the same, tasted the same, felt the same—none of it remarkable. None of it good.

Which is why he got off the bus frequently, sleeping under the sky in fields or in campgrounds. Sometimes he didn't know what state he was in. He passed swamps and bayous. He learned their names from fellow passengers. He saw land so dusty it looked like desert. Then he arrived in the desert proper with its flattop mesas and rock formations so extreme and intricate Ren imagined God had built them.

Last stop on the Greyhound—downtown Los Angeles, a place so abstract to Ren that he only thought of it as the city on the TV in the common room: palm trees and beaches, stucco houses and all that contourless sky. And of course, the sparkling ocean where surfers grabbed the waves like they were riding the subway.

But there was no sign of that city when he got off the bus. The terminal was small and nondescript, no different from those in no-name towns in the middle of the country. Ren had imagined some sort of gateway to the west, a place watched over by a tangerine sun where an archway of palms led to shapely blue waves. But what he got was a drop-panel ceiling and the same vending machines that had been feeding him for weeks.

Another bus pulled into the bay alongside Ren's. He watched the passengers disembark, each dressed in jeans and carrying a cardboard box or large envelope with their name and number on it. Even without these markers he'd have known that ex-con swagger, the way the men looked up at the sky like it was going to bite. How they checked over their shoulders as if they expected to be jumped.

He stood to the side and let the freed prisoners pass. A few of them caught his eye, gave him a nod that said, *I know you, brother, even if I don't.* He reached into his pocket for his bankroll, cupped it in his palm, and when no one was looking, slipped it down his sock so it rested against the sole of his foot.

A couple of churchy ladies were standing at the door to the station. They looked like the social workers who bugged him during his last months in juvie about signing up for job placement and a lot of services he wanted nothing to do with. These women pressed pamphlets into the hands of the ex-cons, talking a mile a minute about the dangers of the street, the ease of cycling back in, the importance of staying straight, being proud but not foolish. A few of the guys took the literature. Some paused to read it, but most let it flutter to the ground a few steps from the door.

Ren unzipped his backpack and pulled out a scrap of paper, faded and sweat worn. He'd read the words so many times that they were burned into his mind, the writing, too. He held the paper out to one of the women. "Excuse me," he said. "You know this place?"

The woman bent over the paper, squinting at the faded script. "The Cecil Hotel? You just head up Seventh right here to Main. And you can't miss it." She pointed at the street in front of the station. Then she pressed a pamphlet into Ren's hand. "Come to my ministry," she said. "When you're low, lost, or lonely."

WHEN REN WAS RELEASED FROM JUVIE, THERE WAS NO ONE TO PICK HIM up. There was no home to go to. He'd returned to his old neighborhood in Brooklyn and found his parents had split for Troy, New York. He'd stuck around for a while, living in an outdoor community by the river, watching his old haunts change before his eyes, trying to figure out where in the hell he belonged. Then one day he'd run across a distant cousin of his mother's. She'd given him the stink eye at first, as if what he'd done was going to rub off on her, as if she'd walk away from this encounter reeking of criminal.

But she did tell him one thing. "It didn't work out for your mama up in Troy. So she split on her lonesome. Turned up in Los Angeles. And from what-all I hear, it didn't work out for her there, neither."

Ren didn't want to beg for intel, but he wanted to know an address so he could find his mother should it come to that. It took a day of hanging outside the cousin's apartment before she coughed up the name of the hotel where Laila was living—the Cecil. Anything, Ren guessed, to get rid of him.

He had no way of knowing whether the info was correct. The hotel didn't have phones in the rooms and when he called, they refused to give out the names of their residents. He didn't leave a message.

During his first couple of years in juvie, his parents visited him three or four times. Then twice a year—for his birthday and near the holidays. During his sixth year they came once. And in his last two years, they didn't come at all.

Just because they abandoned him didn't mean Ren had to return the favor. Because isn't that what all that time inside is supposed to teach you, give you time to reflect on and repent? Not that that's what the other kids were doing. Most of them were planning to be kingpins on the outside and Ren pretty much figured there were only a few ways of doing that.

But he was different even if his parents didn't see that once he got locked up. They forgot all about the little kid he had been and focused instead on the criminal they imagined him to be. So if he had the chance to prove to his mom otherwise and see the whole damn country in the process, it seemed like an adventure worth having.

THE NEIGHBORHOOD OUTSIDE THE BUS STATION WAS INDUSTRIAL— loading bays, wholesalers, and warehouses. It was impossible to tell whether the place was on its way up or down.

Ren headed up Seventh. The streets were bleak, lined with businesses that were either closed for the day or shut permanent—

Famous 99 Cent Diner, Hollywood Banquet Hall (available for film shoots). There were tents along the sidewalks, people pushing shopping trolleys piled with belongings that looked scavenged from Dumpsters. The farther he walked, the more crowded the streets became, overflowing with an untamed community, white, black, Latino.

A man in a baggy red sweatshirt and black jeans stood on the street corner cooking up some sort of hustle. He nodded at Ren. "S'up, brother? What you need? You need anything?"

All around him people were raving and muttering, challenging invisible enemies. There were folks passed out on the sidewalks and slumped against walls. And between them were others who were just getting on with their lives between the junkies and the insane—people reading books or gossiping with a neighbor like they were sitting in a coffee shop or in someone's living room, not outside on the dirty sidewalks of downtown L.A.

He passed a woman braiding hair in an impromptu outdoor salon. Two men were huddled over a crossword. A short, balding preacher shouted gospel through a bullhorn in Spanish to a congregation of six. He wore a sandwich board around his neck proclaiming JESUS ES EL BUEN PASTOR. A man prepped a needle next to a woman eating a bruised banana and reading a decade-old magazine. Two guys in dirty tracksuits sold drugs across from the entrance to the Nazarene Christian Mission. A woman belted out "Backlash Blues," a song Ren's mother used to sing in the shower when he was little.

In lockup, the other boys used to bang on about the cribs they'd have one day, about how they were going to do them up the minute they got flush, articulate them with a lot of nonsense they didn't need. They were always tricking out these imaginary pads with showy flatscreens and preposterous sound systems, a whole lot of business to lock the real world out. They wanted king beds and swimming pool–sized hot tubs. They wanted every excuse never to go outdoors.

Ren had no time for that. The minute he got out, he wanted to stay out, not just out of juvie, but outside entirely. He didn't want a roof over his head. He didn't want to reincarcerate himself in any apartment, phat, dope, or otherwise. He wanted his air to be fresh, not climate controlled. He wanted sky not ceiling. But this was another sort of outdoor living and nothing he wanted part of.

NO ONE GAVE HIM A SECOND THOUGHT, A STRAY GLANCE. SOME PARTS OF the neighborhood looked postapocalyptic—smelled it too—as if they were surviving in the wake of a catastrophe, a bombing, or an earthquake. One street seemed to belong to transsexuals, another to junkies. As the sun began to disappear, folks lined up at a mission for a hot and a cot. A church group set up dinner service on the sidewalk dishing macaroni onto paper plates.

He passed a community center where an open mic night was under way with all sorts of people lining up to sing. Out on the street, folks were dancing to the music that slid out the open door, shuffle-stepping to a cracked and hopeful voice singing Stevie Wonder.

Eventually Ren found his way onto Main Street where the desperation gave way to a derelict business district with cut-rate jewelry stores and half-empty loft buildings—like a bombed-out Midtown Manhattan. He was self-conscious stepping into the cavernous lobby of the Cecil Hotel, like he didn't goddamn belong and everyone knew it. He wasn't sure whether the place was really grand or just faking it. The room was tricked out with marble and ornate wood, but still smelled like the industrial cleaner they used in juvie.

He stepped up to the desk where a short Hispanic man with a heavy mustache was watching soccer on a portable television. The man didn't look up. "You want a room."

"I'm looking for a woman who lives here."

"No information on guests," the clerk said.

"Listen," Ren said. "You told me that on the phone. But I came all the way from New York."

"She's expecting you?"

"No."

"Well," the clerk said. "There's another problem."

"Maybe I'm planning to surprise her."

"I'm not going to let you hang around in the lobby and I'm not going to tell you if she's here."

"So?"

"So you can leave a note or your number. Or you can get a room. Then I can't tell you what to do."

"How much?" Ren said.

"Seventy if you don't mind sharing a bathroom."

It was more money than Ren had spent on anything in his life except for the Greyhound ticket. And he hadn't counted on paying for a roof over his head at all. After all, the Los Angeles on the television had taunted him with ample opportunities for crashing outdoors—on the sand, near the beach, under a palm tree. But that scene outside the hotel? That shit was a different story.

The clerk pretended to ignore what Ren was doing when he fished some cash from his sock. He handed over four sweaty twenties, then filled out a form. He palmed the key the clerk slid across the desk.

"So," he said. "The woman I'm looking for is called Laila Davis."

The clerk shook his head.

"What's that mean?" Ren asked. "You don't know her or you're not telling?"

The clerk turned back to his TV.

"How about this? How about I tell you that she's my mom and I haven't seen her in years."

The clerk messed with the tip of his mustache. "I don't know her," he said. He pointed across the lobby. "Elevator's over there."

Ren shouldered his backpack and crossed to the brass doors

the clerk had indicated. A white kid about his age had just pressed the button. He had lanky blond hair and wore a short-sleeved T-shirt over a long-sleeved one. His nails were ringed with dirt.

"Smoke?" He pulled a scrappy joint from his jeans.

"I'm cool," Ren said.

The elevator came. The small car filled with the white boy's funky weed smell.

"Maybe on the flipside," the kid said, as the doors opened on Ren's floor.

The hallway was dim, the carpet burned and pocked with old gum. It took Ren several loops to find his room. The key stuck in the lock. It felt like he was going to have to rip the whole handle off just to get the damn thing open.

A greenish curtain was half pulled over a window, and the light coming in had to fight through the gray-smudged glass. The carpet was red industrial grade with sharp-looking fibers. At the foot of the bed an old metal radiator was attached to the wall, above it a faded poster of a painting of a pond in a metal frame.

Ren was sure there were better hotels out there, with better-looking beds, and walls not stained with other people's living. But when he shut the door behind him, it was like something he hadn't known he was carrying flew from his shoulders. He locked the door and flipped the deadbolt, then flopped face-first on the bed.

He was going to sleep hard. He could already tell. He wasn't going to have to keep one eye open in case one of the other boys in his hall planned to mess with him while he slept, or one of the other inhabitants of the Brooklyn waterfront community got it in mind to poke around his shipping container, or another bus passenger planned to steal his shit while he was out cold. For once he could sleep on his own terms, undisturbed and alone. Sleep now and tomorrow he'd figure out where Laila had gone to.

3

BLAKE, WONDER VALLEY, 2006

On the highway there were two men and little else. The road was two-lane blacktop. Sometimes the men walked together, other times they kept the highway between them. Except for the occasional car or truck they were the only things moving in the landscape. From a distance it would have been easy to mistake them for a mirage. But they were there.

They were both tanned, their faces the color of rusted pipe with dark furrows that ran away from their eyes and down their cheekbones. Their nails and knuckles were ringed with black. They each carried a ragged pack. Blake knew if a driver passed them on this desolate stretch, he wouldn't slow. So he didn't bother to flag the few cars headed in their direction.

They'd been walking for so long Blake began to imagine their journey from a crow's-eye view, as if he was up above it instead of pounding the asphalt. He wore his Ranger's hat over his greasy black hair. The hat made him sweat but kept out some of the sun. For the last four miles he'd been staring at Sam's back, watching the big man's dark braid bounce between his shoulder blades with each step. That braid was making him nuts. How anyone could have so much hair in this heat was beyond him.

They'd started their trip in Lake Havasu where they'd been holed up in a cabin since September hiding from a Nevada warrant out on Sam for a murder he hadn't meant to commit, or so he said. The men had been smoking in an alley behind a roadside dive outside of Vegas when a jumpy little tweaker bumped into Sam. In no time Sam had his knife out and that knife had found the wrong spot in the tweaker's neck, right at the jugular. Go figure—when Sam wasn't even trying. There was blood everywhere, a goddamn trail that the cops could chase right back to Blake and Sam's trailer.

Sam swore to Blake up and down that he'd acted in self-defense. But with a rap sheet like his, no jury was going to accept that plea. So the men split that night. After Sam had taken him in eleven years earlier, there was no chance that Blake was going to let Sam run without him. He owed the big man that much.

They crossed the state line. The warrant would follow, but at least the Arizona cops might not be so keen on their trail. It didn't help that Sam's face made the papers—a brutal black-and-white sketch that captured his deep-set eyes, his full lips, the hang of his cheeks, and his hollow, violent stare.

In late May the summer people returned to the cabin in Lake Havasu where Blake and Sam had been hiding and the men had to be on their way. They caught a ride down to the Parker Dam then started west on California 62, the Twentynine Palms Highway. Now they needed a new hideout.

Sam had heard about a half-abandoned homestead community just east of Twentynine Palms called Wonder Valley where he promised Blake they could live off the grid and out of sight. Hell, he said, they could probably reclaim one of the old cabins without anyone noticing. A *home for free just sitting there for the taking.* Now this didn't sound half bad to Blake, but the problem was in getting there.

Blake was desert born, desert bred, and he had spent half his life sleeping in Phoenix's parks and alleys or wherever the night left him. But that didn't mean he enjoyed walking under the full-force assault of the summer sun. No man should be out in the open when the temperature hits 112. But that's where he found himself. He'd been cursing Sam for miles.

They had walked out of Parker with a couple of cans of food and little water. After a day on the road they came to Vidal Junction, which they discovered was more of an intersection than a town. There was a diner that had closed, a café with a fiberglass chicken on the roof, an agricultural inspection station, and a minimart with a couple of gas pumps.

They bought two six-packs and drank them by the side of the road. Next to the gas station an old man was selling American flags from a handcart. Sam plucked one without paying and tucked it into his pack. That night they slept in an empty RV park under the awning of an abandoned trailer.

When they headed out the next morning, Blake was stunned by the isolation of the highway—no houses, no gas stations, no stores, just the Granite Mountains to their north, the Mojave Desert stretching out on all sides, and the endless blacktop. After fourteen hours of walking, they'd passed nothing except mile markers and a few highway signs.

"Not even a fucking house," Blake said.

Sam had been singing the chorus from the same country song for two days straight—a four-line refrain with the words jumbled and some missing. It was one of Sam's lifelong habits that drove Blake nuts, made him want to punch the feeble fiberglass walls of their trailer or strangle the big man as he sang. From what Blake could make out this song went something like: *In the dark morning silence I placed the gun to her head. She wore red dresses but now she lay dead.* Blake hummed under his breath to block the sound.

Late in the day they met a man coming the opposite direction.

His face was shriveled like a fruit pit. His lanky gray hair brushed his shoulders. He pushed a shopping cart with patriotic junk tied to it—flags, yellow ribbons, a photo of the Twin Towers, a picture of Saddam Hussein in crosshairs. The man wore an olive army vest and a boonie hat stuck with military pins.

Sam stepped in his path, but Blake held up his hand in greeting.

"You boys got a long way to go," the man said.

"How do you know where we're going?" Sam asked.

"It's at least sixty miles to anywhere with nothing in between so I figure you're going that far at least."

"What kind of nothing?" Blake wanted to know.

Sam had always been a storyteller, and Blake had begun to worry that Wonder Valley was one of his stories, a fantasy grounded in some lost version of the truth.

"What you see, boys, is what you get," the man said, gesturing at the mountain ranges in the distance and the desert in between.

"For how long?" Blake asked.

"First sign of life, if you can call it that, is Wonder Valley. Then comes the Twentynine Palms airport. But if it's food you're after, you'll be seven miles past the airport at the Circle K. So you're looking at some eighty odd miles or so."

"So, where're you headed?" Sam said.

The man pointed to a laminated card on the front of his shopping cart. "'Veterans Walking Across America,'" Blake read. "Why's that?"

"I want to know what I fought for," the man said.

"You got food in there?" Sam lifted the tarp covering the contents of the cart.

"Leave him," Blake said.

"He's closer to food than we are." Sam combed through the man's belongings.

"Leave him," Blake said.

"You can leave him if you want," Sam said. "I'm taking these."

He pulled three cans of franks 'n' beans from the man's cart. The vet didn't try to stop him.

"Get going," Blake said.

The man continued east. Blake watched him until he could no longer hear the creak and jangle of his cart. Then he crossed the highway to get away from Sam.

WHEN BLAKE FIRST STARTED SKIPPING SCHOOL, HIS MOTHER CAUTIONED him, *There's a blackness in you.* Chances were, she didn't mean it literally, but Blake wondered how long it would take before his outside matched his insides. By now he guessed it did.

Even after it was too late—after he'd dropped out of high school and taken up with a rough crowd at the bike shop—Blake's mother liked to remind him she gave him his name because it was soft. She chose it because it was a name without violence, like snow falling. (*Like snow ever fell in Phoenix,* Blake told her.) Snow or not, his mother believed his name would keep him good.

Not long after Blake quit school, his mother was also gone, scuttled east after a software salesman and his two young sons. It seemed like everyone knew how to run from the future except him. But you make family out of whoever's available, Blake figured. Which left Sam.

The men met in jail—both of them pulled in for D&D. Blake was underage. Sam bailed him out, then invited him back to the ratty trailer he called home. Eleven years later they were still bunking together. Sam was fearless. Blake worked hard to be.

Sam's real name wasn't Sam. It was something too difficult to pronounce, a name that caught in your throat and made you spit. But the man claimed to have Samoan blood—or at any rate he looked Samoan. (Blake wasn't sure what a Samoan looked like. Kind of like an Indian or a Mexican but rounder, he guessed.) So the Samoan became Sam for short, not exactly a tough name but a whole lot better than Blake.

Blake was tall and lanky with barely enough skin to cover his bones. At times he felt hollow. His joints and ribs jutted through his T-shirts. His hands and feet were hardened into bark or horn like he was growing a shell. His ID said thirty, but he felt older, worn and brittle like a desert scrub pine.

Sam lived on the same diet as Blake—too few meals, too much beer, and too many drugs—but he had a considerable stomach that rolled over his jeans, and doughy skin that hid his well-muscled shoulders and biceps. Blake marveled at how the Samoan could emerge from a weeklong speed bender looking like he'd just stood up from Thanksgiving dinner.

Blake liked that Sam called them *partners* like they were outlaws or businessmen on the up-and-up. But as he saw it, partnership should come with a goal greater than random havoc, something more productive than grabbing whatever money they needed for the week or month. A life of crime should be just that—a *life*—not a frantic hand-to-mouth existence. Hell, that sort of living is what turned people bad in the first place. But try telling Sam that. The man craved the chaos, the spontaneity, and the thrill of fear in his victims' eyes. Blake, well, he didn't tell his partner this, but for the last year he'd been haunted by the people he and Sam had harmed—a sickening slideshow that kept him up at night and made his dreams bad when he managed to sleep.

THAT NIGHT THE MEN SLEPT IN A BONE-DRY WASHOUT. SAM PULLED OUT his portable chessboard and his battered copy of *The Chess Puzzle Book*. The set was made of expensive wood and the pieces looked Chinese. Although he pretended he'd inherited it from a grand master, Blake knew the big man had stolen it from a pawnshop. Using his lighter, Sam set up the pieces and played by feel and memory in the dark. Blake smoked and stared at the sky where the moon hung like a school clock. He pulled out his pocketknife and tried cleaning the dirt from under his fingernails but only succeeded in driving it deeper.

Sam drank two beers and fell asleep over his game. Blake slipped the board out of his hand and tucked away the pieces, counting each one. Somewhere deep in the desert a coyote howled. The moon grinned stupid overhead. Blake rested his head on his pack and waited for sleep.

They hadn't spoken since they passed the veteran. Blake was used to these long silences and the quick bouts of explosive anger. Before they found themselves in Lake Havasu, they'd spent a couple of years in a foreclosed double-wide in an RV park outside Henderson, Nevada. During the summers, without power to run the air conditioner or even a fan, the place was an oven. It got so hot that the men turned on each other to ease the pain—Sam's knife to Blake's throat, Blake's fist in the Samoan's eye. Before they could do any real harm, they'd burst into the night, directing their violence on others, people in the liquor store parking lot, at the shitty dive bar, coming out of one of the pawnshops on the highways.

THEY STARTED WALKING BEFORE SUNUP—WHEN THE FIRST TICKLE OF pink grazed the mountains to the east. After two hours the temperature was already unreasonable. Even the birds were sheltering until dusk. Blake looked up at the sky. The sun hadn't even reached the top of its path. The mountains in the distance were an inhospitable Martian red. By noon it would be well into triple digits. If nothing else, thirty years living around Phoenix and Vegas had taught Blake to tell the difference between 105 and 112. When he looked back at the road, bright circles had burned into his corneas—sunspots that danced and exploded in the corners of his eyes even when he shut them.

The heat made time drip slow. The blacktop ran on and never got anywhere. Even the insides of Blake's eyes and the back of his throat were hot. His lungs felt like they were pumping steam. His mouth was dry. His thighs chafed, and the straps from his pack had lifted welts on his shoulders. The tops of his boots rubbed the skin raw on his calves. Rivulets of sweat ran down the dust plastered onto his neck. And by his count they were still at least fifty miles to nowhere.

In the early afternoon Blake noticed something glinting in the distance, metal or glass that caught the sun and shot it back in his direction in sharp, blinding fragments. His entire body wanted to give in, collapse and roll off the highway, sleep in whatever shade he could find until sunset. But he kept his gaze fixed on the thing that was shimmering up ahead. It was a beacon that pulled him forward, something man-made in all this bald and barren nature.

The Samoan was lagging behind. Blake pushed on. He fought off discomfort and focused on that shiny object.

After a few minutes, the shiny object was obscured by a curve in the highway. Blake hooked his thumbs under his straps to stop their rubbing. He picked up his pace to round the bend quick.

The road straightened. There were a few hills just off the shoulder and when these flattened, the object reappeared, closer now and brighter. It was moving, spinning, shooting more stars of light in Blake's direction. He pressed on. Two cars passed spraying dust and gravel. One honked at the men, a wail of encouragement or a warning of danger. From back behind him, he heard the Samoan shout something at the driver.

It was a tree or something hanging in a tree. That's what Blake could make out from less than a quarter of a mile away. It wasn't much, but it kept him moving. He shaded his eyes and squinted. The object, or rather objects, got brighter so he lowered his gaze to the road in case the sunspots reappeared.

Five minutes later Blake could make out what he was heading for—a gnarled mesquite tree hung with dozens of sneakers, their reflective stripes and decals catching the sun. He pulled up in front of the tree and stared at the shoes. After the monotonous desert landscape, the primary colors and artificial dyes were a shock. And the evidence of all the other people who had come this way, well, that was just a damn tease, wasn't it?

The tree was dead. Its dried branches reached out in a leafless tangle. It stood in a long, flat stretch of sand, the only tree visible in either direction. Blake shook one of the branches. The sneakers spun and knocked against one another.

"Well, ain't that a bitch." Sam had caught up. He slung his pack off his shoulders and let it hit the asphalt. "Walk all this way for a shoe tree."

The big man stooped, doubling his considerable bulk, and crawled under the lowest branches. He leaned against the trunk, facing away from the sun, looking back down the road they'd traveled. The sun threw a shadowed copy of the sneaker tree into the sand in front of him.

"What's going on?" Blake said.

"Resting," Sam said. "I figure we can knock out another ten miles tonight, then we can get there day after tomorrow."

Blake lowered his pack and joined Sam. He faced north, away from the highway, where the desert ended in the Granite Mountains.

"Ain't this a whole lot of nowhere," Sam said. "A whole lot of fucking nowhere."

"You picked it."

"Well, we aren't where I picked yet are we?" Sam rolled them each a cigarette from his off-brand tobacco. They smoked as if it could ward off the heat.

The sun lingered before it began to fall, plunging back behind the seam where the highway met the horizon. A crow circled just in case. Blake let his head drop to the Samoan's shoulder.

There were awakened by a rustling. At first it sounded as if an animal was circling their camp, snuffling and shuffling in the sand. The sun was gone. The sky was a dull, muted color. The stars were hiding.

The sound was coming from the tree. The sneakers were swaying together—their dried leather and rubber rustling. The wind ran through the arrowwood bushes and sent a spray of sand into the men's faces. They stood up and uncrooked their backs.

"Now this is walking weather," Sam said. He reached into his pack for a can of beans. He popped the ring tab, gulped down half, and offered the rest to Blake. "Don't bother where it came from."

Blake finished the beans and tucked the can into a sneaker that was hanging at eye level. Next to the sneaker was a pair of white leather high-tops, not too worn judging by their soles.

Blake kicked off his own boots and tied the laces together. He dusted the sand from his socks, unhooked the high-tops from the tree, and put them on.

"The fuck you think you're doing?" Sam said.

"Changing my shoes."

"Put them back."

Blake stooped down and felt the toe box. A little roomy, but better than his boots. "How's this bothering anyone?" he said. "Seems a waste just to have them hanging there."

"Put them back," Sam said. "It's like stealing from the dead."

"I'm not sure the dead come all the way out here to hang their shoes on a tree."

"Dead or alive, it's bad luck."

"Since when do you know so much about luck? If you did, you might have noticed ours ran out a few years ago." He finished lacing up the sneakers, then took a few steps to test them out.

"Just put the goddamn shoes back."

"The hell I will."

The Samoan reached into his belt. Blake sprang back before Sam could put his knife to his throat. "It's bad luck, stealing from a spirit tree. I told you the story of my uncle and the coyote grave."

Blake had heard all of Sam's stories, his strange fabricated folktales, too many times to count. And he didn't have patience for one now. "Looks like a sneaker tree to me. Just some dumb shit people do because there's nothing between here and nowhere."

"It's a spirit tree," Sam said.

Blake spat on the ground. The things he had seen the Samoan do—the terrorized families, the men left bloodied and crumpled. There were women all over Phoenix who couldn't sleep at night, haunted by Sam's face. "Since when did you go all spiritual? I don't see any Samoan burial grounds around here." He looped his boot laces over the tree. "I'm calling this a fair trade."

Sam polished his knife on his T-shirt before returning it to its sheath. "It's your blood, brother."

They shouldered their packs in silence. The only sound was the wind running around the sand and scratching through the scrub. Then there was the knock-knock of the sneakers colliding with one another again.

Even though it was dark, the breeze made for easy traveling. The men walked side by side, following the glow of the Samoan's flashlight. The moon was a smudge. The sky hung close and heavy. After several hours, the wind began to whip harder, lifting small pebbles and handfuls of sand. Blake tightened the strap on his Ranger's hat.

To the north, lightning tiptoed along a mountain range, briefly illuminating ragged peaks and tinting the clouds. Sam cast his light off the road. They were in a flat stretch with nothing but a few stunted Joshua trees.

The lightning struck faster, dancing a quickstep. The men hunched their shoulders, lowering their faces from the wind.

The rain started suddenly—an onslaught. They trudged on, struggling through the walls of water. Sam's flashlight was useless. They slipped and stumbled on loosened rock. Finally they were forced off the road.

They huddled in a culvert as the water descended in torrents so strong they had to close their eyes against the storm. When the rain let up, they continued until it began again and they were once more forced off onto the shoulder. The Samoan cast his light into the desert and found a collection of small boulders.

They slipped and slid over the soft sand tearing their clothes. They wedged themselves between the rocks and Sam pulled a blanket over their heads to stave off the worst of the rain.

Beneath the blanket it was warm and close. Blake could smell Sam's rotten herbal scent. It was a smell he was used to after years of sleeping in close quarters—on single mattresses in airless rooms, in jail cells, in cars. He'd gotten so used to it he missed it when Sam wasn't around.

"It was the shoes," Sam said. "They brought the storm." He squeezed rainwater from his braid.

"Well, if that's the bad luck you were talking about, it's not half bad." Blake gathered his bony knees to his chest and fell asleep.

"YOU READY?" SAM REMOVED THE SODDEN BLANKET AND WRUNG IT OUT. The sky was still dark, but the rain had stopped.

"Let's hope those shoes have done their worst." Sam opened a can of beans. When he was finished, he handed the rest to Blake.

Blake didn't point out that it wasn't his shoes but Sam's unchecked violence that had landed them in the sodden desert.

On their way back to the highway, they sank to their ankles in the softened sand. Blake's eyes were heavy and his joints were stiff. He didn't want to come fully awake, hoping that the miles would pass while he was half dreaming.

They walked down the center of the highway. Debris from the storm was scattered in the road. The sun came slow, struggling with the lingering cloud cover, revealing the muddy desert. Water pooled in depressions in the sand. The sky was marbled.

Sam rolled them each a cigarette from his damp tobacco,

which hissed when touched by a match. "Maybe someone'll pick us up today."

"Maybe," Blake said.

It started as a roar in the distance like the sound of a truck rumbling down a dirt road. But there were no headlights. The highway curved and straightened and the noise grew louder.

In an instant, the blacktop became a river. Water rushed toward the men, rolling over their feet, rising to their ankles. The desert around them was mud. Then it was roaring mud. The land was surging, a flash flood that brought them to their knees.

Sam tried to stand but stumbled back.

"Just stay put," Blake said.

The big man tried to struggle out of the flood path. "I'm not planning on getting swept away."

"There's nowhere to get swept away to. Just wait it out."

But if there was one thing Sam didn't do, it was wait. He gripped the straps of his pack and stumbled forward. It was hard to tell the borders of the highway, where the solid asphalt gave way to the softer ground. Sam lurched, trying to high-step over the swirling water. He brought his foot down hard.

Blake could hear the crack of the bone that pushed through Sam's ankle, letting in the dirty desert water. The big man staggered and sank into the mud. He dropped his pack, which opened, sending his few belongings into the flood.

Blake waded to the Samoan's side. The water was easing up. He looped his arms underneath Sam's shoulders and dragged him out of the flood path.

Sam gritted his teeth. A crown of sweat ringed his brow. Blake pulled up the big man's pant leg and saw his anklebone poking through the skin.

"Collect my shit," Sam said, pointing at his open pack.

Blake grabbed the backpack. He found the chessboard and poked around in the wet sand for the chessmen.

"Count 'em," Sam said. "You know how many there's supposed to be?"

"Sure," Blake said.

"Thirty-two."

"Looks like you've got twenty-eight," Blake said. He found the wet blanket from the night before and placed it under Sam's head. Then he put the chessboard in the big man's lap. "We'll play," he said.

"You don't know how."

"Doesn't matter."

They lay on the muddy sand and watched the water roar past. The sun came up full and the clouds blew back. They were too close to the road for Blake's liking, but there was no moving Sam. So he fashioned a shelter out of their blankets and used both their packs to cushion the big man's leg. Using his dirty jeans as a pillow, he lay down and watched for lightning in the distance.

Sam fell asleep. He moaned and thrashed, keeping Blake up. Eventually Blake slid out from their shelter and bedded down far enough away that he couldn't hear the Samoan. The desert rubbed his bare legs. The sand and God knows what else crawled along his skin.

The big man's leg looked bad and would only get worse. But Blake was counting on an upside—a break in the tide of violence that followed in their wake.

4

The night before the chicken slaughter James hadn't been able to sleep. Something had been hunting in the desert. It started with a lone howl then a staccato chorus followed by a chase through the cacti and arrowwood shrubs. Even after four years on the ranch the whip of the wind through the brush kept James up at night. He felt watched by the eyes he swore were glowing in the dark that stretched from the front door to the base of the Pinto Mountains. He was unsettled by the sound of dogs howling over the desolate acres between the homesteads and the way the wolves sometimes returned those calls. Then there were the deep reverberations of bomb tests from the marine base several miles away that summoned a different sort of fear.

His parents' chickens were another barometer of nighttime danger. When the birds were calm, their large enclosure radiated a steady thrum, a comforting, low-grade buzz. But if there was a predator outside—a coyote or a bobcat circling the pen—the coop was seized with a helpless frenzy that jarred James from his sleep and disturbed whatever dreams might follow.

He glanced at Owen in the other bed, sleeping curled toward the window. The moon hung low, filling their room with a puddle of white light, highlighting the mark just below Owen's shoulder in the shape of a child's crude drawing of a flying bird. James stared at the soft V, the spot where he imagined he ended and Owen began, the one aberration to their otherwise identical bodies, until he fell back asleep.

When James next woke, the moon was gone, the sun had started its unforgiving climb, and Owen was gone. He pulled on his shorts and went to look for his twin. The air around the ranch already felt like death. Crows were perched in the palms near the chicken barn like they knew what was coming. They'd arrived early, able to anticipate the bloodlust of the farm. A hawk—the only fleck in an immaculate sky—was circling, the V of its wings tracing the path of its hunt as its shadow slid from sand to bush to tree to scrub.

James watched his father test his ax on a stump, swinging the blade into the hard wood and wresting it back out. His mother was lugging coolers of ice from the main house so the birds could be stored until they could be transferred to the freezer. The interns were up early, looking busy for once, grabbing buckets for blood, guts, and feathers. Owen was nowhere in sight.

He wasn't in the pond or the garage or in any of the unoccupied cabins—all the places the boys hid to avoid the chicken slaughter. James finally found his twin on the backside of the house where a junkyard of fenders, tires, oil drums, old printers, and rebar had bloomed. Owen was sitting on a collapsed bed frame smoking one of the small brown cigarettes the interns preferred.

"Where'd you get that?" James kept away from the interns' cabins. He had no interest in seeing their stuff, let alone stealing it. It was enough to listen to the nightly "sharing" his father conducted with the interns every evening—hearing them berate and attack one another around the campfire as they worked to excavate their most perfect selves.

"Where do you think?" Owen said, blowing a narrow stream of smoke at James.

"Gimme one."

"Since when do you smoke?"

"Just gimme one." James scrambled over the rusted refuse and grabbed for the pink package in Owen's hand.

"Fine," Owen said.

James lit the bidi and tried not to cough as the bittersweet smoke filled his lungs. "You hang out with the interns now?"

Owen tossed his cigarette. "That's my business."

James stared at the tiny ember at the tip of his bidi. He hadn't known that his twin had business of his own.

James didn't like the interns—and he'd thought Owen didn't either—the way they walked as if they were moving through liquid, their wandering speech, how they were always touching each other, rubbing one another's shoulders or braiding each other's hair. Even worse was when they touched him or Owen or let their hands linger on one of his parents. "Your aura matches your bike," the one named Cassidy had told him the previous morning as she drank stinky tea from a large mason jar. "You know that, right?" She'd skipped back to her cabin and returned with a feather on an orange lariat necklace, the same color as James's BMX. She put the lariat around his neck. "It's a hawk feather," she said. "May it guide your day."

James had chucked the necklace behind a creosote bush where the feather would resume being what it was, another piece of desert garbage. He was tired of everyone finding power and meaning in all the objects littered across the sand—squeezing smooth rocks in their palms to release their hidden energies, burning bouquets of unremarkable herbs to heal themselves, making tokens and totems out of teeth, feathers, or bone to ward off evil spirits or to honor animal guides. If he dragged a stick through the sand, someone asked him if he was drawing a mystical sign. If he sat on the deck after dark, an intern praised him for tapping into the lunar power source.

When James was little, the world didn't run on energy currents. People didn't give off vibes or have auras. They didn't require realigning and cleansing. There weren't powers that needed to be coaxed out of everyday stones and plants. The sky was the sky, the wind the wind, the stars the stars—all interesting in their own way, but no more than zoo animals or trains. He wore cream to protect himself against the sun instead of being forced to salute it palms open, inviting it to fill him with its beauty and light.

James finished his bidi and ground it out on a hubcap.

"We better go," he said.

Soon their mother would be calling them, summoning them to the chicken pen.

"Have fun," Owen said.

"They'll make you."

"No they won't."

But at that moment their mother appeared. She was already wearing the heavy rubber apron that protected her from the slime and gore. "Your father's waiting," she said.

Owen slid off the bed frame and followed her.

"See," James said.

JAMES HAD LOST COUNT OF HOW MANY SLAUGHTER DAYS THEY'D HAD ON Howling Tree Ranch. The first couple had been messy and haphazard. A chicken with a half-severed neck had broken free from Grace's grip and run in bloody circles around the coop until Patrick finished it off. Now James's parents operated with grisly efficiency. The procedure was simple: tie the bird by the legs, swing it overhead to dizzy it, place it on a wide tree stump with an ax handle to its neck, then bring a sledgehammer down on the ax. Once the head fell free, the body would be plunged into a bucket of hot water to loosen the feathers. Then someone would reach into the cavity and scrape out the chicken's steamy insides. Finally the bird was hung upside down, so its feathers could be plucked.

In the winter, the harvest wasn't so bad. But in the spring, summer, and fall, the smell lingered for days. It hung on the wind and sank into the sand—a hot, rusty odor that slicked James and dried in the back of his throat.

The twins' job was to pluck the feathers—one of the less gruesome tasks, but it still made James queasy. Even though the birds had been dunked into hot water to open their pores so the feathers would slide out, the quills resisted. Plucking the feathers—touching the bird all over, its skin still warm and almost human—was too intimate. James would rather swing the ax, a quick, remote action that was over in a flash. But that was Patrick's job.

As usual, his parents began the slaughter early, hoping to finish before the sun reached full strength. The day was still—the desert holding its breath. Sound carried from the highway, bringing the roar of trucks heading toward Las Vegas or Los Angeles. The crows circled overhead then settled in the palms to watch. A hawk swooped down on the action.

Before they started, Patrick gathered everyone together. He was shirtless, his graying beard and wild frizzy hair still damp from an early morning swim in the pond. He told the group that they were going to kill two hundred birds that morning.

The interns had tied their hair back in scarves and bandannas and had removed their lariats, necklaces, and rope bracelets. James always expected one of them to vomit or cry as he and Owen had during their first slaughter. But it never happened.

The woman who had arrived the night before stood outside the group. She was dressed differently from the rest of them, in short lime-green shorts and a pristine white T-shirt. Her red hair was brushed back into a neat ponytail. She'd brought her duffel bag to the chicken barn, as if she'd just stopped for a moment on her way back down to the highway.

"Who are you?" Patrick said.

The woman didn't realize he was speaking to her. The other

interns coughed and shuffled as Patrick's question went un-answered.

"The clean one in the back," Patrick said.

"Me? I'm Britt."

"It's a beautiful thing to honor the cycle of life." Patrick swung the ax, driving it hard into the stump.

"If you say so." Britt kicked the sand around her duffel.

A whisper slipped from one intern to the next. Cassidy and Anushna, a blond woman who'd told James her name meant Blue Lotus, bowed their heads together, their braids tangled over their foreheads.

"The world will always sit in judgment," Patrick said. "It is your soul's struggle to remain unjudged. But now there's work to do." He looked around the circle. "Who wants to hold the ax?"

James wasn't surprised when Cassidy stepped forward. Because she was everywhere, a shadow that stretched from his father's feet. When his father sat on the porch, drinking cans of cheap beer, she drifted by, hovering in the driveway, waiting for an invitation to sit. She was next to Patrick at the sharing sessions, her round face turned toward his, even as he and her peers berated her for her vanity and self-deception. And she was there, following Patrick out to the desert for one of his vision quests, returning hollow-eyed and looking more lost than when she'd left.

"I'll do it." Britt had raised her hand. "I'll hold that ax."

She stepped forward, parting the interns, and took the ax from Patrick.

"You have to have a steady hand," Patrick said.

"I do," Britt said.

The first bird was always the worst. Cassidy brought it out of the coop, swung it, and placed it on the stump, waiting for Britt to position the ax. She lingered for a second, waiting to back away until Patrick raised the sledgehammer over his shoulder. James held his breath. His father swung the hammer. The clank of metal striking metal echoed through the coop. The head fell into the empty bucket. Cassidy grabbed the body, struggling to control its flapping wings. Patrick glared at her and she plunged the bird in the pot of hot water, stilling its final wingbeats.

After a few birds, the horror started to fade. The noise of everyone working together distracted James from the clank of the hammer hitting the ax. The bucket began to fill with heads, which muffled the sound of each new one as it fell. And soon he and Owen had too much plucking to pay attention to the killing taking place a few feet away.

The clucking from the pen quieted as the day heated up. Owen was working more slowly than usual and leaving the more unpleasant parts of the bird for James to pluck.

Britt's white T-shirt was speckled with blood. A streak of gore was smeared on her shorts. Blood spatter covered Patrick's bare chest. All around the coop, the other interns, even Cassidy, were talking or singing as they worked. Grace was keeping up a cheerful patter as she moved from station to station ensuring that the birds were perfectly cleaned and quickly stored. Only Britt and Patrick were silent, working in gruesome lockstep.

James's fingers were sore from the quills. The ground was sticky with blood. If you kept working, you didn't notice the smell, but when you walked away it hit you, so Patrick and Grace didn't allow anyone to stop until they were finished and the buckets of innards could be hauled off.

The sun had risen and the land glinted and winked. When they first got to the ranch, James discovered his parents had lied. The desert wasn't really made of sand, not like at the beach anyway. He couldn't walk through it barefoot, bury himself, or build sandcastles. Instead it was rock—rough like gravel, jagged and sharp with pebbles and twigs. Still, his parents had promised that he would grow to love it like he loved the soft, golden beaches that stretched from Malibu to San Diego where he had begged to stay out until evening after the setting sun had stolen the warmth from the air and the water had turned the color of blue ink.

THERE WAS A DISRUPTION TO THE RHYTHM OF THE KILL. JAMES GLANCED at his father and saw that Patrick had frozen with the sledgehammer high above his head, a dazed chicken below him on the stump. "Owen," he said, "you take a turn."

Everyone stopped working and looked at Owen. Britt steadied the bird beneath the ax.

"I don't want to," Owen said, turning back to the bird hanging upside down in front of him. The boys were nearly done with a bird—all that remained was a Mohawk of feathers down its middle. The broiler on the stump twitched, coming out of its daze.

"Owen," their father said. "I'm asking you to do something."

Owen shook his head.

"I'll do it," James said. His hands were sticky with pinfeathers. He wiped them on his shorts.

"I'm talking to your brother," Patrick said.

Owen looked down at the ground and James could feel the tears sting his eyes.

"It'll be over in a second," Britt said. "Do it now and the next time will be a breeze." She beckoned to Owen, drawing him in with a blood-flecked hand.

Owen shuffled over to the stump. He took the sledgehammer. He raised it over his head. His arms trembled with the weight.

In another world, Owen would have been playing baseball. He would have been holding a Louisville Slugger over his shoulder, his eyes trained on the seam stitches as the ball zipped toward the plate. His arms wouldn't shake. He'd put his strength into the swing, driving the ball as far as he could, thrilled by his power. As James watched his brother hold the ax, he imagined being in the stands clapping, urging Owen, or perhaps he'd have been in the game too.

When Owen brought the sledgehammer down, it was with little force. He didn't strike. He just let it fall.

He missed. The sledgehammer knocked the ax, sending it sideways into the chicken's neck, pinning it but not killing it. The bird thrashed. Owen staggered backward.

"Jesus Christ," Patrick said. "Finish her."

Owen dropped the sledgehammer.

"Finish her!"

Owen backed toward the edge of the chicken barn.

Britt picked up the hammer and raised it over her head. In one swift blow she severed the chicken's neck. Then she grabbed the flapping body and plunged it into the bucket.

"Perfect," Patrick said, touching her shoulder. His hand lingered and when he removed it, bloody fingerprints stained her white shirt.

Owen ran from the coop in the direction of the oasis. Patrick didn't call him back. James watched his brother go. Up above him a hawk was circling. The bird began to dive, a controlled downward descent. For a moment, its rippling feathers were the only sound. Then it rose back to the sky with a field mouse in its talons, its wings beating the air like a bass drum.

AS ALWAYS AFTER A SLAUGHTER, PATRICK AND GRACE THREW A PARTY. They filled an oil drum with coals and grilled a few of the chickens, the sweet scent of caramelizing meat hiding the stench of death.

The sun dawdled over the Pinto Mountains. Bruised purple shadows stretched into the sand, creeping from the mountain range to the foot of the property.

Sometimes slaughter days passed without incident and sometimes they got into everyone's bones where they lodged for a week—the sounds and smells of the dead birds lurking everywhere.

Owen hadn't reappeared and James had been too busy picking up his slack, hosing blood from the bird pen and packing the chickens in the freezer, to look for him. In his brother's place, he would have swung the hammer. He would have hit his mark. Patrick would have been proud.

The sun began to set like an explosion—a smoky, red-and-orange violence that erupted across the sky, so beautiful it seemed unnatural. Grace opened bottles of wine. The crackle of the fire, the spit and sizzle of the grill, and the twang of someone's guitar masked the hush and rustle of the desert and made it almost possible for James to love it on Howling Tree Ranch.

The interns danced and drummed and sang as if the noise they made could erase the events of the day. Or maybe the slaughter had excited them, made them raucous and wild.

Grace worked the grill, flipping spatchcocked birds. Patrick stood up from the campfire. All the interns' eyes were on him. He took a few steps in time to the music. Then he held out his hand to Britt. James watched them step away from the circle. His father placed a hand on Britt's waist and the other on her shoulder. Then their bodies merged into a single silhouette as they twirled away.

James joined his mother at the grill, picking sweet, crisp skin from the grate. She looped her arm around his shoulders as they watched Britt and Patrick spin across the sand.

"They always think they're special," she said, "and one day they aren't." She kissed the top of James's head. She craned her neck, but Patrick and Britt were lost in the darkness. "They're just silly kids who will wake up soon and want a hot shower and a three-course meal. Then they'll leave."

"I want to leave," James said.

Grace ran her fingers through his hair and squeezed gently. "But I'm here," she said.

THE SUN LINGERED, CREATING SHARP SHADOWS AND DEFINING THE shapes of birds gliding through the sky. A stubborn ribbon of blue remained overhead, twisted into the evening colors. A hawk hovered and dipped, hunting something behind the coop.

Britt returned and one of the male interns made room for her around the fire. Patrick snuck up to Grace and wrapped his arms around her waist. She stiffened as he pressed his lips to her cheek, then twisted free and refilled their wineglasses.

The gunshot ripped the night apart—a hard crack, like a stone split in two. The Pinto Mountains returned its echo. James looked up at the pink sky as the black outline of the hawk folded its wings and plummeted earthward.

It bucked and tumbled. Then it collided with a rock and bounced once before merging with the dark desert floor.

Owen stood just beyond the oil drum holding their father's shotgun. His arms trembled. He lowered the gun, retrieved the bird, and carried it toward the fire. Its wings were spread across his arms, its body dangling. Blood ran down his forearms. He laid it at his father's feet. The music stopped.

"You wanted me to kill something," Owen said. "So I killed this."

The light was gone.

"How could you be so foolish," Patrick said.

Some of the interns muttered in agreement. Grace silenced them with a glance.

"You won't waste this life." Patrick lifted the bird from the ground.

Grace topped off her glass and returned to the house. She sat on the porch and looked away from the campfire to the road that led to the highway.

The interns packed up their drums and guitars and moved to their cabins.

"You'll eat it," Patrick said. "We eat what we kill."

Owen looked at James.

"He's not going to help you," their father said.

JAMES SLIPPED OFF. HE PLUNGED INTO THE POND WHERE HE COULD SEE Owen. His brother was crouched at the edge of the fire. Their father stood over him as he plucked the hawk's feathers. The quills were stubborn, forcing Owen to yank hard, stretching the bird's tough skin. Every so often Patrick would hold the bird up, examining its half-naked flesh. It took Owen nearly an hour to denude the hawk's body. He left its head intact. When he was done, Patrick handed Owen a knife.

James watched as his brother severed the hawk's plumed head, which Patrick held up in the fire's glow. Then Owen removed its legs and cut off its feet. He followed their father to the oil drum where he placed the legs over the coals.

James ducked under so he wouldn't have to smell the hawk's muscled flesh roasting over the fire. He swam to the far end of the pond, for once not worrying about the coyotes that came to drink after dark. When he returned, Owen was back at the fire, eating one of the charred legs. Their father waited until he was finished, the bones polished white, before handing him a second helping. Owen held up his hand, clutched his stomach, put a hand over his mouth. But Patrick insisted, shoving the roasted bird into Owen's hand and taking the bones and throwing them into the fire. Owen ate slowly, his jaw laboring each bite. When he was finished, Patrick handed him one of the wings.

James closed his eyes, unwilling to assign a taste to the hawk's roasted body. But he could sense it anyway—a bitter, angry taste; a dark, violent flavor.

5

It takes Tony a moment to realize what happened. Grit from the asphalt is pressed into his face, and his cheekbone is sore from where he hit the ground. He's hauled to his feet. Someone presses a hand to the top of his head, forcing him to stoop as he's pushed into the back of a police cruiser.

His lungs are sore from the run. His calves are already starting to tighten. Tomorrow he will have shin splints from running in his loafers. But the adrenaline is still coursing in his blood—that postsprint feeling at the end of his usual run when his body has stopped moving but his mind is still racing forward.

He is handcuffed. The bracelets hold him tight, pinching his wrists and digging into the base of his spine as the cruiser drives off.

Tony's heart rate slows as the car crosses the 110 and slides through downtown. His chest loosens. His breath grows easy. He stinks of his own cologne mixed with sweat. He's missing a cuff link.

He's never been this deep downtown before, away from the familiar office buildings crowned with their reassuring corporate logos that line the freeway. He wouldn't recognize this place as Los Angeles, at least *his* Los Angeles with its palm-tree-lined streets and houses covered in bougainvillea. This is urban—a Newark, a Detroit, a decades-old New York—somewhere between decay and rebirth, a city where life is lived on the streets instead of inside fenced yards and climate-controlled living rooms.

The police car is driving through a sprawling homeless community, the sidewalks filled with tents and other makeshift shelters. The name Skid Row always sounded mythical to Tony, something from a black-and-white movie, a novel, or someone else's city altogether.

The cruiser stops in back of a windowless 1960s-era precinct. The smell when they open the car is unreal—urine and sour sheets and rotting food. The cops don't have to tell Tony to hustle inside.

They book him—take his fingerprints and his mug shot. He allows them to give him a drug test and a breathalyzer even though he knows it should have been done on the scene. They offer a phone call. Tony tries to imagine Stephanie answering in their cream-colored living room, her heels tapping on the pressed wood floor as she listens to him tell her he's been booked for interfering with a police investigation, vehicular endangerment, evading arrest, to name a few. He will have to explain that, best-case scenario, their car has been towed, probably impounded if it wasn't vandalized or damaged where he left it. And that naked guy running through traffic that she'd been concerned about, *that psycho*—well, Tony can only imagine her reaction when she hears he chased the stranger and added himself to the spectacle.

No, that wouldn't fly in their circle where they have a tenuous grip on the city's glamour, where Stephanie works overtime to keep their children in the best private schools, where her butterscotch cookie balls are the toast of the annual holiday bake sale. She's worked too hard for their birthday parties that spare no expense and a hot-ticket holiday party that takes a bite out of their Christmas spending.

Tony is in *the business*, that's all that matters. He works at a studio and has his own office, his own team. Stephanie doesn't explain to friends that he's a legal counsel responsible for overseeing a host of crappy kids' products that are stocked at big-box stores and handed out at fast-food chains. She glosses over that and the fact that her dad got him the job at the studio—a favor they are unlikely to be able to repay. She also glosses over the fact that he was once a snazzy corporate lawyer in Chicago on track to make partner before he let a summer intern walk home drunk after a stupid night out at a stupid club with stupid bottle service. The girl had fallen onto the el tracks. Her parents had sued Tony. They didn't win. But he didn't make partner. His new employers know his history and they keep their eye on him.

Tony can't call his wife. So he calls a friend from law school who has to drive up from Orange County which could take up to two hours during the morning rush.

They put him in a cell. His dress shirt is torn. Somewhere between being shoved to the pavement and hustled into the back of the police car, he has lost one of his Italian leather loafers. Stephanie is going to be furious about the cuff link.

The cell smells like beer and piss and bad breath. There are two other occupants, both slumped in opposite corners. He prays they don't wake up.

He doesn't want to sit, doesn't want to feel the first cramps sneak into his legs. He places one foot on the bench, stretches his Achilles and his calves. He angles his knee outward, letting the stretch reach into his hip flexor.

He walks to the door of the cell and looks out, trying to see if they've caught the other guy, the naked runner who'd created this mess. Even in the stink of the jail, Tony can still summon the tingling sense of freedom the man inspired in him—his unburdened stride, his serene expression that made him seem immune to it all—petty grievances of the nine-to-five, real estate taxes, homeowner's insurance, playgroups, contract negotiations, secretarial gifts. He hopes the man got away. He doesn't want his run to have to end here, in this dismal precinct.

A uniformed officer opens the cell door and calls Tony's name. He takes him to an interrogation room where a heavyset detective is waiting. The man's eyes are puffy. He waits for Tony to be seated before introducing himself as Detective Addison.

"So tell me," Addison says, "what kind of game were you two playing?" His voice sounds like his mind is elsewhere or that this is a routine he's tired of.

Tony fingers the rip in his shirt. "I don't even know the guy."

The detective flips through a manila folder on the table. Tony can just make out what look like grainy aerial shots of the chase through the downtown streets.

"I've seen a lot of shit in my day, but two grown men chasing each other through rush-hour traffic on the 110 is new to me."

"I wasn't really chasing him."

Detective Addison closes the folder and rubs his eyes. He leans back in his chair. "What then?"

"I don't know," Tony says. "I was watching him coming through the jam. And then . . ."

"Hold on," the detective says, looking straight at Tony for the first time. "You didn't know the guy?"

Tony's right calf is cramping hard. He flexes his foot, trying to release the muscle. "No, sir."

"What is it that you do?"

"I'm a lawyer."

"Jesus." Detective Addison closes his eyes. "You know how much shit comes through this precinct on a daily basis? So much shit. Over the phone for starters. Some guy calls, says there's someone lurking outside his house. Says he's afraid to go outside. Says the man has a gun. Sounds okay, right? So what happens? I take his information, try to keep him calm. The routine. Then next thing he's saying it's not a man with a gun, it's five men with sniper rifles.

Says that the president's sent this team to kill him. Says there was a Blackhawk over his house last night. Tells me he's got secrets. Says something about the G8. And that's just what comes in over the phone."

"I get it," Tony says.

"You see that neighborhood out there?" The detective jabs his pen toward the wall. "It's ground zero for chaos. It's not crime like you get in Hollywood or Brentwood—carjackings, B&Es, your run-of-the-mill homicide. There are no rules out here. Hell, people don't even have addresses. Try finding a perp who's got no home and nothing to lose." Addison scratches his stubbled chin. "And now the dealers have started dressing like the homeless to fuck us even harder. Used to be easier. Used to be certain tents were certain colors and sold certain types of drugs. But now they don't even abide by their own order. So you understand what I'm telling you?"

"I'm not sure," Tony says.

"So you saw the naked man and you got out of your car to follow him? You wanted to help him?"

Tony realizes the detective is giving him an out. "No," he says. "I wanted to be him."

"Jesus." Addison pushes back his chair and, with a groan, gets to his feet. "Like I was telling you, we have enough of our own shit down here that we don't need folks like you adding to it. I probably should ship you out for a psych eval." He taps the folder on the short end.

Tony's heart plunges. This is how it will end. This is how he'll lose his job, lose his wife, lose his kids.

He is alone for half an hour. He's missed his midmorning meeting—a conference call about a fast-food animation tie-in. He wonders if his secretary has called his house and what Stephanie has told her if she has. He wonders what his wife is thinking.

If it comes up, she will tell her friends that he had a small breakdown. She will blame the stress of work—*the importance of his job.* In public she will put on a strong face. At home she'll rake him over the coals for jeopardizing his second chance, for risking their tidy life for his stupidity.

Detective Addison returns. He sets a Styrofoam cup of coffee down in front of Tony. The liquid looks like sludge and smells like tar.

"So let's go over this thing one more time." The detective sits in his chair. He sounds like he needs to be oiled. "Okay, so you're driving in your car and then what? You see this guy running down the 110 and you get out of your vehicle to follow?"

That's it, Tony thinks, *that's exactly how it happened.* But he knows this isn't enough of an explanation, not to himself, not to the cop, not to his wife. "It was like he knew something that I didn't."

"Yeah," Detective Addison says, "and what was that?"

Tony knows that any further explanation will only bury him deeper. He can't explain to this guy, or to anyone else, that a couple of hours ago, he'd wanted to be that naked man reverse commuting against the bumper to bumper, that it had seemed easier to leave his car, run against the flow, rewind to something simpler. "I don't know anymore," Tony says. "You know, that commute. It can melt your mind." He runs his finger over a red welt left by the handcuffs.

The detective inflates his cheeks and exhales loudly. "You don't need to tell me. I come in from Santa Clarita." He drums his fingers on the manila folder. "We got a bunch of charges here. 'Willfully obstructing or delaying a sworn officer in the performance of his duty. Fleeing the police on the freeway.' You know it's against the law to abandon your car on the highway? It's going to cost you some dough and maybe even your license. Then there's the question of public endangerment. You could have caused an accident running through traffic like that. You could have been up for involuntary manslaughter." The detective rubs his eyes again. "So let me ask you one more time. You were trying to help your friend out or what?"

"I told you, I don't know the guy."

The detective makes a few notes on the file. "Your buddy's here," he says. "They're going to give you a pile of paper—citations, summonses, the works. Don't miss your court date."

"What about the other guy?"

"In a couple of hours he'll be yesterday's news. You will too, if you're lucky."

IT'S MIDAFTERNOON BY THE TIME TONY GETS OUT OF THE STATION. They've lost the paperwork on his car. They tell him to call in tomorrow.

Peter is waiting for him, dressed in a bold striped shirt with large French cuffs and cuff links that could take out a tooth. "You were sober," he says. "That's a good thing. And you took the breathalyzer so you're clear." Ever since they met in law school, Peter's been working the spin. "This is my advice—friend and lawyer. Enter a clinic, voluntarily. Exhaustion, stress."

"I'm not tired," Tony says. "I feel good." Which is true, surprisingly. His legs aren't cramping. His lungs feel clear.

"No, you don't. You feel like shit. Things have never been worse. It's your job. Your wife. Get marriage counseling. The judge will love that."

Tony rolls down the window of Peter's sports car, his midlife crisis on wheels, and sticks his head out.

"What the hell are you doing? You look like my Labrador."

"I want to feel the air."

"You want to feel the air? Go to Santa Monica. Check in to Shutters for the weekend. Or better yet, move down to Laguna. Get a place near me. We have more air down there than we know what to do with."

But it's not just the fresh air, which Tony has to admit isn't all that fresh. He wants to see if he can glimpse what the naked man was running toward, whether this rotting neighborhood might hold some secret to that overwhelming sense of freedom he'd sensed wafting off the runner as he passed by on the 110.

Peter stops at a light and Tony wedges himself farther out the window, craning his neck so he can look up and down the street. A man is urinating into the gutter. A woman is screaming scripture at every stopped car. He pulls back inside. Maybe he is having a breakdown after all.

PETER LEAVES HIM AT HIS HOUSE IN BEVERLYWOOD. STEPHANIE IS OUT, which is a relief. Tony will have time to spin his story for her, give her the right lines to feed their friends should it ever come up.

He changes into sweats and stretches out on the couch. The neighborhood sounds different in the middle of the day—the distant roar of a leaf blower, the rhythmic tap of someone's home improvement project, a handyman speaking Spanish on the street.

He turns on the television, hoping for news but getting the frenzied drama of daytime talk shows. So he surfs the Internet instead. *Naked runner. 110 streaker. Morning commute.*

He finds dozens of grainy videos, some taken from cars stopped on the freeway, the disembodied voices of the people filming mocking and breathy. Some are taken from the streets. Others from office buildings. Then there is the official news footage—a bird's-eye view from a helicopter of a beige speck gliding through downtown with the news crawl running below.

A few of the videos capture Tony—a fully dressed man running down the middle of the street. But most turn away when the naked jogger has passed. Stephanie will be grateful for that.

Tony is amazed by how many eyes are on everything all at once. And he's fortunate that the speed of information flow is outpaced by how quickly things are forgotten in favor of a new scoop.

He hits refresh on his browser, looking for updates on the naked runner. But the city is transfixed by a singer who overdosed in her hotel room, and has turned away from the morning's first spectacle.

TO SAY THAT STEPHANIE IS ANGRY WITH HIM IS AN UNDERSTATEMENT. "I wanted to do something," Tony says. "Everyone was just sitting in their cars watching."

"So that's what you do. You do what everyone else does. Especially after all we've done to get past that other incident." She's wearing her daytime uniform of form-fitting yoga clothes. Her hair is perfect, her makeup flawless. "They'll drag it up," she says. "They'll start talking about that old stuff and people are going to know." She wipes a tear from the corner of her eye. Her makeup doesn't run. "I can't face after-school pickup."

"Sorry," Tony says.

"What were you going to do if you caught him?" Stephanie lowers her voice to a whisper. "He was naked. You were going to touch a naked man? I told you it was on the news. That's why I called. To warn you. You should have stayed in your car. Or maybe you wanted to be on the news?"

"No," Tony says. "I didn't want to be on the news."

Stephanie checks her small gold wristwatch as if it contains the solution to the mess Tony's created. "It's Thursday," she says, tapping the crystal. "The kids won't go to school tomorrow. You call in sick to work. You *are* sick after all. We all go to Ojai or Malibu, maybe even Santa Barbara. Somewhere nice. Maybe stay through Monday. And you can spend the weekend praying that this will have blown over."

Tony scrolls through the KTLA news blog. "That was Peter's suggestion."

"You should be more like Peter," Stephanie says, peering over his shoulder. "You're Googling yourself?" She snaps his computer closed.

Be more like Peter. Bimonthly cigar nights with the boys, followed by a trip to an upscale strip club and a lap dance everyone pretends didn't happen, a faster, more ridiculous car every couple of years, Sunday afternoon sex dates with his wife while he's thinking of that week's stripper, and a dangerous flirtation with his secretary. Monthly sex dates with his secretary when he's thinking of his wife. Then there are the biannual Indian princess retreats with his daughters where the girls play Pocahontas, the dads try to teach them to tie knots or tell a beaver from a woodchuck but are secretly counting down the minutes until the kids' bedtime when they can all go to the main lodge and get loaded.

Stephanie doesn't know this side of Tony's buddy. She only sees the perfect dad and father—the man who gives the right gifts for the right occasion or for no occasion at all, who is happy (or pretends to be happy) to man the grill, serve drinks, even take the girls to the nail salon. And maybe it's better to see the parts that please you and overlook the rest. Hell, if only Tony had that skill.

But the real world has a way of slipping in and popping the pristine bubble Stephanie is always erecting around their family. Tony knows too well that their bank account sags under the strain of the right private schools and how their older daughter, Danielle, isn't doing well in school to begin with, isn't trying hard enough and doesn't care. He knows that he's lazy when it comes to asking more of her, content to let her slide, chat to boys on the phone, and online shop instead of studying. He doesn't want to anger her, upset the balance, even though common sense tells him it will be better in the long run. On top of it all, he knows his job is a dead end, that if he's lucky he might make a lateral move to a similar department—maybe something in talent contracts or product placement. He'll never have the attractive bonuses and the seven-figure salary of his old job. That dream crashed and burned when he remained in the banquette with the bottle of Grey Goose and let the intern leave on her own.

HE STAYS ON THE COUCH AFTER THE KIDS COME HOME FROM SCHOOL. Stephanie maintains the ruse that he's sick. The television is still tuned to the local news, the volume low. A reporter is posted outside the hotel where the singer ODed. The banner at the bottom of the screen now reads FOUL PLAY? The crawl keeps him up on all the developments—the arrival of relatives, the cancellation of tomorrow night's private performance, a press conference by the singer's estranged father, a vigil being held in the Alabama town where the deceased got her start singing gospel. Then there's a break and the broadcast pulls back to the studio where two lacquered newscasters with laminate smiles and orange tans are bantering.

"Did you ever have one of those dreams where you forgot to get dressed before leaving the house? Well, would you believe this one," the female presenter says in that incredulous and hokey way permissible on the local news. "Traffic was stopped on the 110 today when a naked man began running down the freeway." The shot changes from the studio to the bird's-eye view of the runner as he cuts across two lanes of stalled traffic to exit toward Pico-Union. "The man led the police on a chase along the freeway before they lost track of him near MacArthur Park."

There's a quick shot of the large indoor swap meet across from the park. Tony sits up on the couch, wondering if he'll glimpse himself prone in the middle of Alvarado. But in no time, he's looking at the newscasters. "Gives new meaning to the morning rush," the male newscaster says, shaking his head at either the naked runner or his lame joke.

"Turn it off," Stephanie says from the kitchen. "Just turn it off."

Tony mutes the set but opens his laptop, scrolling for more news. He checks downtown blogs, traffic sites, highway reports. Nothing. When Stephanie pops out to the patio, he places a quick call to Central P.D., where he'd been booked. "Has someone located the naked runner from this morning?" he asks.

"Who wants to know?"

"He looks like someone I know. I'm concerned."

"How concerned? You want to give us his name or yours?"

Tony hangs up the phone as Stephanie comes back into the room. "Who was that?" she asks.

"Work."

"You told them you're not coming in tomorrow, right?"

HE WATCHES HIS WIFE SETTLE THE KIDS INTO THEIR AFTER-SCHOOL routine, monitoring their homework, the number of phone calls they are making or receiving. He watches her prepare dinner using the ingredients that come from the upscale subscription service that allows them to eat home-cooked but easily assembled meals. He has to admit there's an unusual grace to the way Stephanie organizes their house, the way she interacts with their material possessions. He's entranced by how, in her presence, their hundreds of objects and gadgets acquire a symphonic precision, even a strange sort of beauty. He's always bumping up against these things, opening packages with the dedicated kitchen scissors, making his power smoothie in the old baby food blender instead of the Vitamix, storing leftovers in plastic instead of glass containers.

And it's not just the kitchen. The whole house yields to Stephanie as if it has agreed to give her the exact amount of comfort she has asked of it with her carefully chosen carpets, couches, and solar shades. The house knows that Tony doesn't care, that he'd be just as happy on his law school futon or in the worn-out La-Z-Boy he'd lugged around since his frat days. So the house makes no concession to him, doesn't allow him to get comfortable on the eight-thousand-dollar couch although he knows there's comfort to be had there, won't let him in on the secret of the plush pile carpets or share with him the joys of the rain shower in the remodeled bathroom.

Stephanie serves dinner. It looks exactly like the picture on the box that came with the ingredients. Tony is so entranced by her perfect replica that he barely tastes the food. He marvels at the orchestra of dinnertime, the way even Danielle, his disenchanted daughter, passes dishes and clears the table when the meal is over.

"You okay, Dad?" she asks. "You seem kind of spaced."

"Your father's fine," Stephanie says. "His job has worn him down, that's all."

"I feel you, Daddy," Danielle says, pausing at the door between the dining room and kitchen. "It's a grind, right?"

Tony isn't sure whether to laugh or to cry.

After dinner, Stephanie disappears into their bedroom to watch the junk TV she doesn't want their children to know she craves. "Just keep the news off," she warns Tony, "until we know this thing is behind us."

Tony obliges. The story seems to have disappeared from the evening news cycle anyway. He checks his work e-mail and does some damage control—making an excuse for his unexplained absence that sounds serious enough that no one will ask questions but vague enough that he won't be caught in a lie.

He reclines on the couch, keeping the news off but riding the remote just in case something pops up. He drinks a beer he knows he'll regret in the morning.

"Daddy?" Danielle is standing in the doorway between the hall and the living room. She's holding her laptop.

Tony sits up, puts the beer on the side table, and holds out his hands for the computer, ready to be the dad who helps with homework. But when Danielle sits down next to him on the couch, he sees that it's not an essay or a science project on her screen, it's a YouTube video posted on one of her many social media outlets. Danielle presses play.

Tony knows what's coming before the video starts. Unlike most of the footage on the news, this clip has been shot at street level. The runner passes by and the person filming begins to follow.

The frames bounce and jerk as whoever is holding the camera tries to keep the naked jogger in the shot. Then another person comes into view. Tony recognizes his dress shirt, his chinos, his hair still damp from his shower.

Danielle presses her finger onto the screen. Stephanie would reprimand her for leaving a print but Tony doesn't bother. "That's you, right, Daddy?"

The person filming jumps out of the way. The camera catches a city bus, the palms in MacArthur Park. Then there is the sound of police sirens and the footage ends.

"I don't think—" Tony says.

"There's other clips," Danielle says. "In one of them you can totally see your face. It's like a thing online right now."

"A thing?"

"Daddy, don't you know people film everything these days?"

"I guess I didn't, sweetie." He shuts the laptop and hands it back to her.

"Don't worry," Danielle says, "I didn't show Mom."

Tony wants to bury his face in his hands; instead, he runs his fingers through his daughter's hair.

Stephanie is calling him from the bedroom. He gets off the couch. He uses the electric toothbrush and the oat scrub. Then, after removing the bolster and the two decorative pillows on his side of the bed, he slides in next to his wife.

6

Ren slept deep and long. He hadn't crashed in a bed proper since he didn't know when. The bunks in juvie barely counted—thin-ass, rubber-coated mattress, scratchy sheets, and a floppy pillow with about as much cushioning as a flip-flop. When he got out, he'd camped on a lumpy futon on the floor of a shipping container, then floated around Brooklyn's dwindling supply of abandoned buildings. It might have been private, but it wasn't exactly high comfort. So the bed at the Cecil was about as close to luxury as he'd ever come.

He knew there were better mattresses out there with softer sheets and blankets that didn't smell of flame retardant. He knew that pillows probably shouldn't crackle when you put your head down and that comforters shouldn't have plastic threads poking out. But that didn't mean he didn't descend into the sort of blackout slumber he hadn't experienced since before he was locked up.

Ren climbed out of bed, for the first time aware of how much the springs complained. He wondered why they hadn't kept him up at night. He pulled back the curtain. The view looked out across the air shaft toward an identical building with identically spaced rooms, most of which had their curtains drawn. He tried to push one of his windows open, but it was bolted shut.

The shower was down the hall, communal but private. Here's another thing people who've never been locked up take for granted—being able to stand under a stream of hot, or at least warm, water without worrying someone was going to mess with you, that someone was looking at you, mocking you, that someone was just too close for comfort. Washing up surrounded by boys who laughed and hit and tormented you with a wet towel had helped Ren master the art of efficiency—a quick scrub in the places it mattered. And the cold water had its uses—it kept him alert rather than got him clean.

The shower at the Cecil wasn't great. It smelled of mold and some sort of industrial cleanser. The vinyl curtain stuck to Ren's legs if he came too close. There were water stains on the walls and hair clogged around the drain. But the door locked. The water was hot. And there was even a window that let in the outside world.

The warm water kicked up the cheap floral scent of the small bar of soap as Ren worked it into an impressive lather. He washed parts of himself he'd probably never bothered with during his eight years of army showers. He scrubbed until the water cooled then turned cold then reduced to a trickle. He wrapped himself in the institutional towel. What he wouldn't do—no, really, he'd do anything—to keep clean day in, day out.

Back in the room, *his room* if only for a few more hours, Ren was tempted to flop back on the creaky bed, flip through the channels on the old television, relax. But he was only a guest of the Cecil for a few more hours, only allowed to sit in the lobby waiting and watching for Laila until check-out time. He packed his few possessions in his backpack and rode the elevator to the lobby.

From where he sat in the lobby, Ren could tell there were three types of guests at the Cecil—tourists who were expecting somewhere better, long-term residents who shuffled through the lobby in their robes and pajamas, and folks from the surrounding streets who looked like they'd barely scrounged enough cash for a week inside.

Two hours passed. Then three. Then there was only one hour left until Ren forfeited his right to the Cecil's lobby. He watched an older gentleman in a threadbare navy suit enter from the street. He'd seen the same guy three times already, twice passing by in his pajamas, then on his way out in his suit.

Ren intercepted him on his way to the elevator. "You live here?"

"Depends on who's asking." The man smelled like stale cigar smoke.

"Me," Ren said. "I'm looking for someone."

"Someone's always looking for someone."

Ren fumbled with the strap of his backpack. How to describe his mother? The last time he'd seen her she'd seemed weather worn, as if the years of late nights, sweet booze, and 120 smokes had finally had their way with her. She still had her fancy foil curls but her makeup seemed to be falling down on the job, barely hiding her puffy cheeks and swollen eyes. Her curves had overflowed, no longer youthful but fat.

"Her name's Laila Davis," he said. "Looks a little like me."

The man gave Ren the once-over, peering at him through crinkled eyes. "Could be I've seen her." He pulled a stained satin handkerchief out of his pocket and dabbed his dry brow. "But it's not my business who all's coming and going."

The man sidestepped Ren and pushed the elevator's call button.

Ren watched the doors open and close, hiding the man from view.

"So you're looking for someone?"

Ren turned and saw the white kid he'd ridden the elevator with yesterday sitting in one of the lobby's couches. He hadn't changed his clothes—short-sleeved shirt over long-sleeved one, baggy black jeans, and skate shoes—but he now had a small string bag slung across his chest.

"Could be," Ren said.

"This person has a name?" The kid started digging around in his little fabric pouch. He pulled out a battered pack of rolling papers.

Chances were slim that this stoned, skinny white kid with hair like a dirty mop knew his mom. "Laila Davis."

"I know a Laila." The kid didn't look up from the joint he was rolling.

"You know a black, middle-aged Laila?"

The kid was fashioning a filter out of the rolling paper package. "That's the one."

"And?" Ren asked. He wanted to snatch that damn joint out of the boy's hands.

"And she used to live here but she doesn't anymore."

"And?"

"You want me to show you her spot?"

Jesus, Ren thought, *that's what I want. That's exactly what I fucking want. Because why the fuck else would I be looking for her if I didn't want to find her.* "Yeah," he said. "That'd be nice."

The kid stuck the joint behind his ear. "I'm Flynn," he said, offering his hand with its dirt-rimmed nails.

Ren followed Flynn out of the lobby. They exited through a crowd of backpackers speaking a language Ren didn't recognize.

Out on the street, Flynn held out his wispy joint. Ren waved him off.

"You don't smoke?"

"Menthols."

"You're sober?"

"Something like that."

That answer seemed simpler than the truth. Shit like smoking weed and drinking malt liquor—rites of passage for most kids like

Ren—had simply passed him by. Maybe he had a swig or two when he was twelve and free. He might have experienced a contact high from the older ballers he'd been trying to impress when he fired that damn gun across the housing project's courtyard. But drinking and smoking and girls—especially girls—were like foreign countries with unknown languages and customs, shit Ren just couldn't untangle. Add to them the smaller stuff—smartphones and social media—that had blown up when he was inside, things designed to pull people together but did nothing more than keep Ren out.

The sun broke through without apology. It was more white than yellow. By midmorning yesterday's fog had vanished in a brutal blue sky. All up and down Seventh Street, people fought for slivers of shade. They sheltered in the doorways of the SRO hotels. They pressed against the sides of buildings and flopped behind Dumpsters.

Ren was used to the humidity back east that seeped into his skin and made him feel hot from the inside out. There were days when the air in his old housing project or the juvenile hall felt viscous, when it felt like he was inside a dishwasher. But the sun out west was something else. It burned the back of his eyelids and dried his throat. It sizzled and cooked.

"This usual?" he asked.

"This isn't even that bad," Flynn said.

But the way Ren figured, it looked like the sun was bringing out additional crazy. When he arrived yesterday afternoon the neighborhood was jumping. Today it seemed aggressive.

A woman had unfurled a sheet of black plastic and spread it on the ground, baking herself as she insulted anyone who passed. An old white dude in a tattered suit rolled down the middle of the street, sitting backward on his wheeled walker, narrowly avoiding two-way traffic. Two transsexuals were shouting at each other in front of a bus stop. One had a pockmarked face patched with makeup. The other had weight-lifter legs encased in latex shorts.

On the larger east/west streets, most of the tents had been taken down and people stood around with their possessions piled onto shopping carts or wrapped into bundles. "They shake them out early," Flynn said. "They don't let anyone sleep past six. They say it's bad for the business owners."

Ren checked up and down the street. There weren't any stores.

He stuck out, this young white kid moving purposefully between the beached addicts, the helpless, and the hopeless. A few people called to him as he passed. A couple bumped fists.

At the corner of Fourth and San Pedro a middle-aged black man in a Clippers shirt hopped off a wall. "White boy, you got something for me? Medi-Cal stonewalled me. They say I don't have the walking pneumonia." The man's voice was rattling gravel. "They say I have smoker's cough. Ain't no medicine for that. But it's my lungs, boy. I'm telling you. Know what I'm saying?" He held out his hands. "Do your magic."

Flynn reached into the pocket of his jeans and pulled out a plastic Ziploc rolled like a cigar. The hand game was over before you could dial it in. Blink and their palms hadn't touched at all.

They continued down Fourth, then headed south on Crocker. The block was loud with boom boxes and people shouting over the Department of Sanitation truck that was doing a lousy job of sweeping up the trash slicked to the curb.

"So we're heading to Laila's place?" Ren said. Because it didn't seem they were going anywhere at all, just beating time up and down the fetid streets.

"For sure," Flynn said. "For sure." He stopped walking and grabbed Ren's forearm. His eyes were red-rimmed. "You didn't think I was going to lead you astray, brother."

No, Ren thought. But he wasn't sure where the fuck Flynn was leading him. Because after an hour of pacing these streets they didn't seem to be heading anywhere good. They crossed Fifth and came to another busy block packed tight with tents. Folks were lined up for free coffee. Two dudes were slow-rolling on old BMXs. Outside a communal commissary a woman was shouting about stamps. They neared the corner of Sixth where a tight cluster of makeshift shelters rounded the corner. Across the street was the darkened neon sign of the Roger Hotel.

"This is it."

Ren glanced up at the grim façade of the hotel. Compared to this, the Cecil looked downright deluxe. But home is home, Ren figured. And it was more than he had.

He stepped off the curb. Flynn pulled him back. "Where you going? I said, this is it. Here." He pointed at the corner encampment. "This is her spot."

A grizzled man was sitting on a camp chair, a small radio pressed to his ear. He was shirtless, his ribs like a xylophone under sagging skin. A woman lay in her tent half dressed, the rest of her clothing drying from a line overhead. A man in a wheelchair was eating from a Styrofoam container.

"She camps on the end," Flynn said, pointing to an empty space away from the corner. "Guess she's out."

"Here?" Ren said. "Like right the fuck here? On the street?"

The man with the radio looked up like who the hell was Ren to comment on any of this shit. Like Ren better back the fuck up or else.

Flynn held up his hand. "It's cool," he said. "He's just looking for Laila."

"What's she to him?" the man said.

"Is she here or not?" Ren asked. Hoping the answer was no. No, she'd never been here. No, the guy had no idea who the hell Flynn was talking about.

"Can't you see with your own eyes her spot's empty?" The man turned the radio up and pressed it to his ear.

"But that's her spot?" Ren said.

"The fuck I just told you? That's her spot. She comes and goes. I'm not her daddy."

Flynn fished in his bag and pulled out another wrapped Ziploc and handed it to the man. The man sniffed the roll and pocketed it.

"How come you know Laila?" Ren asked as he and Flynn moved away.

"Same reason I know everyone." Flynn patted his string bag.

Of course, Ren thought. No way his mom could ever stay out of trouble. And even when she landed in the lowest of low circumstances, she was still looking for her high.

Flynn stared at the empty square of sidewalk. Something sticky and dark had recently been spilled and was now gathering flies. "You think she'll come back?"

"People come back to their spots," Flynn said. "That's what they do."

"I'll wait," Ren said. Because why the hell else had he trekked all the way cross-country, squandered a few bills on a hotel room, scoured the streets of Skid Row if he was going to walk away?

"It's your day, brother," Flynn said, pulling him into a brief hug. Then he was gone, leaving Ren on the street corner staring at the spot where his mom lived.

HE WATCHED FROM A DISTANCE, A LITTLE WAY UP THE BLOCK WHERE HE could keep an eye on the camp but remain out of sight of the man with the radio and his friends. A young hustler was working the block, the kind of kid Ren had looked up to when he was twelve and stupid as shit. He was a foot shorter than Ren and about the same age. He was dressed like a street tough—baggy jeans, bright high-tops, a Lakers jersey, and an all-black baseball cap twisted to the side. His face was round, his eyes bug wide. He made up for his lack of height by bouncing up and down like there were springs in his shoes.

Five times he passed Ren, their eyes meeting before Ren looked away. On the sixth pass he stopped.

"I can help you with something?" The kid bobbed and dipped and stepped closer. Ren thought he'd be able to take him down if need be, but you never could be sure with the hyper freaks. Chances were they were crazy enough to think they could tussle with dudes twice their size.

"Not that I can think of," Ren said.

"You new?"

"I'm nothing."

"How's that?" The kid jumped forward, his chest bumping into Ren. He was buzzing like a live wire.

"I'm just minding my own."

"Well, I'm minding you. I keep an eye on this block. My block, my turf."

"You can have it," Ren said.

"I can what-what?"

"I said—" But then he saw her, or someone who could be her coming up the block, passing right in front of him, crossing to the spot that was supposed to be hers.

Ren stared, tracked her as she dodged a police car, skirted a man in a wheelchair. The little hustler watched him watching. "The fuck you want with Laila?"

"That's Laila? For real?" Because it was his mother and it wasn't. Like someone had taken Laila and pulled all the softness and style out of her.

"No shit, that's Laila."

Ren moved a little farther down the block so he could get a better look at his mother.

"You walking away from me?" the hustler said. "You got better things to do? You got better things to do than talk to Puppet?"

Ren glanced over his shoulder, hoping this Puppet kid wasn't following. But the little hustler was just staring at him, jumping foot to foot, like he couldn't decide whether to pounce or bounce. Then someone else up the block caught his eye and he hopped off.

Ren stood across from Laila's place. He took his sweatshirt out of his backpack, put it on, and pulled up the hood just in case she glanced his way, just in case she happened to recognize him even though she wasn't expecting to see him.

He watched his mother—or rather, the woman who seemed to have replaced his mother—reach into one of the shopping carts behind the man in the camp chair and pull out a tent. It was yellow, streaked and stained with dirt. She popped it up, arranging the poles and pins in a flash. His mother, who used to have nails so long she made him do the dishes. His mother who spent more money than they could afford on having her hair foiled and colored. His mother who thought a barbecue in the park outside their housing project was nasty.

He watched her unroll her sleeping bag, set up her bed. Then she came out. She was wearing a pink velour sweat suit with a rhinestone heart on the back that was missing most of the jewels. Her hair was cut above her ears, a natural frizz, streaked with gray. Ren had never seen her without her purple or gold coils; he barely remembered seeing her without makeup. When he was a little kid, he'd known enough to see that although she'd been a mess—lit on booze half the day, weed at night—she had still been fine. Whenever she'd come up to visit him in juvie all the other boys would turn their heads, catcall his mom, dare him to step to them for their cheek.

Laila crouched down in front of the man with the radio. He offered her the weed. Ren watched her roll a joint, her movements quick and expert. She sparked it, sucking in her cheeks, amplifying how gaunt she'd gotten. She held in the smoke, then exhaled. She coughed violently, doubling over, her hands on her knees.

He curled his toes around his bankroll. There were cheaper hotels than the Cecil, places outside the city where he could take Laila, buy them a few weeks until he figured out the next step.

Four times Ren stepped off the curb. Once he made it halfway across the street. But each time he tripped up and staggered back to his spot. His mom thought of him as that little banger wannabe, the kid who got caught up in stuff way out of his league. She'd never listened when he'd tried to explain that he'd just been fooling, that he didn't know what he was doing, that the older kids played him. She didn't believe him that he'd never been a bad kid at all.

But what should it matter now that she was living on the street? What should she care who and what he'd been, only that he was there to help. Still, he couldn't bring himself to cross Crocker, reintroduce himself.

One of the women in camp was cooking over a small stove, heating up hot dogs that she served to the group. Someone else passed around leftovers in a greasy box.

Afternoon slipped into evening and evening into night. The street settled in, people tucked into their bags and tents and crawled under tarps. Ren watched Laila zip her flap shut.

Tomorrow, he told himself. Tomorrow he'd come down first thing. He'd pack her tent. They'd get on a bus either back east or out of town. Or they'd find somewhere else to camp, outdoors but clean. But first he'd take one more night at the Cecil, one more locked door. One more shower.

Ren headed back to Main. Things might have been crazy and chaotic during daylight, but at night the streets turned sinister and savage. Sure, it was quiet, but there was a feral element about— prowlers slinking under streetlights and darting from shadow to shadow. It didn't take much to see that the hustle was on in the dark.

Ren had never been to the jungle or any sort of forest. In fact, the closest he'd ever come to countryside was a field trip to Pros- pect Park in the middle of Brooklyn. But he imagined this is what it would be like to be lost in the woods or rain forest at night—the eyes that watched you, the things that breathed and slithered, the shadows that stretched long then slipped away, the footfalls that followed, the crack and snap of things at your back.

He heard the hiss, followed by the chemical burn of a crack pipe. He passed two guys cocooned in their sleeping bags, rolled toward each other snorting something off a dirty envelope. Someone called out as he went by, demanding a fix, a hit, anything.

Women—missing teeth, dirty hair—worked the bigger streets in ripped and saggy dresses that were meant to be sexy but just signaled their trade. Their steps were jerky, uneven. They blew smoke toward the yellow streetlights as they bent into cars, leaning into the windows like that was all that came between them and falling over.

An orderly row of tents had appeared on a side street on the northern edge of the neighborhood. A few men were standing guard, accepting cash or swaps from customers before ushering them through an open flap.

Someone whistled. A coded call came in response. A tall guy in a baggy tracksuit pedaled by on a too-small BMX making slow motion circles across Fifth. There was another whistle. Then an exchange shouted in Spanish. Someone grabbed Ren's backpack, yanking his head back. His neck jerked. He caught a glimpse of smudged sky and they were on him.

They brought him down easy. First came the kick to his side, sending him sliding from the sidewalk into the street. He smelled blood and sewage and all sorts of bodily odors that didn't belong in public. Then came the blow to the face followed by one to the chest that kept him flat. Ren was aware of folks pulling back into the shadows to watch. In the distance a siren wailed. The beating went on.

In lockup he'd had worse. But he'd also known that sooner or later the guards would arrive, pull the boys apart, and punish everyone involved. So inside he gave as good as he got, knowing he was screwed no matter. But the guys out here had the jump on him. This was their beating to give and his to take. So he didn't even try to fight back. He didn't give them the satisfaction, hoping they'd grow bored and move on.

One of the guys reached into Ren's pocket and found the few bucks he'd stashed there. The others began ripping through his clothes, searching for more. They tore the pouch pocket of his sweatshirt. They ripped the seam of his jeans. Ren knew that it was only a matter of seconds before they reached his shoes.

His head throbbed. His eyeball had a pulse. His jaw felt crooked and swollen.

His attackers were speaking Spanish, barking orders at one another. They stripped off his shoes. They peeled back his socks. They found his bankroll. He blacked out as they pried the cash from his sweaty sole.

It was still dark when Ren came to. Someone must have dragged him out of the street and onto the sidewalk. He was sprawled in the middle of the pavement. He wiped the dried blood out of his eyes and blinked. Two men stepped over him as if he wasn't there.

His backpack was next to him, his clothes scattered around it. Ren got to his knees and collected his shit.

He put a hand to his jaw. It felt like a melon, soft and swollen. He prodded inside his mouth, checking for loose teeth. But everything was in place—a small, goddamn miracle.

He stood up. His head throbbed with each movement. Each step rattled his jaw. He pulled a T-shirt and a half-empty bottle of water out of his bag and tried to clean his face. But the pressure was too much. He fumbled in his pockets and the bottom of his backpack looking for a bill his attackers had missed. He found a couple of quarters and two pennies—all the money he had in the world.

So that's it, he thought. Wake up in a hotel in the morning. Take the best shower of your life. And the next night you're brought low, reduced to nothing, as broke and busted as the rest of the people outside.

Ren staggered down the street, sick, disoriented, waiting for what remained of his vision to return. He squinted at the street signs until he found Crocker. Halfway down the block he scored a flattened cardboard box. He dragged it up toward Fifth.

He closed his eyes, tricking himself into believing that this was a precursor to sleep. But he could feel his heart thudding in his bruised cheeks, rattling his swollen gums, pulsing in his split lip.

The first couple of months in juvie Ren was so scared that being scared became part of the everyday. It was his condition—like exhaustion or asthma, so routine that he learned to overlook it. He knew better than to let his fear show. Like the rest of the boys, he put on armor, an exoskeleton. Nothing in, nothing out. But he was scared now. It just took him a moment to realize it. He'd learned to hide his fear for so long, he forgot what fear felt like.

But he recognized it now—a live wire jacking his veins, constricting his breath, making him tense his muscles so tight he shook. He lay like that for hours—his body rigid, his heart battering his chest. Then, exhausted from the effort it took to stay scared, he drifted off. And for the first time in over a decade he slept in the same space as his mother.

7

BRITT, TWENTYNINE PALMS, 2006

The smell of the slaughter was a second skin, a dank, animal odor that crept into Britt's hair, under her nails, and transferred to the sheets and pillow. It felt as if the gore from the chickens had been rubbed into her pores by all the sand and grit—a gruesome exfoliation. The stagnant air in her cabin didn't help. It just made the death scent hang heavy and close.

Britt flung back the stiff sheet and held up her hands to the window. Blood ringed her cuticles. She could feel it matted in her hair. She swore she could taste it.

Grace had been right. After the first few birds, it hadn't been so bad. Once Britt had taken over with the sledgehammer, she'd forgotten about the actual killing, focusing instead on hitting her mark. It wasn't all that different from a service motion—backswing, knee bend, weight transfer, and follow-through. Britt had landed one hundred direct hits. None of the other interns would have posted the same score. Britt was sure of that.

She had worked hard, trying to lose herself in the endeavor, exert herself into blackout exhaustion, where the fatigue in her body overcame the awareness from her mind. With each swing of the hammer, she brought herself closer to the moment when she could cease to be in the present, become nothing more than a mindless machine, lost in the pain and unconscious of the reason she'd found herself in this desert.

Her muscles were sore from disuse. There were blisters on her too-soft palms from the hammer's heavy, wooden handle. Her right shoulder ached. Her bicep, too. She squeezed and flexed the muscle, enjoying the brief, satisfying painful spasm. Because it had been worth it, knocking those heads off, one after another. Britt hadn't taken her eyes off her target but she knew without looking that everyone was watching her as she swung the heavy hammer in one graceful motion. It was grotesque and exhilarating.

This high had carried over into the party. After draining a jam jar of Grace's sweet red wine and taking a few tokes from Gideon's seedy joint, Britt had to admit that the night sky over the ranch really was a miracle and that maybe that big, smiling moon was transmitting some kind of lunar energy into her body like Anushna, the green-eyed, bottle-blond intern with the phony name, had claimed as she twirled around the fire pit, sparks alighting on her long skirt.

Britt's high had continued when Patrick had held out his hands, asking her to dance. It had helped her forget that in the daylight he hadn't seemed special at all. In fact, in his cutoff khakis, his old polo, and his perma tan, he didn't look much different from her father's crew of Florida salty dogs who wasted the day at the marina downing Long Island iced tea and talking marlin. It had allowed her to ignore that, when she'd first laid eyes on him that morning as he'd prepped the interns for the slaughter, she'd nearly laughed out loud that this dude in his weathered piqué shirt and wraparound shades was the magnificent *him* Gideon and Cassidy couldn't shut up about—the man who could *pan for the hidden gold in your soul.* Cassidy's words, not Britt's.

As Patrick had spun her away from the fire, his rough hands

on her back and shoulder, the weed, the wine, and the day's kill had tricked her into thinking that yes, there was something in his touch, something electric or probing, something that slipped beneath her skin. But then that boy had shot the hawk—a thousand-to-one chance, Britt figured—and she'd snapped back to the raw reality of the ranch and the people who lived there.

Owen's bullet had scattered the interns, like he'd been aiming at them. They'd all scurried back to their cabins. But the thick adobe walls of Britt's room couldn't block out the sound of the boy crying as Patrick made him pluck the hawk or the gagging sound he made as he was forced to eat it. Britt had jammed the pillow over her head, smothering herself in her own blood-and-smoke scent, and waited for sleep.

THE DESERT HAD STAYED UP ALL NIGHT AND ONLY QUIETED AS THE SUN broke bright over the mountains outside Britt's window. The day was already bleak with heat when she stepped out of her cabin, a relentless white-hot sear that quickly dried her eyes and lifted her own scent into her nostrils.

Ash from the fire was scattered over the ground, and the sand was littered with refuse from the party that had been abandoned when Owen brought down the hawk. The bird's bones and feathers were piled in a heap, making the place look like the sight of a ritual sacrifice. Britt wondered if the interns would scavenge these for their jewelry or if this particular bird was off-limits.

The sun shower hanging from the dead Joshua tree was empty, its plastic bag limp and heat melted. That left the pond in the oasis.

Britt dropped her clothes on a flat rock and waded in. The water was slick with a slippery film of mud that cupped her ankles. She dipped her head and tried to clean the blood from her hair. She scrubbed her nails and worked the dirt from between her toes.

The buoyancy of the water made floating easy and Britt drifted across the pond, deep into the shadows thrown by the palms. From here all the buildings of Howling Tree Ranch were invisible. There was only the silty water and the whispering trees that framed the sky, reducing it to a pristine blue oval.

There was a chance that her parents, or possibly the police, had been able to follow her movements to the desert. When she'd tried to buy a bus ticket to Palm Springs, she was told her credit card was declined and knew they'd canceled it. They would have known she'd been at the Greyhound depot and it was possible they'd even learned where she'd been headed.

But it didn't matter. There was no way they would be able to track her to this ranch, into this pond, deep in these shadows. And in the water, if Britt closed her eyes, sank below the surface, held her breath a little bit too long, she could forget that drive down the twisted road of Laurel Canyon. She could forget how the small SUV skidded, tumbled once, then landed upside down, caught by two trees. She could forget how she'd been trapped, strapped in tight by her seat belt, the radio somehow landing on a classical music station that she couldn't reach to switch off. Because that's what she needed to do—forget all of that. Outrun it. Keep running.

She heard a splash and felt the water ripple against her body. She came up for air. Cassidy was swimming into the middle of the pond. She dove deep, then surfaced, kicking onto her back so her nipples popped out of the water. Her tangle of braids and dreads fanned out behind her, twisting and turning Medusa-like, letting off oil into the water.

Britt stayed in the shadowed shallows. But Cassidy had noticed. "The water is like a million miracles in your hand. Can you feel it?"

Britt tore her fingers through her tangled hair. "I'm just washing off."

Cassidy kicked backward, sending herself closer to Britt. She reached out and took a lock of Britt's hair in her fingers. She twirled and twisted. "There's blood in your hair," she said, paddling to shore to retrieve a bottle of astringent castile soap she'd brought down to the pond.

She swam around behind Britt and tipped the bottle into her matted hair. Britt could feel Cassidy's soft belly pressing into her sacrum. Her breasts at her shoulder blades. She tensed, as if her stiff muscles could form a barrier between their bodies.

"Relax." Cassidy began to work the soap into Britt's scalp. "Our bodies are beautiful."

Britt had grown up in girls' locker rooms, suffering through her own body's transformation in front of strangers and competitors. So she was pretty familiar with the female body and the lies told about it. Not that she was ashamed. She hadn't been one of those girls who'd cowered in the toilets, changing their clothes hidden out of sight, elbows banging against the walls and sanitary napkin disposal. Nor had she ever learned to contort her limbs to remove her bra and underwear without exposing her privates. But that didn't mean she wanted someone coming as close as Cassidy was.

Cassidy was taking her time, combing her fingers through Britt's hair, twirling the ends and spreading the strands through the water. "You must be haunted by all those dead birds."

"Not really."

"No?" Britt could feel Cassidy begin to twist her hair into a braid. "Owen didn't understand either. It should always bother you to take life."

"It sounded like he was taught his lesson," Britt said.

Cassidy finished the braid and tugged on it once. "You think Patrick's punishment was unfair."

"It was kind of harsh."

"We've all danced with him," Cassidy said. "It doesn't mean you know him." She swam out from behind Britt's back. "He belongs to all of us." Then she pressed her lips onto Britt's forehead. "Together we are abundant."

Britt could smell Cassidy's greasy sage scent and the bitter aftertaste of last night's weed and wine on her breath.

Cassidy pulled back at the sound of someone crashing over the desiccated ground cover beneath the palms.

"Where is he?"

Grace was standing at the water's edge. Her brittle gray-blond hair was wilder than yesterday. Her breasts swung loose underneath one of Patrick's faded polos. She was barefoot.

"Where is he?"

"Who?" Cassidy swam toward the middle of the pond. She dipped her head, turning her face into the full force of the sun.

"You know who," Grace said.

"Patrick?"

"Patrick?" Grace gave a short, bitter laugh, like a twig snapping. "Patrick. Patrick, always Patrick. Cassidy, look at me."

Cassidy went under and emerged in the shallows close to Grace. She stood, water dripping from her buttocks and breasts, and wound her hair into a knot.

From across the pond, Britt could see the whites of Grace's wild eyes. "Not Patrick. Owen."

"I haven't seen him," Cassidy said.

"What about you?" Grace stared over the water to Britt. "Do you know where he is?"

A water bug skimmed the surface in front of Britt's nose. "I have no idea."

"What did you say to him?" Grace said. "Did you tell him that it's okay to follow his own path? That he's on some sort of cosmic trip and he needs to lose himself before he can be found?"

"Grace—" Cassidy held out her hands.

Grace swatted her away. "You might live on my ranch. You might worship my husband. But if you come near my son, there isn't enough universal goodness or spiritual beauty to save you."

Britt stared at Cassidy's back, watching the water slide down her shoulders and pool above her hip bones.

"You think I don't know what goes on around here," Grace said. "You think that I'm just some dumb woman blinded by my husband and his magical powers. But I know."

"Maybe he was just pissed off," Britt said. Because that's how she would have felt if her father had shamed her into eating roasted hawk. "That was messed up last night."

Grace glared at her. "You just got here," she said, "and you're judging us." She stared Cassidy down until her concentration was broken by the sound of wheels coming up the driveway as a cruiser from the sheriff's station rolled into view.

Cassidy flopped back into the pond as Grace went to meet the deputies. She swam over to Britt and laced their fingers together. "We need to be the ones to find Owen," she said. "We need to be the ones to bring him home." Then she started pulling Britt to shore.

"I'll wait here," Britt said.

She didn't want anything to do with those cops or sheriffs or whoever they were.

"Patrick needs us," Cassidy said. "Together we are never alone."

Britt pulled her hand away. "I'm fine."

"Hiding something?" Cassidy said, grasping for Britt's hand again. "Do you have a secret you're not telling?"

Britt could see the rest of the interns shuffling over to the cruiser. It would be worse for the cops to have to come find her if they wanted to talk to her. It would be worse to stand out. "Of course not," she said and allowed Cassidy to lead her out of the pond.

SHE PULLED HER CLOTHES OVER HER WET SKIN. *NO ONE KNOWS YOU'RE here,* she told herself. *They're looking for Owen. Only Owen. And any-*

way, she didn't know what had happened after the SUV rolled off the road in Laurel Canyon. She hadn't stuck around.

She followed Cassidy to the driveway and faced the deputies, a man and a woman whose mirrored sunglasses reflected the distorted bubble of the distant mountains behind her back.

THE INTERNS, PATRICK, AND GRACE STOOD IN A SEMICIRCLE. THE DEPUties' crisp khaki uniforms were in stark contrast to the batik, beads, and sandals of the group gathered in front of them. Patrick had his arm around Grace's shoulder.

"So exactly what goes on around here?" the male deputy said. His slick hair glistened in the sun.

"We raise chickens," Grace said.

"All of you?"

Grace removed Patrick's arm from her shoulder. "What is that supposed to mean?"

The deputy removed his sunglasses and wiped sweat from the bridge of his nose. "People talk about this place."

Anushna opened her mouth, but Patrick held up his palm.

"People say a lot of things," Grace said. "But this is just a chicken farm, and my husband is a practitioner of alternative medicine."

"And who are they?" The deputy put his glasses back on and looked at the interns, their faces stretched into funhouse shapes in his lenses. His partner kicked the dirt, scattering red dust over the toe of her shiny boot.

"Those are our interns," Grace said. "They volunteer."

"You mean you don't pay them."

"They're here to learn," Grace said.

"Jesus. Some life." The female deputy took out a pad and flipped it open. "Now any of you interns have any idea why this kid would want to run away?"

The entire group shook their heads as one.

"Any of you care to say that out loud?" she asked.

The interns muttered and assured the deputies that Owen loved Howling Tree Ranch, that he belonged on the farm, that it was part of his spirit and he was part of its.

"His spirit," the female deputy said. She didn't write that down.

Only Britt remained silent. The woman faced her so Britt saw her dirt-streaked face turned bulbous in her glasses. "And you are?"

"Britt."

"And you agree with rest of them?"

"She just got here the day before yesterday," Grace said. "She doesn't know anything."

"So, Britt," the officer said, tapping her pen on her pad, "is there any reason you can think of that Owen ran away?"

A million and a half, she thought. *And you're looking right at all of them.* But if the deputy was too dumb to see that, she wasn't going to help her out. "No," she said.

"Got a last name, Britt?"

The name she gave wasn't hers. She watched the deputy write it down, before moving on to the next intern.

But that was only a temporary fix. She knew she couldn't leave, not while the boy was still missing. Because, fake name or not, her departure would attract attention—the girl who ran away during a crisis. Then the deputies would be sure to take a second look. Then they'd be able to put together the pieces, the girl who ran from the farm was the girl who ran from the SUV, who'd left the scene.

8

Sam's ankle was bad. The bone protruded, and the skin around it had crusted a purplish black. The dirty floodwater that had entered the wound was going to be trouble if they didn't get some iodine. With a warrant out on Sam for murder—albeit for one that he claimed he hadn't meant to commit—a hospital was out of the question. There was no sense in getting locked up for having the bad luck to get your leg broken.

The men had been fixing each other up for years—sewing stab wounds with dental floss and resetting broken noses. Blake had even spent an entire day removing buckshot from Sam's shoulder with tweezers. But this ankle was a different story.

There was no one around to hear Sam's scream as Blake straightened the big man's foot, drawing the bone shard back inside. He used his cleanest bandanna to wash the cut with his last sip of water, then tied it off with a scrap from a T-shirt. He'd try stitching it up when they got where they were going and hope infection wouldn't set in. The Samoan would never walk right again, but maybe he'd walk. And that was best-case scenario.

BLAKE KNEW THAT NOT EVEN THE ROUGHEST LONG-HAUL TRUCKER WOULD stop for him and Sam. You'd have to be either a goddamn fool or stone blind to pick up someone like the big man. So Blake needed a car and quick.

It didn't sit right jacking a vehicle after he'd sworn off violence at the start of their trip west. Because as Blake saw it, there was no sense in making promises if you broke them the second things got tight. If he wanted the big man to tread a less aggressive path, Blake had to lead by example. But in this particular jam, he couldn't think of another way to transport Sam to safety.

Blake worked the highway, swearing up and down that when they got to their cabin he'd stick to his guns, turn over a new leaf—all that shit. Tread as straight and narrow as their circumstances would allow. He didn't need more faces coming calling at night reminding him of the casual, brutal things he and Sam had done in the last eleven years. There were less violent grifts out there that would keep them in the game and off the grid.

Midmorning a shirtless man driving a pickup slowed. Blake guessed the guy must have been half in the bag to pull over for him or Sam, which made it easy to force him out of his vehicle and relieve him of his wallet. Blake felt bad leaving the driver forty miles from nowhere with a buzz that would harden into a hangover. But he felt worse for Sam.

After driving a couple of hours in the same damn landscape they'd been walking through for days, Sam pounded the dash. "Home sweet home."

Blake followed Sam's gaze north to where a smattering of stripped-down cabins dotted the desert—the first change to the panorama since they hit the Twentynine Palms Highway.

"This it?" Blake said.

"Wonder Valley. All for the taking." The Samoan gestured at the landscape as if he'd built the place himself. A crown of sweat had bloomed on his forehead, and his lip was bleeding from where he'd tried to bite away the pain.

"It's not exactly a *wonder*, is it?"

"What were you expecting, a gated subdivision? No, this is it. This is fucking it. Turn." Sam waved his hand up one of the sandy roads that led away from the highway. Blake cut the wheel and they pulled off, bumping onto the uneven sand. The car hit a rocky depression. The men bounced upward then against the side windows. "Watch the fuck where you're driving," Sam said. "I don't need my back broke as well."

"You think I've driven this road before?" Blake steadied the wheel. "You think I know where the fuck I am?"

"But ain't it glorious?"

"I've seen better."

"The fuck you have," the Samoan said. "This is magic country."

THEY DROVE NORTH. THE ROAD ROSE AND FELL. THE LITTLE CABINS WERE spread out at almost regular intervals just out of sight of one another. Some had been duded up, fenced in and expanded, turned into compounds with jury-rigged satellites and dirt yards filled with old pickups and rusted trailers. But many sat empty, their windows boarded up or missing.

"Would you look at that?" Sam said as they passed a cinderblock cabin, its doors and windows gaping holes.

"Yeah," Blake said, "I'm looking."

There was nothing special about the jackrabbit homestead the Samoan settled on except that it was unremarkable—a pale cinder-block structure with plywood for windows and a rusted chain-link fence. The interior was a single room with a battered mattress and a good-for-nothing bed frame. A black-and-white TV lay on its side, the screen spidered, the rabbit ears bent in on themselves.

The air was close and stale, and trash had collected in the corners. Blake figured that sleeping outside would have been preferable, but he didn't argue with the big man who'd grown angry and irritated as they bumped up and down the rough sand roads. Blake guessed the pain in his ankle was making him jones for a Vicodin or one of the Oxys that usually set him straight.

Blake installed Sam on the mattress and used the big man's knife to cut a narrow strip out of the plywood to let in a little air. Then he ran out to the Circle K on the highway and stocked up on grub and basic medical supplies. He got Sam loaded on three 40 ounces of malt liquor and a handful of Advil and went to work on his ankle. He made a splint out of a scrap of wood to straighten the leg and keep the bone more or less in place. He cleaned the cut with a fifth of vodka and then sewed it tight. He wouldn't win any home-ec awards, but at least he didn't have to look deep into the Samoan's leg anymore.

Blake waited until Sam passed out, then drove the pickup deep into the desert where he shoved a rag into its gas tank and lit it. He jogged a safe distance off and waited for the explosion.

The boom was a release. The moment the windows blew out and the flames rose, he felt that he ceased to exist, that he was annihilated along with the truck's cigarette-pocked upholstery and jerky transmission, that he was blown to smithereens, subsumed into the ether, that he no longer was. In that brilliant moment of heat and light there was no shitty childhood in Phoenix, no cycling in and out of jail, no drugs and their comedowns, no holdups, stick-ups, beatdowns. There were no mangled faces that hovered over his bed that stole his sleep and reminded him of the blackness his mother had spotted in his soul. There was nothing.

The smell brought him back to himself, returning him to the desert made even hotter by the burning car. He put on his hat and found his way back to Sam.

BLAKE FIGURED THEIR FOOD WOULD LAST TEN DAYS, THEIR BOOZE FIVE, IF that. But Sam's foot was getting worse. An ugly purple bruise now inched up his calf and his ankle was swelling, busting open Blake's stitches.

"It's your damn shoes that cursed me," Sam said as Blake washed and restitched the wound. "There's a bad spirit inside of me," the Samoan said. "I can feel it."

"What else is new?"

Sam spat on the floor. "Remember the story I told you about the old man and a panther?"

"No," Blake said. But he remembered. He loved all of Sam's stories about shape-shifting animals and wild holy men. He loved lying on the floor in their trailer back in Phoenix, listening to the big man ramble late into the night, early into the morning, spinning a convoluted web of truth, lies, and spiritual fantasy.

"If I'm not careful, the spirit will steal my soul. Just like the panther. And it's your fault. You and your ugly white sneakers."

"So now your soul's bothering you. After all this time." Blake smudged Sam's spittle into the floor with his shoe. "What you need is a hospital. Or a doctor. When you can travel, we'll head down to Mexico, get your leg reset."

"I'm not going to Mexico," Sam said.

But that's what Blake was planning on. Once Sam's leg was healed, they'd find their way across the border where no one was looking, get lost among people who didn't care about them.

SAM'S PAIN MADE THE DAYS PASS SLOWLY. BUT BLAKE DIDN'T MIND. ANY-thing was better than the anxiety summoned by the Samoan's bent for random violence.

In the evenings, when Sam's fever broke and the heat of the day dropped, the men lay out under the stars scattered across the sky like buckshot, listening to the desert scratch away in the darkness. Blake kicked up a fire from the scrub brush and heated dinner while they watched the satellites blink overhead. If not for Sam's intermittent moaning, Blake would argue this was as close to peace as the two of them had ever gotten.

When the pain got bad, the only thing that took Sam's mind off the hurt was chess. He taught Blake to play using bits of metal and coins for the missing chessmen. But Blake couldn't get the pieces straight, always confusing the bishop with the knight. Eventually the big man would slam the board, scattering the pieces, forcing Blake to crawl on his hands and knees to collect them all.

"You're a good man," Sam said, "but I've seen a mosquito can concentrate better."

THEY WERE THREE DAYS IN THE HOUSE AND THE WALLS WERE CREEPING in. They were down to their last case of Keystone, which didn't bother Blake too much. The warm piss-water didn't do much for him besides pickle his insides.

Sam drained his can of sweet spaghetti. "We're gonna need a plan soon. I'm not figuring to fester in this desert."

"This desert was your idea."

"Well, maybe I'm saying it's time to move on."

Wisdom told Blake to let the Samoan rant. He liked having the big man down for the count instead of having to worry that he was fixing to rough up the next person who crossed their path and add to the roll call of faces that kept Blake up at night.

Back in Phoenix, Blake had tried to hide his bad dreams from Sam. When he cried out in his sleep or woke in cold sweat, he either blamed too much booze or too little. One day Sam had returned to their trailer in Phoenix with a dreamcatcher that he hung over Blake's bed.

Eagle feathers, the big man had said, pointing at the dream-catcher. *Nothing fucks with eagle. Now only the good dreams will get through.*

Blake had no time for Native American nonsense, and to him spiritual doodads were about as legitimate as the Tooth Fairy. But he let the dreamcatcher stay where Sam had put it. At night, buzzing from speed or dizzy with booze, he'd reach up and flick one of the feathers, making the thing spin until he fell asleep.

Sam tossed his empty can into the desert. Blake tried to pinpoint where it landed, figuring he'd be the one to retrieve it later. "How the fuck are we going to get anything done around here without wheels?"

"Wheels are easy. There's a hotel up the way. The man at the grocery said it's filled with foreigners. No one spends too much time searching for a stolen rental."

"Well, take your time. Take your fucking time." Sam hauled himself to his feet and began dragging his busted leg away from the fire and into the desert.

Blake watched him staggering like a drunk, lurching between the low cacti and the scrub brush. Every once in a while he'd bend down and pick something off the desert floor. Finally, he returned to the fire with a splintering plank of wood about a foot long. He sat down and found a long stick and began prodding the coals until the tip caught. He let it burn for a minute, then pulled it from the fire and waved it in the air so flames died out and the point turned to ash. Using the stick like a paintbrush the big man began to draw on the wood.

"What's that?" Blake said.

Sweat trickled down Sam's brow. He jerked his head, flinging his long braid over his shoulder. When he was finished, he tossed the stick back into the flames. Then he turned the plank around and held it out to Blake. Sam had drawn a crude leg—strong and unbroken.

"That some sort of wishing picture?" Blake asked.

"It's a *milagro*," Sam said. "If you aren't going to get rid of those shoes, I'm going to have to start healing myself."

Blake kicked the coals and kept quiet.

THAT NIGHT HE WATCHED SAM AS HE SLEPT ON THE MATTRESS, ARMS splayed wide, his good leg bent, the bad one propped up. He'd leaned the *milagro* against the wall next to the head of the bed. It didn't seem to be bringing him any relief. Sweat soaked the mattress below him, creating a sprawling shadow self. He groaned in his sleep, cursing in the language that he could only speak when verging on blackout drunkenness.

Sam thrashed, slamming one of his hands onto the floor, jolting himself from sleep. He was panting. He looked at Blake as if he were a stranger. Then he closed his eyes and crashed back on the pillow.

Blake tiptoed over to where his pack was leaning against the wall, pulled out the dreamcatcher, and hung it on a nail near a boarded-up window.

VICODIN. VIKES. BENNIES. DEMMIES. CAPTAIN CODY. PERCS. THAT'S WHAT Sam needed. The big man spent two more delirious nights and two brutal days sweating in the dark cabin. He told Blake he couldn't breathe. But when Blake helped him outside, he shouted that the sun was killing him.

On the third day of Sam's decline, Blake kicked out one of the plywood windows, letting in light and air. He opened up two cans of beans and put a six-pack of Keystone next to the mattress. He set up the chessboard and put the puzzle book within reach. He took a last look at Sam's *milagro* and hoped it would keep him safe for the next few hours.

BLAKE HAD BEEN STEALING AND RESELLING SCRIPS AND MEDS FOR YEARS. HE worked the retirement homes in Scottsdale, cleaning out entire floors while the residents were off at bingo or their early-bird dinners. He was an expert in name-brand pills and their generic counterparts. He knew which meds had desirable side effects and which did jack shit but get you well. Once his haul was complete, he'd make house calls at trailers between Phoenix and the first Hopi reservation Although he was a newcomer in Wonder Valley, he got the kind of living that went on out there—the desert isolation that created cravings for pills, booze, and speed. He saw the busted pickups careening down the sandy roads late at night, their drivers definitely lit on something. He heard the random pop of someone firing a gun into the dark to blow off steam. He'd seen the glassy eyes of the greasy-haired teenagers coming down the road on foot. He knew.

Blake put two beers in his pack, along with his knife, and the .45 he'd busted out of a pawnshop outside Phoenix. It was early evening, but the heat hadn't let up. About a half mile from his cabin he found a rusty bike in an empty driveway and figured it was worth the risk.

He rode to Amboy Road and crossed into the northern section of Wonder Valley figuring it was wise to hit houses as far from his hideout as possible. He passed larger compounds, their driveways filled with cars and trucks in various stages of decline.

The first few houses he tried yielded nothing more than drugstore-brand painkillers and meds for conditions neither Blake nor Sam had—hypertension, high cholesterol, and indigestion. Finally he came to a neat white ranch with an empty carport. There was a saggy inflatable pool and a trampoline in the yard. Two satellite dishes on the roof pointed in opposite directions.

He got in through the bathroom window. The interior was dim. A swamp cooler chugged away not accomplishing much. Blake turned on the tap and drenched his hair, then took several sloppy gulps.

In the bathroom cabinet he only found over-the-counter meds, ibuprofen and aspirin. He pocketed these. But in the bedroom he scored. Next to the fat, trashy books on the nightstand was a full bottle of Oxy. On the opposite side of the bed he found Klonopin and Xanax. In the kitchen he helped himself to a two-liter bottle of supermarket-brand cola, a jug of wine, two boxes of cereal, and some cans of soup.

The sun had disappeared and the desert was rusted shadow. He popped the top on the Klonopin and washed a few down with the soda, then got on the bike. He rode slowly, letting the pills take hold as he watched the sky turn from purple to black. Soon his mind softened and Wonder Valley became a maze. In the dark, the sand roads were indistinguishable. One homestead turned into another. He'd ridden by his and Sam's place twice before he recognized it. The cabin should have been dark, but there was light bouncing around inside.

Blake stashed the bike and approached on foot. His legs wobbled and his head felt like it was floating. He could hear voices, Sam's, yes, but someone else's too. He pulled his knife.

He pushed open the makeshift plywood door and stood swaying in the threshold. The knife's hilt slipped in his sweaty grip. The Samoan was reclining on his mattress in front of the chessboard. Across from him a teenage boy sat Indian style.

Blake rubbed his eyes.

The boy looked over his shoulder, then returned to the game. His eyes were curtained by floppy blond hair.

"He's spending the night," Sam said.

Blake tossed the big man an amber pill bottle. "Does he have a name?"

"Owen," the boy said.

"Does he have anyone looking for him? We don't need kidnapping on top of all else."

"What all else?" Sam asked, uncapping the bottle and reaching for his last beer.

Blake leaned on the cabin's wall for support as he watched them play. The kid knew chess. That much was clear. Blake could see him considering each move, staring at the board like it was a puzzle worth figuring out.

He nudged the kid with the tip of his sneaker. "And where'd you say you came from?"

"Let the boy alone," Sam said. "He can't concentrate."

"Not far." Owen picked up one of the castle-shaped pieces.

"How not far exactly?" Blake said.

The kid pointed south, toward the national park.

"The far side? Palm Springs? Indio?"

"Just over the Twentynine Palms Highway and up a couple of miles."

"Shit," Blake said. "You're local. They'll be coming for you for sure."

"I've been gone a week and no one's come looking," the kid said.

"Quit yammering," Sam said. "We're playing."

"How can I be sure when you get tired of playing hide-and-seek you won't go running back to your family, telling them all about the two men you came across over in Wonder Valley?" Blake asked.

"'Cause we won't let him," Sam said. "We're going to be one happy family."

"Christ," Blake said, standing up from the fire. "You hate family."

9

One week after Owen ran away, several of the interns clustered around James on the porch. "What does it feel like?" Cassidy asked. "Was it like having a limb cut off or dying halfway?" She sat at his feet and looked up at him all dopey the way she looked at Patrick.

"Close your eyes," the intern with the stupid Indian name said. "Now try to look here." She pressed her finger into the middle of James's forehead. "Let your third eye guide you." She drilled her finger into his skull. "What do you see?"

James closed his eyes, mostly so he wouldn't have to see her face inches from his own.

"What do you see?" She smelled like sweaty herbs.

"Nothing," James said.

"Look harder," she said. "Look for Owen."

"Leave him alone."

The intern removed her finger. James opened his eyes and saw his mother approaching from the garage where she'd been digging through the refuse of their old life, looking for some clue that might tell her where Owen had gone.

"I'm trying to summon his second sight," the intern said.

"He sees just fine," Grace replied, scattering the rest of the group as she climbed the porch and took the glider next to James.

She and James rocked in silence watching a lizard chase the interns toward their cabins.

Patrick was already waiting at the fire pit, sitting on the tallest tree stump. The interns arranged themselves around him on the low logs that served as benches. The sharing session started before James had time to disappear into the house. He hated this nighttime ritual that somehow managed to seep in through the closed windows and past the sound of the swamp cooler chugging away in his bedroom. Sometimes James could even hear these nightly sessions in his sleep—those same three questions chanted over and over, followed by the escalating anger and the inevitable tears.

The intern sharing was the guy who had turned up with Cassidy.

Why are you here? the group bellowed.

James couldn't make out his response. But the voices of those attacking his answer cut clear across the driveway. *Gideon confuses kindness with truth. Gideon thinks his words are kind but they echo false. Gideon thinks his fancy words disguise the fact that he hasn't said anything honest. Gideon expects us to believe that he cares for the rest of us as much as he cares about himself.* The interns' voices grew louder until they were shouting, until their rebukes and criticisms became one furious torrent of noise. As always, when it seemed the sharer couldn't take it anymore, Patrick silenced the other interns.

Have you learned something? he asked. *Have they brought you closer to the truth?* James always wondered what would happen if the sharer said no. There was a moment's silence before the group launched into their next question.

What do you want? For the first time all day, James wished Owen were around to answer, *I am here to get fucked up in the desert with a bunch of dirty hippies.*

Even the black-and-white TV that could barely tune in a channel was a better option than listening to the interns rip one another apart. But before James could get out of his glider, Grace reached over and wrapped her calloused hand around his wrist. "Let's go dancing," she said.

Sometimes Grace took the twins to the local inn—a collection of wood-framed cabins and adobe bungalows clustered around a restaurant—where the boys would swim in the deep, clean pool and listen to whatever musicians were passing through Twenty-nine Palms. The boys ate hamburgers while Grace drank colorful drinks out of curvy glasses and let the marines from the base twirl her around the pool deck.

WHEN THEY GOT TO THE INN, A TWO-PIECE BAND WAS SETTING UP— a couple in their early sixties. They wore bright western shirts. The man played guitar. The woman sat behind a portable keyboard craning her neck toward a microphone. They played Patsy Cline, Johnny Cash, and Hank Williams.

After two drinks, Grace started dancing with a marine—a master sergeant, she told James. The marine was strong and square, with a regulation flattop. His wide chest tapered down to his belt. He could have lifted Grace with one hand, but instead he looped an arm around her waist and spun her around the small dance floor. James watched them from the bottom of the pool in the shallow end, his eyes open despite the chlorine.

The water and the colored lights above the pool made his mother shimmer. They smoothed the harsh lines the sun had carved into her face so she looked almost as she had before they'd moved to the desert.

James came up for air. His lungs were pinched and tight. His breath came out raw. He grabbed the rough concrete and pulled himself halfway out of the water. His mother had gone back to the bar. The marine was ordering her another drink.

James wrapped himself in a towel and sat on a lounger. Grace had left her last drink half full. The band took up a new song. His mother and the marine emerged poolside.

"You're not ready to go home, are you, James?" Grace asked.

After two more songs, Grace took a break and stepped out of the pool area onto the lawn. James overheard her say she wanted to see the stars undisturbed by the light bouncing off the water. But there were stars enough back at Howling Tree Ranch—stars and stars and stars and a sprawling night sky.

The inn was crowded for a Wednesday—German and Nordic tourists, guidebooks open, planning hikes in the national park. Their pink skin and hiking shorts stood out from the desert natives and grizzled artists.

"You guys do 'Only the Lonely'?" A man in a battered black Ranger hat had stretched out on the adjacent lawn chair. He cupped his hand over his mouth, as if he was calling across a great distance instead of over a small swimming pool. "I said, 'Only the Lonely.' You can do it?"

The woman at the keyboard pointed at a straw hat at her feet. "Put your requests in there. We'll draw them for our last set."

"Maybe I want to hear my song now." The man turned to James. His face was creased like tree bark, but his voice was young. He pulled back, eyes wide. "You gave me a start there," he said. "You look like someone I know." In the low light his eyes seemed flooded with black ink. "You here on vacation?"

"I live here."

"Well, I'll be damned. Must be some kind of punishment to grow up in this particular desert." He wedged a dirty fingernail in the space between his front teeth, scraped, and spit. He crossed his ankles and put his hands behind his head, staring up at the sky. He wore jeans so dirty it was hard to tell if they'd ever been blue, and a pair of chunky, white leather high-tops.

"Is your mother that pretty lady dancing around the pool?"

"I guess."

"You guess she's your mother or you guess she's pretty?" He laughed before James could answer. "So you're one of them base kids. Pretty momma. Marine daddy. Got to be a hell of a way to grow up. Lots of rules and no dating."

"He's not my dad," James said. The marine was sitting on the opposite side of the pool talking to two men from the base. "My dad's back home."

"That so? You think your momma'll let me take her for a spin?"

"She usually dances with the marines."

"Well, we all have our particularities." He patted his jeans. "I don't suppose you want a cigarette." He fished a crushed soft pack from his pocket. "Hell, don't look at me like that. I started way younger than you."

"I'm fifteen."

The man narrowed his eyes. "Well, I'll be." A breeze lifted, rippling the aquamarine surface of the pool and raising gooseflesh on James's skin. "I remember fifteen, although I'd rather not. Now am I right in guessing you don't have a light?"

Across the pool the master sergeant and his friends got up. They shook hands, clapping each other on the back, before heading toward the parking lot.

The man stood up so he could dig into his pockets. He pulled out a white chessman, a pawn. "The stuff you find when you ain't looking for it." He put the chessman on the table next to James. From his back pocket he dug out a battered matchbook. He lit his cigarette and flopped back on the lounger. He picked up the pawn and held it toward one of the colored lights that hung from the palm trees around the pool. It looked carved from wood and had an oriental face. "You play?"

"Sort of," James said. "My brother's better."

"Is that so?" the man said, twisting the pawn before folding it back in his palm.

"He's not a prodigy or anything. But he won the regional middle-school tournament last year."

The man rubbed a grimy thumb over his lips and exhaled a long stream of smoke. "Ain't that something?"

The door to the pool area reopened and Grace appeared. The man stood up. He swiped his Ranger's hat from his head, revealing tufts of greasy black hair. He offered his hand. "Ma'am. I'm wondering if I could interest you in a dance."

Grace looked across the pool to the empty chair where her marine had been sitting with his buddies. She scanned the bar and the other loungers.

"They left," James said.

"Ma'am?" the man said.

Grace drained her drink and put the glass down on the edge of the table. James caught it before it crashed to the ground. "I'm not sure," she said.

The man pulled back his hand. "You are an excellent dancer and it would be an honor." The band struck up "Only the Lonely." "They're playing my song," he said.

"In that case," Grace said.

The man put his hat on and led her over toward the pool.

They danced slowly, mostly moving side to side. Grace tucked her head into his shoulder, letting him guide her. But every once in a while he'd spin her across the pool deck, before pulling her back.

The song ended and the man stepped away. He gave Grace a little bow and lifted his hat.

"A pleasure," he said, bringing her back to the lounger. "And a pleasure to meet you," he said, extending his hand to James. His palm felt like sandpaper.

The man headed for the bar. James felt something pressed into his hand. When he opened it, he saw the wooden pawn with the oriental face.

JAMES STEADIED HIS MOTHER ON THE WAY TO THE CAR. HE HELPED HER behind the wheel. She opened the sunroof, letting in the night air and revealing the web of stars. The tires crunched over the sand and rock of the inn's driveway. James rolled the chessman around in his hand.

They took side streets back toward the Twentynine Palms Highway. They emerged past the Circle K—the last business for a hundred miles. The road was dark—the only illumination came from their headlights, which rose and fell with the blacktop's undulations

"Where is he?" Grace took her eyes off the road and the car swerved. "Where's your brother?"

"I don't know," James said. He'd been waiting for her to bring up Owen since they'd left the ranch.

Grace righted the wheel. "Where would you go?"

"Anywhere," James said.

They passed the tiny airport and its winking purple lights.

"Your father isn't easy," Grace said. "The life we've chosen isn't easy. Sometimes I wonder." She trailed off. The car drifted toward the opposite lane. James reached out for the wheel. "He would have come out to the desert if I'd wanted to or not. He would have left."

"But you wanted to come, right?" James said.

"James, you of all people should understand that no one wants to be left behind."

"We could go back," James said.

"Not without Owen."

"What if he doesn't come back?"

"He's coming back."

"Just what if he doesn't?"

At night, the stretch of highway east of Twentynine Palms was usually empty and dark enough that approaching headlights would be visible far ahead. Whenever his mother felt a little unsteady, she let the car straddle the yellow line in the middle of the highway, using it to help her guide the wheel. Now she pulled into the middle of the road.

The road was straight until just before the turnoff for the ranch where it hooked to the right. Grace kept in the middle of the highway as she took the curve. It was a tight turn and she made it too fast. The station wagon fishtailed and screeched. She struggled to straighten the wheel. Before she regained control, they were face-to-face with the high beams of an approaching semi. The truck had a large LED cross on its grill that towered over their windshield.

Grace stretched an arm over James's chest, trying to pin him back as she yanked the wheel to the right. The nerves in his stomach and legs tingled, anticipating the impact. He held his breath, tensing against the crash.

They careened off the road and barreled into a ditch. The sound of squealing rubber drowned the wail of the truck's horn as it disappeared west.

James's shoulder slammed against the window. His mother doubled over the wheel, then rocked back, colliding first with the headrest then with the driver's-side window. The car shuddered, then hissed, before settling into its lopsided resting place.

Grace gasped and shook James's arm. For a moment he was too stunned to speak. But she didn't let go until James made a sound. Then she turned on the light over the dash. Her breath smelled sour and smoky. There was a thin trickle of blood on her temple. The headlights caught the steam snaking from under the crumpled hood. James's heart was in his ears. His blood pressed hard against his wrists. The LED cross was burned into his vision.

"Promise we can go if Owen doesn't come back."

Grace was crying.

"You have to promise."

"I promise," she said. "You and me, we can go back."

10

Day broke early and hard, bringing with it the ripe smell of everyone and everything left on the streets. All night someone had been coughing like a stalling car engine that turned over and over. Twice someone had nudged Ren awake. The first person had mistaken him for a dude called Baby Ray. The second just wanted to mess with him. Ren mumbled that the man should *back the fuck up or else.* After that, sleep was slippery.

Morning brought the sound of people shouting down the street, the slow roll of cars, a dirty glint of sun. Ren kept his eyes shut, hoping if he slept or at least pretended to sleep, he might wake up somewhere else.

He could feel the camp around him shifting, preparing, readying for the day whatever that meant. He rolled onto his side, pulling himself inward, trying to disappear into his bruised body.

"So you're not too good for these streets now?"

Ren cracked a swollen eye.

"Seems like just yesterday you were saying something like how the fuck it was possible to sleep exactly right there." The man who'd been listening to the radio in his camp chair was squatting down at Ren's side. "Times change quick."

"Leave him." A woman's voice—Laila's but not quite. A little raspier, a little thinner, without the indignant anger that used to rock their small apartment.

Ren flung an arm over his battered face.

"Yesterday this boy was shocked as shit that people could live on the street. Now he sees fit to make his camp next to ours." The man nudged Ren's sore ribs with the toe of his shoe.

"Darrell, I said leave him," Laila repeated before she was swamped by another bout of coughing.

"Last guy who bedded down in this spot you had the police remove," the man said.

"Well, the last guy wasn't my son."

Ren removed his arm, opened his eyes. Laila was standing over him. She wore a different tracksuit than yesterday—still velour, still missing a bunch of rhinestones, but this time purple. Up close, she was even thinner than she'd looked from across the street. The whites of her eyes had yellowed. Her skin was ashy pale.

"'Cept yesterday his face didn't look like he was in a one-way fight. That's right, Renton," Laila said. "I saw you watching me. Saw that you were too chickenshit to come say hi to your mother. Just 'cause I live in the elements doesn't mean I'm blind or stupid." She turned away, barking a sharp, dry cough. "Or maybe you think you're too good for me because I'm living outside."

"No, Ma, that's not what I think." Talking busted open the split in his lip and Ren could feel a trickle of blood drip toward his chin.

Laila put her hands on her hips and puffed out her cheeks, then gritted her teeth. Ren recognized the gesture, the canary before the explosion. That look had sent him to his room too many times when he was small. And when he was bigger, it's what sent him out into the courtyards where he met the older ballers.

"So what all happened to your face?" she said.

"Got beat."

"I can see that. Who and where?"

"Some crew speaking Spanish over on Fifth Street, I think," Ren said. It had to be some sort of badge of dishonor getting jumped after barely twenty-four hours.

"Must have been the Eighteenth Street crew," Darrell said. "Were you trying to cut their turf?"

"Hell no," Ren said. "I was just minding my own."

"That's the way to be down here," Laila said, "though it some-times doesn't work out." She handed him a bottle of water and a small towel. "Keep it clean. If the beating doesn't kill you, the infec-tion will."

Ren sat up and began to tend to his cuts. Compared to the days before, the street was quiet. No one was packing up, no one moving on. In fact, except for the group on the corner, it seemed like folks were sleeping in.

"What's going on?" Ren asked. "Seems quiet."

"Nothing's going on and that's a damn blessing," Laila said. "It's Sunday, so the cops and the boys on the bikes let us sleep."

Ren finished with his battered face and handed Laila the rag.

Laila was taking down her tent. Her sleeping bag was already neatly rolled on the sidewalk next to three large, ripped plastic shopping bags filled with clothes. "What're you doing down here, Ma?" Because even though she was right there, as real and solid as his own arm, Ren couldn't quite believe what he was seeing. Laila, a woman who put on her tightest jeans and brightest shirt to go to the budget grocery store, who ran the power bill up beyond imag-ining because she couldn't live without the AC on full blast, day and night, May to October.

"Mind your own damn business."

"It's—"

"Lemme tell you something, Renton. If you stick around long enough, you'll learn quick that your story is the only thing you have that belongs to you proper." Laila reached into one of her plastic bags and pulled out a big, fake leather purse. She slung the bag over her shoulder and walked to the corner.

Ren watched her check up and down the street, glancing in cars. She crossed her hand over her chest, tapped her foot on the curb. A bus passed and stopped. When it rolled away, Laila shouted something at its back that Ren couldn't hear. She glanced over her shoulder at the encampment. "The fuck time is it?"

"Too early," someone shouted.

A few more cars passed—Laila checking each one. Then another bus.

Laila was craning her neck, straining to see something down the street. Then she put her hands on her hips, nearly pulling down her sweatpants from her bony waist.

A white guy had turned up at the corner. He was dressed kind of like a rocker, kind of like a bum—black hair, black jeans, black leather vest. Laila was sassing him for something. Ren could tell without hearing her, giving him lip about being late or even being there at all. The man didn't seem too interested or troubled by her attitude. It looked like he'd weathered this particular storm before.

Eventually Laila reached into her oversized purse and handed over a bunch of bottles that, from where Ren was watching, looked like prescription medicines. The man slipped her some money, which Laila made a big show of counting right out there in the open. She held out her hand for more, which the man immediately forked over like this was all part of their little dance.

Laila tucked the cash in her bag and returned to the camp.

"What's all that?" Ren asked.

For a split second Laila looked at him like she'd forgotten he'd turned up in the night. Then she wagged her head side to side like he was too foolish to bother with. "Since you are here I might as well get you fed."

They headed to Seventh, retracing Ren's walk from the station two days earlier. On the corner a shirtless man was sprawled half on, half off the curb, a scar clear-cut across his belly. On the far side of the street, Laila had to pause to catch her breath.

"You sick, Ma?"

"I haven't seen you in four years and you come at me with the questions."

Now whose fault it that? Ren thought. *Who left who in a juvie facility upstate and then stopped visiting? Who moved away without a forwarding address?*

Laila led them to an outdoor taco spot with a covered seating area filled with scratched orange benches and dirty tables bolted to the ground. A sign taped to the bulletproof window told Ren the place accepted WIC and food stamps. After Laila ordered for them, she pulled out a crisp five-spot from a small roll in her purse. She caught Ren clocking the cash. "See something you want?"

"You got cash but you sleep on the street."

"I sleep where I choose."

They took their burritos to a table close to the sidewalk. Laila jabbed at her food with her fork. "You ever had Mexican?"

"There was some sort of taco night."

"That doesn't sound too bad," Laila said.

Ren ate fast, a bad habit he picked up in juvie, where lingering over your food led to trouble. But Laila was eating slow, tiny bird-like bites that she struggled to get down. Eventually she slid her burrito over to Ren, only a fraction of it missing.

"How come you don't want it?" he asked.

"I can't give my son some food without a bunch of questions? Eat it or don't, but just know that I'm not in the business of buying a lot of meals."

Ren took the plate and went to work, eating so fast that by the time his stomach caught up it was too late and he felt his gut might bust.

"So," Laila said. "I guess you're going to keep bugging me until I tell you how I wound up here."

"I'm not here to bug you, Ma. I'm here to get you home."

Laila threw back her head and laughed. And for a split second Ren could see how she looked in the early evening when the booze made her light before it brought her down. How she looked when she sang in their apartment when she thought no one was looking. Laila's laughter was cut short by a coughing fit that doubled her over at the waist. "Get me home? How's that now? You only just got here and you got yourself beat up." She wiped her mouth. "You probably rolled into town with grand aspirations, but now you're regulation-grade homeless."

Ren bit his lip to stop himself from spitting out the same kind of childish retort that fueled Laila's anger. He felt blood spring once more from the cut on his lip. "I'm gonna figure shit out, then I'm gonna get you home," he said.

"Who says I want to go anywhere? And what the fuck is home anyway?" Laila crossed her arms over her chest and gave him the look she usually saved for his father when Winston said something she called *dumb as fucking shit*.

"It's not here," Ren said.

"What do you even know about home? Home is where I say it is."

"But—" Ren glanced out along Seventh Street. A woman wearing no pants was using the curb as a balance beam. Two men on the corner were playing a hand game.

"You were out of the house at twelve so you don't know from home."

Out of the house—like he had a choice in the matter.

"And let me tell you a few more things you don't know. I bet you didn't know your daddy skipped up to Troy with his new piece leaving me to pick up his half of the rent should I want to keep on living in my own damn home. And then when he got tired of her he sent for me. And I packed my shit and moved to some gray-ass town upstate because I didn't feel like pulling double shifts to live in that shitty apartment all on my lonesome."

"I didn't know because you didn't visit," Ren said.

"I guess you're not hearing me. I had my own shit going on."

Ren crumpled his paper plates together. "Sounds like it."

"And Troy was no picnic neither. Your daddy said we had a townhome, which sounded fancy as fuck. Turns out it was just another project. Only difference was, we had two floors of shitty living. So I split after four months. Figured I'd see the ocean for once."

"There's an ocean back east," Ren said. "And from what I remember you weren't too interested in that one." Coney Island—only a subway ride away, no need even to transfer, and Laila had never taken him, had told him if he wanted to see the water, he could go look at the damn bay from the docks at the edge of their hood.

"Yeah, well. Truth is I never made it to the one out here, neither. I got waylaid."

Now this was the Laila Ren remembered, using strange words to distract from her own culpability. Like everything happened to her but she did nothing. Because it wasn't her fault was it that her girlfriends had kept her out till three in the morning, that she'd overslept and missed Winston's parents when they visited. She'd been *waylaid*. Because how could she be the first one to leave her little cousin's twenty-first birthday when she was the one who organized it, how could she leave all those girls dancing in a club with a bunch of guys all over them. She'd had to stay, had to chaperone them back to someone's home, had to make sure those guys kept their hands to themselves, had to stay up all night doing it, had to miss work the next day. So it wasn't her fault that she was fired, course, wasn't her fault that she'd been *waylaid* again.

Ren could see it now—Laila arriving in downtown L.A., planning to get out to the beach, planning to start over without Winston, but getting sidetracked by some action on the street, someone promising her the moon but only delivering some booze or drugs, which had been just fine when it came down to it.

Laila took a sip of water, trying to clear the crackle from her throat. "And when I tried to rent an apartment, I learned your daddy hadn't been paying the rent on our Troy shithole in months. Add to that he'd gotten himself evicted after I left. He treated me like a fool and killed my credit permanent. No one's going to rent to me. Three months of hotel living cleaned me out."

"And?"

"And what? And here I am."

"This is no place," Ren said.

"Says who? You? This is a place. My place." She gave him a look, like end-of-subject-or-else, like he was eight years old, a nuisance who didn't know what from what. "Damn," Laila said. "Keep sitting around like this and we're going to be late."

"We're going somewhere?"

"It's Sunday, Renton. A godly day. Or didn't they teach you anything when you were in that juvenile hall?"

"And?"

"And we're going to church."

"For real?" Because when Ren was a boy, he'd listened to his mother and her friends mock the ladies who paraded across the grim courtyards on Sunday mornings, proud in their jewel-toned satin skirt suits, wide-brimmed hats, patent leather heels on their way to one of the storefront churches or local tabernacles. Ren liked their colors, the neatness, the formality. But Laila called them crazy ladybugs, too stupid to see that God, if he existed, didn't give a damn if their shoes matched their purses or their hats, their dresses. "You're going to church?" he said.

"We," Laila said standing up. "We did food, now we do God."

CHURCH WASN'T REALLY CHURCH, BUT A ROW OF METAL FOLDING CHAIRS two wide and twelve deep in a narrow alley. The corridor smelled like the zoo Ren visited back when his memories weren't so hard. Someone had thrown up a few crude religious murals on the walls—a sickly Christ drooping from a frail-looking cross and a cartoonish approximation of what Ren figured was supposed to be the Virgin. If things were up to him, those walls would be blazing with all sorts of heavenly glory—dramatic colors and graphics that damn well made you believe that there really was a better place.

Ren recognized the preacher as one of the women who had been handing out pamphlets down by the bus stop the day he rolled into town. She was light skinned with dozens of moles scattered across her nose and cheeks like three-dimensional freckles. She wore a long purple skirt, dirty at the hem, and a short-sleeved white blouse. Her braids were wound in a scarf. She held a battered-looking microphone plugged in to a single speaker that made her voice crack and boom as it echoed in the narrow alley.

"Sister Cora Dufrane," Laila said, sitting in a chair near the back.

They'd arrived late. The sermon was in full swing. Sister Cora closed her eyes when she preached, her chin tilted toward the slip of sky above the alley. Her voice came like a crashing wave. It took Ren a moment to orient himself in the speech, tune in to the sister's words instead of looking at the group gathered to hear her. Laila broke into a coughing fit and spat. The preacher waited for it to pass.

Most of the seats were taken by people well past Ren's age. A few congregants had pulled up in motorized wheelchairs that whirred and beeped when their drivers jibed the sister's meaning. Ren sat behind Laila at the farthest edge of the congregation, ready to escape should this alleyway god look to confine him.

He only half listened to the sermon. Instead he focused on the graffiti murals. Cup his hand the right way and he could feel the weight and size of a cylinder of Krylon. He could hear the rattle and hiss and get the contact high from the fumes. In juvie he'd practiced his style using printer paper in place of the blank walls he planned to search out when he was released. He painted the world he wanted to step into, and when he got out, he painted a better version of the place he found. He exaggerated his surroundings, made them jump off the walls, hoping he could paint his way into them and find his home. He couldn't imagine exercising his skills on these streets. There was no amount of Krylon that could make them home.

Two women from the front row got up and joined Sister Cora for a hymn. Laila closed her eyes and tilted her head back as she listened. "I always wanted to sing at the tabernacle," she said.

"No shit," Ren whispered.

Laila turned in her chair so she faced him. "Yeah, no shit. Let's just say, I became disaffected."

"The fuck does that mean?" Ren said.

Laila slapped his hand.

The hymn finished. Sister Cora was coming down the aisle, holding out the microphone. "Whose word is going to lift us up? Whose word is going to be the light that shines into our hearts?"

"Me." Laila was on her feet. The microphone was in her hand. And before Ren had a chance to figure that his mother was about to preach to the tattered crowd gathered in the alleyway, she was up front, her mouth open, the few rhinestones on her sweat suit catching a sliver of sun that found its way down between the narrow buildings.

"Someday an old man is going to be knocking at your door and you're not going to recognize him. Maybe it's because he's withered and worn like shoe leather—cracked like a suitcase. And you're going to cover your face, shut your eyes. You won't see the skin gone gray, the bone turned brittle, the pupils shrunk, the tempest that surged up and died out leaving destruction. You'll try to shut the door, but you can't. For this man, he's going to keep coming. This man is you.

"I know, because he's come for me. It was my own damn ghost that grabbed me. Stared back at me from the broken bathroom mirror in my housing project in Brooklyn when I'd been up all night boozing. Looked up at me from the bottom of the bottle I was fixing to throw at my husband. Tapped on my window where I was lying naked with a man I didn't know. Showed me the pain that was permanent. Showed me this skin I can't escape.

"I left home to run away from him. Thought I could leave him behind back on the East Coast. That I could outstrip him.

"I told myself that if I came out here, lived by the ocean, drank in all the light and sunshine, this man wouldn't find me, wouldn't be in me, wouldn't be me.

"You know what? I never did see the ocean. I came thousands of miles only to encounter my own Holy Ghost a continent away, waiting for me the minute I stepped off the bus. He'd beaten me cross-country. He'd been on the express. You know why? Because he knew me better than I knew myself, knew that I'd have to get through him before I'd get to any damn ocean.

"He knew that I was foolish enough to try to run from him when I should have been running to him.

"You don't believe me? You think I'm tripping? Let me ask you this. Who is the Holy Ghost after all? Some man sent down from heaven? No, he's what walks between you, stalking these street corners, slipping in between the whites of your eyes. He's in you already. But you didn't even know. I found him. I saw him in me. I embraced him and he let me go. Which is why I'm standing here talking at you.

"I only have one question for you."

Laila opened her eyes and fixed her stare right on Ren.

"I only have one question for you."

The congregation followed her gaze, everyone turning to look at him at once.

"Who is your Holy Ghost?"

Ren glanced at Sister Cora who was hovering nearby, nodding at him as if his own mother's attention was its own sort of honor.

"I said, who is your Holy Ghost? 'Cause he's in you now and he won't let you be."

Ren shook his head, trying to break free of her stare.

"Oh, I see him in you. I see him in all of you. He's in there. He won't set you free, so don't ask. You need to make room for him in your heart. So I ask you one more time: Who is he?"

Ren was on his feet. He took down two folding chairs in his hurry. He rushed from the sound of Laila's voice, the closeness of the alley and its animal odor. But back on the street the brutality of the high noon sun and the mad noise of everybody else's problems gave no relief.

His mother didn't need to ask and she damn well knew it. Ren was too aware of who his Holy Ghost was—the person who sat heavy on his heart. He took a deep breath, inhaling the strange smell of Skid Row—something beastly but equally antiseptic. He moved as quick as the heat would allow, hoping to outrun the memory summoned by Laila. He passed the Midnight Mission. He passed a group of teenagers wearing matching purple polo shirts advertising their Christian outreach. He passed a woman herding six children into a decrepit hotel.

He crossed from the heart of Skid Row into downtown. He wanted the festering streets at his back. He'd buried his own demons, his Holy Ghost. But a few more nights out here and the man would be as real as if he were still breathing.

Laila knew what she was doing, reminding him of the sin that she would never forgive, letting him know that she knew he was bad. No amount of time inside, no amount of rehabilitation could change that in his mother's eyes.

Ren kept moving, trying to outrun his ghost. He paced the streets, watching downtown get going—a young crowd venturing outside to walk their dogs, take a jog, gather for brunch. The day was theirs, loose and malleable. They'd stay around for drinks, and then start thinking about dinner.

On every corner he could feel his ghost getting closer, growing solid. He could hear the man starting to breathe, his footsteps starting to fall as he began to keep pace with Ren.

Ren walked until the sun slipped over the few skyscrapers at the far edge of downtown. As he predicted, people were filling the few bars and restaurants. Lights were coming on in the loft buildings. The homeless who'd migrated this far west were heading back toward the missions.

He reached his hands into his empty pockets. He was used to having little but never having nothing. At dusk, he joined the shadow march back to Skid Row.

People were already lined up at the Midnight Mission on Sixth. A few tents were handing out food. Ren grabbed a plate and worked his way back to Crocker. He found his discarded box from the night before and dragged it into the spot next to his mother's, which he guessed was what he now called home.

11

BRITT, TWENTYNINE PALMS, 2006

There are things you get used to: the heat, the dirt, the ammonia smell of the chickens. The weird grains and sandy greens. The crappy wine. The cheap weed. The sweet tang of burning sage coming off everyone and everything. Then there are things you don't: the goat-eyed stares of the other interns, the way they are all around you, suffocating you in this wide open space. Grace's eyes watching from a distance. Patrick's watching up close.

Nearly a week on the farm and Britt's skin had already turned nut brown, not quite the terra-cotta hue of Cassidy and the twins, but close. The sand and silty pond water matted her hair, forming textured tangles that she couldn't comb out. There was a layer of dirt on her skin that lingered no matter how hard she scrubbed it away.

At first Britt resisted the desert's insistent takeover. But when she caught her reflection thrown back at her in the large window of her cabin by the night sky, she felt relief, as if the sand and sun and smells would soon hide her self from herself, building a new person on top of the one she'd been trying to escape.

She took on the more repellent chores—mucking out the chicken coop, turning the compost, burning the body of a coyote that had died near the oasis. She wanted to smother herself in the worst the desert could throw at her, drive away the baby powder smell of her teammates' deodorant, the slimy mildew odor of a lifetime of locker rooms, and the heady pop of a can of fresh balls.

If she became unrecognizable to herself, she would be invisible to those who might still be looking. And if she labored hard enough, harder than she thought possible, she could reach that blackout stage of pure fatigue where mind and memory cease, leaving behind the body to do its work.

During farm chores, the interns always started off strong, a burst of industry—singing, whistling, praising the beauty and the power of whatever task they'd been assigned. Then they'd peter out, wandering away to check something inconsequential—a jar of fermenting kombucha, the way the sun was throwing a shadow net of leaves on a flat rock, a snakeskin shed on someone's threshold.

Initially Britt was frustrated by their shirking. But soon she looked forward to the moment they'd wander off, leaving her in the gore and grime. Her muscles were coming back. She could see the curve return to her biceps and feel the bulk in her shoulders. Her calluses would appear soon too. She could see how the weeping blisters from the shovel and sledgehammer on her palms and fingers would heal, then harden. At night, after the sharing session, she'd probe her muscles, prod the ripped red circles on her palms, enjoying the deep ache and prickle of pain.

When the last intern wandered off, Britt was left with Grace. Since Grace's outburst by the pond she had barely spoken to Britt or the other interns, still holding them responsible for her missing son. She worked alongside them in silence, only giving instructions when necessary, saying nothing when they quit for some more abstract pursuit.

When it was just the two of them shoveling out the coop, their arms grazing, their movements in efficient sync, Britt felt the weight of Grace's silence.

The sun was a brutal assault, cooking the coop's already fetid smell, pasting a slick of loose feathers to Britt's arms as she worked. She and Grace had just finished loading a wheelbarrow. Britt blew on her blistered hands to cool them before gripping the cart's wooden handles. Grace was drinking from a mason jar of water. She passed it to Britt.

They sipped in silence, watching a desert hare seek shade behind the garage. Britt glanced at Grace hoping she'd say something. Sweat was pouring down their foreheads. Their hair was dirty and stiff with detritus from the coop. They'd been working for five hours, alone for three.

Britt allowed herself a small sip from the jar. She didn't want to let her exhaustion show.

Grace took the water away. "Take the muck to the far side of the garden. We'll let it enrich the soil."

Britt lifted the wheelbarrow. Her palms stung. "Out of refuse comes beauty," she said. It was something Cassidy had said, or close. Something she imagined was close to the wavelength of Howling Tree Ranch.

She began to roll the wheelbarrow out of the coop.

"What did you say?"

Britt looked over her shoulder at Grace who was staring at her, her brow furrowed, her eyes crinkled, her lips pulled back.

"I said, out of this refuse something beautiful will grow."

"Look around," Grace said. "How can you be so sure?"

"I don't know—"

Grace glanced across the yard at Gideon and another intern making sun tea out of a grab bag of herbs. "They sound so confident when they talk about things they don't know," she said. "I thought you were trying to be different."

IN THE LATE AFTERNOON THERE WERE NO MORE CHORES. BRITT JOINED A few of the interns in the pond where they were floating naked.

Gideon sat on a flat rock rolling a joint. He lit it and swam out, putting it between Britt's lips. "You work too hard," he said. "You'll overlook the sky if you keep your eyes on the ground."

Britt took a deep drag. Seeds slid through the paper and into her teeth. "Work hard with your body. Work hard on your soul," she said. She exhaled, the stream of smoke blanketing her laughter.

"I dig it," Gideon said, wrapping his arms around her. "I dig it. And there I was thinking you were too grounded in the straight world for us."

Britt let him hold on for a moment, then wiggled free, diving down, driving her fingers into the muddy bottom of the pond. She came up and floated. The joint circled. The palms overhead told each other secrets.

Britt stayed on her back, her head just low enough to keep her from hearing the chatter. She watched the wind shake a dry palm frond loose, watched it twirl, then plummet into the water.

THE INTERNS DRIFTED ACROSS THE POND, THEIR VOICES LOST, EXCHANGED for the ebb and flow of the pond's slight current against Britt's ears. Then that too was silenced, replaced by a familiar orchestra. At first Britt thought it was the hum of farm machinery echoing underwater or the reverb of a plane flying low overhead. But then she knew it—the classical piece that had been playing while the Toyota lay trapped by two trees just off the road in Laurel Canyon. Bach, that's what it had been. And now she heard it again, echoing in the silty water at Howling Tree Ranch, haunting her.

She had gone into shock—she realized that a couple of days after she'd fled the accident. Trapped in the upside-down SUV, her mind had locked down, unable to fathom how much worse things could have been, how those trees might not have caught them. The car could have kept on rolling and fallen deeper into the ravine. She couldn't reach out to Andy, who was slumped over the wheel, his face slack, his eyes rolled back. She had tried to touch him, but pulled back at the last minute. She didn't want to know.

Instead, she'd fumbled for the button on the radio, anything to get that damn Bach turned off. And somehow, she'd wriggled out of her seat belt. Her door had swung open, freeing her from the car. She'd slipped, the trees and scrub tearing her dress. She scrambled up the incline toward the road. She hadn't looked back.

She should never have allowed herself to remember the accident. Because the memory made the water in the pond feel too hot and too heavy, like it was trying to drag her down, suffocate her. She splashed to shore with panicked, haphazard strokes. She needed to keep moving, outrun the memory, leave it behind. She needed to force herself into the numbed state that came from either drinking or running, when her body detached from her mind.

She didn't bother to dry off, just shoved her sockless feet into her sneakers. And then she ran. She sprinted, away from the oasis, past the cabins, out into the desert. She pushed herself, hoping for that moment when her exhaustion would vanquish her thoughts and her mind wouldn't go blank but black.

Four hundred meters, then eight hundred—a half mile give or take. Her mind was on the pain in her shins, the tightness in her quads. Soon her focus was turned inward, to the beat of her heart, the struggle of her breath. She ran faster so the blood rushing in her ears swamped her thoughts, drowned out the sound of the crash and the memory of that damn Bach.

But something was penetrating the internal cacophony of her run, an unfamiliar desert noise, a low animal moan, not feral; well, not entirely feral Britt hoped. She stopped. She put her hands on her knees, panting, sweating. Then she lifted her head and looked at the flat rock in front of her.

Cassidy was on her knees, bare chested, her wild hair bouncing around her shoulders, her beads clacking and smacking into her sternum. Her long skirt was bunched up around her hips, her soft belly undulating over the waistband. Underneath her, his wrap-around shades pushed up into his gray-black hair, was Patrick. He reached up, cupping both of Cassidy's breasts, then let his hands fall as if it wasn't worth the effort.

Britt took a step back, her foot cracking through a low arrow-wood bush. Cassidy looked up. Her blissed-out eyes regained focus and she gave Britt a satisfied smile. Then without breaking eye contact, she lowered her mouth to Patrick's ear. Britt could almost feel the hot, wet whisper.

Then Cassidy sat up and shut her eyes, dismissing Britt. She flung her head back, jiggling her breasts from side to side, whipping her wild hair, ramping up her performance, playing to the back of the house, working Patrick like a sorority girl riding a mechanical bull.

Britt took a deep breath, ignoring the tightness in her lungs and the burn in her calves, and kept running, not back to the farm but farther toward the national park, like nothing had interrupted the rhythm of her run.

THAT NIGHT IT WAS CASSIDY'S TURN TO SHARE. AND AS USUAL THE INterns were brutal on her. She sat at Patrick's feet, looking at him as the shouted accusations and defamations reached a fever pitch, absorbing the interns' cruelty without looking at them.

Anushna piled on. Then two of the other guys. Then Gideon again.

"Britt?" Patrick said. "You have nothing to add? You think Cassidy's response to the question is perfectly honest? That she has achieved her true self?"

"I think Cassidy prefers performing for others rather than focusing on herself," Britt said. "I think Cassidy only pretends to want to be part of the group but instead would rather be above it." It felt good, she had to admit, this reasonless attack, savaging Cassidy for her exhibition out on the rock.

"Good," Patrick said.

"Cassidy needs to be loved by everybody," Anushna said, "but she only values the love of certain people."

"Cassidy mistakes sex for love," Gideon said. "Cassidy confuses sexuality with spirituality."

"That's a lie," Cassidy said. "You're a liar."

When the session was over, lingering aggression hung in the air. The interns drank heavily, groped and pawed, and quickly got sloppy. Britt joined them for a bit, but her work in the coop and her run made her an easy drunk so she dragged herself back to her cabin before she made a mistake.

She had no idea how long she'd been asleep when the door to her cabin opened. At first she thought Gideon had come to press his luck because she knew all the hippie-dippie bullshit would fade away the moment she told him no.

She reached for the light.

"Don't."

It was Patrick's voice. Britt pulled her covers up to her chin.

"Shh." He sat at the edge of her bed. Her body tensed as he slid under the covers.

Britt kept her hands pressed to her sides, her toes curled, her calves tense, her stomach taut. She could feel every detail of his body where it touched hers—his wiry arm hair, the bump of his elbow, the knob of his shoulder, his knuckles and fingertips against her hip, his ankle bone against hers.

She waited for the migration to begin, the casual crawl of his hands over the waist, the first tickle of toes, the incremental invasion until he was on her, in her. But Patrick didn't move. He didn't speak. He just lay there in the dark until their breath fell into sync. Until Britt started to lose herself in the in-out rhythm of their chests rising together. Until she slept. And when she did, she didn't hear the desert and she didn't dream of the accident.

12

TONY, LOS ANGELES, 2010

When Tony wakes up, the sky is the color of eggplant—an imperfect black that is the result of light pollution or immanent dawn. The clock on the table tells him it's not even six. He feels the familiar punch in the gut followed by the tightening in his chest as the list of things to do, things to pay, and all his other ambient stresses reach him at once. He feels for his phone under his pillow, ready to check his e-mail, then remembers he's taken the day off—Stephanie's idea and a good one. His chest loosens. His heart slows. He can breathe.

Careful not to disturb Stephanie, Tony slides out of bed. He knows the moment she opens her eyes the morning will be flooded with preparations for their weekend away—luggage, clothes, dinner reservations. He will be asked to check the timers on the sprinklers then go fill up the car and bring it around front to load. He will keep his mouth shut when he sees how much his wife and children are bringing for their three-night escape.

Tony knows how the weekend will go. Once they are on the road heading north he will relax. He will enjoy the ride, enjoy the lunch spot Stephanie picked. He will enjoy the complimentary glass of wine at the hotel.

The weekend will be flawless. It will have no surprises. There will be no talk of Tony's breakdown or of their impounded car. On Sunday Tony will wake with the same panic in his chest as today. He will try to tamp it down while Stephanie checks her watch, counting the minutes until she has to begin to coordinate their packing.

Tony slips into the bathroom and puts on his running clothes. He figures he can fit in a long run, maybe even ten miles, and be back in time to help mobilize his family. He logs into his Map My Run app, chooses his "Long, Slow, Steady" playlist of rock anthems, and slides his smartphone into an arm strap. He slips a credit card, a house key, some cash, and his ID into the pouch behind his phone—precautions Stephanie insists on.

In the living room he checks to see if Danielle has left her laptop out, if he might scroll through her social media outlets for more footage of the naked jogger, scanning the blurry videos for a fleeting shot of himself. The computer is nowhere in sight. He goes to her room, cracks the door. He watches her sleeping, the soft rise-fall of her bedspread. He can see her laptop winking on her desk across the room. He leaves it.

Tony steps out onto the lawn. The only hangover from yesterday's run is a slight sting in each shin. He stretches his calves against the eucalyptus tree in the yard then hops foot to foot, testing the spring in his step. The music is pumping in his ears, helping his adrenaline rise to meet the needs of his run. He jogs to the end of the driveway and looks up and down the street. Other than a cat scurrying between the garbage bins, he is the only thing moving.

Normally, he heads south, under the 10 and toward the Kenneth Hahn State Recreation Center where he carves a five-mile loop through the three-hundred-acre park before heading home. But today he doesn't want to escape the city so he heads north, toward Pico, a busy east-west boulevard usually avoided by runners.

From his cocoon of music, Tony watches the city get into

gear—delivery trucks, lumbering buses, the early commuters heading off in their cars. As he turns onto Pico, he passes a woman pushing a tamale cart. He watches a white van pull to the curb and a man lean out the driver's window calling to the vendor.

Tony whips off his headphones. Now he can hear the vendor crying, "TA-MA-LAYS," as each car passes her stand. He can hear the rumble and sigh of the buses, the birds calling down the morning, the guard dogs barking behind cyclone fences. He can hear a car speeding ahead and a siren wailing. He can hear his breath and his heartbeat in his ears, the internal soundtrack of his run. No longer controlled by the rhythm of his music, he picks up the pace.

He turns right on Pico, passing shopping centers and shuttered taco stands. He runs through a Hassidic neighborhood with Glatt supermarkets, orthodox schools, even kosher Thai and pizza restaurants.

The miles slide by. He doesn't bother to check his app to see if he should turn back. He passes car washes and a few big-box stores and soon he's in an unfamiliar section of Pico, run-down and gritty, part Mexican and part black with old burger and pastrami stands, their windows greasy and cracked. He passes a row of upholstery shops and used appliance stores. He passes El Salvadoran panaderías, Oaxacan panaderías, and dozens of carnicerías. He runs by Pentecostal storefront churches, a large Ethiopian church, a Greek Orthodox cathedral.

He's run at least six miles. He should turn back, pick up the pace, get home, but his legs are loose, his breath easy. His feet keep moving.

He's back in Pico-Union—the neighborhood of Honduran and Salvadoran restaurants, calling centers, pawnshops, and places advertising CASH PAYDAY LOANS where the cops had caught up to him. He passes the L.A. Convention Center, a green-glass-and-white-steel behemoth that straddles Pico.

To his left are the downtown office towers, their tops illuminated by the first glint of sun. To his right, the wholesale district. In five blocks Pico dead-ends at Main. Tony takes a left. He runs a few blocks then heads east into the heart of Skid Row. He's not sure if he could have predicted it when he took off, but his jog ends at the police station.

He checks his phone. He's run over nine miles, averaging below eight minutes per. It's a solid outing. He'll log it into his app and one of his online training buddies will comment: *Good effort, bro. Beast.*

He ignores the looks he gets from the homeless packing up their tents as he does a few stretches against the low wall outside the station. For a moment he's ashamed of the luxury of time, of being able to run unencumbered by the basic necessities of survival.

But he's not entirely unencumbered, not really. He's still plagued by the worries of his family and his job, his panic that he's flatlining and dragging his wife and kids with him. No matter where or how far he runs, he always arrives back at this. He's ashamed that the problems of people toughing it out on the street make him think of his own. Life is turning him into an asshole. And this is another problem.

He wipes the sweat from his forehead and heads into the dim interior of the precinct. There are a few people waiting to talk to one of the desk sergeants. A couple of tourists are trying to locate a lost passport. And good luck with that. A young man is complaining that the window of his car was smashed outside a bar last night. A middle-aged woman is trying to report a crime that sounds like it only happened in her imagination. When an officer emerges from the back to lead her away, Tony approaches the desk and asks to speak to Detective Addison. He tells the sergeant that he's a lawyer and needs Addison's help with a case. The desk sergeant gives him a look—assessing his running clothes, his sweaty body, his flushed face. Then he pages the detective.

It takes ten minutes for Addison to appear. Tony's cell buzzes twice but he ignores it.

"You're back," Detective Addison says, leaning on the high desk. "Looks like you're actually dressed to run this time."

"Did you find him?" Tony's tightening up. He jogs from foot to foot to stay warm and keep loose.

"You seem pretty concerned about a guy you don't know." The detective shifts his weight. His tie clip knocks against the wood.

"I'm just curious."

Addison scratches his florid neck where his razor has run rampant over irritated skin. "Everyone turns up eventually."

"So that's it?" Tony says. "It doesn't matter what happens to him."

"It matters," Detective Addison says, "but just not to the LAPD Central Division. At least not today." He looks over his shoulder, like something is hovering behind his back. "Listen," he says. "That naked guy is only the tip of the iceberg when it comes to the kind of crazy that came in overnight."

The waiting room grows loud. Two young men are looking for their mother who gets lost downtown. Someone is shouting that his tent has been set on fire. A good-looking young woman also in athletic clothes is standing at the desk, half shouting, half crying, and not listening to whatever the sergeant is telling her.

Tony backs away from the desk. A woman with wild gray hair shoulders past him waving a photo at the sergeant, telling him that the man in the picture is her husband and that she has a restraining order but no one down on the streets bothers to enforce it because, she guesses, rules don't apply down there. A middle-aged man complains that the government has stationed a spy outside his hotel room.

Detective Addison catches Tony's eye. *Now you get it?* Then he disappears.

Tony begins to retie his shoes. He watches as the young woman steps away from the far end of the desk. She's got glossy red hair pulled into a sleek ponytail. Her workout clothes are worn and faded.

She's yelling at one of the desk sergeants over her shoulder, telling him to do his job, asking them how the LAPD could lose someone in plain sight. But soon the crowd of people waiting with complaints of their own push past her, force her away from the desk.

Tony's staring. He can't help himself. And he hates himself for being drawn to this person. She sits on a bench, exhausted or frustrated. She glances up, sees Tony, gives him a look that tells him to turn his attention elsewhere.

He finishes tying his shoes then hurries out of the station. He can feel the woman driving him out with her eyes.

Tony pauses on the steps to the precinct. The hiatus has nearly frozen his legs. The return trip is going to be brutal. He checks his phone. Stephanie has called three times. He should find a cab, spare himself the pain of the run. He'll jog a few minutes, get himself into downtown, find a place he won't mind waiting while his ride arrives.

He starts slow, a walking pace. It's embarrassing, but there's no one around to call him out, no other runners to shame him. He passes Los Angeles Street. The pedestrian cross light is flashing. He'll have to accelerate to make it. The effort nearly floors him.

He is almost at the far side of Los Angeles when someone grabs him from behind. He's jerked backward. He wheels around, fists up.

The woman from the police station is clawing at his shirt. But the moisture wick fabric is slipping in her grasp. He swats her away, but she grabs at him again. A delivery truck is barreling down on them. Tony grabs her wrist and yanks her onto the sidewalk.

She writhes and jerks in his grasp.

She's slightly out of breath.

"What the fuck?" Tony says.

"It was you," the woman says. "You were the one chasing James."

"Who's James?"

"Where is he?"

"Hold on," Tony says. "Hold on." He lets go of her wrist. "Just slow down."

"I saw you on the news. And now you're at the station. Tell me where he is."

"I don't know," Tony says.

"You don't know? You don't know?" The woman pushes him. "Don't tell me you don't know. You were chasing him down the street? Why?" She's screaming now, hitting his chest when he isn't quick enough to sidestep her blows. "Why?"

"I don't even know him."

"James. His name is James. And you're lying."

Tony searches the block for somewhere where they can continue this conversation in private. Because the last thing he needs is for the cops to see him in a confrontation with this woman. The last thing he needs is to be hauled back into the station. Up the street, he sees a door open to what he hopes is a coffee shop. "Come on," he says. "Let's go somewhere and talk."

His calm tone seems to quiet her and she follows.

A few people are coming and going through the door on the corner. The sign says THE KING EDDY SALOON, but Tony figures that's got to be some sort of hipster joke because it's only eight o'clock and no bar would be open this early.

But he's wrong. The King Eddy is the diviest bar he's ever seen, let alone entered. He can imagine Stephanie's reaction if she saw the cracked vinyl booths, the sticky floor, the bar smudged with greasy soap and thousands of fingerprints.

Tony orders two beers that come in cheap plastic cups. He

takes a seat at the bar; the woman sits next to him and sips her drink as if boozing with a stranger at breakfast time is the most natural thing in the world.

The bar is dark. The only window is a floor-to-ceiling gate in a far corner that lets smoke out onto Fifth Street from a cabin walled off from the rest of the space by dirty plexiglass. Except for the clientele, the place isn't too different from a college bar, dirty and cheap with stiff pours in plastic cups.

"So," Tony says when he's finished half his beer, "let's start over." The booze hits him hard. "I'm Tony."

"Britt." The woman is drinking almost as fast as he is. "Now tell me how you know James."

"I don't," Tony says. "I really don't."

Britt is about to object when he cuts her off.

"I promise you the first time I saw him was when he was running down the freeway. Then I got out of my car and chased him."

"Why?"

The same damn question he's been trying to answer for twenty-four hours. But the beer is helping. "Because I hate my job. Because I should have gone running over the weekend, but instead I drank too many beers and pretended to be interested in my daughter's friends' parents and their school fund-raiser. Because I have to attend the damn fund-raiser to make up for the fact that my wife and I are in the bottom tier of contributors to a school I already pay too much for my daughter to attend." Tony takes a sip of his beer.

"Yeah?" Britt says. "And?"

"And your friend James. It's like he was giving a big fuck-you to the everyday."

"And that's what you want to do?"

"I wouldn't mind," Tony says.

"So why'd you come to the station?"

"I was just passing by on my run."

Britt looks at him over the top of her plastic cup. "Sure you were," she says. "So you really didn't know him?"

Tony finishes his beer in two big gulps. "Swear," he says.

"What happened?"

He tells Britt how he left his car on the 110 and began to run after James. He explains how they jumped the barrier so they were running with traffic then ran up the ramp and emerged on Seventh Street. He tells her that he made it up to Alvarado before the cops brought him down.

"Then what?" Britt crushes her cup on the bar.

"That's it," Tony says. "I got arrested."

"I mean what happened to James?"

"I don't know."

"What—"

He can hear her energy ramping up, her voice about to get loud. He puts his hand on hers. Somehow in the dark bar, in the morning, the intimacy of this gesture, of touching a stranger, doesn't seem out of place. "All I know is the cops got me instead of him." He signals for the bartender and orders two more beers. Stephanie would kill him. In fact, she will kill him when he gets home late from his run, stinking of beer and other odors from the King Eddy.

The beers come. Two drinks in and Tony's finally able to admit to himself that he had been unable to catch up to the runner. He didn't have the strength for that final acceleration, that last kick. Or maybe he did but he was too complacent, too happy to trail behind the guy instead of reaching him. Coasting, almost. Doing just enough but failing at the final hurdle. He still runs regularly but he's losing ground, letting go of the college runner he used to be. He's growing solid. Soon he'll be grounded like the commuters stuck in their cars he'd left behind on the 110.

"You promise?" Britt is staring at him.

"Promise what?" The beer is making things fuzzy and making him loose and a little floppy.

"That the cops didn't get him."

"I—" Tony says. But then he has an idea. He pulls out his cell phone and dials Danielle. She picks up on the third ring.

Tony can hear the tail end of a disagreement with Stephanie in the background. "Jesus, Mom, it's Dad calling. Hold on." He can hear Stephanie fall silent or maybe Danielle left the room.

"Danny?"

"Mom's losing it. Where are you?" Danielle's tone is both curious and tickled.

"You know that thing you were showing me last night?"

"Are you okay, Daddy? You sound funny."

Tony clears his throat and tries to find his sober dad voice. Britt's looking at him across the bar, mouthing—*You're calling your family?*

"You know that thing you said was a thing online."

"The thing I said was a thing?" Danielle says.

Tony holds the phone away from his mouth and sips his beer. How fast must information and interest pass by for these kids? How many things have come into Danielle's orbit since last night? How many other things have there been since the thing she brought to his attention?

"Oh," Danielle says, "the video."

"Yeah," Tony says. "That." He hopes he sounds casual. But there's nothing casual—nothing innocent—about calling up your daughter from a dive bar at eight A.M. where you're drinking with a strange woman. "How do you find that stuff?"

"It's called a hashtag, Daddy. You just type in hashtag whatever into whatever place you're searching."

"Hashtag whatever?"

"I mean not literally whatever. So, like, hashtag nakedrunnerLA, hashtag freeballingonthe110, hashtag lettingitallhangout, hashtag—"

"Oh," Tony says, "I get it."

"So are you coming back soon?" Danielle asks. "I think Mom is going to blow any second now. She already packed your bag."

"Tell her I'll be home in less than an hour." He'll rinse off in the bathroom of the King Eddy. He'll take a cab. He'll tell Stephanie to upgrade them to a suite.

He pulls his seat over closer to Britt and clicks on one of the social media apps Danielle installed on his phone and types *#nakedrunnerLA*. It takes a while for the results to load. Britt's angled away from him, like she's unsure of what he's going to show her, like she might have to watch baby videos or something much worse.

A few videos load. Tony selects one that from the blurry still seems to show the moment after he was arrested. He clicks on it. Britt watches a ten-second clip of police cars and shouting. She clicks on another video and another. The bartender brings them new beers they didn't order. Tony drinks his without thinking.

Britt keeps scrolling through the videos until she lands on one that she replays several times. Tony can hear two people shouting in Spanish. Then someone catcalls and the video ends.

Britt turns the screen toward Tony. "Where is that?"

He watches the video—the naked runner passing down the middle of a two-way street with two lanes of traffic in each direction. The man holding the camera seems to be the one who catcalls. "Looks like the edge of Koreatown maybe."

Britt watches the video one more time. "Okay," she says. "Okay. So he got away."

"So I'm off the hook?" Tony says.

"For now." There a song in Britt's voice, a lilting note that Tony doesn't find unpleasant. It's been so long since he had a playful conversation.

"So?"

"So what?" Britt says.

"Do you live around here?"

"Tony," Britt says. "Let stop pretending to get to know each other and just have fun. Because in a couple of hours you're going to come to your senses and head back to whatever west side neighborhood you jogged over from and you're not going to care about my life story."

They sip their beers while Britt keeps scrolling through Tony's phone, clicking on new videos and replaying ones she's already seen.

"Is he your boyfriend?"

"James?" She laughs, spraying beer on his screen. "No, his father."

"His father is your boyfriend?"

"Was."

"That's fucked up."

"Fucked up is relative."

Music comes on. The bartender flips a switch and a disco ball that's missing half its mirrors rotates, bathing Britt in intermittent, lurid light. "Smoke?" She glances at the smoking cabin.

She slides off her stool and Tony follows her to where two smokers are caged like zoo animals in the plexiglass box that looks into the bar. Even though part of one wall is open to the street, the air is revolting.

Britt pulls some hippie-dippie cigarettes out of her bag—thin coils of brown paper.

"Is that a joint?" Tony asks.

"Do you ever get out of the west side?"

"How do you know that's where I'm from?"

"Because it's where you're from," she says. "I'm guessing Brentwood."

Stephanie wishes. "Beverlywood."

"Beverlywood." She drags out the name of his neighborhood, making it sound as contrived as it is. Then she pops the brown cigarette in her mouth.

"That's really not a joint?"

"I thought all you middle-aged rich folks had medical marijuana cards and vape pens you charge off your computers."

Tony only has the vaguest idea what a vape pen is. But he can imagine the look on Stephanie's face if he started plugging marijuana devices into his laptop.

"It's a bidi. From India." She flashes a pink package covered in Sanskrit. "They're supposed to be healthier than regular cigarettes, but they're not."

"So why do you smoke them?"

"Because fuck it." She lights the bidi, takes a drag, then places it between his lips. "Live a little," she says and pulls out another for herself.

The cigarette isn't awful. It's harsh and unfiltered and tastes a bit musty like a spice jar. Tony exhales and watches his smoke join the communal cloud hovering over his head.

The smoke makes the bar swim and sway. Tony feels as if he's floating inside himself. Then everything takes shape. And this whole adventure suddenly makes sense. And Tony realizes why he's here, what he's doing here. Now it's essential that he tell Stephanie about this, tell her that what they've been doing wrong in their attempts to "reconnect" with each other (her word)—their overnights to Ojai or Shutters in Malibu, their dinners in pricey West Hollywood—only dig them deeper into their mutual isolation. What they need to do is to come close to each other without the swag of their comfortable lives.

Something like what he's doing now—as crazy as it is. Because he feels real. Like really real. Like himself, but better. Like how he was before he got distracted by all the crap that clogs up his calendar.

He wants to tell Stephanie this. Needs to. Right now. He looks around for his phone and sees that Britt's holding it. He forces himself to focus and sees she's watching another video. The video ends and she replays it.

"That's right up the street," she says.

The video seems to be shot by a tourist who's speaking Italian. It starts with a shot of another tourist—a woman wearing her backpack on her front—standing at a bus stop. She waves at the camera. Then she points at something over the cameraperson's shoulder. The shot whips and finds the naked jogger coming down the street. The person filming says something like *Forze Los Angeles* before he's shouldered aside. A man in a black hat blocks the shot. He turns and scowls at the person filming, then takes a few steps in the direction James was headed. Then the clip ends.

Britt yanks the phone away. She presses play. Her mouth is hanging open. She watches the video two more times. Then she hits pause as the man in the black hat scowls at the Italians.

"Oh my God," she says. She holds the phone toward Tony. "Oh my God."

The guy looks mean, sure. In fact, he looks like he might bite the head off the tourist with the camera phone if the guy takes a step toward him.

"Oh my God," Britt says again. She takes a sip of her beer. Her hand is shaking. She nearly spills the rest of her drink. "Did you— Do you— This man . . ."

Tony takes the phone from her. He squints at the screen. "What about him?" He looks like the kind of guy who might be hiding out in the corners of the King Eddy.

"Did you see him?"

"Just now. In the video."

"But not then? Not yesterday."

"No," Tony says. "The only person I saw was James."

Britt replays the video again, then makes Tony watch—the Italian woman, the naked jogger, the mean-looking man stepping into the street. "You didn't see Blake."

"Who's Blake?" Tony asks.

Britt holds out the phone and makes Tony watch the video again. "Does it look like he's chasing James?"

It's hard to tell. It certainly looks like the guy takes a few steps in James's direction. But then the clip ends. He might have chased him or he might have resumed waiting for the bus. "Maybe," Tony says.

Britt watches the clip over and over.

The air in the smoking cabin is suddenly stifling. Tony's stomach is doing flips. He reaches behind Britt for the door. But she grabs his arm. "Where are you going?"

He tries to shake free.

"You have to help me."

"I have to go."

Britt's got him tight, digging in her nails. "That man in the video—you have to help me."

Tony needs air. Not the air of the King Eddy. Not the air in downtown L.A. Not even the air of Beverlywood. But the perfectly calibrated air of his house. "I can't."

Britt's drawing blood with one hand and using the other to jam the phone close to Tony's face. "This man," Britt points at the phone. "Oh my God, Blake—he found James."

It seems too crazy now. Everything—the bar, Britt, James, and now some mystery assassin. Tony wants out and home and away from all this. He manages to break free of Britt and out of the smoking cabin and back into the main room of the King Eddy, which is an improvement, but not much.

Britt's at his side. "You have to help me. You have to."

The bartender stares Tony down like he better not be making trouble.

"Go to the police," Tony says.

"The police?" Britt says. "The police?" She is verging on hysteria. "I'm not going to the police. Not now."

"I need to get home. I'm going to Ojai." His excuse sounds so lame, so conventional, so exactly like the reason he'd chased the naked runner down the 110 in the first place.

"Ojai? Fuck you." Britt shoves him and heads for the exit. She's unsteady on her feet. And then the door opens and closes and she's gone.

13

Sam liked the boy, which was strange because he didn't care for most people. And this should have given Blake hope that something was softening in the big man.

But the problem remained—the kid had family close by and Blake had seen them, a pretty mom and a matching brother. Any day now the boy would run back to them or they'd come looking. Or worse, the sheriff would get it in his mind to do door-to-doors through these damn jackrabbit homesteads looking for the kid but turning up two felons instead. Then all the cop's Christmases would come at once—snag a wanted murderer, drug dealer, armed robber and his partner when he wasn't even looking. Blake could see it now.

And what's more, he hadn't done himself any favors by giving the boy's brother that damn pawn in some girlish display of petty jealousy about Sam and Owen bonding over the chessboard day and night. Between him and Sam and this kid who had become a barnacle on his ass, it was like they were setting off fireworks, letting the whole goddamn world know where to find them.

Four days after the kid turned up, rain blew in. The sky was the color of shale. Lightning tapped along the mountains followed by the thunder's boom.

The rain made the interior homestead smell like wet dog. Sam's stench had gone from fetid floral to downright rotten. Blake had tried to restitch the wound that morning, but the bloated, busted skin made sewing impossible.

"Want me to help you outside, rinse you off?" Blake said.

Sam was cloudy and disoriented from his last dose. "The fuck I'm running around in the rain."

Blake rolled him a beer and a can of spaghetti and watched the Samoan knock out a few pills. He could hear the near-empty rattle in the bottle. "Something's not right with the world that we're getting all this rain in the desert. Someone's telling us we're fucked." Sam dry-swallowed his dose.

"Some people might say rain's a good thing," Blake said.

"Nothing's going to get better for us until you get rid of your damn sneakers."

"Just keep taking your pills."

Sam threw the nearly-empty bottle across the cabin. "You know what this kid says? He says these pills are keeping me sick. He says his father believes you need to heal the spirit before you can heal the body."

Owen began setting up the chessboard. Blake had a mind to stomp the thing and fling the pieces far into the desert, ending the game for good.

"Is that so?" Blake said.

Sam slammed his beer on the ground and glared at Blake. Owen flinched. "The fuck I've been saying all this time? I've been saying my spirit's sick. That's what I've been saying."

"Your leg's broke," Blake said.

"And now a kid comes along and tells me that I've been right this whole time?" He looked at Owen. "Blake didn't tell you it was his shoes that did this to me?"

"No, I did not." Blake moved to the window and stuck his face out, breathing in the scent of wet desert.

"And what would your daddy say about my poisoned soul?" Sam asked.

"That it's fatal," Blake said.

"I'm not asking you." The big man was staring at the kid.

"He'd say you need a cleansing or a realignment."

There was a break in the storm, but to the south another thicket of clouds was massing over the Pinto Mountains.

"Well," Sam said to Blake, "you better take me there."

"The fuck I'm taking you to the father of the runaway we've been harboring."

The big man pounded the floor, scattering the chessmen. His eyes were glazed. His pupils minute. The kid was probably right about one thing—those pills were beginning to poison Sam.

They needed wheels. They needed out of the desert. They needed to put distance between them and the kid before he ran off home.

BLAKE WAITED ON THE WET SAND UNTIL DARK. HE COULDN'T WATCH another goddamn chess game. He couldn't take any more of Sam's comments about his shoes, about how he'd made the big man's spirit sick, or how he'd better hoof it to Owen's dad's clinic.

He was going to get Sam on the road bad leg and all. If he had to break his promise about perping to do so, so be it.

When it was dark enough for Blake to make his move, he took the boy's BMX and cased Wonder Valley for a truck, figuring if you weren't at home out here by nightfall, you weren't coming back for a while. Because where the fuck would you be in this whole lot of nowhere? About three miles away he found a vintage Ford pickup, orange and chrome detail, sitting in the carport of a dark, tidy ranch. The truck was a little snazzy for his taste—the kind of fetish ride that stuck out—but way easier to hot-wire than these damn keyless entry cars everyone was driving.

He kept the lights off as he rumbled back to the ranch. The truck had a throaty diesel chug that Blake was sure was booming all across Wonder Valley to Twentynine Palms and farther.

The lights were on in the cabin, which was a disappointment. Blake had been hoping that he might somehow sneak the big man out without waking Owen. Not that it was likely he'd get a 270-pound man with a busted, infected leg out of that cabin without making noise, but it was worth a shot. There was no chance of that now. No chance he'd even be able to get on the move once those two were bent over the chessboard.

Blake cut the engine. He'd give them two games. After that he was running the show.

When he entered the cabin, he saw the chessboard pushed to one side. Sam was sitting up, his broken leg out to one side. Owen was crouched down in front of him, his hands on Sam's busted calf. He was muttering something under his breath. The sight of the boy's hands on the big man's leg—his sweaty little palms on Sam's infected flesh—turned Blake's stomach. He felt he had stumbled onto something grotesquely intimate.

"The fuck is going on here?" Blake grabbed the boy by the shoulders and pulled him back. He let go and Owen tumbled into a far corner of the cabin.

Sam's irises were ink black, large and roving. "He's healing me."

"Is that right?" Blake said.

The kid got up, brushed himself off.

"Now back off and let him finish the job," Sam said.

"Don't tell me. You feel better already?" Blake said.

"How the fuck would you know how I feel?" Sam said. "You've done nothing to help me. Up to me we'd already be at this kid's place so his dad could get to work."

"Jesus." Blake kicked the chessboard. The fuck hadn't he done to help Sam—jacking a car, boosting pills, cooling his heels while the big man played chess with this kid. "Jesus," he repeated, scattering the chessmen as wide as he could.

He could feel Owen at his back, waiting, just waiting for him to step aside, like he had every right to be there.

"Be my guest," Blake said.

The kid crouched down and put his hands back where they'd been.

"And what is this shit you're doing exactly?"

Owen looked up from Sam's leg. "It's what my dad does. I'm pulling out the bad energy."

"And he showed you how to do that?"

The kid didn't respond.

Blake nudged him with the toe of his sneaker. "And he showed you how to do that?"

"Ask anyone around here what my dad can do," Owen said.

"I don't see anyone around here."

"Shut up and let the kid work," Sam said.

Blake watched them for a bit until he was sure that the boy wasn't doing anything more harmful—or more helpful—than mumbling nonsense under his breath. Sam's eyes started to close. He fell back on the mattress.

"You can stop this shit now," Blake said.

"It's working," Owen said.

Blake picked up the chess handbook off the floor and dragged his bedroll out to the fire pit. If chess was all it took to get back into Sam's good graces, he figured he'd better get studying. He pulled out his penlight and cracked the book. But the narrow pinpoint of light bouncing over the black-and-white diagrams and the small print made his head spin. And he slept.

BRUJO. BRUJO.

Blake's eyes snapped open to the sound of Sam's voice. He couldn't have been out for more than half an hour.

Brujo.

It was the worst of the big man's curses, his most evil condemnation.

Brujo.

His mother, for instance, who had abandoned him for a rich Texan, or so he said. His uncle who stole from him and lashed him with a rope.

A scream followed—not Sam's but the boy's.

Blake flung open the cabin door so hard he ripped it off the hinges. Blood spatter streaked the floor and dripped from the wall.

"*Brujo!*" Sam cried.

Blake glanced at the big man's leg. His bandage was oozing as usual, and his calf was the same mottled purple-green mess, but there was no fresh blood. It took him a second to dial in Owen huddled in the corner, bent over his arm.

"*Brujo,*" Sam said. His voice was distant and foggy, now an old man's wobble. "He tried to steal my soul."

"He what—"

"In my sleep, he tried to steal my soul," Sam said. His eyes were rolling back. "So I cut him. Here to here." He traced a line from underneath his elbow to his wrist."

"I—I—I . . ." The kid was stuttering.

"His hands were on me. He was stealing my soul. He was pulling it out through the wound in my leg."

Blake coaxed Owen out of the corner and turned his arm over. Blood had soaked his T-shirt and the top of his jeans. The cut was bad, two flaps of skin pulling away from each other and exposing parts of the boy he didn't need to see. This kid wasn't dying on Blake's watch. He wasn't dying on account of Sam's delirium. He wasn't fucking dying period.

Blake took off his shirt and wrapped it around Owen's arm. "Let's go," he said.

"Where—"

"Hospital."

"No," Owen said. "I want to go home. Take me home."

14

Monday came in loud with the sound of semis booming up Sixth and the slow roll of garbage trucks kicking up an even worse stench than what already hung in the air. The streets were up early, banging with the rattle and clatter of shopping carts being loaded and pushed away before the cops or the red shirts came.

Ren had slept, if you could call it that, jerking awake each time someone passed too close to his square of sidewalk. He was up before the rest of the camp listening to Laila's sandpaper cough and foggy breathing.

The sun was still hanging back when his mother unzipped her tent, poked her head out. She hurried to the curb, doubled over, hacking and rasping, spraying the sidewalk with blood. The fit over, Laila wiped her mouth, straightened the bottom of her sweatshirt.

Ren shifted on his box.

"What?" Laila said, catching sight of him.

"What's wrong with you?"

"This damn air is what's wrong with me." Laila waved her

hand in front of her face like she was searching for unpolluted breathing room. Her voice was tight and raw.

"That's it?"

"What'd I just say?" Laila patted down her wild, puffy hair. "Now how come you're asking questions before I've even got my day started? That's what they taught you in that place?"

That place. Even living out here on the streets she was too good to admit that Ren had gone to juvie.

Laila ducked back in her tent leaving Ren to his box and backpack. Eventually she emerged and began taking down her camp. "You just sitting there?" she said, giving Ren a side-eye.

"I'm figuring shit out," he said.

"Well, take your time then. But I'll give you some advice. The missions aren't going to feed you before nine, but the cops are going to shake you out before that."

"How come Darrell and the rest of them aren't moving?"

"A cocktail of stubbornness and longevity." Laila finished with her tent and stashed it behind Darrell's shopping carts, between which he draped a tarp to provide cover while he slept.

While Laila was packing, Darrell had emerged and was sitting in his camp chair, a fat black book open in his lap.

"My kid can stash his box for the day?" Laila asked.

"I'm not going anywhere," Darrell said. He pulled out a pen and put it to the paper.

Ren craned his neck to see what was on Darrell's pages.

Darrell glanced up like he was fixing to tell Ren to mind his own. Then he spun the book round so Ren could see. "My masks," he said. He thumbed the pages, showing a flipbook of masks— some African, some Native American, some Asian. Then he turned the book over and fanned through the pages in the opposite direction and a whirlwind of faces passed by. "My faces. Down here everyone's got both. I've filled seven books since I came downtown. It's my routine."

"I'm taking a break from routine," Ren said. Eight years in lockup. Eight years of the same wake up, the same lights out, the same hour of exercise, the same damn meals in the same damn order.

"You're what now?" Laila asked.

"All I'm saying is, I'm living unregimented for a while," Ren said.

"*Unregimented?*" His mother spat the word out like a fancy food she didn't have the taste for. "Seems like that sort of living is what landed you in trouble in the first place."

That and the fact that Laila and Winston didn't pay heed to anything he did, just turned him loose and hoped for the best.

"You should listen to Darrell. They had a show of his stuff over at the community arts center and at the Skid Row Museum." Laila strung her large white purse over her chest. "I remember you doing some drawing when you were a kid, always locked in your room with crayons. Too bad you messed shit up for yourself. You could have done something with that-all."

Who was she to know what he did? Just because he was trapped in juvie didn't mean he didn't put marker to paper, didn't mean his imagination died along with his freedom.

"You still draw?" Darrell asked.

"No," Ren said, which was a half-truth. He didn't draw. Never had. He painted—paper, walls, roll gates, anything that would hold still long enough for one of his pieces, his blowups, or tags. There were buildings and stores all over his old hood in Brooklyn that bore his artwork, places people paused in the middle of their everyday business to take a long look, to consider all the mad color on their streets. *Go back home,* he wanted to tell Laila, *see what-all I didn't do with my gifts after I got out.*

"Draw or don't draw," Darrell said. "All I know is you need a routine."

"No need," Ren said, "since I'm not sticking around."

"Where are you going?" Laila said.

"Home," Ren said. "Both of us."

Laila crossed her arms and shook her head. "Not that non-sense again," she said. Then she picked up her big white purse. "I'm out. Darrell's not the only one with a routine. I got to go to the clinic and pick up my scrips."

"Because why?" Ren asked.

Laila gave him a look that told him to quit it with the questions. She adjusted the strap of her bag and headed north toward Fifth, leaving Ren behind.

THE NEIGHBORHOOD WAS FULL ON AWAKE NOW. PEOPLE WHO'D CAMPED on the out-of-the-way corners kept their tents up. But on the main thoroughfare of Seventh and the surrounding side streets, all the overnight living was gone. But just because tents were down it didn't mean the hood was calm. In fact, the streets were filling. New folks had arrived at the missions waiting for food, then spilling out onto the streets, getting in the way of buses and cars.

Ren didn't need a routine but what he did need was a plan, a way out of this hood with Laila, or, worst case, without her, but he hoped it wouldn't come to that. The bus back would run them about one sixty each, give or take. More cash than he could hustle in a few days' work—because that's longer than he could imagine hanging around these streets. But a phone call, that he could hook up for free. Get Laila's cousin on the line, the one who let fall that his mom was out here in Los Angeles. Get her to understand the situation. Get her to send some cash. Get Laila to listen to reason. Problem was, Ren didn't have a phone. But Flynn did.

So here was the plan. Wait the day out. Wait for Laila to come back from that business she called her routine. Tell her they were taking a walk, a break from the dark heart of Skid Row, that they were going to breathe the somewhat cleaner air of downtown. They'd go to the Cecil, wait in the air-conditioned lobby—fuck the clerk who would tell them to leave—until Flynn showed. They'd borrow his phone. Maybe even ask to borrow his room until they could work this shit out.

That was the plan. But here was the problem: Laila was ghost. Morning heated up into afternoon, which sweltered into evening, and she hadn't returned to her camp. Darrell told Ren to chill because this was a neighborhood like any other—people did their jobs, stuck to their routines, hell, some even went to college, then came home at night. *Just because folks live on the streets doesn't mean they don't have stuff to do all day,* he said. Which made sense until every other tent on the block was up but Laila's was still folded behind Darrell's carts.

Stop your fretting, a woman from the camp told Ren as he paced. *These parts, people come and go. A man sleeps next to you for two years, then up and leaves, then a year later he's back like no time at all.*

What about Laila? he asked her, Darrell, anyone who he thought would know, anyone who would listen. *What's her schedule?*

Laila, everyone said, *she always around.*

She always come back.

Maybe always. But not now, not this evening when Ren was waiting, hoping to take her up to the Cecil, get her on the phone with her cousin, then get her home.

It was dark and the streetlights on Crocker were out. Ren walked the block, then rounded the corner, headed up Fifth, and looped back. People were lined up on the sidewalk like casualties. They were hidden in tents and under tarps. If Laila had crashed somewhere else, for whatever reason, there would be no figuring it out until morning, if at all.

Ren came back to his camp. He headed around back of Darrell's carts where he'd stashed his box.

A hand reached out and grabbed him. "Whoa, whoa, my man. Who you messing with, my man? Not your shit to mess with, you feel me?" Puppet, the little thug, was tugging and twisting Ren's shirt. You could feel the extra energy coursing off the kid. He wore a different baggy basketball jersey and cap twisted forty-five degrees off center.

"I'm just getting my stuff," Ren said.

"Not your stuff if it's in Darrell's cart, you feel me?"

The last thing Ren wanted was this jumpy motherfucker buzzing up in his face. "Maybe I keep my stuff with his stuff."

"This is my block. I know the what-what," Puppet said. "I know you don't camp with Darrell. You feel me?"

"No," Ren said, "I don't feel you."

Puppet jumped forward, his chest nearly bumping into Ren's. "What happened to your face?" he said. "First I saw you, you were looking smooth, like these streets hadn't touched you."

"What's it look like?" Ren said. "Got beat down."

"Hold up," Puppet said. "I heard about you from Uncle Darrell. He told me you got jumped by the Eighteenth Street motherfuckers."

"Darrell's your uncle?"

"Why the fuck else you think I'd keep watch over this particular block? He's my uncle and someone messes with his shit, I'm-a know about it."

Ren laid his box on the ground. If only this twitchy fool would back off, he'd be able to lie down, cradle his head on his pack, allow himself this one remaining comfort.

Puppet's eyes were jumping from Ren's busted lip to swollen eye. "You're not proud of taking a beating?"

"You have to be one dumb motherfucker to be proud to get beat down," Ren said.

"Uncle D said you took it like a man. He said you hard, you feel me?"

"I'm not hard, I'm tired."

"You do time?"

"I do what I fucking want," Ren said, although that was far from the truth, especially at this particular moment. Because here he was, sleeping on the street, talking to some hyped-up junior-G, the exact type of person he'd sworn to avoid since the day he got taken away.

Puppet stopped bouncing. His bug eyes narrowed. And for a split second Ren thought the crazy kid was going to come for him. Then he cupped a hand over his mouth and laughed. "*I do what I fucking want*," he said. "*I do what I fucking want*. Motherfucker, you don't mess around and you don't take shit. You hard. For real, you feel me." He offered Ren his hand.

"Sure," Ren said. "I feel you. We're copacetic," Ren said.

"Cop-a-what-what?"

"We're cool."

"Listen," Puppet said, twisting his hat farther off kilter. "You're young. You're smart. I can help you."

"I'm good," Ren said. How the fuck this hyper kid planned to help him was something he didn't want to discover.

"You sleeping on the motherfucking street. Nothing good about it." Puppet bounced from foot to foot like he was stepping over a snake. "Maybe me and my crew need a favor. Maybe we do one in return. Maybe I help you get your paper up. Everybody needs some bank. 'Specially you by the looks of it."

"I'm not in the favor business," Ren said.

"Maybe not right now, but tomorrow is another day, you feel me?" Puppet reached into the pocket of his saggy jeans and pulled out a roll of cash and wagged it at Ren. Then he tucked it away. "Your call, boy."

After Puppet bounced off, Ren bedded down and searched for sleep. But there were things you don't think about after dark, things you do your best to lock away until morning. And for Ren his old, childish desire to be tough, to be a baller, to be in Puppet's words *hard* was one of those things. Because if he let the memory in, he knew it would be better to stay awake than to go to sleep. But Puppet's talk brought back the whole mess, making it come to life like a video game on the backs of Ren's closed eyes.

A rat found its way onto his box, tugging on his sleeve like it had something important to say. He sent the creature away and tucked his arms tight. But no matter. His skin kept tricking him into sensing the scutter of little feet, the whip of a hairless tail.

Ren rolled side to side, searching for a second of comfort. Now where the fuck had Laila gone? Maybe the Laila who lived down here was different from the one who half assed raised him back in Brooklyn, the one who stayed out all night with her girls, sometimes coming back in the early morning smelling of sweaty perfume, sometimes staying gone for another day. Maybe this new Laila *always came back*, like her friends promised. But trust her to up and leave when Ren showed. Trust her to fuck stuff up for him worse than it had to be, to strand him out here with only his damn Holy Ghost for company while she got busy with who knows what. That's the Laila he knew. Even still, he'd get her home.

15

BRITT, TWENTYNINE PALMS, 2006

Prepare like it's competition. Stay inside yourself. Nothing in. Nothing out. Know that they are jealous. Let that make you stronger. Tougher. Know that they are here to kill you. They want to take you down. Repeat: nothing in, nothing out. You are not there.

They gathered at the fire pit. It must have been ninety with the sun gone, but Gideon kicked up a minor inferno with a couple of bunches of dried sage that sent heavy, sweet smoke into the air. Anushna passed around a mason jar of something earthy and fermented. She rubbed Britt's shoulder. "We come from a place of love," she said. "Always."

Britt wasn't so sure. She'd seen the way the interns eviscerated one another during the sharing sessions, insulting and demeaning in the service of so-called truth—shaming one another to save their souls. And she'd joined them, feeling the visceral thrill of unbridled vitriol. And it sure didn't come from a place of love.

"No one does it right the first time," Cassidy said. She wound a piece of Britt's hair around her finger and kissed her forehead, then took a seat on the bench closest to the tall stump which was Patrick's place.

Another intern hung a beaded necklace over Britt's head to *allow truth and honesty to flow.*

After a few sessions, Britt had detected a sort of electricity in the air as they waited around the fire pit for the session to start. At first she'd thought this was in anticipation of Patrick's arrival, excitement for the moment he turned his focus over to the interns. But soon she realized that this jittery current passing through the group was simply eagerness to let loose on one another.

They watched her, their stoned eyes mining hers for any sign of weakness, any hint that she wasn't up to the task of being insulted for an hour. She steadied her game face—drew her focus back to something only she could see. Like it was all happening to someone else or not even happening at all.

Britt knew Patrick was coming by the way the interns shifted in their seats, put down their guitars, stopped petting and grooming one another. They extinguished their joints and tossed them in the fire.

Patrick stood at the edge of the circle behind Britt. She hadn't spoken to him since he'd come into her room the previous night. She hadn't felt him leave her bed. He put his hand on her shoulder. "Your turn."

How bad could it be? A brutal training session might last an hour. A disastrous match in front of coaches and parents and teammates could go on even longer. How many times had Britt failed, her hands and mind and legs letting her down as the score slipped away and time ticked slowly forward? Out here by the fire, with a dozen people who didn't really matter, all she had to do was endure.

Patrick's hand lingered. Britt felt his fingertips against her collarbone, pressing, probing like he was playing chords on a guitar, transmitting something she didn't understand. The interns shifted, ready, waiting to chant the first question, holding their breath until he signaled their release. When he sat, it wasn't on his stump where the rest of the group could look up to him but on an empty bench next to Britt.

"Okay," Patrick said. "Let's begin."

Before he held out his hands for the first question, Cassidy moved onto his stump. She crossed her legs and pulled back her hair, her beads and bells clattering and clacking.

"All right?" Patrick said.

Cassidy's smile was like that of a mother wolf.

There was a split second of silence. Britt heard an owl calling out. She heard the one-two beat of either James or Grace sitting on one of the rockers, listening from the porch.

Don't make eye contact. Don't look at them, but through them. Let them have their way. It will be over soon.

"Why are you here?" The interns' collective voice ripped through the fire.

Britt knew the first question. She'd heard it repeated over the last nights, chanted until the sharer sputtered out an answer. She'd prepared. Or she thought she had. But now her mind was blank.

The firelight licked the interns' faces as they stared at her, enjoying her silence, counting down until they could chant again.

"Why are you here?"

A stick in the fire snapped, spraying sparks at Britt's feet.

"Why are you here?" they chanted again. "Why are you here?"

"I don't know," Britt said.

Then it began.

"Britt is lying," Anushna said.

"Britt thinks that by appearing humble she can fool us into thinking her intentions are noble," Cassidy said.

"If Britt doesn't know why she is here, she is not ready to share."

The responses came fast, picking up speed, until Britt couldn't tell who was talking. She was weak. She was deceiving herself. She was deceiving the rest of them. She was wasting her time. Their time. She thought she could impress them by working with her hands, but they knew she was too scared to work on her spirit.

She'd imagined it would be easy to sit there and to absorb the insults, let them wash over her. She thought it would be easy not to react.

"Britt is afraid of herself," Cassidy said.

Britt's head whipped round. She caught Cassidy's eye, the unmistakable vicious joy.

"Britt is afraid of her true self," Cassidy repeated.

"Shut up." The other interns must have been drugged or doped out of their minds to accept this shit in silence, because the words were out of Britt's mouth before she could stop them.

Patrick held out his hand.

"Shut up," Britt said again.

"See," Cassidy said. "Britt's fear makes her angry."

"Britt is aggressive."

"Britt only pretends to be brave."

"Britt thinks she can hide her aggression behind her work ethic."

Britt was glaring at Cassidy whose placid smile couldn't hide the fierce delight in her eyes. She dug her nails into her thigh, distracting herself with the pain, and punishing herself for breaking her vow not to make eye contact and to let this nonsense into her head.

But it was too late now. She was in the game. And she was losing.

The interns pivoted into the next question. "What do you want?" They were shouting, bellowing, their voices louder than the roaring fire.

"What do you want?" they repeated.

"To become someone else." That's the answer Britt had prepared the night before as she listened to Gideon being ripped to shreds. It was the sort of vague half-truth she thought might get her through this section quickly, win some sort of approval from the group.

Gideon leaped first. "How can Britt become someone else when she doesn't know who she is?"

"Britt doesn't understand what she wants because she doesn't want to be here."

"Britt thinks her answer will impress us."

"Britt wants to impress us."

"Britt thinks she is better than us."

Just who the fuck do these people think they are? And why do they think they know the first thing about someone they'd met less than two weeks ago? Britt stared at her feet so she wouldn't have to see the hungry, gleeful faces leering through the flames.

"Britt is turning away from the work," Cassidy said. "Britt is afraid."

"Look up," Patrick said.

She tried to drown out the accusations, concentrating instead on the game itself, trying to figure out how exactly it makes you a better person to endure this. And because you've endured it, do you win the right to dish it out heavy and hard on the next night's victim? And is this a game of personal improvement or a cycle of revenge? And what would she say the next time it was Cassidy's turn to share?

And if she hadn't killed all those chickens and if she hadn't danced with Patrick, would they be taking it easier on her? And if she'd accepted Gideon's or one of the other guys' advances, would one of them at least have let up?

The fire was making her skin itch. She'd been staring into the flames and her eyes felt scorched.

"Britt is just a rich college kid who thinks she can slum it for a while."

"Britt is blinded by her privilege."

"Britt believes it's her privilege to become someone else."

"Britt takes her privilege for granted."

The interns fed off one another, their insults a never-ending riff that gained steam, came at her from all sides, accelerating with the leaping flames.

At a nod from Patrick, the circle fell silent, took a deep breath before they pounced for the last time. "What do you fear?"

"What do you fear?"

Britt tried to put her mind elsewhere—in the pond, in the coop, back in Los Angeles. But the chanting voices and the fire rooted her in place.

"What do you fear?"

"What do you fear?"

Britt's mind went blank, and her mouth moved without her being conscious that she was speaking. "I fear myself."

The circle was quiet.

"Britt—" Cassidy began.

But Patrick silenced her. "Say that again."

"I fear myself," Britt said.

"Britt—" Cassidy tried once more.

"Say it again," Patrick repeated.

"I fear myself."

Over the lick of the flames, her own heart in her ears, she could hear the interns' ragged breath as they recovered from their verbal torrent.

"That's it?" Cassidy said. "She just gets to have that answer."

"Maybe it's the right answer," Patrick said.

"We don't know anything about her." Cassidy slid off the stump and sat next to Gideon, her head on his shoulder, their long dirty hair twisting together.

"You know enough to insult me for an hour," Britt said.

"That's the game. Get used to it." Cassidy twined tighter into Gideon.

Britt's blood rushed, her adrenaline spiked. She had them

now, she was on the verge of victory, winning their little game. All she had to do was twist the knife—go for the kill and send it home.

"Okay," she said. "Okay. Now I have some questions for you."

"Patrick—" Cassidy said.

"Shut up, Cassidy," Britt said. "Shut up and listen. Or are you too taken with your own voice? *Does Cassidy prefer to talk but deafens her ears to others?* Is that right? *Does Cassidy have selfish ears? Does Cassidy prefer the game when it's not her turn?* Well, fuck that."

Britt looked around the circle. Patrick had crossed one leg over the other and was encouraging her with a flicker of a smile.

"So, question: Why is Britt here? Because Britt is a working-class kid from Pensacola, Florida, who got a tennis scholarship to USC then lost it because she partied too hard."

"Patrick," Cassidy said, "this isn't the process."

"She earned it," Patrick said.

Cassidy rolled her eyes and studied one of her braids.

"Question: Why should you care? You shouldn't. It doesn't matter, except that you are happy to insult me without knowing shit about me. Like that brings you closer to the truth."

"But—" Anushna said.

Patrick held up his hand.

"Okay, so I guessed right," Britt said. "I played your little game and I won. I fear myself. But is that really enough of an answer? Is it?"

None of the interns spoke.

"Don't you need to know why?" She stared at Cassidy. "Don't you?"

Cassidy wouldn't meet her eye and focused instead on digging her bare feet into the dirt.

"*Cassidy is turning away from the game,*" Britt said. "*Cassidy is afraid of the truth.* And here's truth. I got cut from the team right before the women's champs. I had to stay home, but fuck it because there was an awesome party up in Laurel Canyon. I convinced the captain of the men's team to drive me because I couldn't afford a cab. The party was epic, the kind of thing that makes you forget you're a Florida girl, about to lose your one shot of getting out of Pensacola for good." She glanced around the circle, making sure to catch each intern's eye. "And don't you all act like you think partying is stupid. Because that is what you're doing right now. Always. Partying. You just give it a different name." Britt took a breath, preparing for the next round. "Even Goody Two-shoes Andy had fun. Even without drinking—because I promised him I wouldn't make him drink and wouldn't tease him about his commitment to stay dry until the end of the season. I didn't even mind when he told me he wanted to leave to practice in the morning. All I said was, *I used to be just like you.* Then we got in the car."

Cassidy tried to stand up, but Gideon pulled her back down. "We weren't going fast," Britt said. "It was impossible to go fast. I was messing with the radio when the car skidded off the road down into the ravine." Britt curled her mouth into a thin, nasty smile. "Now this is the part of the story where I should tell you that the universe was holding out its hand to me. That the big wheel of fate had swept me along in its wake. Because the car was caught between two trees. So there's a fucking blessing, right? There's something to marvel at in the whole damn universal equation."

The fire sparked. The interns were staring now. All of them, even Cassidy.

"Let me tell you how I counted that particular blessing. I ran. I didn't even check to see if Andy was okay. He wasn't moving. And I didn't want to know. I got myself out of that car and fled. Because I'm selfish. Because I fear myself. Because what I want more than anything is to be anyone but who I am. And that's why I ran. And that's why I'm here."

She'd crossed the city on foot, then on a bus, then on foot again. Then into her dorm. Then, before the sun came up, before her coaches, teammates, parents, or the police could call her, off campus, out of town. First up to Santa Barbara, then into the Inland Empire. And now the desert.

Andy could be dead. He could be in the hospital. Or he could have won the goddamn NCAA Men's title like he was supposed to before she'd dragged him to that party. Britt didn't know. She told herself she didn't care.

"So," Patrick said, standing and placing both hands on Britt's shoulders. She could feel the electricity course out of his palms now. It was undeniable—a current that penetrated her skin, sped right to her heart. He knew. She knew. They were in this together now. "You are right to fear yourself. But that is only the beginning. Once you have confronted your fear, then you must overcome it; otherwise, our little game around the campfire will have been worthless. Are you ready?" His hands kneaded Britt's shoulders as if coaxing out her answer. "Are you ready?"

"Yes," she said.

"You will have to trust us. You will have to trust me. I will lead you back to a place without fear where you can begin again."

Through the fire, Britt saw Cassidy roll her eyes again and whisper something to Gideon. But Gideon wasn't paying attention to her. He had clapped a hand over his mouth and was pointing in the direction of the driveway.

Patrick and Britt turned to look behind them. Someone was staggering from the driveway toward the fire pit.

"James?" Patrick said. "What are you doing?"

But it wasn't James. He was sitting on the porch in his glider. "Dad?"

Owen stumbled forward. He was holding his arm against his chest.

"Dad?"

Patrick stood and caught Owen as he lurched forward, his son's blood streaking the front of his faded polo shirt. Patrick gently peeled Owen's arm away from his body, turning it toward the firelight.

A deep gash ran from his elbow to wrist.

"Grace!" Patrick bellowed. "Grace!" He picked Owen up.

"I can walk," Owen said. But Patrick didn't let go.

The interns rose and followed. They paused at the foot of the porch, left outside as the screen door swung closed.

Cassidy came to Britt's side. "We all have stories. It doesn't make you special."

"I know," Britt said.

They could see Grace hold the screen door open for her son and husband. They could see her instruct Owen to sit at the kitchen table as she began to clean the wound.

Owen's back was to the window. James sat facing him, Patrick over his shoulder. Grace with her head bowed to Owen's wound. From a distance, they looked like a normal family, playing a game, working on homework, sharing a newspaper story together, in their brightly lit kitchen after dinner.

"I know what you're thinking," Cassidy said. "But none of this changes anything—not you, not Owen. Patrick will still come to my cabin tonight. Sit up and watch if you doubt me."

"I believe you," Britt said because it was easier to lie.

16

The sirens on Glendale set off the coyotes in the ravine a block east. At first their high-pitched yips and howls were indistinguishable from the wail of the police cars. But soon the yelping pulled away into feverish cries, a frenzied hunger calling down the night. Then the dogs in the nearby houses came to their gates, barking low, warning one another of the threat. After a few minutes, the coyotes fell silent. They rustled through dry underbrush, slinking into the hunt. The dogs barked themselves hoarse then pulled back into their houses. Two more sirens screamed down Glendale.

Blake rolled over on his mattress, knocking his knees against the camper's fiberglass wall. He sat up looking for Sam. But Sam was dead, four years now. Blake couldn't kick the habit. He fucking missed him.

The big man seemed too tough, too solid, to be murdered. And if Blake hadn't been there as the Samoan's blood gushed from the gash in his neck—more blood than Blake had ever seen before, warm, sticky, and metallic—he'd have trouble believing it possible. For days he found blood crusted on his clothes and under his fingernails, like the big man was clinging to him.

And to think a woman had done that. It was almost beyond imagining. Except that it wasn't. Because the memory haunted Blake day and night, reminding him that, although he'd tried, he'd done nothing to restore the balance that had been tipped by the big man's death.

Here's what kept Blake up at night: if it had been him bleeding out over that rusty blade, Sam would have wasted no time in seeking revenge. But Blake had failed his best friend, his only friend, and the big man wouldn't let him forget it. Late at night, when Sam's voice kept him awake, Blake swore he'd find the lady and make her pay.

When he'd first come to Los Angeles, he'd had days when he'd thought he saw her everywhere getting on with her life, always happy, as if she was set on reminding him of his misery. He'd made a fool of himself a couple of times, barging into a swank coffee shop and a boutique, placing his grubby paw on some redhead's shoulder, then realizing his mistake and scramming before she hollered for the rent-a-cop. He'd begun self-medicating to keep these visions at bay.

THE INTERIOR OF THE CAMPER SMELLED LIKE SMOKE AND OLD CLOTHES. Blake should have opened the windows, popped up the canopy, and sat out waiting for the air to change. But he didn't have the patience to spend the day guarding his shit against people who saw an open window as an open invitation.

His camper was third in a row of six lined up on Alessandro from Ewing to Oak Glen Place—all of them stranded without cars to tow them away. Blake inherited it when its owner headed north to pick grapes. A few people had knocked on the door claiming the camper had been promised to them, but when they saw Blake, they didn't insist.

Except for the Jesus freaks—a middle-aged Mexican couple who'd decorated the outside of their trailer with bilingual urgings to praise the Lord and crude paintings of the Virgin and Christ—Blake ignored his neighbors. (*Keep your face hidden and your plans secret*, Sam always said and Blake still listened to the big man.) But he gladly suffered the smudged tracts about revelation and rapture Santiago pressed into his hands in exchange for the tortillas and spicy frijoles Soledad cooked up on the propane stove behind their camper. Sometimes they even gave him a chicharrón.

Street camping was illegal. But the cops didn't pay much attention to this strip of a street at the base of Echo Park. Instead they focused on the dwindling drug busts in the gentrifying neighborhood, the remnants of crime that kept housing prices somewhat attractive to rehabbers and flippers.

Up on the hills overlooking the ravine that dropped down to Alessandro were an assortment of houses in stages of disrepair and rehabilitation—Craftsman bungalows, Spanish-style haciendas, modernist homes—houses that had been desirable before the 5 interstate was built. Most of the residents were families who couldn't afford the trendier neighborhoods or kids just out of college who were trying to start bands or make art or do something besides nine to five.

These kids weren't Blake's style. They pretended to be hard when they were as weak as generic beer, but they provided a market for the pills Blake scored from nursing homes and shitty clinics in East L.A. and the folks down on Skid Row. So he went to their parties and peddled his goods.

His dirty clothes and battered Ranger hat gave him cover among their grungy uniforms. He lingered in their backyards, listening to skinny girls with black-rimmed eyes and carefully ripped T-shirts talking about art and industrial music (or was it industrial art and music?), and wondered if they tolerated him because they thought that he'd once been like them. More likely, they didn't give a fuck as long as he had a pocket full of Oxys or Vikes. Blake wasn't sure when or why hard drugs had gone out of fashion—in his day he'd only resorted to pharmaceuticals when the dealers ran dry—but this trend worked in his favor.

Between the houses where the kids lived and the nicer places owned by families were tumbledown cabins and disintegrating shacks, their windows boarded with plywood and their porches and walkways missing steps. These places were of no use to Blake, but their inhabitants, an assortment of hermits, interested him. They managed to blend into their environment—off the grid but smack-dab in the middle of the city. Wasn't that something? Sam would have loved it.

One of these hermits had kept Blake up the whole night, a woman who lived in a two-room shack that seemed ready to give into the hillside—in the little off-road warren of Fellowship Park. She had a dog that looked more like a pig than any dog should. Blake had peeked into her place a few times. It was hard to see much behind the dirty windows and the screens studded with leaves and twigs, but he could just make out the slippery bodies of her cats slinking through the dusty shafts of light. There must have been twenty of them, rattling empty tins of cat food and clawing at the shredded screens.

How she could keep track of her cats was beyond Blake, but last night she was pacing up and down the Oak Glen stairs from Lake Shore to Alessandro, clapping her hands in threes and calling out for Ernie. For two hours she was at it, that three-beat clap followed by a drawn-out two-syllable wail. In her place, Blake would have welcomed Ernie's loss.

Sam would have done something about those cats, picked them off when they wandered out of the cabin, culled the population. He was good like that, sitting up on the roof of their trailer outside Phoenix, sharpshooting feral creatures. But Sam was gone.

The loss still felt like a shot in the gut. He could have prevented it—he could have stopped messing around the campfire with those stoned farmhands who called themselves "interns," listening to their tripped-out nonsense and, instead, spent the evening at Sam's side. Maybe then he would have seen Britt slip into the cabin. He couldn't think about that—at least he tried not to think about it. But the trying was the hard part.

While the hermit was beating time up and down Oak Glen, Blake turned on his LED lantern and took out the chessboard. Over the years he'd replaced the missing pieces. Although the set was complete, it didn't look right. Some of the pieces were too big for their squares, nudging their neighbors and messing Blake up. Others just didn't look right and he had to give them a good stare to remember what was supposed to be what.

ANOTHER BURST OF COYOTE NOISE SHOT OUT OF THE RAVINE, A QUICK YIP and howl. Blake stepped from his camper. The sky hung like a camp blanket. Nearly half a decade in Los Angeles and he still couldn't get used to the run of gray days that didn't hold the promise of rain. The city felt smothered, the sky that same bathwater gray, the air still, making everyone stir-crazy even outdoors. It would have pushed Sam over the edge.

One of the guys down at the Midnight Mission, where Blake sometimes grabbed a free meal when Soledad wouldn't feed him, called it "earthquake weather." They'd been standing in a line that ran from the door of the Mission all the way down Sixth to Maple. The man had looked at the sky and told everyone around him that he'd lived up and down the coast and knew earthquake weather better than anyone. He could *feel* it, he said. Then the whole crowd standing in line for a hot tray of nothing good latched on to the idea, as if an earthquake—a real trembler—was exactly what was needed to pull back the gray blanket and reveal the sun. Like it would solve problems, put a roof over their heads and money in their pockets so they wouldn't have to line up for hot slop.

This kind of madness—the contagious crazy of Skid Row— was what kept Blake in business, made it easy for him to get ahold of people's meds for bottom dollar. Tell them that shit was government poison and they'd nearly give it away for free. For five dollars he could relieve someone of her antipsychotics, downers, and painkillers and resell them to the kids on the hill for ten times that. Everyone was on something and everyone needed a buck.

He felt bad. But then again, he didn't.

BLAKE LOOKED UP AND DOWN ALESSANDRO. A FEW CARS WERE TURNING up the hill, heading toward somewhere better. He went behind his camper to relieve himself in the scraggle of dried-out bushes that blocked him from full view of Glendale. He could hear Santiago shouting. He shook and zipped and checked the street to see what possessed the little man. For someone who lived semi-illegal, it struck Blake that Santiago sure made a lot of noise, yelling at cars that came too fast or passed too close to his camper, heckling joggers and dog walkers, basically raising hell in the direction of anyone he suspected didn't possess his holy-mindedness.

Blake shaded his eyes against the strange glare that came with the gloom. Santiago and Soledad were standing outside their camper staring at something on the ground, hopping around and wringing their hands like a couple of nitwit grandmothers. Blake figured it was worth checking out in case he could score a meal.

They were looking at a cat that had been run over. One eye was dangling from its socket and there was a break in its spine so its back legs swiveled out at a right angle. Its black fur was matted with blood. Reddish drool pooled below its mouth.

"Alive," Santiago said, poking in the animal's direction with a broom. "All morning like this and alive." He was dressed in a yellowed guayabera shirt, and his horny toes curled over the edges of old shower sandals. "The Lord says to pay attention. The devil works day and night."

Blake towered over Santiago and stared down at the shiny

dome of the man's head trying to figure out exactly where the communications from the Lord entered his brain.

"*Es un signo del diablo,*" Soledad said. She kicked in the cat's direction, her flip-flop nearly slipping off her dirty sock. Blake had seen women like her before—breasts, stomach, and neck, carved from wood and sold to tourists by the road in New Mexico.

"No, no devil. No *diablo,*" Blake said. "It's just a dying cat."

"*No es natural,*" Santiago said, crossing himself. "*Un signo.*" He pointed first to the sky and then to the ground as if he wasn't quite sure who had delivered the sign. "You move, please? For us."

"I pick that thing up, it'll fall apart in my hands. Let him pass on his own. Then I'll deal with it," Blake said. Sam would have killed the thing right there. But Blake had enough problems without a dying pussy's juju in the mix.

"He die here, he curse us," Soledad said. "Then we move the camper. We leave and no more frijoles. *No más cena para ti.*"

Blake ran a jagged fingernail down one of the deep creases in his cheek. "Jesus," he said. He patted his pockets for a cigarette he might have forgotten about and headed up the hill.

He took the staircase at Cove Avenue and up to Cerro Gordo, where he climbed a flight of stairs carved into the hill, then descended into the strange enclave of Fellowship Park—a hidden collection of houses and cabins connected by dirt paths.

The two-room cabin was partway up the path. The pig-dog was digging underneath the small walkway that led to the front door. Blake banged on the screen. The entire cabin shook. Several of the cats mewled. He shaded his eyes, watching the felines slither in and out of the light. He banged again.

The woman who came to the door was younger than Blake had imagined—closer to fifty than seventy. Over her shoulder he could see moving boxes stacked to the ceiling, so many moving boxes it seemed they were holding the place up.

She wedged her foot between the screen and the door frame and looked at Blake though a four-inch gap. "Do I know you?"

"There's a cat down the hill," Blake said. "Got hit."

"And?"

"I thought you could come take a look."

Behind the woman the cabin rustled with animal noise. A large tabby snaked between her ankles, walking figure eights around her feet.

"It's not mine," the woman said.

Blake peered into the dim interior. "You sure? What about Ernie?"

"What about Ernie? You came up here to tell me I don't know my own pets?"

"No," Blake said.

"So?"

"Maybe there's something you can do?"

"What exactly?" She tried to step back from the door, but Blake elbowed halfway inside.

"I don't want the thing to die undignified," he said.

"Death isn't dignified," the woman said, pushing his arm away and pulling the screen shut behind her.

HE COULD HEAR SAM—YOU AIN'T NOTHING BUT A LITTLE GIRL. CAN'T EVEN *kill a cat that's mostly dead. You'll be too fucking chicken to avenge my own damn death when the time comes, which reminds me, motherfucker, why hasn't the time come?*

What Blake wouldn't tell Sam, couldn't tell him, was that the time had come and gone and come again, and he hadn't pulled the trigger. For two days after Sam had been killed, he had watched and waited, lingering in the dark at the edge of that goddamn farm, getting cactus pricked and even spooked by things that crept through the sand, watching the remaining interns smoke and drink and praise Mother Fucking Nature as if Sam had never passed through their lives. He'd had his chance and he'd blown it. And if he'd told this to Sam, the big man would have said—*Like I said, too fucking shit-scared to kill a girl.*

But that was early days, back when the sight of the big man's blood all over that cabin, all over his own hands and chest, was still fresh in his mind, when it didn't seem that adding more blood into the equation was going to help matters, before the reality of Sam gone set in. That was before he understood the mass and weight of his own loneliness—that he was going to spend the next five years talking to himself at night, drinking alone, trying to remember the big man's smell, his stories, even his anger. Because if he'd understood that in the days immediately after Sam was killed, when he haunted the farm, there was no way his knife would have remained in its sheath. If he'd known that the Sam-shaped hole in his life would grow larger, darker, filled with all the anger, depression, and desperation the big man had helped him keep at bay, there was no way that the woman who killed him would be alive right now. That's what Blake told himself.

HE HOPED THE CAT WOULD PASS BY THE TIME HE REACHED SANTIAGO AND Soledad. But when he got down to Alessandro, he could tell by the way they were poking and leaping back that he still had work to do.

Sam's acts of violence that Blake had witnessed, encouraged, even participated in—stabbings in alleys, barrooms, and parking lots—he remembered all of it. Sucker punches for no reason other than he had nothing better to do. Stickups for money or amusement. The women who'd have said no if he'd given them the chance. The liquor store where they'd found one of the clerks sitting on the can. The bank teller with breasts you could fall asleep in—and didn't they look good hanging out of her blouse right there over that name tag that said CARRIE CONNORS: ASSISTANT BRANCH MANAGER. The college kid meth heads so spun out they handed over their stash and their cash even before Sam pulled his gun.

Blake squatted down next to the cat. "All right," he said. "It's all right."

Santiago and Soledad scooted back into their camper and shut the door, as if the dying animal's soul was going to leap from its body and jump down their throats. Blake tried to think of all the roadkill he hadn't given a rat's ass about—the flattened raccoons and snakes and skunks Sam called *God's street meat*.

"Please take it away or we get the devil's fever," Santiago said.

"How's that?"

"The cat spirit becomes poison in your blood."

"Okay," Blake said. "Sure."

He reached under the cat's body. Its blood flowed hot, but beneath its fur the animal was cold. As he lifted it, it hung between his hands at all sorts of unnatural angles. A few drops of blood fell onto his sneakers.

He cradled the cat as best he could, pretending that he was transmitting some sort calming energy from his calloused palms to the dying animal. Pretending was as close to belief as Blake got and he prided himself on getting that far.

The cat was dead before Blake got to his camper. He didn't have to look down to know. He just felt the life go out of it, a brief electric current that momentarily touched his hands before fizzling out. That's how Sam had gone—a flicker, a spark of hope as his energy passed into Blake's arms. Then lights out.

He turned and headed back up the hill to where the ravine ended in a tangle of chicken wire. He pulled back a gap in the fence and placed the cat inside hoping to help the coyotes on their hunt. He looked at the cat. He wasn't sure death offered it much peace.

17

Owen was tan—the deep, leathered hue of the desert rats and their children. His blond hair had turned darkish and yellow. His clothes were dirty. His collarbones poked out of his T-shirt and his cheekbones were high and pointed. His eyes were sunken and wide, too large for his narrow face.

As their mother sterilized a needle, James glanced at their reflection in the window over the sink. They were no longer twins. Owen been gone for nearly two weeks, but it looked as if a year had passed and James had become the younger brother.

Owen's wound was gruesome. The white flap of exposed flesh turned James's stomach. Still, he couldn't take his eyes off his mother's needle and thread pulling the flesh taut, closing the gash with small crisscrosses that looked like mosquito wings. "Is it going to scar?" he asked.

"Of course, stupid," Owen said and held up his arm to examine the ladder of thread that ran from his wrist to elbow. "A big one." Like he was proud. Like the best thing in the world was that there would be no confusing the twins anymore.

"Where were you?" James asked, because his parents hadn't.

"At the beach," Owen said. Then he gave James an unfamiliar, nasty smile. "Like my tan?"

For a split second James almost believed him and for a split second he was almost jealous. Because that's exactly what he would have done. But of course Owen hadn't made it that far. He probably hadn't even passed Yucca Valley.

"You don't believe me?" Owen said.

JAMES STRUGGLED TO SLEEP WITH OWEN BACK IN THE ROOM. HIS TWIN'S breathing, his rustling, his indistinct muttering broke into his dreams, jolting him awake. But he must have slept, because he woke to Owen's face inches above his own. Owen had one hand on James's shoulder and was shaking him hard. In the other he clutched something small that he was jabbing in front of James's eyes.

James tried to wiggle free, but Owen had him tight.

"Where did you get this?"

He couldn't see what Owen was holding.

"Where did you get this?" Owen repeated.

"Get off," James said, twisting underneath his brother's grip.

"Get off," Owen mimicked in a child's falsetto. His face was rigid with anger. He smelled of stale smoke and old clothes. His hot breath flooded James's face.

"Tell me," Owen said.

James bucked onto his side and sat up, pitching Owen off him. He fumbled for the bedside light so he could see that his twin was holding the pawn the man from the inn had given him.

Owen got up and held out the chessman toward James. Despite their mother's careful stitches, some blood had soaked through his bandage. His breath came in short, sharp bursts. "Where did you—?"

"A friend." James tried to grab the pawn.

Owen pressed James back against the mattress. "Tell me where you got it."

"I said, a friend."

"You're lying."

"I'm lying? You're the one who won't tell anyone what you've been doing for the last two weeks."

"I was hiding out with a couple of criminals," Owen said.

James managed to push him away. "Now who's lying?"

"Whatever." Owen went to the window and opened it. "Now tell me where you got this."

"I already did. A friend."

"You don't have friends."

James lunged for his brother and tried to grab his arm. But Owen was too quick and chucked the pawn out into the sand. The room was silent, and when James went for Owen again, he didn't know what he wanted to do to his brother.

This hesitation was his mistake. Owen's punch landed on his forehead, just above his right eyebrow, splitting his skin, freeing a sticky trickle of blood. James balled his fists to strike back, but Owen ran from the room.

James sat on his bed, feeling the warm blood run down his face. He knew it wouldn't be long before his eye blackened and swelled shut.

When he was sure that Owen had left the house, he went outside, circled to his bedroom window, and began to comb the sand for the pawn.

He shaded his eyes and scanned the property. He saw his brother hovering behind two of the male interns as they weeded the pathetic garden their mother struggled to keep alive. He was shirtless, a bandanna tied in a triangle over his dirty hair. From a distance it would be hard to distinguish him from the others plucking weeds from the sand.

That night Owen ate with the interns and hung around the campfire waiting for the sharing session to start. James sat in bed with a book, pretending to read, but really staring out at the group around the fire. Owen could bead necklaces, drink their gnarly tea, even let them insult him for hours under their father's direction. James wanted no part of it.

Patrick wasn't sitting on his stump but on a bench alongside the new intern. They were waiting for Cassidy who hadn't come out of her cabin. James could see her shadow passing back and forth on the far wall of her adobe. Eventually she emerged and walked slowly toward the group. She stopped at the edge of the circle, clearly confused by the seating arrangements. Then she plopped down next to Owen. She took off one of her necklaces and placed it around his neck. Then she ran her fingers through his hair before turning to Patrick.

James closed the curtain. He didn't need to see any more. But even still, the sounds of the sharing seeped into his room.

Anushna was up. Cassidy was being especially vicious. James heard her voice rising above the group.

Anushna thinks if she is honest about lying to us, then she is not lying.

Anushna needs to attack the lie that is the cornerstone of her soul before she can answer with honesty.

Anushna has a liar's heart.

Anushna isn't here for herself but to use us.

Anushna thinks she's learned something, but she also thinks she knows everything.

They moved on to the second question, then the third. The accusations grew louder, turning into frenzied shouts. If Owen had joined the chorus, his voice was lost among the others. James didn't want to hear any of it. He covered his ears with his pillow, until he fell asleep.

He woke to what sounded like an animal circling the embers of the campfire, cracking and crackling the sticks that hadn't made it into the blaze. There was a shuffling noise—muffled breath that sounded almost human. He pressed his nose to his window. Something was out by the fire circle—two large shapes barely visible in the night.

Then a match flickered in the dark. In its quick, thin flame James could see Owen and Cassidy.

He got out of bed and went to the porch. A sliver of moon showed him his brother's shadow as he half danced from the fire toward the oasis with Cassidy at his side. James heard the water splash once, then again. Owen let out a howl, a wild wolf cry.

James left the porch and crept across the driveway. The chickens clucked and fluttered as he passed. He made a wide circle around the oasis and approached the water under the cover of the palm trees.

Owen and the intern were in the middle of the pond. The water was lit by the moon's reflection. The intern dove under, then surfaced. She rolled onto her back. She was naked, her skin—her breasts—as white as the blank-faced moon. Now she let out a howl. Owen joined her, their voices rising and falling, carrying across the water and out over the desert.

Owen swam across the pond and began to climb onto the low, flat rock that the boys used as a dock. He too was naked. The bandage had come off his cut, showing the jagged stitches that ran across his arm. He looked feral.

James ran his fingers from his own elbow to his wrist, probing between the fine bones in his forearm, trying to figure out how this entirely new brother had emerged from such a narrow wound.

Owen looked up. His eyes were wild. He crouched down and grabbed two handfuls of water that he flung over his head. He opened his mouth as they rained down on him. Then he stared at his palms, turned them over, and held his hands up toward the sky. His cut was caught in the moonlight and, in the bald, white glow, it looked even darker and deeper.

In the pond, Cassidy was submerged to her neck. She had her arms stretched out in front of her and was staring at the ripples her fingers made in the water.

"Sshhh," she said. "I can hear it talking. The world whispers to us underwater."

Owen went to the water's edge, cupped his hands in the pond, and brought the liquid to his ear.

"You can feel it too," she said. "You can feel its words in the water. It's telling secrets." She clapped, sending up a spray of water. "Come back. Let's listen."

Owen slid on his belly into the pond. He swam to Cassidy's side—their naked bodies hidden underwater.

James slipped away.

18

REN, LOS ANGELES, 2010

One week and Laila was still ghost. Her tent remained where she'd stashed it behind Darrell's carts. And if Darrell wandered off for the day, he took her stuff with him, which in some foolish way gave Ren hope that she'd return.

Ren went to Central P.D., waited behind a throng of people, each clamoring about his or her own injustice—stolen car, stolen wallet, being stalked, feeling threatened. The desk sergeant asked him for Laila's address. *Sixth and Crocker,* Ren replied. *Can you be more specific,* the sergeant said.

On the northwest corner.

The officer put down his pen, like living on the street made it okay that Laila had up and vanished.

Did you check the hospitals?

Ren hadn't.

Check the hospitals. The sergeant looked over Ren's head, calling forward the next person in line.

Another week passed. Then another. And without knowing it—without meaning to—Ren became a part of life outside.

HERE'S WHAT YOU NEED TO SURVIVE ON THE STREETS: A TENT OR A TARP (Ren got his tent from an outreach organization doing drop-offs in Skid Row), a sleeping bag, a backpack, travel-sized toiletries from the 99-cent store or community donation center, some kind of music device to block the noise, some kind of flashlight so you can read or startle the person kicking you awake.

Here are a few rules to live by: Keep one eye in front, the other in back. Avoid the worst of the addicts. Avoid the slingers. Avoid those out to exploit whatever remains of you. Find the right crew—people who will look out for you, who are down but not entirely out, who are trying to elevate, to get housed, to get their medical and mental needs looked after. Find the neighborhood's activists, the men and women trying to make Skid Row a better place, who fight against the thousands of tickets given to the homeless for loitering, for the public possession of their own private property, for jaywalking, who fight for the liberties and human rights of the undomiciled.

On Saturdays, have dinner provided by Jackets for Jesus. Before it gets cold, make sure you score a coat. On Sundays, get fed by one of the charities dishing out hot lunch or dinner along Seventh or San Pedro. But don't cycle back. Be good. Be honest. Don't take more than your share.

Nearly a month outside and Ren got the rhythm of Skid Row. He learned how the streets got wild on the second Thursday of the month when the welfare checks came in. The party started gentle, first with booze—malt liquor and beer. But later the hard stuff made folks mad, and then they retreated into themselves until the whole neighborhood was tumbled down and passed out.

After that the streets cleared a little. Those smart enough to pocket some of their checks moved into a hotel until they ran out of bank. Welfare bought you two weeks. Unemployment, three. Social Security, for those lucky enough to have it, four. But by midmonth most everyone was back, surviving in the open. Even some of those who could stay inside returned, drawn to the chaos, craving the on-street action.

The other type of wild came when the streets were running dry, when the dealers were low on dope, crack, and speed. Then the place was angry, crazy with folks prowling all night long in search of a little relief.

It didn't take Ren long to be able to categorize the different folks downtown. There were those who couldn't help themselves, who fell down next to their wheelchairs, who slept on the streets unsheltered by a sleeping bag, tarp, or tent, who were barely lucid, barely aware of where they were, how they got there, or how to move. There were those who were just getting by, neither part of the problem nor the solution, who took minimal handouts and relied on scant services. Then there were those like Darrell who saw Skid Row as a community, who could look past the dirt, grime, and noise, past their own addictions and illnesses, who relied on religion, prayer, art, dance, or music to lift the place up, who took classes, went to college, attended meetings, lent a hand even if they were on the streets. But most visible, especially come night, were the masters of chaos, the people who thrived on the madness and the lawlessness, who sold drugs or kept the dealers in business. You either joined them or gave them room.

Ask him a few days after he started sleeping outside and Ren would have said that cash was the thing he craved most—money to get him and Laila back east. But a few weeks in, it was sleep. No matter how tired he was come evening, his mind wouldn't shut off, alert to the disturbances on Crocker and haunted by the memories he'd once worked overtime to keep in check. Kill someone at age twelve, shit don't really start haunting you until you understand what life is, how breakable people are. And down here there was no turning away from folks' fragility. So Ren avoided sleep until he couldn't. He paced the streets until his legs buckled and he had to hurry back and make his camp before he collapsed.

He and Puppet circled each other on these rounds, the little hood monitoring Crocker, checking that his dudes on bikes were rolling in to replenish his dealers' stashes, and keeping an eye on his crew as they worked their various corners. Puppet watched Ren too, calling out, "my man," when they passed. Ren only ever replied with a nod so small he might have been blinking something out of his eye.

"You play a cold game, you feel me?" Puppet said each time. "You too stubborn to get on the up-and-up."

WAY TOO LATE AND CROCKER WAS ROCKING. A MAN AND A WOMAN WERE having it out going on two hours now, one yelling from the middle of the block, the other standing across from Ren's camp. Around the corner, a dude wouldn't shut off his radio and was threatening anyone who said they'd make him. Puppet's crew were sending coded calls up and down. And in one of the tents nearby, a couple was having loud, hard sex.

Ren had been trying to sleep—pointless, he knew. He flung off his sleeping bag, unzipped his tent, stepped out into the air that was no fresher than where he'd been tossing and turning. Sometimes he felt like the only straight man on the street—the only person who didn't rely on drugs, booze, meds, or weed to get himself through the day and survive the night.

He shouldered his backpack but left his tent up, too tired to give a fuck about his sorry possessions. He had an idea, if not a plan—head to the Cecil, find that kid Flynn, take him up on the offer of a joint, smoke until he passed out even if doing so meant he broke his own code of conduct. Because Ren had promised himself when he got out of juvie to stay on the straight and narrow. He planned to live his life clean, repentant. He wanted to make his small slice of world better, not partake in the things that poisoned it.

But he guessed you could call these extenuating circumstances. Because if he didn't sleep soon, good and hard, he was going to become part of the problem, cracked and crazy and capable of who knows what. So if he broke his personal prohibition on weed or booze to make sure that didn't happen, that was okay for the time being.

Ren had seen Flynn a few times during the last month, sometimes passing by the camp to do a quick exchange with Darrell, sometimes smoking on San Pedro with a cute girl in tight jeans, shiny combat boots, and a bleached mini 'fro. He'd spotted the kid in Gladys Park, chilling under a statue of an angel with an older Rastafarian, dreads gone gray, and caught him once checking out a guy and a girl freestyling for a small crowd in San Julian Park. But one thing Ren learned quick-smart was that in Skid Row, when you want to find someone, that person becomes straight-up invisible.

He passed the row of tents where hookers set up. He watched two women work the streets, keeping out of the streetlamps' glow.

Ren didn't like to be on the move so late. The neighborhood's desperate energy this time of night made him jittery, like his skin was turned the wrong side out. Two men made a handoff under the tattered awning of a closed convenience store. On the corner of Wall, a stone's throw from Central P.D., Ren smelled the chemical burn of a crack pipe.

A few police cars rolled down Sixth, slowing whenever they passed someone moving instead of sleeping, turning their flashlights on the bodies lined up against the roll gates, revealing faces with dilated pupils and twitching lips.

At the corner of Seventh and San Julian, he caught sight of Puppet and ducked his head. But it was too late—the little hood had clocked him and in no time he was bopping down the block, attracting way too much attention. "My man." Puppet tried to bump fists, but when Ren didn't mirror the gesture, simply landed a light blow on Ren's chest. "My man, my man, my man. Where're you off to, my man?"

"Taking my constitutional," Ren said.

"Your what-now?"

"Just walking."

"You always walking. Walking around and around. 'Specially this time of night. 'Specially around my turf. I'm starting to get ideas about you, my man."

"Such as?" Puppet was buzzing up and down, not doing much to alleviate the persistent dizziness in Ren's head brought on by lack of sleep.

"Such as you're playing your own game out here. You're running your own business."

"I'm just taking a walk."

"Not the way I see it," Puppet said. "Not the way I got you figured out. You up to something. Which is why I want to bring you in, cut you into my game. I picked you for smart with all your big words. I could use a fool like you."

Ren tried to sidestep the little dude, but as usual Puppet was standing too close, able to intercept his getaway.

"Where you running to? Because I can see you're running. Got business of your own and I'm gonna know what it is."

"No business," Ren said. "Promise." He wanted away from this tiny banger quick. Each second he spent around Puppet took Ren back to that apartment in the projects, reminded him of wanting to hold that gun, wanting to be hard, wanting to be like the little hood bopping up and down in front of him. Each minute he stood there listening to Puppet's nonsense was another minute of sleep stolen from him. Each moment he remained solidified the ghost of the man he'd killed.

Ren juke-stepped and this time Puppet couldn't keep time.

"Go your own way," the little hood called at his back. "Just remember, you my number one draft pick."

Ren held up his hand in acknowledgment but didn't look back.

REN DOUBLE-TIMED IT. HE'D SPENT TOO LONG WITH PUPPET AND NOW could sense something moving at his back, something keeping pace with him. He didn't want to check but needed to know if the ghost who'd followed him during his first years in juvie—the middle-aged man's bloodless face he saw when he looked at himself the mirror—had returned. But when he glanced over his shoulder he saw it was a cop car creeping along the curb.

Ren slowed. The car fell back. Then he picked up his pace. The cruiser gave him a beat, then accelerated. Two blocks, three blocks—the car was nipping his heels, then retreating, then catching him again. When Ren crossed into downtown, the cruiser pulled away for good.

On Fifth Street, just before Main, Ren got lucky. There outside a late-night deli, he saw Flynn. The kid was talking to a middle-aged women with lank gray hair and baggy men's clothing. Ren watched as he passed her something from his string bag, then hugged her briefly, before they parted.

"Yo," Ren called.

Flynn spun around, like someone had just run fingers down his flesh.

"Easy now," Ren said.

"Dude. You know the shit that goes on out here at night?" Flynn looked a little jumpy, his eyes a little too red, and a little too narrow.

"Looks like you're part of that shit," Ren said.

"Me?" Flynn gave him a dopey smile. "I'm offering compassionate care." He patted his string bag.

"Which is why I'm searching you out." Ren glanced at the bag.

"Last I heard, you were sober, brother."

"Don't mind what you heard," Ren said.

Flynn worried the thin strap of his bag.

"Do you think if I start smoking weed, things are going to get worse for me? I thought you said that shit was compassionate."

Flynn reached into the bag. "Dude, this stuff is nature's antidepressant. All those meds people are lining up for at the clinics—

that's the stuff that will kill you." Ren could hear Flynn's fingers working the little, rolled packages. But he came up empty-handed. "I can't sell what you can't buy," Flynn said. "So I'll make you a deal. Come back to the Cecil, I'll smoke you out. First time's on the house. Dealer's special."

On the way back to the hotel, Flynn smoked a thin, brown cigarette that smelled like a botanica candle. He tossed the butt as he pulled open the smudged brass doors to the lobby.

The interior of the hotel looked different, larger and more imposing. Or maybe Ren's perspective had changed since he was on the streets.

They rode the elevator to the top floor and entered a room like the one Ren had stayed in, except that Flynn's pad was filled with all sorts of weird crap. A few rocks were lined up along the window ledge. A bundle of what looked like charred grass stood in a clay holder. Next to the bed was a stack of yellowed books on energy and sacred spaces and healing herbs.

Ren picked up one of the rocks.

"That's a powerful one," Flynn said. "Hold it tight and you can feel its energy."

Ren squeezed the rock, but all he sensed were its sharp edges cutting into his palm.

He sat on the desk chair, while Flynn flopped on the bed and began to roll a meticulous joint, fashioning a filter from a matchbook and tapping the whole thing together with the clip from a ballpoint pen.

"How're you liking L.A.?"

"For real? How the fuck you think?"

Flynn held up his hands, like, *Don't blame me for asking.* "Listen," he said, "just because you're living in Skid Row doesn't mean you need to spend the day downtown. It's a big city."

"So what do you suggest? I should take a tour?"

"No, man, all I'm saying is you need a place to clear your head. You've been to Griffith Park? The Observatory?"

"Naw."

"How about the beach?"

Ren shook his head. Just like Laila, came all this way to get waylaid.

"That's a trip," Flynn said. "The man's never been to the beach. But I dig it." He looked out the window. "Staring at this shit all day, it's easy to forget that it's there. But when you remember"—he popped his fingers open like exploding fireworks—"bam, it's like you've been saved. I grew up in the desert and each time I see all that water, it's like I realize that for the last months I've been forgetting to breathe." He exhaled loudly.

"Maybe I'll have time when I figure out my way out of my present situation," Ren said.

Flynn licked the edge of a paper. "What you need is a hustle."

Ren pursed his lips and exhaled loudly. Back in Brooklyn he had enough game to rustle up the cash he needed to put him and Laila on the bus. But the streets downtown had drained him. Anyway, the game was rigged against him. Everyone had the jump on him and no one cut him in. The folks who'd been out longest went about their jobs like pros and guarded their turf like gangsters—recycling, window washing, collecting cardboard, or selling beers from shopping carts to feed the two A.M. drinkers when the stores closed.

"I'm too tired to hustle. What I need is sleep."

Flynn held up the nearly rolled joint. "Almost there, brother."

"So that's your hustle then?" Because even the lowest-level street dealers Ren knew in Brooklyn, the ones who sold dimes of schwag, lived better than Flynn in his dingy room at the Cecil.

Flynn spun the paper closed at the tip. "It's a medical service." Then he took the charred grass from its holder, lit it, and waved it around the room, until the flame turned to embers and it began to smoke. "Sage clears your space," he said, replacing the herbs in the holder. "It also hides the smell of the weed." He sparked the joint, took a long drag.

"But you could play that game anywhere, offer your *medical services,*" Ren said. "I mean, wouldn't you rather play that game somewhere else? Like the beach for instance."

Flynn exhaled an impressive gust and held the joint out to Ren, filter first. "Down here is where I play. These streets are my beat. And my people need me. I undersell the clinics."

Ren put the joint to his lips. The hoods in his housing project smoked blunts—fat and brown and sometimes sealed with honey that hot boxed a room in no time so that even though he had been too chickenshit to smoke back then, they assured him he was getting a contact high. *Joints are for hippie-ass motherfuckers,* one of them had said. Now Ren dragged deep and the smoke stung his lungs. "How's this your beat?" Ren asked. He passed the joint back.

Flynn hit it then examined the cherry like it was going to tell him something. He took another drag and shot a stream of smoke up toward the ceiling. "You ever get the feeling there's nowhere you belong. Like the world isn't made for you?"

"Sure." But in Ren's case it wasn't a feeling, it was a certainty, something he was as sure of as the fact of his own heartbeat. Despite the administrators' best efforts, he didn't jibe with the JV hoods in juvie, the violent kids from similar backgrounds as his. He had no place back in the housing project where he'd been raised, and the rest of the neighborhood where he'd grown up had passed him by while he was inside. And it wasn't just the neighborhood. It seemed that the whole world had rushed on ahead, leaving him behind, closing the gap around the small space that had been meant for him. So, yeah, he got the white boy's drift.

"Well," Flynn said, making some small adjustment to the filter, "this is the place to be when you don't belong anywhere else, when you've done things that make the straight world an impossible place to live."

Just like me, Ren thought—*just like killing a man when you're not even old enough to get into a PG-13 unaccompanied.* "I hear you," Ren said. "Problem is, maybe I belong, but maybe I don't like it."

"Make your peace with it or don't," Flynn said. "But down here your past is your past, no better or worse than anyone else's. People don't ask questions and they don't judge. We've all got stories. And trust me, there's always someone whose story is worse than yours."

Ren doubted that, but he didn't want to share his story with this kid, didn't want to summon the ghost of the man he killed. And what's more, he didn't need to know this kid's story to add misery and anxiety to his own.

He hit the joint in silence one more time, then signaled that he was through.

"Trippy," Flynn said. "This is your first time. You must have been a sheltered kid."

"Something like that," Ren said.

Flynn pocketed the roach. "You want to take a shower or something? Not that you need to, I just thought it might be groovy after so much time outside."

"Yeah," Ren said. "Cool." His words were like bubbles, rolling up slow from deep inside him.

He took the towel. The hallways expanded and retracted in front of him. He found the bathroom. The hot tap released cold and the cold ran hot. It took him ages—or was it just minutes—to calibrate the temperature. He washed his hair and his body, marveling in the foam on his limbs, the rivulets of dirty water running off, the clean drip that eventually followed.

The shower filled with steam. The hot water disappeared. But Ren kept the faucet on, enjoying the sharp sting of the cold. When he began to shiver, he stepped out and rubbed the abrasive towel over his body.

His head felt light, his thoughts floating somewhere. When he got back to the room, Flynn was standing by the door, his bag strung across his chest, like he was on his way out.

"The room is yours for the night," he said. "My guess is you could use a real bed." He ran his fingers through his floppy blond hair. "Anyway, I'm not much of a sleeper, at least not during regular hours. Shit just keeps running through my head."

Ren knew and he didn't object as Flynn closed the door. He didn't ask where Flynn was going. To the ocean for all he cared. He just lay down, felt the give and groan of the springs, listened to the door click behind him, and closed his eyes. And for a few moments, he was convinced that he was going to sleep, tumble into the same blackout slumber as he did during his one night at the Cecil.

But his eyes popped open. This room wasn't his, didn't feel like his. He didn't have the key and couldn't come and go as he pleased. It smelled strange, like that burning sage, and someone else's sweat.

He rolled from side to side, trying to pull back that split second of peace that had come when he'd first lain down. It was gone— replaced by the walls coming in, the ceiling crashing down, the un- familiarity of being in someone else's space, breathing in someone else's life. Like juvie. Too much like juvie.

Ren flung back the covers. He scrambled for his clothes. His mind was flipping over. He pressed back against the walls he swore were coming close.

Down the hall, into the elevator, across the lobby, and outside. For a few moments the fresh air settled him, brought everything back into balance. But as he headed back to Crocker, things began to shift around him, moving at the edges of his vision. Shadows stretched, became solid, got up and followed him down the street.

Ren knew what was up. He'd long suspected that it was only a matter of time, what with Laila's and Puppet's reminders and his constant lack of sleep, before the ghost of the man he killed stopped confining itself to his mind—to his dreams—but took corporeal form. Now he saw Marcus waiting at the crosswalk. There he was coming down the middle of the Sixth.

Ren quick-stepped back to Crocker. But the ghost was everywhere, jumping right ahead, then falling behind. Ren unzipped his tent, momentarily comforted by the sight of his sleeping bag. But before he ducked inside, he caught Marcus standing across the way, just to the right of where Puppet kept his lookout.

He zipped the tent shut. But he was certain the ghost had crossed the street and was now standing outside, biding his time as Ren passed another sleepless hour, waiting until Ren's mind let go of reason and welcomed him in.

19

Blake spent the morning hovering near the free clinic on Sixth Street in Skid Row, waiting for the right kind of homeless to emerge, the people who were jonesing to sell him their scrips. In two hours he had a pocket full of Klonopin, Percs, Vikes, generic Ritalin, Oxy, and Valium. It was a cheap scam, easy and quick with a whole bunch of upside and very little risk. When he was loaded up, he scuttled out fast, turning a blind eye to those unmedicated fools raving in the street. Not his fault, Blake told himself. No one forced them to sell.

On the bus back to Echo Park, he helped himself to a couple of the Valiums. Back in his camper, he closed his eyes, waiting for the pills to erase the hours between then and evening when he'd search out a party up the hill to unload his haul.

As his mind floated a few inches above his skull, Blake tried telling himself one of Sam's stories, but he forgot the good part. The big man always had something to say—some yarn about a man who found himself alone on top of a mountain with only a crow for company. A tale about an old woman with a soup pot and a magic husk of corn that kept her fed for weeks. A story about a boy and a girl alone in a forest, hunted by a great panther. Sometimes he recounted his own adventures, his violent romances, his scrapes with death, his drunken, drug-fueled craziness that got wilder with each telling.

Sam also had stories about his family: his grandfather who'd killed a bunch of Germans, his uncle taken prisoner in Vietnam, his grandmother who worked in a brothel in a border town. Sometimes these stories merged and mutated, the grandmother escaping the brothel and finding herself on top of the mountain with the crow, the uncle surviving with only a magic grain of rice for months. But Blake didn't mind. He'd never been much concerned with the truth.

But the story didn't materialize. Instead his mind dragged him back to that godforsaken ranch—Sam's last-ditch idea to save himself and a bad one. It took him back to the campfire, to the kids and their crappy weed and cheap booze. And if Blake was honest with himself, he had to admit he'd been longing for an out from Sam's sickbed, something to distract him from the fact that his friend was probably dying, no matter what the hippie doctor was telling them.

And for what it had been worth, he'd been enjoying himself, never mind the interns and their spiritual gobbledygook, because he couldn't remember the last time he'd enjoyed a drink and smoke with someone who wasn't Sam. For a stupid split second, he'd liked this freedom.

The rest of the scene he had to imagine because he'd been too wrapped up in watching one of the farmhands spin in circles, her skirts skimming the flames. For whatever reason, Britt had gone to Sam's cabin, maybe trying to bring a little of the party to the big man's bedside. Blake hadn't seen her go. He'd been lost in the fog of weed and wood smoke and burning sage and the fungal odor of communal sweat. But he could almost visualize it—Sam grabbing her, pulling her close, taking things too far and too fast. He probably had his knife stored somewhere under the mattress. Blake could nearly see it as the big man pulled his blade to get Britt in line. And it wouldn't have been too hard for her to pivot that blade around, forcing Sam to fall on his own sword.

THE VALIUM HE'D TAKEN ON THE BUS FOGGED HIS BRAIN, AND THE STORY he was trying to recall just wouldn't come. But it wasn't just the pills—certain memories were softening, losing their edge. Sometimes Blake had to ball his fists into his eyes and press hard to conjure the sooty crags of Sam's face. He was losing the big man all over again.

He kicked the wall, cracking the brittle fiberglass. The dreamcatcher above his bed lurched and swayed from side to side. He flung off his sleeping bag and stared at that tangle of beads and feathers until he slept.

Someone was knocking on the camper's door. Blake opened his eyes and pulled back the ratty curtain. It was evening but barely.

Santiago was standing on the street, hopping from foot to foot. "She sick, Señor Blake. Very sick."

"Get a doctor," Blake said. "Take her to the clinic."

"No clinic. The cat brought the devil's poison."

"Come on, little man. Just take her down to the clinic and leave me alone." The fog of the Valium hung heavy and thick. Blake had to will his eyes open.

"She needs prayer. No doctor."

"You've come to the wrong guy." Blake blinked and shook his head side to side. He'd have to dip into his supply, swallow a few Ritalins to bring everything back into focus.

"You come look." Santiago grabbed Blake's shirt. The camper shook as Blake resisted. He heard his chess game clatter to the ground. "You come now."

He staggered onto the street. The asphalt was cool on his bare feet as he followed Santiago to his camper.

"Very, very sick," Santiago said.

"You want me to catch it?"

"This sickness comes from the devil. It's not contagious."

"In that case, there's nothing to worry about. I've already got that."

Inside the camper the air was thick with the smell of prayer candles. "You're going to melt the walls," Blake said.

Santiago was making the sign of the cross and muttering a prayer under his breath.

Soledad looked sick all right. Not as sick as Sam had, but pretty bad.

Blake stood in the door. "There's a clinic down on Alvarado. But for now." He reached into his pocket where he'd stashed some of the pills. He shook them in his palm until a long, pink capsule rose to the top. Percs might not take the fever down, but at least they'd help Soledad forget her illness for a bit. He held it out.

"No *medicina*," Soledad said.

"We don't believe in medicine," Santiago said. "Only prayer. All the help we need come from *el Señor*."

"Well, you better get praying then."

"Yes, yes." Santiago yanked Blake's hand and fell to his knees. "Yes. You pray with us. The more voices, the better he hear us." He jerked his chin to the camper's roof and pulled on Blake's hand again.

Blake fell to his knees, half in, half out of the door. The lingering Valium made him wobble and nearly tip over. He steadied himself by gripping the door frame. "I don't know if God's gonna listen to me."

With one hand Santiago held on to Blake. He took Soledad's hand with his other. He pulled Blake closer to the bed so he could complete the circle. Soledad's palm was cool and clammy. He closed his eyes, as if that might help him block the smell of the candles.

Santiago began to pray. Blake couldn't follow, but whenever the little man jerked his hand, he bellowed an *amen* in unison with them. The man had fervor to spare. That much was clear. Blake had seen him doing his sermons on the street corner near the 101 freeway ramp, praying a mile a minute without pausing for breath.

Blake's knees began to ache. His palms were steaming. He cracked an eye to keep from drifting off. Santiago was praying with his head thrown back, his gaze upward if he could see right through the roof of the camper into God's house. Beads of sweat were dropping down his forehead. He took a deep breath and squeezed Blake's hand. He shouted a final *amen* so loud that the camper rocked. Then he got to his feet and went to sit by Soledad.

"That's it?" Blake said.

"He heard," Soledad said. "You pray. He hears."

Blake staggered out of the camper. The sun was disappearing over the hills of Silver Lake. Hopefully tomorrow would be clear. He didn't need any more of this earthquake weather.

He made it to his pad and swallowed a few Ritalin. A few minutes later he heard Santiago's flip-flops slapping down the street. Blake put a pillow over his head.

"Señor Blake?" The doorknob rattled. "Señor Blake. I know you're in there."

Blake held his breath as if that could transport him elsewhere.

"Okay, Mr. Blake, I'll leave it out here."

There was the sound of a dish being placed on the camper's aluminum step, then *slap, slap, slap* as Santiago padded away.

Blake cracked the door and darted the bowl of rice and beans inside. *Just like prison*, he thought. *Too much like prison.* He watched the dreamcatcher spin. It hadn't done its job. His dreams were still evil.

All the pills he'd swallowed had made him sweat. He changed into a cleaner T-shirt and pulled out the sneakers that had made everything go wrong for Sam. He owned better, sturdier shoes. But he liked to wear the sneakers sort of as a fuck you to the big man (may he rest in peace), to prove to him that he'd been wrong about that spirit shit back in the desert. Because Blake was still up and running, wasn't he?

An hour after dark, music started coming down the hill, the screech and reverb of equipment being set up. How the fuck the neighbors dealt with this noise Blake didn't want to know. But the music meant cash to him and he knew where the sound was coming from—a dirty white stucco house perched above three garages carved into the hillside with a backyard filled with battered lawn chairs balanced around a fire pit.

Whoever decided it was a good idea to dig a fire pit in an L.A. backyard hadn't watched the flames consume the San Gabriels a few years back. They hadn't watched the daytime sky turn an apocalyptic black. They hadn't noticed the smoke that crept east across the city for days. They didn't see the hillsides crackle like they were running with lava. Blake was surprised the kids on the hill hadn't burned the place down, lit fire to the neighborhood, and sparked a citywide emergency.

The backyard was crowded by the time he turned up. Strands of Christmas lights dangled from the balcony and wrapped around a tree. A bunch of kids were sitting in a circle around the amps that had been dragged outside. A splintering table was piled high with booze—six-packs and half-empty bottles of harder stuff. There were no mixers, no ice, and the beer was getting warm. This didn't bother Blake. He helped himself to a can of Bud, then found a folding chair off in a corner.

Soon the kids started coming up to him. They used their cell phones to light the stash he held out. He walked them through his wares—warning them what they shouldn't mix, what they shouldn't take more than two of. Whether or not they listened wasn't his problem.

The band took a break. Other musicians took over, fiddling with the dials on the amps, getting their sound right. It was all one big noise to Blake. He wandered to the table of booze for another beer to chase whichever pill rose to the top of the pile. He didn't have to take his own advice about mixing and matching.

He settled back into his chair waiting to see what developed in his bloodstream. He could usually guess what he'd popped in a blind taste test by whether his fingers itched, if his stomach felt like a washing machine on spin cycle, or his blood flowed slow.

Soon the first opiate rush hit his bloodstream. His vision flickered and resettled. He felt as if his veins were melting. He glanced around the garden. If he wasn't careful, the Perc would trick him into liking these people.

Someone got a fire going. A group gathered around the flames, feeding them scraps of paper, cigarette butts, dried twigs. Ash blew into the garden. Sparks shot into the trees.

Burn the whole place down, Blake thought. *Let the motherfucker burn.*

A few of the kids near the fire looked his way.

So maybe he was speaking aloud instead of in his head. Anyway, fuck it, he was rolling now.

The fire was pretty tame. It wasn't a burning meth shack or an exploding car. It didn't give Blake the release brought on by combusting metal and steel that made him feel as if he was standing outside himself. No, this was just a campfire and these were just kids who think it's enough to slide through life ass backward.

Someone was plugging into the amps. The sound of reverb shot through the garden. A few musicians started warming up, playing competing songs on different instruments.

A couple of girls came looking for Valium. He was almost sold out. He had a nice little roll in his pocket and a couple of pills to send him off to sleep should it come to that.

The new band started grinding away, pissing off the neighbors and making the partygoers look stupid with their down-with-it-ness. There were three of them playing some sort of repetitive, tinny crap, while a singer delivered panting vocals. One of the guitarists had arms completely covered in tattoos—flowers and birds on one, strange antique machinery on the other. The concoction in Blake's bloodstream made the birds on the guy's arm look like they were flying. He let himself get lost in the hallucination, watching the birds flutter as the guy ran his hand up and down the guitar's neck.

"The fuck is this?" He'd said that aloud too.

A group of girls swaying or staggering next to him stopped moving and stared. Then they shuffled away, giving him room.

"What?" Blake said. He must have been talking loud, louder than he meant to. But fuck it. And fuck them. They all had one another and their crappy music. He had no one. Him and his god-damn empty camper.

Another girl stepped out of the shadows to join the little posse. Blake had to squint to make her out—red hair, pale skin made even paler by black jeans and a black tank top.

"Fuck me," he said.

Everyone turned. The band stopped playing for a beat.

Someone took Blake by the arm and tried to pull him away from the musicians. The thing is, even wasted, Blake was stronger than these pussies who probably broke a sweat just lifting their guitars or paintbrushes. It only took him a second to twist free.

"Take it easy, buddy," the guy said.

"I know her," Blake said, pointing at the redhead. "I know her."

"Sure you do."

There were two of them now, corralling him like a couple of sheepdogs, herding him away from the fire.

What had he promised Sam? That this time there would be no second-guessing, this time no mistakes. And now the woman who had killed his friend, who had knifed him, was standing a few feet away surrounded by people, nothing better to do than enjoy the night high on Blake's fucking pills.

There she was. There she fucking was.

WHAT HAD SHE SAID WHEN HE'D BURST INTO THE CABIN AND SEEN HER and the boy from the ranch smeared in Sam's blood? "He attacked me. He tried to—" She didn't need to say the word. Everyone pushing in behind him at the door could fill in that particular blank.

And for a moment Blake had believed it—that Sam had taken advantage of a little alone time with a pretty girl to get her to do what he wanted and she didn't. Because that was Sam's way—the big man wasn't big on no. It had seemed plausible in the bloody frenzy of that room that Sam had provoked this mess. That in some state of delirium, Sam had found the strength to grab the girl, force her on top of him. It was only later when Blake could hear his own thoughts over the blood roar in his ears, the explosion of his heartbeats, that he realized how unlikely this was. Sam could barely make it through a chess game without falling asleep.

She'd killed him and then she had blamed him. And she'd lied to Blake.

"WHERE THE FUCK DID YOU BURY HIM?" BLAKE SHOUTED. HE POINTED AT the woman. It took her a moment to notice that he'd singled her out. "Yeah, you," he said. "Why the fuck did you kill him? Don't lie to me this time."

She gave him a look that showed him how fucked up he was.

Squint and he could see her still covered in Sam's blood. Close his eyes all the way, tune out the band's whining, and he could hear her excuses for the killing.

He took a step toward the woman and she ducked behind her friends. He reached for the knife in his pocket. Then stopped. Because what was he going to do in front of all these people? He needed to get her alone.

Three scrawny dudes were standing in front of him, marching him out, like riot cops advancing on a crowd. Blake held up his hand. "Yeah, yeah," he said. "Yeah, yeah, yeah."

He backed up, falling twice. He didn't want to take his eyes off the woman, didn't want to lose her again. He tumbled through the garden gate, then made a big show of heading away from the party, letting the guys know they were rid of him.

But they were suckers, back at the party in no time, holding cans of cheap beer. Blake only waited a few moments before he was back too, watching, lurking, ready for the moment the woman separated herself from the group.

His plan was ill formed, especially now that so many people had seen him, especially people who knew more or less where he lived and what he did. But still—he'd promised.

AFTER HE'D BEEN IN LOS ANGELES FOR THREE YEARS, BLAKE HAD RE-turned to the ranch to correct the balance tipped by Sam's death. He'd boosted a car and driven east. He stashed the car just off the Twentynine Palms Highway and walked the last mile or so to the farm. The place was in bad shape. The chickens were gone, the coop collapsed in on itself. The windows of several of the cabins were cracked or gone.

He'd camped out in one of the cabins, smoking, not giving a fuck if the boy or his dad noticed his cherry lighting up in the dark. But no one was home. Finally, the boy turned up, driving his dad's old truck up from the highway. He was tan and scrawny, with small ropy muscles that poked through his skin. He looked like any other desert stoner. The dad and the redhead were nowhere in sight.

Blake had brought a fifth of Evan Williams that he cracked as he watched the boy smoking a joint out his bedroom window. What the fuck had they done with Sam's body? Had they burned or buried him? Had they left a marker, anything to indicate Sam had passed through this world at all? Or had they simply dumped him so that the desert creatures could have their way?

He'd finished the bottle and swore that he'd wait until he was sure the kid was sleeping, then take him by surprise and demand to know where Sam was buried and where the redhead had gone. He'd tie him up, hold him hostage, until he had the answers he needed. But he'd passed out before he got around to his plan.

He'd woken to a lurid sunrise. His back ached and sand had crawled into his clothes. The first thing he noticed was that the pickup was gone. Blake had barreled into the house and flung open the door to the boy's room. It was empty. His bed was made. Drawers hung open. A few items of clothing were strewn on the floor.

He'd taken a bottle of cola and a couple of beers from the fridge. Then he'd turned on the gas on the stove. He'd held his lighter to the cheap curtains in the master bedroom. He'd sparked the bedclothes. Then he'd stepped outside. The coop was easy, like it was waiting to ignite. He'd tried a few of the cabins. Some burned easy, some resisted.

The main house was going great guns—crackling and releasing a noxious chemical smell when Blake hightailed it to the highway hoping for the satisfying release of an explosion that didn't come.

THE PARTY HOUSE IN ECHO PARK WAS ON ONE OF THE STEEPEST HILLS IN Los Angeles—a place where skateboarders played chicken with runaway vehicles. Blake sat on the opposite side of the street from the house, hidden behind a recycling bin in someone's driveway, trying to make himself comfortable on the angled asphalt. Around one A.M. the music stopped and thank fuck for that. Soon, people started filtering out, getting into old Hondas and twenty-year-old diesel Mercs.

At one thirty, the redhead came out alone. She'd parked down the hill—and that was lucky. A short walk. A dark street. Anything could happen to her.

See, he said to Sam, *who's a pussy now? Who can't take care of a girl?*

Blake nicked his finger as he pulled his knife. Jesus, he was out of practice.

Throat or in the side prison style? He had about twenty feet left to decide.

She was fumbling with her keys, having trouble figuring out her own damn door lock—a sure sign she shouldn't drive. Blake stopped. If he was lucky—and he usually wasn't—maybe she'd lose control on the downhill, kill herself, and spare him the trouble.

Pussy, Sam said.

"Fuck you," Blake said.

The woman turned. She'd heard him. She got her key in the lock and was jiggling it. Blake ran, knife out, not sure he was going to hit his mark in any meaningful way. She got the door open.

He was a few steps away. If she was smart, she'd get in the car without turning back, pulling the door shut, barring him outside.

But she looked, her face terror-white. And in the weak light from the car's interior, Blake saw his mistake—he didn't know this woman. Not at all.

He staggered past her, lurching into a bush, then righting himself. He lost his footing on the steep hill and rolled. He felt asphalt scrape his face. He scrambled out of the road so the woman couldn't hit him as she drove past.

20

Tony stands in the King Eddy. His phone is vibrating. He checks it. He's missed five calls from Stephanie. And now there's a text from Danielle. *Call Mom. She's really losing it.* Tony searches for the number of a cab company. But he doesn't dial.

The Filipino bartender's still staring at him, her lip curled, her eyes narrowed. There are smudges under one of her eyes that Tony now realizes are tattoos.

"What," Tony says, peeling off two twenties and dropping them on the bar.

"You just let her go off like that?"

"I don't know her," he says.

"So you just let her go off." The bartender pockets Tony's bills, mistaking his generosity. "It's your life."

Jesus. The room is swimming. Tony's not sure whether or not he's about to puke. And now the bartender at the scummiest dive bar he's ever set foot in is calling him out for his lack of chivalry.

She pulls a beer for a man who's barely managing to sit upright. "This world," she says. "A woman says she needs help."

She doesn't need to tell him. No one needs to tell him. Tony knows. He knows. But it's not his problem. Not at all. He has others. Many others. He wants to tell the bartender this—wants to explain that he's drunk and it's nine thirty and he needs to get home and somehow sober up and somehow pacify Stephanie and somehow drive his family to Ojai and somehow make it through the weekend. So, problems. Right?

Fuck it. Fuck it. "Fuck it," he says.

The bartender looks over and shakes her head like nothing Tony could do or say would please her. Like his presence—his existence—is an insult.

"Fuck it," Tony says again. He can't let Britt go off like that. He can't let her escape. Because that's what he'd done with the naked runner. He'd let him go. He hadn't caught him. He hadn't tried hard enough. And the guy was in trouble. Or at least Britt thought he was. And she was drunk, staggering around Skid Row. And Tony was going to Ojai.

He's been in this situation before. And look how that ended for him. Dead-end job. Pretending to care.

It wasn't really his fault that the summer intern had wandered onto the el tracks. Not entirely.

Tony lunges for the exit, then pauses in the doorway to the King Eddy and takes a deep breath. He shakes his head side to side, feels his brain knock into his skull and settle. Then he runs.

For a few steps he feels terrific, like why doesn't he run after a few beers all the time. Like he's invincible. Like he could go on and on to the goddamn ocean if need be. But then he wants to vomit. In few steps a sickly perspiration erupts on his forehead. His legs feel boneless. He is nauseated. He has vertigo. He can't keep a straight line.

He plunges down Fifth weaving wildly through the middle of the street. He turns south on Los Angeles. Then he dry-heaves into a wastepaper basket. He approaches Sixth.

Where the hell is she? Where did she go?

Downtown is waking up. The dingy stores on Los Angeles

have lifted their roll gates, revealing windows filled with crap—gaudy, synthetic fabric, dusty disco lights, off-brand toys in sun-bleached boxes—that Tony can't imagine anyone buying.

He runs another block then doubles back toward the King Eddy. Again he has to stop, support himself on a lamppost and take deep gulps of the unpleasant air to combat the urge to vomit.

This is dumb. This is fucking dumb. And pointless. Because she could be anywhere, could have run in any direction. And what he should do is go home. Get a coffee on the way and maybe some hand sanitizer. He should call the hotel from the cab, get an upgrade, a couple's massage, organize an on-site sitter. Max out on all the comforts and pay his way out of this mess.

But then he sees her about half a block away talking to a man in a tent. He calls her name. She turns and begins to stagger north. He follows.

If the cops come, he's screwed. It doesn't look good—a drunk man chasing an equally drunk stranger through Skid Row. Especially after yesterday.

He calls her name again. She stops. He catches up to her and she catches him before he collapses. "Okay," he says, "I'll help." Although he has no idea what he's promising, no idea how helping her on this ill-formed quest is even possible.

"You'll help me find James?"

"Yes," Tony says. "Yes."

He thinks back to his run earlier that morning, his mind scrolling through all those neighborhoods he'd never seen or noticed before—the unknown city stretching out on all sides, spreading inland, climbing toward the mountains, flowing down to the beach towns. And somewhere in all this is the naked runner. Maybe. Because he could be anywhere by now. He could have left the state. He could be dead.

"That guy," Britt says, pointing to the phone in Tony's hand. "We need to find James before that guy does. He'll kill him."

Tony almost laughs.

"Blake will kill him," Britt repeats. Her tone is stony serious—sober as hell despite the way they'd wasted the morning.

"Why?" Tony asks.

"Revenge."

But before he can ask Britt to explain, his phone is ringing again. Stephanie, of course. He switches it to Do Not Disturb. He's in it now. "And the police?" Tony says.

"I told you before. You can't go to the police. Promise? Promise?" Britt's shaking his arm like she wants to tug the promise right out of him.

"Okay," Tony says. The second promise in just as many minutes to a woman he doesn't know.

Britt takes his phone and presses it to her head, like it's going to transmit a revelation of where they should start their wild goose chase. "He was running down Main," she says. "So the hotel, maybe. Maybe that's a start."

"What hotel?"

"There's a place around here where James used to crash. Maybe he still does. Who knows. Who knows what he does."

"And you haven't checked?" Tony says. If she hasn't checked, there's a chance this could be over before it starts.

"Let's go." Britt slaps him on the back like they're partners now—Nick and Nora.

She smokes a bidi on the way. Tony has to breathe through his mouth to avoid the smell.

They stop outside an enormous building on Main near Seventh while Britt finishes her smoke. The sign says they've arrived at the Cecil Hotel and from the people coming and going, it's pretty clear this is a place Tony will never spend the night.

The doors to the hotel are dingy brass and the glass is smudged. While Britt grinds her butt in a large planter by the street, Tony shades his eyes and squints into the lobby. It's grand

and gaudy and run-down all at once. He can see some cheap brochures for tourists unfortunate enough to have mistaken this hotel for somewhere in the middle of it all.

A skinny blond man is checking in, presumably because he doesn't know better. The clerk is giving him a hard time about something. Their conversation is getting tense, a fraught pantomime muted by the thick glass of the doorway.

Britt's back at Tony's side, their reflections obscuring the scene in the lobby. The man turns, pointing out onto the street—gesturing large, waving. The clerk is shaking his head vigorously.

Tony grabs Britt's arm. Because it can't be. It can't be that easy.

That's James—the naked runner right there, standing at the desk.

"Oh my God," Tony says. He's relieved. Not just that he doesn't have to spend the day looking for James but that he's okay, alive, standing in the hotel where he supposedly lives. He hasn't been hit by car. He hasn't fallen into some train tracks. He hasn't been killed. Because if something had happened to him, if the kid turned up dead, missing, or whatever, it would always be hanging in the back of Tony's mind that he hadn't caught him—that he could have but didn't. And whatever happened—that would be Tony's fault. Always.

"Oh my God," he says again. He wants to cry, which is probably partly due to the booze. "I can't believe it. I can't—"

He exhales deeply, setting free a tension he hadn't noticed gripping his muscles and chest.

Britt pulls the door open. She barrels past Tony into the lobby, running full tilt. "James." The man at the desk turns, but he doesn't approach.

Britt skids to a halt. "Oh, fuck this."

Now Tony can see his mistake. It's James but not quite. Because this man's arms are covered in full sleeve tattoos that Tony hadn't noticed through the glass door. And there's a sharpness to his features, an angry angularity he hadn't seen on the naked runner.

The sour, vicious look on his face when he sees Britt is enough to stop Tony from coming closer. "Why are you here?" he says.

"Same as you—looking for your brother."

"Go," the man says. "Get out."

"Excuse me?" Britt says. "Excuse me?"

"Last time I checked, this isn't your life."

"And when was the last time you checked? Let me see," Britt says, tapping her lips. "I lived with your brother for years, and as I remember the number of times you checked was never."

"Who do you think is paying for this hotel?" James's brother turns back to the clerk as if that settles it and Britt should leave. But she stays where she is. The man turns. "Go," he says. "Go!"

"No," Britt says. "You're the one who left and never came back."

"Don't tell me anything. Don't talk about my family." The man bangs his fist on the counter, scattering the desk clerk's pens and sending a pile of brochures to the dirty marble floor. "Don't—" He turns and takes a step toward Britt.

"You left him there," Britt says. She's shouting now, her voice echoing in the vast marble-floored lobby. "You left him—"

"I left him with you. And now you tell me that's a bad thing."

Britt lunges for him, but Tony catches her, pulls her back. She's writhing and clawing like an animal.

"And who the hell are you?" the man says with a glance at Tony. "Who—" Then he looks from Tony to Britt and Britt back to Tony. "Oh, I get it. You're the new one."

"Owen, fuck off." Britt is shaking in Tony's grip.

"So she's wrecking your home now?"

"No," Tony says.

"Oh, I bet she is," Owen says. "I bet she is. Or she will. And you don't even know it." He points at Britt. "You're a dirty, fucking home wrecker. Now get the hell out and let me figure out what happened to my brother."

"That is one thing you ll never understand," Britt says. She sounds confident, satisfied.

"I don't know what you and my dad did to James. All I know is he got good and fucked up staying out in the desert with you."

"That's right and I'm never going to tell you," Britt yells. "Ever. And you are not going to find him because you have no idea what kind of danger he's in. You probably think he's just off on his own trip. That it's some cute and stupid adventure. But let me tell you— you have no idea. None." Britt's shouted herself hoarse. She's kicking, spitting almost.

The desk clerk steps out from behind the desk. "Get her out," he says to Tony. "She's disturbing the guests."

Tony looks around the lobby. The only guest he can see is an elderly man passed out in a fake leather chair, a free newspaper sliding off his lap.

Tony wrangles Britt out onto the street. Eventually she relaxes and lets herself be led. Just before the heavy door swings shut behind her she turns, "Fuck you, Owen Flynn!" Then she and Tony are on the street. "Asshole," she says.

Tony steers her away from the hotel. After a few blocks, she calms.

"He's an asshole," Britt says. "I barely knew him, but that's my lasting impression. Looks like he hasn't changed." She pulls out a bidi. "They're twins, but he didn't treat James like a brother. He just looked down on him because James stayed in the desert while Owen went to some rich kid school in the Palisades. And look at him now." She's fumbling with her lighter, and Tony has to help her get her smoke lit. "After the ranch burned, James went to him for help. His dad and I were God-the-fuck-knows-where. When James got to Los Angeles, Owen ignored him, pretended to his friends like he didn't have a brother at all. So James drove all the way back out to the desert and lived in the ruins of the farm until his dad and I got back." She grabs Tony's arm. "He lived in a burned-down building in the desert for weeks all because Owen was too good for him. James was a weird kid before, especially after what we did. But after that trip to see Owen and those weeks alone on the burned ranch, he was totally changed—no more real world."

"What did you do?" Tony asks.

"You know what? Maybe Owen's right. I should go." She starts walking east along Seventh Street, into the heavy heart of Skid Row.

"Where?"

"Home. Back to Indio. I'm a tennis coach. Can you believe that? I teach tennis to half-dead people at a retirement community."

Tony can't quite believe it. Except for the fact that she's dressed in athletic clothes, he's almost certain that she's lying.

"I got lost and that's where I wound up. So I get it. You think I don't but I do. I fucking get it why you chased James down the freeway. I understand being stuck. I'm fucking stuck. And I know that you could see that he was unhinged from the everyday—that he had never played by the rules because the rules had never oc-curred to him. So you were right."

With the last hour's drinking beginning to congeal into a hangover, Tony can't imagine he was right about anything—that he had ever once in his life been right about a single thing.

"Here's what I know. Chasing James won't do a thing. It won't help you at all. Because what you need to do is find your initial mis-take, the thing that got you stuck in the first place. That first error you made that made you the way you are now. And maybe if you find it, you can undo the damage."

Tony knows what that is—or he thinks he knows. But maybe it went deeper than that stupidity back in Chicago. Maybe it was whatever took him to that bar, whatever deluded him into think-ing bottle service and private tables and partnerships in fancy law firms were the thing.

"I know how you felt when you saw him running down the freeway," Britt says. "And for a moment I was happy for him too. But, then, I know too much." She flicks her cigarette toward an approaching bus. "You can't change yourself by grafting your life onto someone else's. I know," she says. "I tried."

At the corner of San Pedro she stops walking. "What the fuck are we doing, Tony? What the fuck are we doing? This is a huge city, and he's the most untethered person I know. He could be anywhere. Literally anywhere."

Tony agrees but doesn't say anything. They cross the street, avoiding a woman in a motorized wheelchair with a boom box strapped to the front.

"You know what my biggest mistake was? I tricked James into thinking that you could escape the worst thing you ever did by ignoring it."

"What did you guys do?" Tony's not sure he wants to know. But knowing will make this story complete.

"What did we do? We killed someone."

Tony feels sick. Because this has finally gone too far. The smells and sights of the neighborhood are creeping in on him. He can't breathe. He can't think. And there's something else in the air—a heady odor of fresh paint. "You what?"

"And now that man's buddy is looking for James. Or maybe he's already found him and it's all too late."

This is the moment when Tony knows it's time to walk away. He takes Britt's shoulder, draws her to a halt. He's going to buy her a ticket back to the desert. He's going to put her on that bus. Because she's right—they won't find James. But he can extract her from this mess. See her safely gone. That's the least he can do. And that is what he has to do.

He takes a deep breath, searching for his serious dad voice. It's time to cut their losses. And then he looks over her head. A

young black man is rattling a can of spray paint. He aims the nozzle at a mural he's painting on the side of the building that wraps
around Crocker to Seventh. It takes Tony a second to understand
what he's seeing. And instead of finding the sober words to tell Britt
that this charade ends here, he spins her around to show her the
art on the wall.

21

It was as if Owen hadn't come back at all. In the morning, James's family was scattered just as they had been during his twin's absence. His mother had gone out early and was nearly finished with the chickens in the coop, their feed thrown, their water changed. Patrick was in his consulting room, the smell of sage and piñon thickening in the hallway.

James ate breakfast alone. He sat with his back to the window that looked toward the interns' cabins. He didn't want to catch sight of his brother. He didn't want to think about what Owen and Cassidy had done in the water after he'd slipped away. That was one secret he'd let his twin keep. But he couldn't shake the vision of Owen naked on the flat rock—his brother's winnowed body and his savage expression.

James was wheeling his bike over the gravel drive when he heard the first scream. It sounded like more intern nonsense. They were always pushing each other into the pond or pranking each other with scorpions or snakeskins. They didn't realize how far their voices carried across the desert or how shocking their cries sounded. James propped up his bike and straightened the handlebars.

There was another shout. Then another, more urgent. Someone was being chased behind the cabins.

James let his bike fall.

The interns appeared at once, gathering in front of the adobes. Grace ran out of the coop. Patrick hurried from the garden. The group moved as a unit, circling around the cabin closest to the oasis.

Someone was scurrying behind a creosote bush. The figure dashed from one cluster of brush to the next, doubled over into a half crouch. It was Owen.

Patrick turned to the interns. "Get back," he said.

The interns shuffled in place. A few of them tried to offer suggestions.

"I said, get back." Patrick's voice was thunderous.

The interns backtracked and disappeared to the far side of the cabins. But James could feel them watching through their windows.

Owen darted to another group of bushes. There were small cuts on his body, scrapes and scratches.

"He's been out all night," James said. "I saw him swimming in the pond before I went to bed."

"Go back to the house," Grace said.

James didn't move. "What's wrong with him?"

His parents began to approach the bush from opposite sides. Owen howled. His words were half formed, half coherent. His expression was feral. He shook his head wildly. "They're coming," he said. "They're coming." He turned and began to run. Patrick was there and caught him. Owen flailed and thrashed. Patrick fought to control his writhing limbs. Grace rushed to them. She stroked Owen's hair and tried to comfort him in a steady voice.

Owen didn't so much calm as freeze, his eyes wide and panicked, his mouth half open and his limbs rigid. Patrick held him. Grace cupped his cheeks in her hands. Owen's eyes pinwheeled.

"What's wrong?" James asked.

His parents glanced at each other then turned back to his brother. Owen twisted in Patrick's grasp. He howled.

"What's wrong?" James shouted. "What's wrong with him?"

"Tell him," Grace said.

Patrick didn't take his eyes off Owen. "He's tripping."

"On what?" Grace's voice was cold.

"It doesn't matter," Patrick said.

"On what?" Grace repeated.

"Peyote." Owen thrashed. Patrick restrained him. "Owen, look at me. Owen."

Grace tried to stroke Owen's cheek, but he jerked sideways. "How did he get peyote?"

"You know—" Patrick began. "My cactus."

"He stole your cactus, then figured out how to extract it and boil it all by himself?"

"It doesn't matter how he got it."

"It doesn't?" Grace said. "You really think it doesn't?"

"Not right now," Patrick said.

She inserted herself between Patrick and Owen. "Go. Go back to the house. To your consulting room or whatever. Go play with your potions. I'm taking care of this."

"Grace, this is what I do."

"No," she said. "Not this time. This is your fault. Now go. Go away."

Patrick kicked a rock toward the national park.

"James," his mother said. "You, too. Go with your dad."

James didn't move.

"I'm serious. I need to be alone with your brother. I know you're scared. But believe me, it's a million times worse for him."

"They're coming!" Owen screamed.

Grace gripped Owen's face. "Jesus," she said. "Owen, honey. No one's coming. No one. You're home. You're safe."

"Yes, yes, yes, yes, yes!"

"No. No, they're not. Look at me." Grace brought her face close to Owen's. "Look at me. Look at me."

James watched his twin try to focus, trying to steady his roving vision on their mother's face.

"Okay," Grace said. "It's going to be okay."

She led him to an abandoned cabin. James followed, but she shut the door, forbidding him to come inside.

He stood in front of the door trying to count the differences between him and Owen. There were all the little ones he'd tried to ignore over the summer, the small superficial likes and dislikes. But since Owen had shot that hawk a chasm had opened between them. James had remained a little kid, a shadow on his parents' farm. But Owen had plunged into a fast and shady world of nights spent alone or with mysterious criminals, encounters with interns in the pond, and psychedelic journeys.

He heard a whoosh of swirling fabric, the jangle of bracelets, and felt Cassidy's hand grip his wrist. She too was wild-eyed. But unlike Owen, she didn't look scared.

"I asked for the father, but I got the son," she said. She twined her fingers into his. "We get the gifts that we are given. He was beautiful, like a moon rock unexplored."

She smelled sweaty and swampy. James twisted his wrist to get away, but her grip was strong.

"I took him into the water. I told him we could see the galaxy in a single drop of water. Do you want to see?"

"Not really," James said.

"My fingers hold the water's whispers." Cassidy waggled her free hand in front of his face, then pressed her fingers to his ears. "Listen. What do you hear?"

He heard the sound of Cassidy rubbing her hands into his ears, his hair rustling as she combed through it.

"He saw through my eyes. We saw the desert rise into the sky.

The palm trees told us a story," she said. "Let me take you." She tried dragging James toward the pond, but tripped, tangling with her mess of skirts and falling into the sand where she drew circles in the dirt with her fingertips.

James looked from her to the door of the cabin he knew wouldn't open for him, then made his way back to the house.

THE SETTING SUN LEFT THE SKY OVER THE SHEEPHOLE MOUNTAINS THE color of the flesh of an overripe plum. Patrick had locked himself in the consulting room all day. James killed time in front of the TV, not really watching the blurry picture. For a few hours, he'd been able to hear Owen's intermittent cries coming from one of the cabins. But now the ranch was silent. Grace shuttled back and forth between Owen's cabin and the house. Each time she passed James her expression was stony. She gathered whatever she needed to help Owen then hurried back to his adobe.

It was almost night when a car started in the driveway, sputtering loose gravel. The kitchen door opened and slammed. James heard his parents on the porch. Their voices were low, but their sharp, angry tone was unmistakable.

James moved to the kitchen and watched through the screen door. His mother's station wagon was pulled up to the house. Owen lay in the backseat, wrapped in a blanket, his head on a pillow. His eyes were glazed.

"You know where he got it?" Grace asked. "One of the interns." She loaded a bag in the hatch and slammed the door.

"Okay," Patrick said. "She'll leave."

"It's a little late for that. And you know what else? She took advantage of him. In the pond."

"He's fifteen," Patrick said. "I don't think he was unwilling."

Grace shook her head. "I should have known that this would happen. You always think you can control things, but you can't."

"So what?" Patrick took a step closer to Grace. He was shirt-less and barefoot. "You're going to leave because your fifteen-year-old son had a bad trip?"

"No," Grace said. "I'm going to leave because you've created an environment where I'm supposed to think that my fifteen-year-old son having a bad trip and having sex with a twenty-year-old is no big deal."

"It's not—"

"You see, Patrick, that's the problem. If this isn't a big deal, what is? What's next? What will be a big deal?"

"Grace, please."

Grace looked past Patrick and saw James standing in the kitchen. "James, let's go. I've packed some things for you."

"Me?"

"Come on." Grace stepped toward the car. "We're leaving."

James opened the screen door. "Where—"

"L.A. To stay with Grandma."

"For how long?"

"Yes, Grace, for how long?" Patrick said. He grabbed her arm to stop her from getting in the car. "Why don't you tell James what you just told me? Or were you pretending to keep that a secret too?"

"Tell me what?" James looked at Owen in the backseat.

An owl hooted from somewhere near the oasis—a lonely two-note cry. The western sky was darkening, no longer the color of a plum's flesh but of its skin. The interns had come out of their cabins and were watching the scene on the porch.

"She's not coming back," Patrick said. "She's taking you and your brother to live with your grandmother."

"Now?" James said.

Grace broke free of Patrick's grasp. "James, this is what you want." She drummed her fingers on the roof of the car. "I should have done this ages ago. I shouldn't have waited for something terrible to happen. Owen needs to go. You need to go. Get in. I've packed everything you need." She got behind the wheel. "Come on James, our secret plan, right?"

But it wasn't, not exactly. If this had been their plan, she would have let James in on what was going on. Because this departure was his dream, not Owen's—running away from Howling Tree Ranch, leaving his father and the interns behind. He and his mother were supposed to go to Los Angeles. She was going to let him get a car when he was old enough, take surfing lessons, hit the beach in the morning before school. But now his brother had stolen it. It should have been him in the car and Owen on the porch, invited at the last minute.

If his mother had told him that she was leaving, made him part of the adventure instead of a bystander, he would have made a different choice. If she'd planned to leave because he wanted to instead of when Owen needed to, he would have climbed into the seat next to her.

James listened for all the noises that made him hate the desert—the scratching and shuffling—but he didn't hear them. He looked around the ranch, taking in the sleeping coop, the pond in the oasis that held the moon's reflection, the silhouette of the meditation rock.

"Can't I come later, on a bus or something?"

"James, please," Grace said. "This is what you want. How many times have you told me?"

James felt his father's arm encircle him. He smelled Patrick's sage and piñon odor, and this time he didn't mind it. "You can go whenever you want," his father said.

"I love you, Mom," James said.

"Jesus," Grace said. "Jesus." She slammed the door. James watched her put the car into gear. The wheels spat loose rock. The station wagon began to roll toward the dirt road to the highway.

Patrick left his arm on James's shoulder until the car crossed the yard. As the taillights dipped and bucked on their gradual descent toward the highway, Patrick rushed from the porch and ran toward the road. His arms pinwheeled as he stumbled over the bumpy ground. He let out a wordless bellow. He stopped, bent over, picked up a rock, and flung it toward the disappearing car. Then he continued down the road, half running, half staggering in pursuit of the dwindling taillights. After a few minutes, James could no longer hear the wheels of his mother's station wagon. He listened for his father's voice or the car's return.

The chickens were scratching in their pen. James sat on the edge of the porch. Soon he heard Patrick coming up the drive. He was limping as he crossed the yard. His hair was wild, his shorts torn. When he stepped onto the porch, James could see that his feet were cut and bloody. He didn't stop when he saw James. He just stormed into the house and reemerged with a six-pack of beer.

James left his father on the porch, but kept watching the driveway through the kitchen window. His mother's departure didn't seem real. She'd turn around. She'd come back. She'd drag him into the car instead of leaving him behind so easily.

He waited. The evening shadows stretched into darkness. Patrick finished his six-pack and jumped in his truck and headed to town.

After his father left, James went to his room and slammed the door. He dragged his bed over the invisible line that divided his half from his brother's and began to sort through the disarray of their belongings—the haphazard pile his mother had left behind in the closet during her furtive packing. Then he stopped. There was no Owen's and his anymore. There was no Owen and him. There was only James.

PATRICK WAS STILL OUT WHEN JAMES WENT TO BED. IN HIS SLEEP JAMES was vaguely aware of the pickup rolling into the driveway, the headlights casting into the house before extinguishing. He turned away from the window and resettled into his dream.

The first crash jarred him fully awake—an explosion of breaking glass. Another followed. Then another. James stuck his head out of his window. His father was standing near the fire pit. He watched him pick up a beer bottle then hurl it at one of the interns' cabins where it shattered against the adobe wall. Patrick's motion was wild, an unstable windmilling release, but he hit his mark more often than he missed. James counted as ten bottles connected with the wall.

A light came on in one of the cabins, and Cassidy appeared in the window. Another bottle crashed into her cabin. Her door opened and she stepped out.

"Bitch." Patrick father hurled another bottle. "You killed my cactus. You killed my fucking cactus and you drove my wife away."

She stepped into the doorway. Her hair was wild, her clothes more disheveled than usual. "You're a liar."

Patrick reached for another bottle. Cassidy ducked.

"You said you would come to my cabin. You lied."

"You only hear what you want to hear."

She lunged at Patrick and tried to wrap her arms around him. But he shoved her off. She stumbled sideways, then righted herself. "You drove your own wife away," she said. "You did that yourself."

Patrick hurled another bottle over her head. "You don't know how to listen. You have selfish ears. You have a selfish mind."

"You're a liar." She grabbed a handful of dirt and pebbles and flung it at Patrick. She raked her fingers through the air and down her cheeks. "You said we were on a journey together, that we were reaching out for each other across the desert."

"Did I?" Patrick said. "Did I?"

"Yes," she said. She doubled over, her body shaking. "Yes, you did."

"I was wrong. I can't help you. No one can help you." Patrick lifted another bottle and threw it at her cabin. It crashed to the left of the doorway.

Cassidy hurried inside, slamming the door behind her. The next bottle hit the window, spidering the glass. The light in her cabin went out.

James could see the silhouette of his father's spent figure. His shoulders were hunched. His arms dangled. He was out of bottles. He sat down at the edge of the fire pit. Then he wobbled for a moment, before collapsing to the desert floor.

22

REN, LOS ANGELES, 2010

The sun was up, filling Ren's tent with dingy yellowed light, but the street was quiet. Ren had slept, he wasn't sure when or how long, but he emerged from a near blackout, feeling rested but disoriented. His head was foggy with last night's weed. His tent had a strange smell, not putrid exactly, but wet and metallic, like rusted metal. Then he remembered—the last thing he'd done before passing out was give up, invite the ghost that had been standing outside his tent inside. And then he'd crashed.

His neck hurt. He must not have moved all night. He reached behind him to adjust his backpack that he used for a pillow. But it wasn't there. He sat up and searched the tent, worried that he'd slept so hard someone had snuck in, relieved him of his shit. He rubbed his eyes, trying to beat back the fog that lingered in his brain, pressing hard until he remembered—*Flynn*. Chances were he'd left his pack up at the Cecil when he'd fled.

At least he was clean. At least he slept. He could live without his few possessions for a couple of hours.

He unzipped his tent. People on Crocker were going slow. Darrell was standing in the street looking at a large collage that a man was wheeling around on his bike. He bent low to read what was written on the canvas's border. A woman was passing out copies of day-old newspapers. A dude from a nearby camp had scored a box of donuts that he was offering around.

Ren was so distracted by the casual routine unfolding in front of him that it took him a few minutes to notice that Laila's tent was up, right there in the square of sidewalk next to his. He must have been mad high last night to have missed it.

He stood outside his mom's camp, listening, checking that she was in there. He thought he heard the ragged edge of her breath, but it was hard to distinguish from everyone else's noise. He had to check, had to make sure that it really was Laila in there and that someone else hadn't co-opted her spot.

He tugged on the zipper. It caught and shook the tent. He worked it free just enough to peek inside. Someone was sleeping curled on Laila's pad, a pillow over her head, the sleeping bag unzipped and tossed over like a blanket. A skinny arm, flesh loose and gray, protruded. Ren could see a lean cheekbone.

"Laila?" he whispered.

The sleeper didn't move.

"Laila? Mom?"

The woman—at least Ren thought it was a woman—under the bag rolled to the side and groaned. "Don't Laila me," she said. The pillow slipped off her face, revealing the harsh, sharp line of her jaw, the thin cracks of her lips. "Don't come into a woman's tent. Don't wake a woman up."

Her voice was dry, like she was near choking on her words.

"It's Renton."

"I know who it is. And I still want to sleep."

Ren couldn't take his eyes off his mother's ravaged face.

"I can feel you watching me, Renton. I know you're about to start with your questions."

Ren tried tugging up the zipper, but it snagged.

"And now you're shaking the place on top of all else." Laila sat up and drew the sleeping bag up to her chin. Ren almost had the zipper up. "I'm awake now, so don't bother. And stop rattling my tent."

"Where've you been?"

"Me?" Laila said. "I went to check out the ocean. Got a front-row seat and couldn't take my eyes off it."

"For real?"

"What do you mean *for real*? Yeah, for real, for real. It's big and blue and makes all sorts of noise."

"You spent a month at the ocean?"

"And you spent a month living on the street," Laila said. "You tell me which sounds crazier. Now let me put myself in order."

REN SAT OUTSIDE HIS TENT LISTENING TO LAILA GET DRESSED. MUSIC WAS coming from down the street—old soul from crappy speakers. He watched a woman who camped on the far side of Darrell begin to jive to the beat in her motorized wheelchair, zipping to the curb, then doing a one eighty back to her tent, over and over again. She was white, midfifties, and wore purple fleece pajamas patterned with comets. She'd been living in assisted housing for a year but had lost the rights to her place. Had them stolen from her is what she said to anyone who asked. That was three years ago.

She was a talker—a mile a minute, all day and all night. She gave Ren her story. Mental health issues, addiction issues, anxiety issues, and an eating disorder. Overeating, not under.

She said her name was Nancy and before she'd become disabled, folks had called her All-Night Nancy because she was the queen of these streets. Things were different now.

She turned her wheelchair and headed in Ren's direction, stopping in front of his tent.

"I am an artist," she said. "You know that, don't you? A local artist. They got my work at the community center up the street. You been there yet? You better go. And when you do, you can see my stuff, right in the window. They gave me my own show. Photos, paintings, sculptures, collages. Some I make for myself. Some I sell. You got a piece of graph paper in your tent? I don't like ruled paper. You got graph?"

"I—" Ren said.

"Gimme me a piece of graph. I'll make you a drawing. But you better hold on to it when I'm done. One day I'm gonna be a big, famous artist. Already am around here. But one day they're gonna have my stuff over in the museum. The for-real museum."

"I don't have graph."

Nancy reached into the wire basket at the front of her chair and pulled out a few paintings on thick paper. Most of them were crude images of trees and houses. But there was something to Nancy's work, Ren had to admit, something in the way the colors came together, how you could see her individual brushstrokes, the way the simplicity of her art gave it life.

"Rad," he said, flipping through the stack of paintings.

"Lemme take your photo," Nancy said. "It's for my class. I'm doing portraiture." The long word took its time coming out of her mouth. "Normally I take pictures of my friends from back in the day. But lots of them are drug dealers. They don't want their picture taken for a show. They don't want to be hung on the wall. Lemme take yours?" Nancy wheeled the chair right up to Ren and tugged on his sleeve. He stumbled after her, trying to avoid crashing into the chair.

Ren allowed himself to be posed in the middle of Crocker facing north, the street running off behind his back. He tried not to laugh when Nancy pulled out a small disposable Kodak and squinted through the tiny viewfinder.

"Light's wrong," she said. "You got to get the light. That's the most important thing. Light, light, light."

Nancy reached into a basket at the back of her chair and pulled out a piece of cardboard covered in tinfoil. She zipped over to Ren and held the thing under his chin. The board was floppy, the tinfoil dull.

"That's the light," she said. Still holding the cardboard she lifted the camera to her eye. Ren pulled back, dodging the proximity of the lens. The shutter clicked. "Gotcha! I'm gonna make you a star. You ever think of drawing anything yourself? Bet there's an artist in you somewhere. Take my marker. I got a pencil, too. If you ever get yourself some paper, maybe you could draw something."

Ren waved her off, but she pressed the Crayola marker into his hand.

"I have a show next week. But I'll get your photo up before then."

He didn't tell her he expected that by then he and Laila would be gone. One look at his mom's face told him the streets were going to kill her if he didn't make his move.

After Nancy drove off, Ren rolled the marker over in his palm, then gripped it, scribbling in the air, making the shape of his old tag—RunDown. In juvie he'd spent hours practicing his tags, his graffiti skills, his throwups, and burners, so he could color the world when he got out. He'd studied the oriental writers, the Wild Style masters, and the blockbusters, crafting his own aesthetic from others' work.

He found a week-old *LA Times* in Darrell's camp and scrawled his tag across the front page. He stared at the name he'd chosen for himself, running his finger over the crisscross letters. RunDown—it was meant to let folks know he had the drop on them, that he knew the score. That even though life had tried to run him down, he was still in charge. But on these streets, his tag had a different meaning. Run-down, run aground, grounded, brought low.

He flipped the paper over and tagged the weather page. Then he pulled out the business section, hitting the stocks on one side and the article below the fold on the other. He hit the calendar section and California. Ren was still tagging the paper, covering the news with his name when Laila finally made it out of her tent. "You still messing around with those drawings?" she asked.

Ren stuffed the paper away.

"And still ashamed of it too," Laila said. "Never could quite figure out what's good for you."

Ren was shocked at his mother's transformation. She was now just an ounce or two above skeletal—her parchment skin doing a shit-poor job of protecting the bones underneath.

She'd tried her best to distract from her condition with another bright sweatsuit, all sparkles and sequins, loud makeup that made her gaunt face look clownish, and a psychedelic headscarf over her hair.

Ren stared at her sunken eyes gone spooky beneath bright yellow eye shadow. "What are you staring at?" she asked.

"Where you really been, Mom?"

"Didn't I tell you, the ocean. Camped right on the beach. Got the sand in my toes, the wind in my hair." Laila put her hand on her bony hip. "These streets aren't the only place in town you can sleep out in the open."

Laughter came from Darrell's quarters. Laila turned. "What?" she asked the tarps. "He's my boy, so I have to school him."

Darrell poked his head out. "Tell him where you really been, Lay."

"Who told *you* where I've really been? I'll tell you all where I really been, and that's the beach."

The exertion of sassing Darrell made Laila double over, coughing out the bad air and searching for something fresh.

"Mom?" Ren asked. "Let me take you somewhere. Let me get you some help."

She waved him away.

"I'll take you up to the clinic," he said.

Laila stopped coughing and fixed her stare on Ren, her yellowed eyes hard and cold. "You even think of taking me to that clinic or any sort of clinic, I'll beat you on the spot."

Ren had to bite down hard to avoid talking back. "You need help."

Laila looked from Ren to the street corner. "There's the only help I need."

Ren followed her gaze and saw Flynn coming down the block, his string bag slung across his chest, Ren's backpack on his shoulders. He bumped fists with Darrell, then nodded at Laila. If he was shocked by her transformation, he didn't let it show.

"You always know when to show," Laila said. "Like magic."

"It's a wavelength thing," Flynn said.

He did a quick handoff to Darrell, then gave Ren his backpack. "You must have been in some heavy shit to have run out and left your stuff," he said.

"I slept," Ren said.

"Groovy." Flynn sat down on one of Darrell's camp chairs and began to roll a joint, pausing now and then to whip his lanky hair from his eyes. His nails were dirty, and he smelled of burned herbs.

He held the joint out to Laila. "Ladies first."

"You sure that's a good idea," Ren said.

But Laila was already lighting it. Ren watched her smoke, cough, smoke, cough, until she'd finished half the joint. Then she passed it to Ren.

"I'm cool," he said. Maybe tonight. Maybe when he wanted to sleep. But for now he needed to keep his head in the game, start putting two and two together, and take the first step to getting Laila out of downtown.

He knew that there was trade in selling beer after the last late-night deli closed down. He'd seen dudes wheeling carts filled with cheap tallboys, offering them for a tidy profit. He closed his eyes and did the math—figuring what the buy-in needed to be.

In his juvie math class it had gone something like this. *If Paul buys ten apples for three dollars and sells them for five dollars, how much money would Paul make if he bought sixty-five apples?* The answer was always the same, or similar. *Paul be a fool with those apples. Paul do better to be slinging rock. That shit turn a profit at least ten to the dollar.*

No one was going to take him seriously if he started out selling a single six-pack, so he needed a case, which meant fifteen bucks—nothing crazy. If he banked fifteen bucks a night, selling those beers for double what he paid, it would take him nearly a month to get enough cash to get him and Laila back east on the Greyhound. He didn't have to be a fortune-teller to know that a month was too goddamn long.

"The fuck you thinking about?" Laila had her voice back.

"Just running some numbers," Ren said.

"If you can do two things at once, come with me to get some food. I can't remember the last time I had an appetite proper. What time is it?"

Someone told her, although Ren couldn't see how it mattered to her hunger.

"Shit," she said. "We have to hustle."

Ren took her arm and helped her to her feet. Her bones felt like twigs beneath her sweatshirt. "Hold up," Laila said, doubling back for her large white purse.

Flynn stood up, gave her a quick hug. "Just breathe," he said.

"My number one medicine man," Laila said. "Better than a million and one doctors in a million and one clinics." She gave Ren a look that told him for his foolishness—like only someone with no brain at all might suggest a sick lady see a doctor. Then she shook her arm, letting Ren know it was time to move.

They rounded Sixth just in time to see a bus pull up on the opposite side of the street. Laila tugged and Ren helped her across.

"We're taking the bus?"

She was about to give him another look when the doors opened and a white guy dressed in all black stepped out—the same quasi-biker dude Laila had met up with before. She broke out of Ren's grip. "Gimme a moment to do my business."

The man looked startled to see Laila looking like she did. Laila pointed around the corner on Crocker, and the two of them stepped away, leaving Ren at the bus stop like he had nowhere in the world to be. In a few minutes Laila returned. Ren watched the white guy cross Sixth, his pants pockets bulging and a prescription bottle in one hand.

"What was that all about?"

"The fuck I'm going to tell you," Laila said. "I thought we were going to eat."

The weed had put some spring in her step. At the taco stand on Seventh, Laila ordered for them both—quesadilla plates with rice and beans. She paid from a large wad of sweaty-looking cash that she tucked away before Ren could ask any questions.

By the time the food came, her energy had begun to flag. While Ren wolfed down the melting, cheesy mess, Laila had only managed the edge of one of her triangles of quesadilla. "I prefer to eat on my own time," she said.

Ren boxed up her food. He dangled the plastic bag from one hand and used the other to support Laila as they made their way back to Crocker. Laila didn't talk. He could feel her breath shaking her rib cage. When they got to her camp, Ren lifted her. Laila's body felt like a bag of sticks, brittle, light, and easily snapped. He settled her on her thin camping mattress and covered her with her sleeping bag.

"Lemme tell you about the beach," she said.

"Go on, Mom." Ren cushioned her head on a folded sweatshirt.

"Lemme—" she said. And then she was asleep.

On the ground next to her bed was an old newspaper. Ren unfolded it and found a fairly empty page. He dug in his pocket for the marker Nancy had given him, and while Laila slept, he began to draw the ocean.

23

Nine A.M. and Blake was already three drinks in at the King Eddy on Los Angeles. A few smokers were hot-boxing the plexiglass cigarette cave and the Filipino bartender was half asleep over a small Styrofoam cup of coffee. Blake knew the bartender, not that she acknowledged him. She had a line of stars tattooed beneath one eye that had once been tears. One night, she'd quit her shift right in the middle and demanded that someone take her to an all-night tattoo spot to fix her ink. That someone was Blake. He had to look away while a bald dude with black tats crawling down his forehead and creeping up his neck transformed the teardrops into tiny stars. The bartender hadn't flinched.

Blake crackled his plastic glass. He'd really screwed the pooch on this one and he knew it—verbally assaulting, then attempting to attack a woman at a party where he did reliable business so near his camper. Sooner or later they'd be coming for him. His guess was sooner.

Across the bar were two rich kids—a couple it seemed—on the tail end of what looked like a pretty rough night. They'd either staggered over from one of the refurbished lofts nearby or cabbed it crosstown knowing the King Eddy was the only place they could get a drink this early. Despite their glazed, jittery eyes, there was something smug about them—a story to tell on Monday—*you won't believe where we wound up.*

Blake cased the newcomers. They didn't look like they needed his business. They probably had Westside doctors to write them legitimate scrips for illegitimate ailments. He watched them pound ill-advised shots then start making out halfheartedly.

There'd been women in the years after Sam's death. Mostly one-night stands or a weekend, tops. One had even stuck around for a couple of months, moving a bag of clothes into the camper. But then she had to go ahead and get drunker than Blake thought a woman should and asked him if he and Sam had been lovers. It was a struggle not to slap her senseless. He settled for shoving her out the camper door and hurling her clothes after her.

But mostly Blake was alone and he didn't need to be reminded of that fact first thing in the morning, in a dive bar where all he wanted to do was have a few drinks in peace and figure out his next move. Because he was going to have to move on, clear out of that camper. The smart bet would be to quit the city altogether—the state even—before the kids up the hill crawled out from under their hangovers and brought the cops down on him. But leaving the city meant giving up on setting things right for Sam.

He finished his beer, hoping the swill would bring him some inspiration. But the booze was only making him sad. Drinking was never as much fun without the big man. But he kept at it, sipping away the thought of the redhead holding Sam's knife, his friend's blood on a stranger's body.

Blake crushed the plastic cup on the table and ordered another, telling the bartender to drop a shot in it for good measure. It tasted foul. He drank quickly, each sip making him wonder how the most despondent folks can pair up in a pinch. Except for him. The seat next to Blake was always empty.

Blake patted his pockets. He had made some good cash from the party last night. He had enough to split town, keep him afloat for a while until he reconfigured his hustle. He was just over a mile from Union Station. If he'd been thinking clearly, he'd have brought his bag so he could grab the next train to San Diego, then cross on foot in TJ, then, when he got to Mexico he'd do his best to trick himself into believing Sam's tales, believe them so hard that he'd make them true. But he didn't have his bag. He didn't have shit besides the cash in his pocket.

Then again, what was to stop him from leaving now, abandoning his sorry possessions in the camper? He didn't need that crap. He didn't need Sam's chess set, his chess puzzle book. He didn't need to wait around for a snowball's chance encounter with the redhead who'd killed the big man.

Sam's voice was just a voice. So what if the Samoan nagged him till kingdom come. He'd finish this drink. Then he'd go.

Blake's phone buzzed. He flipped it open, squinting through the beer and low light at the small blue screen. He didn't recognize the number—his Skid Row hookups often borrowed phones—but knew the message.

Bus stop. 6th Street. Ten minutes.

Well, what was the harm in one more transaction? He'd restock, he'd move his product, then he'd split a little bit richer.

The meet was only a few blocks away but Blake snagged the bus. His legs were wobbly and his brain too liquor lazy to walk. He got off on Sixth and Crocker.

Laila had beaten him to the stop. She always did, then acted as if he were standing her up when he showed. She looked like hell and for a split second, just one, Blake thought about telling her to keep her meds. But then it passed. She had the good shit—the 'zpams—and the more cash he made, the longer he could travel, the farther he could get out of town.

There was a skinny black kid with her, nearly blocking her

path. He didn't look too pleased to see Blake. But Laila shoved him aside like he didn't matter, then dragged Blake around the corner.

Her hands shook and she pulled bottles out of her purse—everything his customers craved from anti-psychs to tranqs.

He checked a few of the labels. They were all current and they all had her name—Laila Davis. They had been filled by the pharmacy at the hospital over in Boyle Heights. "How'd you get all this shit?"

"I'm anxious and I'm hallucinating and I can't sleep." Laila laughed. It sounded like she was gargling pebbles. "Truth is I'm only dying, but I let the docs keep on scribbling." She held out her hand, and Blake began to peel bills off his roll.

There were too many bottles to stash in his pockets. He had to hold some in his hands.

"I did good by you," Laila said. "There may not be a next time."

Blake fished out another twenty, like that would make a difference. At least she knew time was up. At least she could contemplate the road coming to an end. Sam hadn't had that opportunity. In fact, the big man had spent his last days convinced that the wacko doc out in the desert was going to heal him. Then he goes and gets himself stabbed to death.

"Life's a bitch," Blake said.

Laila stashed the cash in her purse. "Not really."

The skinny black kid was standing at the corner, tapping his foot and looking at Laila and Blake so hard and anxious that there was a chance he'd snag the cops' attention. Laila clocked him and scowled. Blake left first, the pills rattling in his pockets.

He crossed to the corner where Laila and her friends made their camp, trying to decide how he felt—whether the booze was inspiring him or dragging him down, whether he needed another drink or to get home quick so he could crash. Reason told him to grab a coffee at the free spot on Fifth, sober himself up then start moving the meds.

SAM HAD A STORY ABOUT COINCIDENCE. IT WASN'T HAPPY. TWO DISTANT cousins of his grandfather's had a falling-out after the older brother slept with his little brother's wife. They were both bad men—sometimes Blake wondered if there were any good men in Sam's bloodline—and their argument quickly turned violent. The older brother escaped with a stab wound in his chest. The younger brother swore that he would finish the job one day. Several decades passed and the older brother didn't reappear. The younger brother grew rich. His wife died. Their children left for Texas. He remarried a beautiful young woman. *Lucky bastard,* Sam called him.

One summer he decided to take a bus up to the States to visit his children. (*If he was so rich, why did he take a bus?* Blake had asked.) In the middle of the night, in a remote section of road that cut through the Sonoran Desert, the bus ran off the highway and overturned in a ditch. The younger brother was the only survivor of the crash. He had a concussion and, instead of staying with the wreckage, he set out on foot through the desert. It was the hottest month of the year, and it wasn't long before he was suffering from sunstroke. He needed food and shade, but there was nothing in sight.

He walked for three days with the sun beating down on him. (*Sounds familiar,* Blake said the last time Sam had told the story.) When he was just this side of dead, he stumbled across a cabin—the only human dwelling for miles and miles. The cabin was inhabited but no one was home. The younger brother crawled inside. He found a small cup of water, drank it quickly, and fell asleep.

An hour later, he woke to the sound of footsteps. He opened his eyes and saw his older brother standing in the door to the cabin. The older brother had been living in the desert for twenty years, surviving like the hares and foxes. The younger brother stood up. Without thinking, he grabbed a cast-iron pot off the table and swung it into his brother's head, killing him.

That's a terrible story, Blake said.

Depends on your perspective, Sam said. *The younger brother got everything he ever wanted.*

What happened to him? Blake asked.

Died, Sam said. *Dehydration.*

BLAKE STARTED UP CROCKER, PASSING LAILA'S CREW AND THEIR TENTS and tarps. The middle-aged black dude who seemed to run the corner was sitting in a camp chair, some old soul squeezing out of a handheld radio. Next to him was a white kid, head bowed over a joint he was rolling. He looked up and lifted the rolling paper to his lips to seal it.

Motherfucker. This time Blake was careful to keep his voice inside his head. *One of the fucking Flynn twins. Right here. Right in my own backyard.*

He kept moving, but stopped halfway up the block, checking over his shoulder. The boy sparked the joint. He hit it and passed it. Blake crossed the street and doubled back, playing it cool behind a minivan, checking to see if the boy had a scar on his arm or not.

It had to be James. This kid had the same vague quality as the boy Blake had watched getting stoned from his bedroom window on his failed and final visit to the ranch. And since James hadn't had the sense to split from the desert with his mother and brother, it didn't seem to be much of a stretch to imagine he'd wind up here.

The beer was catching up to Blake and fast. His vision was blurry. His head felt heavy. He swayed forward and leaned on the van. Folks on the street probably figured him for another junkie nodding out.

He was sure it was James—or possibly Owen—but after last night, he was suspicious of his instincts. And he wasn't making any more mistakes. He headed up Crocker to Fifth. He needed that free coffee like it was a fix. It would be bitter to the point of undrinkable and strong enough to make his veins dance. But it was just the thing to bring his head back down to this shoulders.

He took the coffee down in one gulp and held the cup out for more. Then he hustled back down the street.

The things you find when you stop looking. The things that happen when you give up.

Sam would have called it a sign, an omen. Sam would have told Blake that seeing the Flynn kid was all the proof he needed that it wasn't in the cards for him to split town without doing the big man's bidding.

Shit, Blake thought. *Shit.*

He shouldn't have met up with Laila. He should have stuck to his original plan—headed to the station, grabbed the train, then walked to TJ.

He approached the camp. A few of the tents had come down. Soul music was still oozing out of the radio. A white woman in a motorized wheelchair was jerking along to the beat.

The Flynn kid was gone. His chair was folded and stashed against one of the carts.

Figures, Blake thought.

He waited. The coffee and beer were doing a dance in his stomach. He was starting to sweat. He needed another drink or to dip into one of Laila's bottles.

Flynn had looked pretty comfortable with Laila's crew, like Blake would have no trouble finding him again when he sobered up. And he would sober up, later that night or tomorrow. And he'd find the kid and he'd force him to tell him what happened to the redhead. And then he'd find her. And Sam would be happy. Then Blake could go.

24

JAMES, TWENTYNINE PALMS, 2006

Cassidy left in the night. No one heard her go. In the morning, her cabin was empty except for a tie-dyed scarf, a sandal, and some joss sticks. James watched Britt and Gideon clean out her cabin, throwing her stuff onto the junk pile behind the house.

Patrick slept by the fire pit where he'd passed out. The interns skirted him as they went about their morning routines, letting the sun launch a full-force attack on his skin.

There were no chores that day. There was no sharing session. The following night, two more interns slipped away in the dark, as if they were ashamed.

The ranch felt dead. The chickens languished in their coop. The coyotes came at night. James saw four of them drinking from the pond and another two pressing their noses through the chicken wire of the birds' enclosure.

Sand crept into the abandoned buildings. Wind blew open their doors in the night. Three days without water and Grace's plants died.

Anushna and Gideon drove Patrick's pickup into town and returned with bags of potato chips, frozen pizzas, and cut-rate cola. Britt found an old boom box and took it out to her cabin. A Top 40 station poured into the night. From his bedroom, James watched the interns dance. He watched them pass joints, polish off the wine his mother had left behind, then move on to Patrick's booze, and finally their own. His father joined them—no longer their leader, just another person in the disorder.

James knew it had been foolish to stay. He tried not to think about Owen in their grandmother's Spanish-style home in Los Angeles, of the clean sheets, central air-conditioning, cable television, and of Grace somewhere else in the house cooking him meals, signing him up for a new school.

His mother called every day. But James didn't answer. He didn't know how to tell her he'd make a mistake, ask her to come back. He didn't want to see Owen's face if he rolled into L.A., following in his twin's footsteps, finishing in second place as always.

He tried to avoid the ranch as much as possible. He rode his bike into Twentynine Palms, swam in the inn's pool until a guest reported him to the management. He explored the empty cabins in Wonder Valley. And he hung on the edge of an empty lot on Baseline Road, watching shirtless kids take aim at beer bottles.

EARLIER THAT DAY, THE SKY HAD GROWN STEELY AND THE WIND HAD kicked up, threatening a rainstorm that wouldn't come. Now in the darkness the palm trees in the oasis were bending together. It seemed to James like they were telling one another stories, laughing at the people on the ranch.

A new sound joined the rustling farm, the crunch and swish of tires coming up the sand road. James looked down toward the highway and saw headlights bumping and dipping, dancing over the palms and sparse cacti. For a second before the car came into view, James let himself think that it was his mother's station wagon, but when the vehicle crested the small hill, he recognized the truck—a vintage Chevy Silverado with chrome and orange trim. It belonged to the father of a kid in the class above him who lived in Wonder Valley. A few times, the truck had slowed for him and Owen as they were riding their bikes to school. The kid's father invited them to climb in the flatbed before roaring off down the Twentynine Palms Highway.

The truck scattered the gravel then came to a stop. The headlights stayed on, illuminating the porch, the house, a few of the cabins, and the edge of the fire pit. The driver's-side door swung open and the man who'd danced with Grace at the inn stepped out. He still wore his Ranger's hat and clunky white sneakers.

He looked at James like he knew him but couldn't quite place him. "So?" The man shaded his eyes. He seemed to be staring at James's arm.

"Are you looking for my mom?"

"Is she around? Or is she off dancing with the marines?"

"She's gone," James said.

"Permanent?"

"She took my brother back to L.A."

The man cracked a small smile, like he was relieved. "And left you here."

"I stayed," James said.

"You told me your daddy wasn't a marine; you didn't tell me he was a healer."

James glanced at the fire pit. His father hadn't moved from where he reclined against the split log bench, but he was looking over his shoulder at the truck in the driveway.

"I need his help," the man said.

James waved at his dad, beckoning him away from the campfire. "What's wrong with you?"

"You know I can't tell you that," the man said with a wink. "Doctors and patients and all that." He swiped his hat off his head and tucked it into his back pocket. "Anyway, it's not me; it's my friend."

Patrick joined them in the driveway. "What's wrong with your friend?"

The man gave Patrick the once-over. "So you're the great and powerful Oz?"

"Excuse me?" James watched his father try to widen his eyes, straighten his posture.

"You can heal people just by touching them?"

"Who told you that?" Patrick said.

"A little bird," the man said. "All that matters now is that my friend is real sick. And he's got a bee in his bonnet that you're going to be the one to help him. He thinks his spirit's infected."

Patrick rocked back on his heels. "And what do you think?"

"What happened is, he broke his ankle clear through the skin a couple weeks back. We were in a flash flood to the east. I tried resetting it myself."

"So you're a doctor?"

"Amateur pharmacologist. I treated him with some painkillers and antibiotics. But now his fevers don't break anymore."

"Let's take a look," Patrick said.

They went to the truck and opened the passenger door. The cab's light came on, illuminating a slumped figure with a long black braid. He looked Mexican or Native American. His dark skin had an unhealthy sallow tone. He was much bigger than his friend—broad shouldered and overweight. Despite his girth, his face was gaunt.

Patrick threw one of the sick man's arms over his shoulder. The man from the inn took the other, and together they half carried, half dragged the big guy past the fire pit and into Cassidy's old adobe.

James followed his father into the cabin. The interns watched through the window as Patrick laid the big man on the bed and rolled up his pant leg to look at the break. "Best case you're going to have to lose this leg."

"What's a better case?" the man from the inn asked.

Patrick bent over the sick man. He sniffed his breath and his forehead, then placed a hand on his heart. James couldn't understand how he could get so close. The entire adobe smelled like rot. "I'll see what I can do," Patrick said and headed back to the main house.

James tried not to look at the sick man's blackened leg and the scab of flesh that hid the place where the bone had broken through the skin. He stood near the door, where the air was better. The sick man groaned.

The man from the inn pulled a crumpled cigarette from his jeans and struck a match against his teeth. "Is your daddy a miracle worker?"

"That's what people say."

"How about you? What do you say?"

"I guess," James said.

"Is that why you stayed behind? You want to learn his tricks?"

They stepped out of the cabin. The interns had returned to the campfire. Gideon pulled out his guitar. Anushna was spinning in a circle, the flames nipping at her dress.

The man from the inn exhaled in the direction of the campfire. "Who are they?"

"Interns," James said.

"What do they do?"

"Not much." The Silverado's headlights were still on. "I like your truck," James said. He wondered if the man had noticed the sticker on the gate from the local high school.

"Do you now? I think she's a bitch. These antique vehicles are all show and very little rock and roll."

"Where'd you get it?" James asked.

The man ran his thumb over his lips. "You sure ask a lot of questions." He exhaled in the direction of the truck. "I don't need you or any of these kids making any noise about my truck or anything to do with me or my friend. Believe me, trouble can find you even all the way out here. Especially all the way out here. And I don't want to cause you any trouble, do I?"

"I guess not," James said. He looked over his shoulder into the cabin. The sick man had passed out, his long braid hanging over the edge of the bed. "Can I ask you something?"

"What did I just tell you about the questions?"

"Do you know my brother?"

The man crushed his cigarette with the toe of his sneaker. "Why? Does he know me?"

"It's just something he said."

"And what was that?"

"Nothing," James said.

A stick in the fire cracked and split, showering sparks onto Anushna's dress. She screamed and batted the fabric.

"You ever see a meth trailer explode?" the man from the inn asked. "Out in Arizona they light up the desert." He spread his fingers wide against the sky. "Pop, just like that. Pop. If it wasn't for the smell, they'd be a thing of beauty. I used to climb on top of my own trailer and watch them go off. Better than television. I even lit one on fire myself just to see the show."

He raised his eyebrows and widened his eyes, like he was watching the trailer burn all over again.

"Why are you telling me this?" James asked.

"Because you need to know the world ain't pretty and there's not much you can do about it. You still got my pawn?"

"Yes," James said.

"You might give my friend Sam a game sometime. He doesn't take to boredom too well." Then he offered James his hand. "I'm Blake," he said.

25

With Owen back (and then gone) there was no reason for her to stay. The sheriff had no reason to come around to pay attention to the woman named Britt who now looked like the rest of the group at the farm, just another lost kid pretending to find herself in the middle of nowhere. And when she left—if she left—her departure would be camouflaged by the general intern exodus, someone else twisting away on an aimless voyage.

But Patrick's words at the sharing session had rooted in her brain—it wasn't enough to acknowledge her fear without working to overcome it. It was a process Britt understood now, and one she was good at. She'd knocked it out of the park on her first time out, answered one of the questions perfectly, truthfully. So how could she give up?

There was something else that kept her up on the farm, sleeping on the sagging twin bed, staring at the planes winking in the sky as they passed overhead. An unexpected euphoria had arrived after her sharing session, a high that came from confessing her deepest secret, her worst crime, propelling the story into the vastness of the desert. Like she had finally come face-to-face with the enormity of what she had done. She'd abandoned Andy—dead, alive, she didn't know.

But the comedown was hard. Now that she'd admitted what had happened in the SUV—what she had caused to happen by dragging him to a party he had no intention of attending—given it shape and texture, the memory of the accident, the strange slackness in Andy's face, the way she'd been unable to touch him, to discover what she'd made happen, never left her. And it wasn't just the accident. It was all the things that had led up to it, all the moments of carelessness—the late nights, the questionable company, the drunken drives. The decision to keep the party going even though everyone else had packed it in, to forfeit the next day's training which would most likely mean losing the next weekend's match.

It was a maddening tangle, a complex and horrifying puzzle, figuring out when she had first put her foot wrong, and which foot, and where. And how that led to all the things that put her in that car with Andy and that car rolling down the ravine and killing him or hurting him or nothing at all. Because there must have been a first error, something that set the whole disaster in motion.

You can find this moment in every blown match, that split-second what-if that might have sent the ship sailing in the right direction—the return that didn't sail long, the second serve that clipped the line, the volley that skimmed the net, the look you didn't give your coach, the cheer from the stands you ignored. All of it discoverable, each wrong decision easily pinpointed, addressed, advised against on the next go-round. If you hadn't done that, you would have avoided the entire landslide, the descent into chaos. So it had to be there, that initial mistake.

And there was a chance that if the Toyota hadn't skidded, or if she hadn't made Andy go to the party, or if Coach hadn't told her about losing her scholarship that weekend and she hadn't been so dead set on getting off campus, Britt would have pulled it together next year, rediscovered the adrenaline rush of working herself to the limit, exhausting her muscles, and, more important, of being the best. But now it was too late. Because there was no way she would be welcome back on campus. No way she'd get another tennis scholarship anywhere.

So this was where she belonged until she no longer feared things she was capable of, the danger she posed to herself and others. Or until she could pinpoint the precise moment when she'd made the error that brought her out to the ranch. Or until Patrick helped her not just to acknowledge her fear but overcome it. Because that's what he said he would do just before Owen arrived. He'd promised they'd do it together.

But for the last three days there had been no more soul-searching, no more questions and answers. The gardens of the interns' souls had gone untended. Their reasons, fears, and desires unquestioned. And when Britt's fear had not been addressed, it had become magnified, as if once acknowledged, it had been allowed to grow, rampage like an invasive weed.

And now these rough men had come, bringing a different sort of danger than what Britt had sensed scuttling in the desert behind her cabin—a dark, real-world violence. Two men in this wide-open ranch, and somehow they managed to make the place feel cramped. Like they had their eyes on everyone and everything. The air between the campfire and Cassidy's old cabin hung thick with Blake's cigarette smoke, his sick friend's rotten smell and the cloud of sage that Patrick burned to make everything better.

Released from their spiritual questing the interns dropped their hippie shoptalk. They loafed and lounged like your average stoners. When Blake wasn't sitting with his friend he joined them chain-smoking off-brand cigarettes and popping the odd pill from a dwindling supply in his pocket.

The interns avoided Sam's cabin. They worried that Patrick was going to ask them to assist him with whatever herbal healing he was doing. Whenever he attended the sick man, they'd scurry away, plunge into the pond, refill the sun shower, or pretend to be busy with the neglected coop or garden.

But Britt didn't mind. She helped Patrick clean the festering wound, apply herbal compresses and ointments to try to take down the swelling. She fanned the sage around the cabin. She reorganized the power rocks around the foot of Sam's bed. She even assisted with Patrick's laying on of hands, although touching Sam's unnaturally warm flesh made her stomach rise.

She changed the sheets every day, rinsing the sick sweat from the towels she held to Sam's forehead. As she helped, Britt stared deep into the blackish-green cut and at the swollen purple skin and wondered what Sam's first misstep had been, what mistake had he made that had landed him here, rotting away in a crappy cabin?

Blake and Sam had been there for three days. There didn't seem to be much change in Sam's condition. He was lucid part of the day but toward the afternoon he began to rave about magic animals and Mexican witches. By evening he'd stopped speaking a recognizable language.

On the fourth night, the interns gathered around the fire pit out of habit. The vicious excitement that preceded the sharing sessions was gone. But still they came together waiting for Patrick. That night he didn't sit among them as he had for the last few nights. He didn't reach for one of the circling joints or take a swig from the container of booze. Instead he took his old place on the tall stump.

The few interns snuffed their roaches, put their drinks down, and stared at him. There was no electric current, no excitement, no sense that a session was about to start.

Patrick crossed his legs. He smelled more powerfully of sage than usual, as well as of Sam's sick stench.

"Whose turn is it?" He glanced around the circle. No one volunteered. "Gideon," he said. "Be brave."

Gideon's eyes were loopy, his movements even more noncommittal than usual. "Sure," he said, like he couldn't have cared less.

"Okay," Patrick said.

Why are you here? The group's chant was out of sync, some people starting early, others trailing off, and a few barely raising their voices.

Gideon pursed his lips, biting back a lazy smile. "I don't know," he said.

A few interns laughed like that was their answer too. For a moment no one took up the attack.

"Do you think Gideon is telling the truth?" Patrick said. "Do you think Gideon has earned that answer?"

The fire cracked and snapped. An owl called from behind the main house.

"Gideon isn't trying," someone said.

"And?" Patrick stared at the interns in turn. "And? And? And?"

"Gideon has given up on the game," Britt said.

"Gideon thinks he's being honest, but he's only being lazy."

One by one the answers trickled in. Soon they started coming faster, not quite at the usual manic pitch but close. The detached expression left Gideon's face, replaced by simmering frustration.

The interns were in it now. They were no longer the drifting, dazed stoners they'd been a few minutes ago. The sharing gave them clarity. It sharpened their edges, sharpened the whole ranch. Brought a solidity to the drifting desert.

Energy was coiling around the circle, a current winding tighter and tighter, transferring from one intern to another. Their attacks were less specific, less focused on Gideon's answer than usual. But Patrick didn't seem to care.

Britt's voice climbed above the others because the frenzy of the sharing crowded out the memory of the skidding Toyota. She wanted to keep going, build the session up, use it to restore order, bring purpose to the ranch.

She could tell they were approaching the end of the first question. The answers were slowing. Patrick was looking pleased, Gideon defeated.

The door to Sam's cabin opened and Blake stepped out. He struck a match on his teeth and lit a cigarette. The circle began to quiet. Anushna shouted out a final answer.

"Good," Patrick said.

Blake's laugh cut the silence that preceded the chanting of the next question.

"The fuck is all this then?" He took a seat on a vacant bench between Britt and Patrick. "You playing some sort of game?"

"It's a sharing session," Patrick said.

"Is that so?" Blake said. "How about one of you share some of that weed with me."

"Not until the session's over." Patrick held up his hand, signaling the next question.

"Well, okay, then. Don't mind me." Blake took off one of his sneakers and began cleaning it with a dirty bandanna.

The group stayed silent.

"Like I said," Blake repeated. "Don't mind me."

The interns chanted the second question. Gideon gave his answer. But he sounded tentative, not just uncertain of his response but uncertain about the game itself.

The group started their attack but the venom wasn't there. Every once in a while one of them glanced at Blake who'd begun picking at his cuticle with a match. He flicked the match into the fire. "How come you're all so sure about this shit?"

"They're not," Patrick said. "I'm here to show them they're not sure about anything."

"I could have told you all that." Blake extended his hand over to Gideon, waggling his fingers until Gideon passed the roach. Blake put it between his lips. "Continue," he said.

But the current had died. The interns were slouched on their benches.

Blake sparked the joint and passed it. "Sorry," he said. "A man needs to be high to listen to this shit." The weed circled. No one spoke.

The mason jars of booze reappeared. Anushna turned on the boom box. Patrick slid off his stump. Gideon went to his cabin and came back with a plastic handle of whiskey. The bottle circled three times before it was half done.

Anushna started her fire dance. Blake reached up as she passed, grabbed a handful of her batik dress, and pulled her toward him. She laughed and fell onto his lap. "Let me read your aura," she said.

She straddled him and held her hands in front of his face, tickling the air. "I'm not sure what you're doing, sweetheart," Blake said. "But I sure as shit don't mind."

Britt had accepted the bottle several times and had taken a few too many hits of the joint. The interns grew wild. Their language turned rough. Their stories dirty. It was as if Blake had sliced the air with a knife, letting the outside world in. They played drinking games, chain-smoked their way through Blake's last cigarettes, popped some pills from his stash.

When Anushna and one of the male interns began tangling together on the ground just behind the fire pit, Patrick stood and staggered back to the house. Britt watched him climb the single step to the low porch, then steady himself for a beat against a glider before lurching through the door.

Blake had returned to Sam's cabin. Which left Britt.

She was on her feet, crossing the driveway, stumbling over the loose gravel. She tripped on the porch step. The screen door slammed behind her.

The house was dark; the door to James's room was shut.

Britt fumbled down the hall, knocking something on the wall askew. She could hear the swamp cooler chugging in the master bedroom. The door was cracked. She nudged it open.

Patrick lay on the bed like a dead man. He didn't budge when she lay down next to him. The room spun. Britt put one foot on the floor to steady herself and Patrick reached for her, pulling her back onto the bed.

It wasn't that bad, she told herself later in her cabin. She'd wanted to do it. She'd left the campfire, crossed the driveway, entered the house. Of her own free will. She'd wanted to be wanted like he'd wanted her after the chicken slaughter. Wanted to be wanted more than Cassidy or Grace, because at the end of the day, she'd stuck it out when they couldn't. And she wanted Patrick to want her enough to help her like he'd promised.

It had been quick, that was something Britt had to be thankful for. Like Patrick had some urgent need she was helping him fulfill— not sexual but visceral, a need for motion, activity, a need to shake himself free of everyone's abandonment, a passing desire to escape the ranch itself into a blackout pool of sweat and breath and skin.

When he was done, he flopped on his back. "Jesus Christ."

Britt pulled her knees to her chest, unsure whether to touch him or to leave.

"What a fucking mess."

The swamp cooler gurgled. The house resettled.

"You mean with Sam and Blake?"

Patrick raked his fingers through his bristly beard. "Them and the rest of it."

"Can you help him?"

"Who? Sam?" Patrick kicked the sheet off the bed. "No, Britt, I can't help him. I can't help any of you."

26

Darrell knew all about the guy Laila had met by the bus. He told Ren his name was Blake and his hustle was buying folks' meds and reselling them. He even knew where he lived—in a trailer, in a neighborhood just northwest of downtown. But there was no need to search him out, Darrell explained, Blake always turned up. Which was exactly what Ren wanted to prevent. If Laila couldn't sell her meds, there was a chance she might take them, and that might buy him a little more time to make some scratch to get them off Skid Row.

Laila was feeling good that morning. She was up before Ren, sitting in a chair next to Darrell, finishing a joint, and picking at the edges of yesterday's untouched lunch.

"You got somewhere to be?" she asked, eyeing Ren and his backpack. He ducked into her tent, retrieving the marker he'd left there the previous afternoon. He'd done three broadsheet-sized drawings of the ocean, his fat, black lines rippling across the newsprint in a way he hoped made the waves and clouds he'd drawn move and sway. The drawings were tucked into the tent poles where he'd left them, hanging so that they would be the first thing Laila saw when she sat up.

"I have plans of my own today," he said, popping out of the tent.

"A man with a plan," she said. Then she glanced at the marker in his hand. "A boy with his toys."

REN GOT ON THE WRONG BUS TWICE ON HIS WAY TO GLENDALE BOULE-vard. No one had told him there was a Glendale Freeway and no one mentioned that there was a whole other part of the city called Glendale. Eventually he found the spot Darrell had described.

There was a line of campers on the west side of the street opposite a steep hill. One of them was painted with all sorts of religious shit—crosses, Bible passages, a baby Ren assumed was supposed to be Jesus. Others had windows that were either blacked out, covered with dirty cloth, or piled high with too much crap to get a look inside.

Ren paced the street, trying to guess which one belonged to the guy with his mom's meds. Finally, a little Hispanic dude stepped out of the religious camper. He was shirtless and wearing shower sandals. He slap-slapped over to the embankment at the base of the hill and started scraping something out of a frying pan onto the ground. Whatever had been in that pan smelled pretty damn good.

Ren came up next to him, making the little man jump. "You know a guy called Blake?"

The man looked Ren up and down and backed away.

"Blake," Ren said. "White guy. Looks like he might have been left behind by a heavy metal band."

"Señor Blake not in a band," the man said.

"No shit."

The man shuffled from foot to foot making his sandals squeak.

"So which one of these is his?"

The man pointed to the camper next to his—a smallish white

bubble with a gray-washed sheet hanging over the window. "Señor Blake sleeping now," he said.

"Perfect," Ren said.

He meant to bang on the door, rattle the man awake. But he hadn't figured on his fist shaking the fiberglass wall, making the camper vibrate and rock. From the inside Ren heard the sound of someone startled from sleep, the sound of something getting knocked over, something else scattering on the floor. The whole camper shook as the door opened.

The man was wearing only a pair of black jeans. He was skinny, with loose flesh at his waistband. His black hair was sleep matted on one side.

"The fuck—"

"Are you Blake?" Ren put a hand on the camper door so the dude couldn't shut it.

"The fuck you care?"

"I care," Ren said, "because you've been messing with my mom."

"Jesus," Blake said, patting his pocket, like he might have slept on a pack of smokes. "What the hell is all this now?"

"I saw you yesterday and a month before that."

Blake held up a hand. "Not guilty, Judge."

"Yeah," Ren said. "Yeah, you are. You been scamming off my mom for years now. Least that's what folks downtown are saying."

"Are they?" Blake reached behind him and fumbled on a fold-down table until he grasped his cigarettes. "You better step inside. I don't need all the nice folks around here thinking I'm a criminal, now, do I?"

He made room for Ren to pass but stayed in the doorway to smoke. Ren stood, wedged between the bed and the wall, his shoulders stooped and his chin tucked into his neck. The camper was cramped and smelled like stale laundry. Some kind of tribal weaving—a round hoop hung with beads and feathers—dangled from the ceiling over the bed. A chess set with mismatched pieces sat on the folding table. "Why don't you make yourself comfortable?" Blake gestured at the bed.

Ren sat, making the chess set jump.

"Now what's this about your mom?" Blake angled his chin up and blew smoke away from the camper, like it made a difference.

"The way I see it," Ren said, "you've been scamming her for a while now. And I'm here to put an end to it."

"Listen, kid," Blake said, "back in the day you might have made your case but it's been years since I scammed anyone."

"I saw you just yesterday. You got off the bus, met my mom, went around the corner. Next thing, your pockets are fat with her pills and she's got a roll of cash in her pocket."

"You're talking about Laila?"

"Yeah," Ren said.

"Well, it's not exactly a scam if I'm buying what she's selling."

"She's broke, living on the street. My guess is she'd do anything for money, selling her meds if necessary. So from where I'm sitting, it looks like a scam. A con. You're taking advantage of a lady who doesn't have any other options."

"Well, you're right about that. Laila is out of options."

"How's that?"

"Didn't you say you were her son?" Blake said. "Well, then, I don't need to tell you that she's dying."

"The fuck you talking about?"

He knew, but then he didn't. Ren had hoped to get Laila out of downtown before someone put this truth into words, made it real, solid, permanent. And now this dude—this Blake—some tenth-rate con artist had been the one to do it.

"I asked, the fuck you talking about?" Ren repeated.

"Come on, son. She's half the woman she was a month ago and about a quarter of the person she was when I first met her. She doesn't need her meds. So she might as well turn a profit on them, buy herself whatever comfort she wants."

Ren's stomach was rising, his fingers tingling; every nerve in his body seemed on fire. "You let a dying woman sell you her medication?"

"It's her choice," Blake said. "When you're dying, they give you the good stuff for your sleeplessness, your anxiety, your depression. That's what keeps the kids happy these days."

"How come you know she's dying?" Ren said.

"She just got finished a monthlong stint in the hospital. I'm guessing they told her there wasn't anything more they could do. Gave her the meds, sent her on her way. It's her right to die at home."

Ren had been pretty sure Laila was blowing smoke about her sojourn at the beach, but he never figured she'd been in the hospital. The desk sergeant at Central P.D. was right—he should have checked.

"The streets aren't home."

"Listen, I'm not one to judge who lives where. All I know is, we'd all be blessed to get to die where we choose."

For a second, Ren thought the guy sounded choked up. But he must be tripping, his brain in free fall.

"Okay. Okay, okay, okay. So she's dying." The words tasted foul. "I'll make you a deal. You leave her alone till she passes. And any meds she has left, I'll give to you for free. I don't need you profiting off Laila's last days." What he didn't tell Blake is that both he and Laila would be gone before she died. Because no way in hell was he letting her pass on the streets.

Blake ran his hands though his matted hair. "A deal?" he said. "All right if I counter? There's this white kid I've seen hanging around Laila's camp. I don't think he lives there."

"There are a couple of white boys on the corner."

"About your age. He's got dirty blond hair and his eyes are some sort of strange gray."

"That sounds like Flynn."

Blake gave a crooked smile. "It certainly does sound like *Flynn*." He drew the name out. "If you tell me where to find him, I'll leave your mom be until . . ." He trailed off.

"Yeah, until."

Blake pulled out another smoke and held it in his mouth without lighting it. He looked expectantly at Ren.

"He lives at the Cecil Hotel," Ren said. "Top floor."

LATE AFTERNOON AND THE SUN STILL HADN'T FOUGHT THROUGH THE gray-washed sky. It had been the same shit for a week now, like a wool blanket had been thrown over the city, damming the light, casting a ghostly pallor over the streets. Back east overcast meant rain and promised some sort of release. But here rain didn't come and the heavy-hung sky did nothing more than raise a whole bunch of expectations it couldn't deliver. Folks downtown had their theories—some said it was the start of an El Niño, others prophesied an earthquake, and some even called it the June Gloom although summer was still months away. Whatever was coming, Ren wasn't going to be around to see it.

As he waited for the bus, he tried to figure what *dying* meant. Days? Weeks? Months? Maybe years. Because we were all dying, some slower than others; it was only that Laila's deadline had been moved up. And if they'd let her go from the hospital, didn't that mean they expected she'd have some living to do? Otherwise, they'd have kept her around, let her pass supervised. Had to be, right?

It didn't seem fair that he'd made his way cross-country, found his mom down in Skid Row just in time for this messed-up finale. He tried to be good but the world treated him bad. He tried to atone and the world turned away.

So what the fuck? What did he have to lose? Folks imagined

he was bad—he might as well do bad, especially if it helped him get on the up-and-up and get Laila out of downtown. If it helped her die dignified, why the fuck not?

He got it now—how the boys in the PJs and the tougher kids in juvie kept a spring in their step. They owned their choice not to play nice, abide by the rules. They'd taken control, chosen a path they knew they could stick to, bad as it might be. And there was power in ownership. It gave you something in a world that denied you the rest.

That's how it happened. That's how easy it is to step over the boundary of good and bad, to stop pretending to be one thing and decide to be another. Now he was walking faster. He felt lighter. In control.

He began to look for Puppet.

The cops were doing shakedowns on Skid Row, which only made Ren's anger harder. Some of the police were mounted on horses, towering over the people in their tents. Others, wearing plastic gloves, even masks, worked the sidewalks, rousting folks from their camps, shaking out tents and sleeping bags, confiscating shopping carts and other things they felt the homeless shouldn't have.

Health hazard. Safety hazard. Pedestrian hazard.

Abandoned property. Discarded belongings. Waste material.

Any excuse.

The hood was chaotic. People stood on the streets, watching their possessions torn through, piled willy-nilly as if everything was trash not personal property.

Activists and community organizers had arrived, shouting at the cops, pulling aside the people whose stuff had been taken, trying to explain their rights and where they needed to go to file a complaint.

A few folks were taken away in handcuffs. Several dogs were hauled off to a shelter, their owners howling and spitting after the police. Some people chased after the trucks carrying their stuff. A few shouted coherently about civil rights, illegal searches, invasion of privacy. Others just yelled freestyle curses.

A man in an army jacket and red cap jumped up on an overturned shopping cart. "We gonna get your stuff back, but first we gonna paint a mural right here." He pulled two cans of Krylon out of his backpack. "*Private Property*. That's what it's gonna say. Tell the police they can't be messing with our possessions. Can I get a crew with me?" He uncapped one of the cans, rattled it, and sprayed it on the wall.

Ren was too far away to hear the shake and hiss of the can as it released its paint. A day ago—that morning even—he'd have rushed over, asked for one of the cans, eager to leave his mark, let folks know that he had been here before he split town. But now he just pulled his hood low over his eyes and hustled off.

He found Puppet in the third spot he checked, on some steps on Fifth Street watching over the action in San Julian Park. Puppet sure kept his shit obvious, but Ren assumed he had his reasons.

"My man." Puppet bounced to his feet when he saw Ren. He was wearing a pair of shorts so long they might was well be pants and a T-shirt that could be considered a dress. He had his black baseball cap pulled at a right angle to his face, the straight brim knocking against his shoulder as he bobbed and dipped.

"Whoa-ho, my man," he said as Ren stopped in front of the steps. "You didn't walk on by this time? You stopped for me."

Two of Puppet's minions came down the steps, joined up with a kid on a bike, played a quick hand game then retreated.

Puppet gave Ren the once-over. "You don't look so good, you feel me? You look motherfucking abused."

"Your offer still good?"

Puppet smiled and swiveled his hat round to the opposite side. "The man's looking to do business, is that it?"

"I need some bank."

"That's a cold game, coming up to a man and straight-up asking for some cash."

"Yeah," Ren said. "But call it an emergency. Extenuating circumstances."

"Ex-ten-u-a-ting." Puppet drew the word out. He turned to his crew. The boys behind him nodded, then returned their gaze to the streets. Their eyes looked dopey, but chances were they didn't miss a move over in the park. "This boy's got a lot of big talk. A lot of hundred-dollar words. But he needs to get his paper up."

Puppet bounced down to street level and clapped Ren on the shoulder. "You feel me?"

"Puppet, boy, I always feel you," Ren said.

Puppet stopped bouncing. He stood on his tiptoes so his bug eyes were level with Ren's. Then his eyes widened and how that was possible Ren didn't know. Ren stared him down, unsure whether the kid was going to bark, bite, or back off. Puppet bumped shoulders with him. "You one funny motherfucker." He sprang back up the steps, whispered something in one of his boys' ears, then was down by Ren again. "So you want to get your paper up? Time to get up off those streets?"

"I need three hundred and change," Ren said. He figured that three C-notes plus whatever Laila had in her purse would be enough for the tickets and some vending machine feeds.

"Whoa. Whoa. Whoa. How come you think I'm gonna pay that large? That's a whole lot of paper, you feel me?"

"It's what I need."

"Well, now it seems like there's a whole lotta room between what you need and what I can give."

Ren jammed his hand deeper in his sweatshirt pocket, reflexively feeling for a pack of smokes he was too poor to have. He looked over at San Julian Park—a dance of users, dealers, and folks just trying to enjoy a little public peace. "I'll do whatever."

"And who says I got whatever for you to do?"

Ren glanced down at his dirty jeans, his sockless feet. He wasn't going to beg. He wasn't even going to ask again. "Mother-fucker!" Puppet hit him on the shoulder. "I'm just messing with you. I'm just playing hard to get. I don't want people out here think-ing that Puppet comes easy. That he's a motherfucking fairy god-mother. But matter of fucking fact I got a job that needs doing and coincidentally you the perfect dude to do it."

"How's that?"

Puppet laughed. "Because you look motherfucking homeless."

In his mind's eye, Ren had held himself separate from the rest of the folks on the street but there was no mistaking him now.

"But it's cool, you feel me?" Puppet said. "See we got a few workers who live up in these SRO hotels and these subsidized build-ings. Idea was, they're supposed to be selling to their neighbors, keeping the business hidden from the streets. Problem starts when they begin keeping it all to themselves. Now they're messing with the cash flow because me and my boys can't get inside to make it right. We're what you call a known quantity. Dudes at the security see us coming a mile away. What we need is a homeless mother-fucker we can trust, you feel me? Someone who got half a head left."

"So you want me to get your money?" Ren asked.

"Motherfucker, I need you to send a message. Not silence these fools but let them know they best never mess with my busi-ness again." Puppet swiveled his hat again, then crossed his arms over his chest. "Then if you can get my money, that'd be the moth-erfucking bomb, you feel me."

"And you'll give me three large?"

"Hell no," Puppet said. "I'll give you thirty percent of the bank or product you recover. We got four instances of these motherfuck-ers in four separate buildings. Sum total, I'm guessing these fools owe nearly a G. That's with the interest."

"What kind of message?" Ren asked.

"Tomorrow I'll have one of my boys hand you a piece you can borrow."

"No guns. I don't do guns."

"How you gonna send a message? You gonna shout at them? You gonna ask them pretty-fucking-please? You do this with a piece or you don't do it, you feel me."

Ren shook his head.

"No one's asking you to kill a motherfucker."

What had he expected? That Puppet would ask him to wash his car, fold his goddamn laundry? That he'd make three hundred by, worst case, carrying dope from one spot to the next?

"So?" Puppet was bouncing less than a foot in front of Ren's face.

One thing's for sure, Ren thought, if he was housed, if he had a roof and door, a bed and even a window no matter how shitty the mattress, how crappy the view, he wouldn't ruin it by slinging drugs. He wouldn't contaminate his space with all the sickness out on the street. His room would be precious, perfect, a place to escape the crazy instead of inviting the outside in. How folks could be so careless, so spoiled was a wonder. How they could ruin their SRO or hotel for others was a straight-up crime.

So fuck it. Teach these fools a lesson. Knock 'em back to the streets so they might not have the bank to get back inside where things were supposed to be safer.

"Sure," Ren said. "I got you."

Puppet stood still. "My man," he said. "I knew I could count on you. I know you're gonna bring the hard logic to those fuckers, set them straight." He reached into the pocket of his saggy shorts and pulled out a ten-spot. "Get yourself a feed. I need you on point, you feel me? You need to do me proud. You need to collect. Come back tomorrow night."

Ren swiped the bill.

"You my boy now," Puppet said.

27

A week after the men arrived at the ranch, James woke up and saw that the Silverado was missing from the driveway. Without bothering to put on shoes or a shirt, he hurried to the cabins, hoping to find Blake and Sam gone.

But when he got to Sam's adobe, he saw the sick man lying on the cot surrounded by a ring of rocks and burning herbs. Patrick sat at his side, dressing his wound and pressing a compress to his brow. Underneath the smell of burning sage Sam's odor hung heavy in the cabin. It smelled like death or what comes after.

James watched him from the doorway. Sam's matted braid hung over the edge of the mattress. His pupils were lost in his inky irises. The whites of his eyes were yellow. His gaze locked on James. "You," he said.

Patrick turned and saw James.

"You?" Sam said. "You're back." He thrashed on his cot.

Patrick placed a hand on Sam's chest to quiet him, then gave James a look that told him he'd better beat it. He lingered for a moment, until Sam's lids fluttered, his eyes rolled, and he slept.

James backed out of the cabin and wandered over to the

oasis. The palms were still. He took off his shirt and shoes and walked into the pond, letting his feet sink into the soft cool mud. He waded up to his knees, turning in circles to animate the stagnant water.

He hadn't been in the pond since the night Owen shot the hawk and he'd hidden, half submerged, trying to ignore the smell of the bird's roasting flesh. The water seemed murkier. He kicked onto his back and floated, staring at the sky through the trees.

James dipped his head and went under, hovering just below the surface. The water jolted with a muffled sonic boom. He came up for air, waiting for an aftershock or the vacuum of silence that always seemed to follow a bomb test from the military base. He swam for shore, grabbed his shirt and shoes, and hurried to the house. He could see a curl of black smoke rising several miles from the ranch—a narrow, noxious-looking coil.

James fell asleep in a glider and woke to steps on the porch. He opened his eyes and saw Blake. There were rivulets of sweat dripping from under the brim of his Ranger's hat. He smelled of smoke and gasoline.

"You don't need to ask about the pickup anymore," Blake said.

"What happened to it?"

"I told you, you didn't need to ask. But seeing as you are, all you need to know is, I never liked the damn thing in the first place. It didn't run smooth." He brought a cigarette to his lips. His fingers were streaked with some sort of grease that he wiped on his pants before reaching for a match. "Fact is, you start to like some things better when they're gone. Like that brother of yours."

"I don't really like him," James said.

"You don't wonder how he's doing in the big city?"

"Never."

"I like that," Blake said. "A man of principles. Someone betrays you, you stick to your guns. You've got spine, kid."

THAT NIGHT THE PARTY AROUND THE CAMPFIRE STARTED EARLIER THAN usual. In fact, it seemed to be less of a party and more an outgrowth of an afternoon of smoking and drinking. By six, Anushna was dancing topless. By seven, Gideon had roared into town for more booze. At eight, Britt came into the house to find James.

"Don't you want to join the fun?" she asked, draping an arm around his shoulder.

James wriggled free.

Britt tugged on his arm. But he pulled away so hard that she stumbled backward. "I'm sorry," she said, then grabbed some beer from the fridge and rejoined the party.

Not even the TV could drown out the boom box, the shouts, the laughter.

James went to his room. He pulled his curtains against the noise. He jammed a pillow over his head. But it was too hot and he threw it at Owen's empty bed. The pillow bounced off the bed frame and something hit the floor. James turned on the light and saw the pawn Blake had given him down at the inn. He picked it up. He looked at the small Asian figure that had made Owen so angry.

Blake was lying, that much James was sure of. He knew Owen or something about Owen. He pocketed the pawn and hurried out the door, across the driveway in the direction of the cabin and fire pit. Blake and Patrick were drinking whiskey out of Grace's mother's teacups.

Britt sprang up when she saw him. She pulled him into a sloppy hug, then took his hands and together they spun in a circle. James tried to break free. But her grip was strong.

"Dance with me," she said. "Dance."

"I-I-I—" James said.

She was whipping him faster now, her face thrown back, her red hair streaking behind her. Four, five more revolutions and she let go, sending him careening sideways, until he tumbled to the ground. "Live a little," Britt said, helping him up.

"He looks alive to me," Blake said. "But you seem dead set on killing him."

Britt pulled James back to the fire. "I want him to have fun."

"Then give him a drink," Blake said.

James glanced at his father. "What are you looking at me for?" Patrick said.

Britt poured a glug of whiskey into a large pickling jar.

James winced as the liquid burned his tongue, then his throat. He drained the glass quick and passed it back to Britt and started for Sam's cabin.

"James?" Britt called. "James?"

JAMES TAPPED ON THE CABIN DOOR, THEN PUSHED IT OPEN. SAM HAD fallen asleep, a battered book on his chest. A chess set sat on the small nightstand. Several of its pieces were missing, replaced by odds and ends—a couple of bottle caps, a rock, and a paper clip. But the ones that remained matched the pawn in his pocket.

Sam's eyes opened. He looked angry and disoriented. James fumbled for the pawn in his pocket. He held it out.

"You stole that?" Sam asked.

"I found it." It seemed better to lie.

"So you do have magic in you."

"I guess." James approached the bed and put the pawn next to the chessboard.

"So are you going to set it up or not?" Sam asked.

"You want to play?"

"The fuck you think." The sick man pushed himself up to sitting and whipped his braid over his shoulder.

James hated chess mostly because Owen always beat him. He only retained a vague memory of what piece went where, which could move in what direction and why.

He put the pawn in its place and lined up the rest of the pieces, not quite sure if he'd mixed up which of those went on the right or left. Then he looked at the makeshift pieces. "What's what?" he asked.

"Christ," Sam said, snatching the board away. "You got a worse memory than Blake." He slammed the bottle caps and the rocks into place. "Remember now?"

James looked at the chessmen. It sort of made sense and if everything stayed in place he could keep track. But once the pieces were scattered across the board it was going to be hard.

"You waiting for anything in particular?"

"No."

"So you gonna open or what?"

James's hand hovered above the board. He couldn't remember whether black or white moved first. His fingers came to rest on a black pawn. Sam slapped his hand away. "The fuck's happened to you?"

James quickly snatched a white pawn and slid two spaces forward.

The music outside switched from Top 40 to classic rock. And soon Blake's voice rose above the rest singing along to every other word.

James was able to hang with Sam for a few moves, shuffling around pawns and hoping the rock that was supposed to be a knight. But after that his pieces began to disappear while Sam took over his side of the board.

"I'm sick as fuck," Sam said, "but you're playing like you're brain-dead. I guess I must have been taking it easy on you."

James had thought it was another one of Owen's stories invented to make him feel small and naive. But his twin hadn't been lying. He had been camped out with Blake and Sam—the two criminals.

"You know my brother," he said.

Sam looked up from the board. "Nope," he said. The sweat was coming down his nose.

"He was in the cabin with you."

"You think because Blake's got me all hopped up on pills that I'm crazy."

"He was in the cabin with you. He told me."

"No, boy. The only person in the cabin with me and Blake was you. Except you were different then."

"I wasn't—"

"You were different. And don't act like I'm too far gone to know better. You were smarter, tougher. Not so much of a pussy. But now look at you. Asking all sorts of questions. Tiptoeing around like you're afraid. But I know the truth. I know what you are."

"No, you don't."

"Oh, I do. And just because you're back home doesn't mean you can hide it from me. The world needs bad men as much as it needs good ones. You don't believe me, but you've got a darkness in you. I can see it from here. I can smell it and I'm never wrong. You're more like us than you think." He flung his braid to his other shoulder. "Your move."

James reached across the board. He was pretty certain Sam had lured him into a trap so the next move would be checkmate. He took the sick man's queen. As he picked up the piece, Sam's hand wrapped around his wrist and twisted so James's underarm was facing up.

Sam's grip was clammy and strong. James's skin burned as the sick man rotated his arm back and forth, running his eyes from James's elbow to wrist.

"*Brujo*," Sam said.

James tried to pull his arm away. Sam held tight.

"*Brujo*. Where is it?" Up close James could see that Sam's pupils were constricted to pinpricks. He pulled James closer, dragging him up toward the head of the bed.

"Let go." James wriggled his wrist side to side.

With his other hand Sam traced the skin of James's forearm. "I cut you there to there. Deep. Down to the bone." His breath was sour, like the decay was bubbling up. "Now there's no scar."

"Let go!" James shouted.

"In the cabin you stole my spirit. I fell asleep and you stole my spirit so I wouldn't heal. I had to punish you."

James shook his head. "It wasn't me."

"Of course it was. I'm sick but I'm not blind."

"It was my brother."

Sam narrowed his eyes. Sweat dripped from his brow. "It was you. I cut you there to there," he repeated. He yanked on James's arm, making it burn worse. "I cut you so my soul could fly out. So I could have my spirit back."

James thought of the cut on Owen's arm, the dark, crusted wound, and the white flicker of bone beneath.

"The scar is gone. You are a *brujo*. You've come back to try to take my spirit again." Sam's eyes were wild, widening, showing the yellowed whites.

James yanked his arm harder now. But Sam pulled him closer and reached under the mattress. In the dim light of the cabin James saw the knife. Sam held it up. Its blade was speckled with rust.

James screamed, hoping his voice could be heard above the music.

Sam tried to find his mark. James grasped the hand holding the knife and managed to turn it away from him and toward the sick man. Sam was exhausted by their brief struggle. His arm wobbled.

There was a moment when he could have pushed Sam's hand in any direction he'd wanted, down toward the mattress, behind his back. James had the upper hand. He could have freed the handle from Sam's fingers and fled the cabin.

Instead James pressed harder, bending Sam's arm back, not

stopping until the big man plunged the knife between his own col-larbone and neck.

Behind him he heard a scream. He turned and saw Britt stand-ing in the doorway holding the whiskey. She dropped the bottle and it shattered on the threshold. She rushed to James, pulling him off Sam. She yanked the knife free and a fountain of blood flew up from the wound, soaking them both, splattering over the walls and ceiling.

James was thrashing, but Britt restrained him, pinning him in her arms. He could smell the wood smoke on her clothes and hair.

He could hear footsteps outside—Blake then Patrick, then the rest of the interns. Blake rushed to the bed, taking Sam in his arms.

The two men lay on the bed, Blake cradling Sam as his life leaked onto the thin mattress and down to the floor. The sick man's body went slack. Blake shook him once, then again as if he could restore his pulse, restart his breath. Then he stood, letting his friend's body slump onto the bed.

He looked around the cabin with a savage expression. The sound that came out of him was an untamed wail.

Blake ripped his hat from his head and raked his fingers through his hair. He wiped them away, then locked his gaze on James. "You," he said. He lunged forward.

"No," Britt said. She still held James tight. Now she scooted in front of him, blocking him from Blake. "It wasn't him. It was me."

Blake looked from one to the other. James's heart went wild. He tried to speak, but Britt drove her nails into his arm. "It was me."

"What—" James said. Britt dug deeper.

"It was me," she said. "He wanted me to-to-to . . ." She was stammering. "He had a knife."

PATRICK KEPT WATCH FROM THE PORCH, HIS EYES ON THE CABIN WHERE Blake was slumped at Sam's side. When Blake left his friend and headed away from the farm, he intercepted him. Blake would not be returning. He would not be reporting whatever happened in the cabin. He had too much at stake. Patrick made certain of this.

When Patrick was sure Blake was gone, he and Gideon loaded Sam's body into the back of Patrick's pickup. Along with Britt, they drove deep into the desert, along the unmarked sand roads only Patrick was familiar with. They didn't invite James.

When he was alone James stood under the shower until he ran out the warm water, until gooseflesh popped on his arms.

Deep down he'd always imagined that one day he'd join Owen, that he'd take the bus or demand his father drive him. That would never happen now.

Owen and Grace would live in a Dutch colonial house not too far from their grandmother's. Owen would join the swim team in high school and go surfing with his friends. He'd save up for a nice car in a flashy color. He'd cruise down the PCH with his girlfriend who would put her feet on the dash. He'd watch the sunset from Matador Beach and camp out in Paradise Cove.

James could see it all. And he would have to settle for the desert sand.

He turned off the shower. He didn't bother drying off, but walked straight out of the house, past the campfire, past the cabins, toward the national park. When he found a patch of ground clear of arrowwood and creosote bushes, he lay down. He tried to dig his toes into the sand, tried to recall the feeling of the cold, wet sand a few feet below the surface near the water. He closed his eyes and tried to imagine the sound of the wind sprinting across the desert was the crashing sea.

28

They say the condemned sleep because why the fuck not, and the guilty because it's game over. In juvie Ren had noticed that boys who didn't give a shit about what they'd done, no matter how messed up their crimes, slept like babies, relaying their dreams of filthy trysts with video vixens in the mornings. Their unimaginative porn fantasies didn't interest Ren. What interested him was that they'd slept.

The night after Ren had signed on with Puppet, he slept longer and deeper than he had in months, in years even. He slept through Laila's racking coughs. Slept through Darrell crooning along to Teddy Pendergrass. Slept through the smells, sounds, and suffering around him. He slept way past the time when the rest of the folks on Crocker were packing up their camps, moving on to whatever got them through their days. He slept until the sun had finally fought its way through the gray haze that blanketed the sky.

Laila's tent was up but she was out. And that was a blessing. Because Ren had a feeling his mother would be able to read it on his face—his decision to go bad. Because she'd suspected all along and always that there was something dark inside Ren that had made him pull that trigger, shoot the corrections officer who had been crossing the courtyard, bring down an innocent man in front of his ten-year-old son.

There had been no explaining to Laila that it had been not simply an accident, but the dumbest luck of all. That Ren hadn't aimed, hadn't even looked.

But if she saw him today, she'd see it written all across his face. She'd know that he'd become what she thought he'd always been. And that would make Ren lose his nerve. So he kept away from Crocker until dark, until it was time to find Puppet's boy.

THE DEPUTY WAS WAITING BY THE PARK, A RED HOODIE COVERING HIS face. He gestured for Ren to follow him. They marched to a doorway where he slid a paper bag into the pouch pocket of Ren's sweatshirt. The gun made the material sag, so Ren held his hand under the fabric until he could transfer the piece to his pants.

The deputy gave Ren an address, told him what floor he'd find the dude. "Alls you do is leave your ID at the door. But don't forget it on the way out. Motherfuckers do stupid shit," he said. "Now Puppet don't expect you'll recover shit. Motherfucking junkies use it all and trade the rest."

"So—" Ren asked.

"So you supposed to send a message, is what Puppet says— send a good message, make some good paper."

So that was the deal. Puppet didn't expect him to deliver cash or goods, he expected Ren to hit hard.

"Now we not saying lay the motherfucker out. Just let him know he messed with the wrong motherfuckers." The guy pulled his hood farther over his face and turned tail before Ren could object.

Ren watched the deputy slip away, just another Skid Row regular on the make or take. He felt the gun sagging in his sweatshirt. It was cold consolation that he didn't have to kill his target. Because what he had to do gave little relief—beat the dude or scare him shitless.

He stuck his hand into his pocket, crinkling it through the paper bag until he hit cold metal. He couldn't believe the weight of the thing, couldn't believe that his twelve-year-old hand had lifted something similar.

He tried to remember raising that gun, nosing it through the busted blinds in the project window. There must have been a recoil, a kickback that sent him flying. But his only memory was like a movie or video game, visual not physical. Because he hadn't marked the action at the time and hadn't ascribed any particular importance to shooting that gun. He hadn't expected it would hit anything and fuck his shit up for good.

He wrapped his hand around the shaft, trying to remember if it had felt the same before, if he'd marveled at the weight. Two hands. He'd used two hands—he could see it now. It was only later, when the older bangers fled, that he'd posed with the gun execution style, turning it sideways, sighting his own third eye in the mirror, his other hand cupped over his mouth like a bandanna. Bang.

He measured his gait. He didn't want to look like he was on the prowl or fleeing some scene. He didn't slink or keep to the shadows. He even took down his hood so any passing cruiser might see that he was carrying on out in the open, nothing to hide, nothing worth stopping for.

He ran his fingers over the trigger, the raised ridges on the grip. He felt for the opening out of which the bullet would fly.

He didn't have to fire the gun. He just had to hold it. He could take the bullets out. He should. He just needed somewhere out of the way.

Ren crossed Fifth and turned up Wall. On the smaller street he realized that he wasn't alone. Someone was at his back in lockstep.

He tensed his hand around the gun. At the next corner he paused under a streetlight and glanced back. Except for people rolled up in their bags, he was alone.

He headed west. Now his pursuer was at his side, bumping his elbow, crowding his space. And he knew. The gun had brought the ghost, not that Marcus's specter needed an invitation these days. Ren walked faster, but his companion kept up, never breaking stride. He gripped the gun tighter. The ghost came closer, his cold, liquid presence chilling Ren.

"It's not like I have a fucking choice," Ren said. "I don't have a fucking choice."

He stopped under another streetlamp, hoping the glow and radiant electric warmth might drive the ghost off. But the man crowded in, merging his body with Ren's, filling him with a cold current.

His heart beat double time and then for a split second seemed as if it didn't beat at all. His nerves were brittle like steel wool. He had to do the job quick before this particular bout of crazy took over and he did something that snared the cops' notice and he got hauled in on vagrancy, then booked for possession of a firearm. And who knew where that gun had been, how many bodies were in its rearview.

Do it quick.

Get home quicker.

Ren turned into the small alleyway church, the dimmest, narrowest place he could think of—a place out of cops' view. He squatted down against the wall and took out the gun. There wasn't enough light to make the black metal glint or gleam.

HE'D GRIPPED IT WITH TWO HANDS, RAISED IT, BLINDLY AIMING AWAY from him. He'd closed his eyes. Now he remembered that, too. He'd been afraid. And he'd squeezed the trigger fast, wanting to get the dare done quick so the older bangers wouldn't tease him anymore.

The kickback had bruised a bone at the base of his palm. He remembered that as well, remembered pressing a finger into the bruise during the first days he spent waiting to see if he'd be tried as an adult or a kid, as he listened to the juvie rep tell him what he'd done, what he was up against, what was happening. He drove that finger into the bruise, grinding toward the bone, trying to summon any sort of feeling at all.

I can hold your piece?

The older boys had laughed, mimicking his prepubescent voice.

Fuck y'alls. Lemme hold it.

Let him hold it. Let lil banger hold it.

Only if he's got the balls to fire it.

You gonna put yo money where your mouth is, lil banger.

You gonna play with it like a doll or you gonna pull the motherfuck-ing trigger.

Lemme see it, Ren had insisted.

Give it him.

Shoot out the window, not at your foot.

Shoot in the direction of Stone Cold Boys. Show 'em you hard. You hard, lil banger?

Less than sixty seconds. That's all it had taken from the moment one of the older kids had put the 9 mm in Ren's hand to the moment he'd nosed the thing through the curtains and fired. And that was it. His life. Done.

HE PULLED OUT THE CLIP AND EMPTIED THE BULLETS INTO HIS HAND.

Somewhere someone was singing. A prayer it sounded like. Or maybe he was imagining shit, what with the ghost on his case and all. Ren closed his eyes. Shook his head. The song disappeared, or maybe the blood rush in his ears dammed it back.

He jiggled the bullets, rolling them like dice. Hard to imagine something so small landed him here.

Ren stood up. He tucked the gun in the waistband of his pants.

He cracked his neck side to side. All he was doing was coming down on some junkie dealer, someone who spread poison where folks were trying to stay safe. He narrowed his eyes in the dark, drawing his focus inward, blocking out everything but the task at hand. He'd used the same technique when zeroing in on one of his larger murals, beating back the outside world, the other areas of the wall, even the other sections of his piece in order to bring whatever small corner he was working on to life.

The muttering started again. He pulled his hood over his ears, listening instead to his hair rubbing the fabric. He booked it out of the alley.

He wasn't looking left or right. He wasn't even looking ahead. He was zoned in on what he had to do, thinking about it so hard that he wasn't even thinking about it at all, more thinking into the black space around it. He didn't see the person kneeling on the ground at the far side of the alley before it was too late and he'd tripped, sending the gun skidding along the ground.

Ren fumbled for the gun, launching his body over top of it like it was a football. He recovered it and jammed it back into his waistband. Then he got to his feet, ready to hustle off.

"Aren't you going the wrong way?" It was Flynn's voice.

Ren flicked his lighter. The white boy was on his knees, a small mound of rocks in front of him. His hands were pressed together like he was praying.

"What's it to you where I'm going?" Ren said. He was sure Flynn could hear his heartbeat. Sure he could detect the gun sagging his pants.

"Where've you been all day?" Flynn asked.

"Around."

It's like Flynn knew. And maybe he did. Maybe Puppet had said something to someone and the word got around that Ren had been drafted.

"So you don't know about Laila," Flynn said. "People are saying she won't make it through the night."

"Shit," Ren said. The gun felt cold against the small of his back. "Shit."

Flynn resettled on his knees.

"You're praying for her?" Ren asked.

"For her, for me. For everyone."

Ren hadn't noticed that he'd been sweating. And now the sweat had dried cold, making him shiver. Marcus's ghost was suffocating him, standing too close, making it hard for him to breathe.

Flynn returned to his prayer. "You'd better hurry, brother," he said.

Ren needed to get rid of the gun. He needed to wipe it clean. He'd figure out what to say to Puppet and his crew later.

At the eastern edge of the alley he found a half-full can of soda, which he poured over the 9 mm. He took off his sweatshirt and rubbed the sticky liquid over the gun. A few blocks from Crocker he dropped the thing down an open sewer. He listened to it rattle and clatter. He crouched down and sparked his lighter. He saw nothing glinting down in the dark.

Only then did he remember he hadn't mentioned to Flynn that Blake had been asking about him, that the dude sounded like he had bad business in store. But it was too late to double back.

THE WEARY STREETLAMP HALFWAY UP CROCKER WAS FLICKING ON AND off, showing a crowd of people in front of Laila's camp.

"It's blood, man," someone said. "Stand back. You don't want what she's got."

"Someone take her to the medic spot. She'll die better over there."

"That place only kills you quicker."

Ren shouldered through them.

Laila was flat-backed on the sidewalk in front of her tent. A dark streak ran from her mouth down to her chin.

"Who's gonna take her to the doc?"

Laila raised one hand and shook it back and forth.

"She's saying she don't want to go."

"How you can tell what the lady's saying?"

Ren squatted down. He slid his arms under his mother's frail body. "Don't let them take me," she whispered.

"Ma," he said. "I'm not letting you stay here."

Her fingers fumbled for his wrist, clawing at him until she got a grip. Her hand was all parchment and sinew. "You of all people should know what it means to be locked away somewhere you don't want to be."

"Ma—"

"We all make mistakes," she said. Ren had to press his ear to her lips to catch her words. "It doesn't mean we should be denied a few graces."

He lifted her. He could feel every bone—the protruding wings of her shoulders, the snaky climb of her vertebrae.

"Careful boy, she might have the TB."

"Back off," he said to the crowd. "She needs air."

"Not this air."

Laila coughed again. Ren could see the tendons on her neck strain and her rib cage press against her T-shirt. She squeezed Ren's hand. Ren loosened his grip, worried his mother's bones would crack. The fit subsided and Laila went limp.

"Get that woman to the health center," someone said. "We don't need bodies on the street."

"No," Ren said.

"Dying don't cure a woman of foolishness."

"Leave us alone," Ren said, shooing the crowd away as he lowered his mother into her tent.

The group shuffled off but loitered nearby.

Laila's lips parted and fluttered, but no sound came out. Ren found a half-empty bottle of water and helped her drink. The liquid dribbled down her chin.

A police car rolled down Crocker, slowing at the curb. The remaining crowd scattered, retreating to their shadows. The white beam of a flashlight shot from the passenger window, blinding Ren.

"What's the trouble here?"

"No trouble, sir," Ren said.

The flashlight bounced from Ren to Laila. "What's wrong with her?"

"She's having trouble breathing," Ren said.

"You want to tell us if you've got anything on you that you don't want us finding before we get out of the car and take a look ourselves?"

The gun was in the sewer. "I got nothing," he said.

The door to the police car opened and slammed shut. "Save it," the cop who'd been sitting in the shotgun seat said.

The cop told Ren to back out of the tent and stand against the wall. He patted him down. He dug deep into Ren's pockets, pulling out the last of his loose change—a single dime—which he let fall onto the sidewalk.

When the cop was finished, he spun Ren around, blinding him with the flashlight. "What's up with your lady friend? What's she got in her tent?"

"I don't know," Ren said, blinking and looking to the side to regain his vision. "Nothing."

"Which is it? *I don't know* or *nothing?*" He jabbed Ren's chin with the flashlight. "Look at me when I'm talking."

"She's sick. Maybe TB, maybe worse. That's how come she's choking."

His partner cast his flashlight over Laila. "Take a look at this." He let the light bounce around Laila's stick-thin limbs, ropy neck, and sunken cheeks.

"I'm taking care of it," Ren said. "I'm taking her to the medic."

The cop turned the light on Ren. "Be sure you do. A person dies on the street it becomes our problem. And you don't want to be creating problems for us, do you?"

"No, sir." He hoped his voice sounded steady.

The police got in their car and pulled off.

Ren crouched down. Laila fumbled for his hand. She was saying something, but her words sounded like static—a dry, indecipherable crackle. Ren leaned closer. "The ocean," she said. "You got to see that ocean." She broke off on a coughing fit. "It's beautiful." She pointed at Ren's drawings hanging from her tent frame.

Laila's breathing was jagged—sometimes pinched and high-pitched, others a painful rattle like something in her lungs had come loose.

Ren sat cross-legged, his back to the street. He placed a hand on Laila's forehead, wiping away the sweat that ran hot and cold.

Laila's eyes flickered below her slitted lids. Her lips were open, drying out as she struggled to breathe. It looked like she was forming words that wouldn't come. Ren wet a cloth with water and squeezed a little liquid onto his mother's mouth and tongue.

Laila's hands rested on her legs. They twitched and fluttered, like she was typing or playing the piano, like she was sorting through some invisible objects.

Ren couldn't tell how much time was passing. He hoped that the sun was far off. He didn't need the cops shaking them out.

He poked his head out of the tarp. The sky was still black. He could hear a few folks rustling around prepping for morning. He ducked back into Laila's tent. The air was tight and close. His hands were clammy. His legs cramped. He wanted to close his eyes but he feared sleep, worried that when he was out he'd be carried off along with his mother. He dug his nails into his palms to keep himself alert.

The first trucks were rolling past in the semidark. A couple of voices carried down the street. Someone approached the tent, paused for a second, then continued on.

The air in the tent changed. There was a release, like a pin-popped balloon. Ren reached out to wick the moisture away from Laila's forehead. Her skin felt different, more like paper than flesh. Her face had shifted, not slack but calm. Her semiclosed eyes were still. Ren reached out and brought her lids down. He let his hand linger, hoping. His mother didn't move.

He got up and opened the tent flaps wide, pinning them back, and letting in as much air as he could. He found another water bottle behind some balled-up clothes. He kneeled down next to the body. He began to wash his mother's face, removing the flecks of blood around her mouth, the city grime wedged into the creases of her cheeks and below her eyes. Ren moved on to her hands and feet, trying to wipe away as much of the streets as he could.

A few people gathered in front of the shopping carts, watching him work. Someone brought him a couple of towels. Another gave him two liter bottles of water. Ren lifted Laila's thin shirt and cleaned her stomach and the brittle hull of her rib cage.

Outside the tent a woman was singing a hymn Ren didn't recognize. She kept her voice low, trying not to draw attention to their congregation. Ren replaced Laila's shirt. Someone handed him a clean sheet—a rare commodity on the streets. He wrapped his mother from toe to crown and backed out of the tent. The small crowd parted for him. A few people patted him on the back and squeezed his shoulders. Then a woman he'd never seen before came up and stood directly in front of him. She pulled a handkerchief from her bosom and wiped away his tears.

He walked down the gray street, hoping Darrell's crew would keep Laila safe until he returned. He knew what he needed to do—one tiny criminal act, sure, but he needed wheels if he and Laila were going to get to the ocean. No more getting waylaid.

He rounded Sixth and turned on San Pedro passing the community arts center. He was hustling, which is why he almost missed it—his own face staring back at him from behind the window, proud as anything. In the photo he was squinting in the sun and his crinkled eyes made him look like he was puzzling something out. There was something in the background—a flash, a trick of the light, some weird aftermath of Nancy's jury-rigged, tinfoil light bounce.

Ren leaned closer so his nose was almost on the glass. That thing in the background, that diamond-shaped starburst, he swore he knew what it was. Because if he narrowed his eyes a certain way and let the thing come into focus, it was clear. There was no mistaking his ghost disappearing. Vanishing into the ether. And just like that. Gone.

29

It was all falling into place, that's what Sam would have said. He would have said that there was no denying that this shit was pre-ordained, that it was predestined, that whatever spirit had been watching over him in the afterlife had swooped down to earth and was guiding Blake now. And who was Blake to deny the spirit's assistance? Who was he to resist this call? *You're a stupid motherfucker. You look an omen in the face and turn away,* Sam said.

After all, what were the chances of Laila's boy turning up at his camper? What were the chances of him knowing where to find the Flynn kid? He'd saved Blake a day's work and Sam would have claimed there's a blessing in that.

I'm counting them, Blake said to the empty camper. *One by one.*

You'd better, Sam said.

He spent what remained of the day moving most of Laila's meds. He spent the night half asleep in case the kids from up the hill had figured out that he was the sort of person they should report to the cops.

He rose before the sun began its losing battle. He put the dreamcatcher, the chess set, and his battered white sneakers in his pack along with his few clothes and set off for the Cecil Hotel. He had a day's work ahead of him. The boy, then the redhead. Then the next bus to San Diego.

Bribing the clerk at the Cecil was easy. The guy looked like he was on the wrong end of too many graveyard shifts. It only cost Blake a half bottle of Ritalin to score the Flynn kid's room number. "If he's not there, check the roof," the desk clerk said. Then he pinched his thumb and forefinger and pressed them to his lips, slitted his eyes, and made a deep sucking noise.

The boy wasn't in his room. So Blake braved the fire door to the roof, guessing, rightly, that like everything else in the Cecil the alarm was busted.

The roof was blackened by years of pollution and urban grit. Trash had blown into its corners where it had become bleached and faded. There were birds' nests and debris nestled in the industrial air vents and the scattered remains of a few beds and dressers. And there, leaning on the low wall overlooking Main, his back to the fire door, was the Flynn kid.

"I guess you could say this is better than that desert," Blake said. "But then again, maybe you couldn't even say that."

The kid turned.

"James," he said. "I've been looking for you."

The boy went white under his dirty street-streaked tan. He dropped the joint over the edge of the roof.

"Careful," Blake said. "Don't be wasteful."

James backed up and pressed himself into the wall like Blake was going to come for him, like he was going to do a back dive down to the street.

"I've been looking for you," Blake said again, "and here you are, not too far from my own pad. Funny how our paths cross."

"You l-l-looking—me." The boy was stammering.

"You sound like you've been smoking too much." Blake reached into his pocket where his knife was folded in its sheath. It was funny how easily it all came back, the old menace, the casual threatening voice.

"Did you talk to Britt?"

Blake smiled. He knew he looked nasty when he showed his teeth—that his smile was anything but welcoming. "No," he said. "But you guessed why I'm here."

James seemed to relax. He peeled himself away from the ledge. "You haven't talked to her?"

"I haven't," Blake said, "but I'm guessing you might have. In fact, it's better for you that you have and we can wrap up this little chat quickly and painlessly."

"I saw you," James said. "You came out to the ranch a few years ago. You stayed in one of the cabins."

"I did."

"You were smoking. You were watching me." James was worrying his hands like an old grandmother, rubbing his thumbs. "You stayed out there all night. You didn't come in the house. Why?"

"I didn't see what I was looking for. It seemed to me you were all alone."

James was chewing his lip, staring at his fingers, anything but meeting Blake's eye.

"My dad and Britt had split for a while. They were at some trailer in Malibu."

"So you do know where she is."

"I mean, I did—I don't. She's not at the ranch," James said.

"That much I know."

Now James looked at him straight. "You—"

"Yeah, me. But you knew that." It had felt good but not great, watching the flames consume Howling Tree Ranch, like it was a job half done.

"So if she's not at the ranch and not with your daddy in Malibu, where is she?" Blake said.

James lips moved. He muttered something Blake couldn't

catch. He knew and he wasn't saying. "She left him. A few years back."

"And?"

"What are you going to do if I tell you?"

"To you or her?" Blake gave James another nasty smile that would have made Sam proud.

James inched along the wall, like he was somehow going to slip away. Blake took two steps and pinned him. James leaned back, his floppy blond hair dangling down toward the street.

"Where is she?" Blake said.

"I don't—"

"I will find her," Blake said. He hoped it sounded convincing.

James crumpled. He doubled over and sagged, then slumped onto the tarry roof. The kid smelled like the farmhands with a little of the fetid downtown tang in the mix. Blake crouched down and leaned close to James's face. "Did you leave a marker? Any sign that Sam passed through this world?" The kid started worrying his damn hands again. "I didn't think so."

"He was dying," James said.

"You think I didn't know?"

"My dad said he only had a few days left."

"So that makes it okay that he was murdered. I'll remember to tell that one to the judge next time I'm called up."

"It was self-defense."

"Kid, I know Sam. I know him better than I know my damn self. I hear him in my head every night. I know that he's got a violence in him that would scare the darkest creature on earth. I also know he didn't have the strength to slap that girl. So when she says self-defense, I'm going to say bullshit."

Blake inched forward, pinning James to the wall. "It was," James said.

"Imagine this," Blake said. "Imagine someone murders your best friend. Imagine she lies to you, telling you it was self-defense.

And imagine you will never have the opportunity to prove her wrong because you can't report your friend's death on account of the life he lived and the trouble it would bring to you. Now imagine you have to spend the rest of your life knowing you let him die undignified. That he just gets erased from the earth like he didn't matter." Blake pressed his nose right against James's face. "Can you imagine that? Can you imagine living with something like that for the rest of your life?"

The boy was crying now and Blake didn't even have the knife to him.

"Are you trying?" Blake said. "Are you trying to imagine that?"

James either nodded or started crying harder, it was hard to tell.

"Good," Blake said.

"I don't know where she lives," James said. "She was with my dad for a few years, but they split. She's in the desert somewhere around Cathedral City. She teaches tennis."

"Tennis?" Blake rocked back on his heels. "Tennis?" he repeated. He stood up. His knees popped. He cracked his neck and stretched. He shouldered his backpack.

"What are you going to do?" The kid was standing now.

"Too late, kid," Blake said. "Too late to ask questions." He hoped he sounded hard. He hoped he sounded like Sam.

Blake turned and headed for the fire door. But James was on him, tackling him from behind. He got ahold of Blake's backpack, yanking it and pulling Blake backward. Blake struggled free of the straps. The zipper ripped open, the contents spilling onto the roof.

Blake squatted down, but James pushed him aside. He'd picked up the dreamcatcher. "This was his," James said. "Sam had it above his bed in the cabin on the ranch. You must have hung it there."

"I must have," Blake said.

James sifted through the rest of the stuff that had burst from Blake's bag. "You have all his stuff." He picked up *The Chess Puzzle*

Book, thumbed the pages, and let it fall. Then he opened the chess set. He selected a pawn and flipped it over in his hand. He stared at that pawn so long and hard that Blake worried he'd gone into a trance.

"You kept all this." James held the pawn up to the gray sky.

"You think I'd just discard my best friend's stuff? You thought I'd throw it aside like you probably did with his body." Blake dug in his pocket for a cigarette, then stopped himself from wasting time.

James was staring at the pawn. "They buried him out in the desert. My dad and Britt and two of the other interns. They didn't let me come."

"Did they leave a marker?"

"I don't know."

"You probably think people like me and Sam don't matter. But we deserve to be remembered."

"I think about Sam every day."

Blake pushed James aside with the toe of his shoe and began gathering his stuff. "I bet you do."

James was crying again, harder now. "I do," he said.

"Sure, kid, whatever you say." Blake didn't have time for this boy's trauma of seeing Sam get murdered.

"I can't sleep. I never sleep."

"I'm sorry Sam's murder turned you insomniac," Blake said. He fished in his pack for a mostly empty bottle of Klonapin. "For what ails you."

"It won't help," James said.

Blake finished stuffing his possessions into his bag. "In my humble opinion, pills help."

"Not me."

"Yeah," Blake said. "What makes you special?" He'd shouldered his bag. He was ready to go.

James was sitting on the roof, his knees drawn up to his chest, his head bent low. "I killed him. I killed Sam."

Blake dropped his bag. "How's that now?"

"It was me. He thought I was my brother. He grabbed my arm looking for the place where he'd cut Owen. When he didn't see it, he called me a *brujo* and grabbed his knife."

Brujo—that damn curse. The one that had undone him in the end. "Jesus," Blake said. "Fuck."

He could see it. He could finally see it—how the big man died, undone by his spiritual mumbo jumbo, too drugged or delirious to understand that there were two boys, too stubborn to listen. No wonder Blake's mind had never quite wrapped around the scene in the cabin with the redhead. No wonder his imagination had failed.

Five years of seeing it wrong. Five years of halfheartedly hunting the wrong person.

"So," James said. His eyes were red. His nose was dripping.

"So what?"

"What are you going to do to me?"

Blake's knife was in his pocket. He reached for it.

The kid looked pathetic, crouched on the grimy roof in the drab early dawn. So he'd killed Sam? Look what it had done to him. Look where it had landed him.

"Shit," Blake said. Because the kid wasn't that much different from him from time to time—wallowing, weeping, messed up on whatever it took to get him to silence Sam's voice. The big man had done that too, done it to Blake. Sam had brought Blake low enough. He wasn't going to let the big man sink him further.

"Fuck it," Blake said. "Fuck it all." He took his hand out of his pocket and found a smoke instead. "Look at you. Look at this place. If this is what killing Sam did to you, I think we're even. If he haunts your dreams, we're square."

Somewhere an ambulance was screaming through downtown. Blake glanced across the rooftop toward the building opposite with its grimy row of darkened windows.

He picked up his pack off the roof and slung it over his shoulder a final time. Then he opened it and dug out Sam's shit—the dreamcatcher, the chessboard, the chess book. He dropped these on James. "I thought I needed his stuff to remember, but fuck me if I'll ever forget."

He headed for the fire door. He didn't look back. He didn't need to see the kid sniffling and sobbing. He knew too well what that looked like.

Outside the hotel he lit his smoke, then walked to the bus stop.

The sky was the dull color of dirty sheets. Downtown was waking up. People from Skid Row were trekking west for their daily hustles. Hipsters were walking clean pit bulls and yappy Chihuahuas. The traffic was already thickening with delivery trucks, cars, and cabs.

Blake should have left ages ago. From the side pocket of his pack he pulled out the same road map of California he and Sam had used to get to Wonder Valley. He ran a jagged thumbnail down to the border, to where the Sonoran Desert began east of San Diego. He was sure somewhere in that hot, wild place there was a cabin for him.

There were two tourists at the bus stop, both of whom were wearing their backpacks on their chests. One was filming the other, like there was something worth remembering about this particular moment. Blake opened his map again. It nearly came apart in his hand. The paper was soft, the lines and print faded. He had to bring it up close to his nose to make it out.

Blake was so engrossed in the map that he almost missed him. If it hadn't been for the angry screech of wheels, he wouldn't have even looked up.

James was running down Main, not on the sidewalk, but threading his way through traffic. He was moving quickly, weaving in and out of cars. He was stripping off his clothes. People were rolling down their windows, shouting at him to *getthefuckoutofthestreet.*

Blake watched him pass the bus stop. James was naked now. The tourist filming his girlfriend turned and trained the camera on James, catching him as he skirted a bike cop. James darted in front of a city bus coming in the opposite direction. Blake stepped onto the street, cutting in front of the cameraman to get a better look. He saw James slow for a moment and then stagger slightly.

The bus came. Blake got on. Bystanders were holding up their cell phones as James passed, making this scene permanent.

Main was a chorus of honking horns, screeching tires, enraged drivers shouting at James as if he was the source of all their frustrations—as if this one man, moving on foot through traffic, would bring ruin to their days. Blake took a seat and folded his map, silently urging James on, hoping he'd keep going, that he'd snarl and snag these drivers, tangle their commute. Sitting behind their wheels, moving from point A to point B, they didn't understand what it was to need to escape.

30

The mural is beautiful, which is what caught Tony's eye in the first place—muted colors on the right showing a ribbon of road, a freeway to be precise, slicing through the drab downtown skyline. Then as it crawls to the left, the colors begin to brighten, grow bold, leap off the wall in a fluorescent tropical explosion ending in collision between the sand, the ocean, and the sky.

It's only when he takes a closer look that he sees that the artist has painted the outline of a man crossing the threshold where the freeway gives out to the beach. And the man is naked, or rather he's flesh toned.

Tony's gripping Britt's shoulder and staring at the wall. People have scooted their tents and carts to either side to make way for the painter to do his work.

"What?" Britt says.

The artist is a young black man. He's wearing a dark hoodie and his hair sticks up in unruly tufts. He rattles his can and unleashes a spray of paint, electrifying the sky above a stand of palm trees.

"What?" Britt says again.

Tony pulls her over to the wall. "Is that—" He's pointing at the shape of what must be James. "Is that?" It has to be. There's no way this scene unfolding on the wall is anything but the naked runner coming down the 110. Because it's exactly as he experienced it, an event brimming with possibility, something containing a secret beauty to those who knew how to look. "Oh my God," he says.

The artist rattles the can again but before he hits the wall, he checks over his shoulder and sees Tony and Britt watching him. He pulls his hoodie over his head and resumes his work.

"Excuse me," Tony says.

The painter finishes a patch of sky and turns. "You're breaking my flow," he says. He picks up a different can and returns to his mural. Tony and Britt watch as he shades the sky with brilliant streaks of yellow.

"Is that yesterday?" Tony asks.

The artist drops the yellow paint. "That's some philosophical shit you're asking. This here is today." Then he points at the wall, "And this is forever and always."

"But is that James?" Britt says.

"I don't know a James." The artist steps back and tilts his head side to side. "Do me a favor," he says. "Walk by it real fast. Tell me what you think."

Neither Tony nor Britt moves.

"You're not going to do me this thing? You're just going to ask me questions about my work?"

Tony walks along the wall left to right. The mural is still beautiful, but not different from when he was standing still. "Nice," he says.

"Other direction," the artist says. "And double-time it."

Tony figures he'll humor him just in case.

He trots along the mural, his eyes trained on the wall. And then it happens—like the wall is coming to life, like he's back on the 110, leaving the dull downtown skyline behind, like he's really moving, dancing, accelerating while the city stands still. Except that this time he gets somewhere. He's not taken down by the cops on the grimy outskirts of MacArthur Park. He makes it out of the city, out of the stop and go. He arrives at the ocean. He comes unstuck.

"Oh my God," he says. Because it's so real, so perfectly perfect that it takes him a moment to come back down to the grim reality of this street corner. "That's exactly what it was like," he says.

The artist gives him a wry half smile. "This your story too?"

"Not really," Tony says. "But I'd like to know how it ends."

"So is that James or not?" Britt asks.

"That nude dude?" the painter says. "I know him as Flynn."

"James Flynn," Britt says. "Did you see him on the news or something?"

"In the flesh."

Britt steps closer to the mural. "Where?"

"This is some detective-level inquiry." The painter begins searching through his cans. "On the freeway. That's where I saw him. And then again later."

Tony wants to ask the guy if he saw him, too, if he noticed him coming down the 110 after James, if he'd struck the artist enough to commit Tony to his mural.

"Where later?" Britt asks.

"At the beach."

"You followed him to the beach?"

"Lady, my business is my own. All I'm going to tell you is I wasn't following your boy. I just encountered him, fortuitous like." The guy finds the can he was looking for. He rattles it and steps back from the wall, considering.

Tony wants to stop him before he adds more to the mural. The artist uncaps the can, but doesn't aim. "So I'm guessing you two are just going to stand there until you squeeze the whole damn thing out of me. Here's the basics. There I am driving down the 110.

I'm going south. It's my first time. I'm not much for four wheeling. So I'm looking out my window—you should see the shit drivers get up to in this city—and there's your boy headed in my direction, but across the divider, running against traffic. I'm guessing you know that he was in his birthday suit." He cocks his head side to side, searching his mural. "I called out to him. But let's just say, I didn't need anyone looking into my driving credentials. So I wasn't about to draw unnecessary heat. And I thought that was the end of it."

He finds a spot on the wall that suits him.

"Then I saw him again where the highway lets out onto the beach." He turns and looks from Britt to Tony. "You two ever been to the beach?" He shakes the can again. "The fuck am I asking? Of course you have. But that was the first time for me and my mom. I promised I'd take her. Not to the tourist area, mind you. We went north until I was sure we were the only people around. I found a cove or some shit, just a place for the two of us to see what's what with the water. No one but us."

He sounds sad, like the memory of yesterday's beach trip might be too much.

"So when I drove back, that's when I saw him. Still running. Still naked. Still looking like he didn't have a care in the goddamn world. So I pulled over just before the road curved back to the freeway. Almost hit a dude riding a bike and balancing a surfboard. I watched him run to the edge of the water."

"I know the place," Tony says. It's just down from the fancy beach club his wife wanted to join.

"Did he go in the water?" Britt asks.

"I don't know. I had to get a move on." He rattles the can and approaches the far left corner of the mural. For a moment it seems to Tony as if he's signing his name. But when the words blossom, the script reads *Laila Davis, RIP.*

It's been nearly twenty-four hours since James took his run, but Tony knows that he and Britt are going out to the beach to the place where this graffiti artist had seen him head out over the sand. But he wants to jog past the mural one more time before they go, wants to reach back for those twenty minutes when he'd been unencumbered, when he'd felt free to run, to chase something that was unreachable. When he hadn't minded that he couldn't catch the very thing he'd wanted. Because, he realizes now, it's okay to know some things exist without grasping them.

"Let's go," he says. He'll leave the mural for now and only return when this whole episode has faded to a dream that he can barely recall—when he will need to remember.

THEY TAKE THE BUS, SOMETHING IN TONY'S TWELVE YEARS IN LOS ANGE-les he's never done. He doesn't mind that it's going to take more than an hour to make it to Santa Monica because he knows this is the last stop on this wild ride. The bus crawls through downtown and then gets on the 10, where it stop-starts through the dregs of the morning commute.

They pass over the old homes of West Adams, the freeway-sooted Victorians and Craftsmen. Baldwin Hills rises on their left. The Hollywood Hills on their right. They bring the sun with them as they go, as if the bus is pulling back the drab sky, rolling it out to sea.

The bus exits the freeway at Bundy and wheezes through the wide, clean streets of Santa Monica until it emerges on Ocean a block from the beach.

Tony and Britt get off. He's always surprised by the temperature drop by the ocean and by how the Pacific doesn't have the same briny smell he associates with other beaches. They head to the spot he believes the artist had been talking about, the place where the PCH curves onto the 10.

He's not sure what to expect and is reconciled to finding

nothing. He's pretty sure a naked man wouldn't have made it through a day and a night on a popular public beach without getting rounded up.

Britt barely spoke the entire ride. All she said was, "Blake couldn't have followed him that far. Could Blake have followed him that far?" She repeated this or some version of this until she had convinced herself that it was the only truth.

Tony has to agree.

They leave the paved walkway, dodge surfers and people on beach cruisers, and head onto the beach. They take off their shoes. The sand is cool.

The strand is filling up. The sun's out and the clouds are stripped away. The water's sparkling, catching the crystalline sky. Britt's looking to the left and the right, scanning the sand for James. But Tony's got his eyes trained on the water. It's like he's never seen it before, or noticed it—the whole reason people flocked to this city, just a few miles from his front door and he took it for granted, like it didn't matter, like it belonged to someone else.

He counts back through all the years he's lived in Los Angeles and realizes that he's never swum in the Pacific, never even dipped a toe. Was it too obvious? Too convenient? Was it because he and Stephanie weren't members of the beach club just up the beach from where he and Britt are walking?

There's a light breeze kicking up a pleasant smell. Two gulls are circling, taking turns plunging into the ocean, their bodies creating small whitecaps as they submerge. Tony wants to walk into the water. He wants—needs—to rinse the sweat and booze and stink of downtown from his body.

He's making a beeline for the ocean when he feels Britt's hand on his shoulder. "There," she says.

She's pointing at a small mound of rocks. She pulls Tony closer. It looks like the work of bored children or snarky teenagers messing about with occult nonsense. Tucked into the stones are a few feathers and twigs.

"He was here," she says. She falls to her knees.

On the north side of the rock pile, a string of stones has been positioned in a pattern. Tony stands back to get a better look. He tilts his head, trying to find meaning in the arrangement.

"Sam," Britt says. "It says Sam. That's the man James killed."

"I thought you killed him together."

Britt shakes her head. "It was James. I lied for him because I thought it would help him. But here's the fucked-up thing. I thought I was helping him, but deep down, I was really trying to help myself. I thought if I took the blame for what James did it would correct the balance of all the things I did wrong. The world doesn't work that way."

"Maybe it does," Tony says. But he knows that she's right. He'd chased James to make himself feel better, to outrun what had happened to him in Chicago. He'd done it for himself of course. Always for himself. And he'd woken up the next day feeling no better.

Britt places a stone on the small mound, making sure the structure won't topple. "We didn't leave a marker. We should have. We should have acknowledged the whole disaster instead of pretending it didn't happen. But we continued on like James didn't do anything. Like Sam's death was just another fucked-up thing that came from living in the middle of that goddamn desert."

She checks up and down the beach. A last look, just in case.

"He's somewhere," she says. Then she begins to walk back toward the PCH.

Tony lets her go. James is somewhere and Tony's own part in this story is over. It's time for him to go home. Because his life is lovely and peaceful. He's earned his comforts and he knows that he can enjoy them. He turns his phone on and texts Stephanie. *On my way. Sorry.*

Then he takes off his clothes, stripping bare. People are watching but he hardly sees them. He doesn't care. He doesn't hear them whistle or laugh. He doesn't hear them catcall.

Then he begins to run. He feels good. The sea air is fresh in his lungs. The wind pings sand into his face. He sprints to the water's edge. It's cold. It stings but he keeps going, lifting his knees out of the surf until the water gets too deep. He's up to his chest now, half running, half swimming.

He wants to scream partly with pain, partly with pleasure at the chill that bites and pierces. He goes farther. Chasing no one. On his own. Then he goes under.

He feels the currents dragging back and forth against his body. He hears the surf break overhead. He feels lifted by a wave, then pulled into its furrow.

He curls his body into a ball, sinks as low as he can toward the sandy bottom.

You think you have it all figured out—you've timed your commute, you've fit in your weekend run or you haven't, you've got life down to a science, a mathematical equation of time, interest, and energy. But one day something stands up to you, surprises you in a place where you've determined never to be surprised. And that's when you run. You move fast the wrong way through traffic. You think it's working. But something deep inside, driving the rhythm of your steps, tells you that it isn't. So you try again. You search for that tiny space hidden in you, untouched by everything that you've experienced or survived.

He can hold his breath for fifteen more seconds, maybe thirty. And that's all he has, that is all he will be granted. These are his last moments to find it—and he does—what he'd been reaching for when he'd run after James. That place that is essentially and undeniably him. It's small and solid like the sea-smoothed rocks beneath his feet. And he will come up for air. And he will swim for shore. And he will go home.

ACKNOWLEDGMENTS

I am thrilled to have had the chance to work with the terrific, clever, and creative Zachary Wagman at Ecco, whose belief and guidance were indispensable to me in the writing of this book. Thanks, of course, to Dan Halpern, who was able to see where I was going from the beginning and liked it, as well as Kimberly Witherspoon and William Callahan at Inkwell, who did the same. To all of my readers who acknowledged my novel's flaws and strengths and took the time to help me correct the balance—Elizabeth Pochoda, Philip Pochoda, and Sylvie Mouchès. And to those dedicated to getting this book out in the world, Ashley Garland and Lyndsey Blessing. And to those who encouraged me along the way—Justin Nowell, Louisa Hall, and Matthew Specktor.

But this book really belongs to the people who inspired it and who shared their time and stories with me, especially the artists and writers at the Lamp Arts Program: Linda Leigh, Sir Oliver, Garrison Alecsaunder, Marianna, Nick Paul, Simone, Myka Moon, Karen Zaldaña, and Ramiro Puentes. And to Hayk Makhmuryan, thank you for building such a wonderful community and allowing me to be part of it. Finally, to Robert Barratt, who took the time to tell me everything.